About the Author

Chris Bailey-Green was born in Suffolk, and has lived in Norfolk for most of his life. He has a degree in philosophy and lives in the rural heart of Norfolk with his wife, Debbi, and various pets. He became a full-time writer after spending twenty years in the police, both as a civilian worker and a police officer. You can follow him on Twitter @cbgreen9.

Chris Bailey-Green

Apnoea

Olympia Publishers

London

www.olympiapublishers.com
OLYMPIA PAPERBACK EDITION

A CIP catalogue record for this title is
available from the British Library.

ISBN: 978-1-78830-127-5

This is a work of fiction.
Names, characters, places and incidents originate from the writer's
imagination. Any resemblance to actual persons, living or dead, is purely
coincidental.

First Published in 2018

Olympia Publishers
60 Cannon Street
London
EC4N 6NP

Printed in Great Britain

Dedication

For Debbi,
Who makes it possible.

Acknowledgements

I would like to thank:-

Debbi – my wife, who has always been there for me and enabled me to believe in myself and the only reason you are holding this in your hand is because of the faith that she had in me that it was possible for me to do it. This book, and every one that I write, is dedicated to her.

Dr Phillipe Grunstein – of Norfolk and Norwich Universtity Hospital for guiding me through sleep apnoea and always being there to help with the troubles and issues that were raised by those that did not understand the problems. A tireless fighter for the cause.

Kerry Barrett – for being my first editor and making the important changes and suggestions to the book that enabled it to take the shape that it is today, and for teaching me that, despite what I learnt at school, you don't put two spaces after a full stop any longer.

Jess Brooks – for designing the cover and believing in the story.

Apnoea

Apnoea (æpˈniə) *n* a temporary inability to breathe

One

There were many events in my life that took my breath away, before I found out that I medically suffered from the temporary inability to breathe and literally was robbed of my breath.

That's something that features later in my story though; this is my story. It is a story that will feature love (a fair amount of it), sex (not enough of it) and sleeping disorders (too much of it).

I have lived a normal life and I guess that means that I have met a lot of girls, fallen in love, fallen in lust, fallen out of both of them and then fallen back in again. Some people meet someone and that's it, they are with that one person for the rest of their life; they have never been with anyone else and never will be with anyone else. Other people are unfortunate enough to never meet anyone and to be destined to spend the majority of their life alone. That hasn't been my story.

'I'm really not all that bothered about being with someone,' a friend of mine had once told me while we were having a coffee one day.

'Really?'

'Really. I can't stand the idea of someone else being there that I have to kowtow to, and is always in the way. Plus, of course, I wouldn't be able to be myself in front of them. It would just be so much effort all of the time.'

'I'm of the opinion that the best partner… ' I had gone through several by this stage, '…is someone that you can be totally relaxed with.'

'Well, I've never experienced that.'

'I think if you can't fart in front of your partner without them minding, then you are not really in a good relationship.'

She turned her nose up at this, as if I had just farted in front of her. She probably felt that I was trying her out to see if she was likely to be partner material, in which case she made efforts to destroy this possibility.

'I don't think I could ever do that. Plus, of course, I would have to put up with having his "things" all over the place.'

'Things?'

'Yes. I like things in my house to be the way that I want them to be. I couldn't cope with someone else's stuff lying around all of the time and what if he didn't put things back in the place where they belong?'

'Or left the top off the toothpaste?'

'Well exactly. Razors and hair all over the sink. I couldn't cope with that kind of thing in my life.'

I don't care what people say, you have to be a very strange person to truly want to spend your life alone. We seem driven to seek out companionship and the will to procreate is imbedded in us. It is going against Nature to say that you don't want to be with someone. I think that is why there have been so many issues over priests. The Catholic Church have forced people to go against nature and won't even let you toss one off without frowning on you and saying it's a sin. Is it any surprise, therefore, that the tension builds up and eventually all kinds of criminal activities explode, rather than just letting nature take its course? No; I think if you say you are happier alone then you are probably just lying. If you still deny that, then you are probably lying to yourself most of all.

I am going to tell you my whole story. I thought about this long and hard over the years and I will try and tell you from the very beginning until smack bang up to date, the things that have happened, 'warts and all', as Oliver Cromwell wanted his portrait to show.

Well, my name is Max Durant, which is probably something that I should have said earlier, but it's nice to meet you anyway, even if it is in this weird, distanced manner. If I am being honest, I should say that my name is Maximillian – that's what it says on my birth certificate at any rate.

I really hate it.

Maybe I should explain how I got the name; it's all the fault of my father. My father is a huge Jack Lemmon fan and his favourite Lemmon film was *The Great Race*. Did you ever see that? An epic of a film, where Tony Curtis is the good guy all dressed in white with sparkling teeth, whilst Jack Lemmon is the bad guy all dressed in black with a moustache to twirl. Total comic book caricatures, of course and as subtle as being ravaged by a rhino. Anyway, they race across the world from New York to Paris; hence the title of the film. It used to be a film that I loved when I was growing up. The only thing that bemused me and still does to this day was if my father was such a huge Jack Lemmon fan, then why did he name me after the character in that film played by Peter Falk?

My mother only really called me Maximillian whilst I was growing up because she said that was what they named me and she didn't like nicknames. She was of the opinion that if she wanted to call me Max, then that is what they would have christened me. Eventually over the years, I wore her down and she started to get used to the idea of calling me Max, but she would always resort to Maximillian whenever I was in trouble. Parents have a way of doing that I have noticed. Anyone who calls me Maximillian today is a surefire contender for being someone that really doesn't know me. Either that, or they are taking the piss.

***

At this stage I will gloss over my early years and I beg forgiveness if my memory shoots about all over the place and later on I tell you something that you really think that you should have known about earlier. I was born in 1973 though, so you can at least get some idea of the context.

My memory of school is very strange, like many distant memories. When I look back on it now, it all seems to have blended into one; so many years made up of so many individual days and yet when I think about it now it's just like a blur all condensed together like a ball of plasticine. I suppose that is a useful image given how primary school was probably the last time that I ever held plasticine in my hands. I used to feel faintly upset that it would come in such long, ordered strips, which would then be rolled up into a ball and pulled apart by someone, as it was manipulated into whatever shape the user wanted it to be put into. You would then have to spend ages making sure you didn't drop it and tread it into the carpet. You would never be able to get it back into those ordered strips once again though, and I couldn't stand those individuals who rolled all the different colours into the same ball.

I remember the art room in my primary school. I remember the big long wooden tables that dominated the room and how it smelt of woodwork and paint. I suppose I most remember the mixing up of paints that you squeezed out of plastic bottles in much the same way that I would later squeeze mayonnaise out of bottles. I remember mixing up the colours and how our teacher tried to teach us about the primary colours and how you could make other colours up by mixing primary colours together.

'What happens if you mix blue and yellow together, Maximillian?'

I was still a Maximillian at this stage. I didn't know the answer; whenever I mixed anything together it just seemed to end up as a gunky mess somewhere between pus and vomit in colour.

In one corner of the art room there was the big walk-in store cupboard that only the teachers were allowed to go into, but I remember standing at the entrance as if I was standing in front of Aladdin's cave being privy to all kinds of secrets. In the other corner was a caged-off kiln where one of the teachers used to put all the clay things that we had made. God knows what monstrous creations that machine saw over the years. Any skill that came out of that room was more by luck than judgement. Probably not even allowed to do this kind of thing in primary school these days; health and safety have probably closed down anything that is remotely fun.

My next memory of primary school was the brave, but futile attempts to introduce me to music. Now, I love music. I have a vast CD collection now which I hardly use because most of my music is downloaded and on an iPod. I have never had the remotest talent for playing music though. It was compulsory at my school to play the recorder which was torture for me as I really couldn't get to grips with it and I can't listen to *Frère Jacques* to this day without breaking out into a cold sweat. Why they thought it was necessary for us to learn this French nursery rhyme I have absolutely no idea at all; naturally, we had no idea what it was that we were singing about. I still don't know what it was all about. My problem with playing an instrument is that I have never been able to get my hands used to the idea of doing different things at the same time. I think the problem is that I think about it too much, so whenever I have tried to play the guitar, or the piano, it has just become confusing to try and co-ordinate it all in my brain. I just don't think I have the kind of brain needed for playing music.

When we weren't engaged on pointless recorder practice, we were singing hymns in assembly - things like *Kumbaya*, praising a God with all our hearts, and at full lung capacity, that the majority of us would probably grow up to not believe in. Probably no reason why we should when we later discovered that everything else that adults told us was true turned out to be a lie; you know, Tooth Fairy, Father Christmas, Easter Bunny, a decent politician, that sort of thing. Lies that we still go on to tell our children today, incidentally.

Then there were flash cards. Now I don't know if this was something that was just what we had at our school or if this was a nationwide thing, but these were small cardboard cards that either had a letter of the alphabet on them, or a word – I can't remember which now, it might have been both. We had them so that we could learn the alphabet and so on, presumably called flash cards because people would randomly pick one and hold it up and you had to say what it said. All basic stuff now, but you have to start learning somewhere. It's probably all done on computers these days. What I do remember is that we used to keep them in those little metal tobacco tins that you used to keep your roll ups, in rather than the packets you get these days. I still remember the tinny-tobacco smell that came from these boxes all these years later.

Probably the most dominant memory for me of those early years was the classroom at Christmas. Christmas is an extremely exciting time when you are a kid. We all bought into the myth 100 per cent. I remember the classrooms would be so warm and it would be so cold outside that the windows would drip with condensation as we all made decorations which involved glue on a brush in little pots and lots of glitter. The classrooms in my memory seemed to smell of stale urine and other odours that you get when you put thirty or so kids together in a hot room for long periods of time. More singing here, of course, lots of *Good King Wenceslas* and *The Holly and the Ivy*, again sung at full aptitude. Now I think about it, singing seemed to feature as a major part of my childhood schooldays.

I never really got into sport at school, probably because of the policy in the 1970s that if you forgot your gym kit then you would 'have to do it in your pants'. The trauma that was created by this policy is incalculable to numerous children over the years and it is something that I suspect that they would never be able to get away with these days without allegations of child abuse being thrown all over the place. We never really thought about it back then. The term 'paedophile' that would become so familiar in later life, was unheard of by us. Decades later we would get the revelation that so many of our childhood heroes – men we had grown up watching on television - had all been at it in one form or another. Sex is a driving force in humanity and seems to be what so many of us are preoccupied with in some way or another. The majority of lives seem to be about pursuit and conquest of sex of some description.

The thing that I do remember about sport at primary school was the coach that used to arrive every Tuesday, that we would all clamber on and then be driven to the local sports centre where we would all go swimming. I was never particularly good at swimming and I just used to mess about a lot of the time. I remember that when you managed to swim a certain distance, 10m, 30m, 50m and so on, you were presented with a certificate in the school assembly to show what you had achieved. I was the last person in my year group to get my 10m certificate, which was the lowest that you could get. There were people years younger than me that could swim like anything. In my case, it was obvious that I would have 10m to get from a sinking ship to safety, or drown. I never progressed beyond my 10m certificate and I am out of practice now, so I doubt that I could even do that.

I also remember the school sports day held every July on the field at the back of the school. We all had to carry our chairs out from the classroom to the field and place them down for the parents to sit on whilst they watched us perform. We had to chalk the classroom number onto the bottom of the seat of the chair, presumably to prevent other thieving teachers from stealing chairs from each other. I don't remember too much about it other than the various races you had to do - the egg and spoon race, three-legged race, sack race. Things which were largely determined to be of no use for anyone who had aspirations to be an Olympic athlete. However, if the Olympic committee decided to add an egg and spoon race to the agenda, then I think Britain would lead the field. I won the egg and spoon race myself. Only one year mind. Well, I didn't like to show off.

They were simpler days, but it would have been nice if they had spent some time trying to teach us and prepare us for what the outside world would have in store for us instead of spending all our time singing

***

Primary school is where I came into my first real contact with girls. Women and girls will feature heavily in my story and outside of the family, this is where I met girls for the first time. Females within your own family can often shape attitudes towards women that you will later have relationships with. I have always had a tendency to reject women who wear a lot of make-up. This is because I remember an aunt of mine that tended to wear makeup so thickly that she must have spent hours trowelling it onto her face each day. Or maybe she never

17

washed it off so built it up, layer upon layer, day after day. I remember it gave the impression of a waxy imprint to her face that made her look like she had been rejected by Madame Tussaud. Even to my juvenile mind, it looked to me like painting a corpse to try and make it look like it was still living. Since then until this very day, I have never been attracted to women who feel the need to hide their real face behind another fake one. To me, there has always been something so false about it. Shakespeare, of course, said it best: *'God has given you one face and you make yourself another.'*

It is also funny to remember how, in the early days of primary school, if you were a boy and you hung around with girls you were considered a little strange and could be thought of by your contemporaries as 'a bit gay'. This isn't particularly logical, of course, but that is what my fellows thought like. You didn't hang around with other lads and play football and do the things that all the other young lads did. You hung around with girls, which obviously meant that you must want to be one. Later on, if you kept away from girls and hung around with other guys, they would think you were gay then as well. Very little logic applied to any of this at all. If they suspected you were gay at that age then they called you 'a bender', a phrase that I have not heard for a number of years, but I suspect that we haven't moved on that far in terms of tolerance for the word to never be used any longer – or maybe it has just been replaced by worse words now. The invention of social media seems to have perfected the art of insult and allowed insulting, nasty little people to inhabit its pages in the darkness of the night.

The first girl that I was vaguely interested in was a girl called Ellen. I am ashamed to say that I can't remember her surname now, but then I am more ashamed to say that there were girls I knew more intimately later in life that I can't remember their first name, assuming I ever knew it. I can't remember how old we were, probably about eight. Nothing happened between us, of course, we just used to hang about with each other and occasionally sit next to each other at school which caused much amusement to the obviously much more heterosexual male classmates who all sat at the back of the class together.

My friendship with Ellen is something that I remember vividly because I suppose she was the first female that I was ever friends with. We were never 'dating' as such; we were far too young for that sort of thing. We just used to hang around with each other a lot. I have no idea what happened to her and where she is now. To be honest, I couldn't even tell you what she looked like. We drifted apart and found other friends.

I will tell you a couple of things that I have discovered over the years though with regards to sex. The first is the well-known saying that there are two kinds of people in life: wankers and liars. This is true as far as I can tell. I don't think I have ever known anyone who has not had 'one off the wrist' from time to time and for some, it's frankly something they could enter the Olympics for, and I would include myself in that category. I am sorry to say that masturbation will probably feature a fair amount in this story so I apologise in advance if this is the kind of thing that you object to on moral or religious grounds, but it's a fact of life. It's something that we all do and yet we don't talk about it, it's time that we brought masturbation out into the open.

Okay, that sounded wrong.

The second thing that I have observed is that when it comes to us men, you women should know that there probably isn't one of us who has not at some stage looked at every female that we have known and wondered what it would be like if we had sex. Obviously, this hopefully excludes family members. It is true though, we men have looked at all our female friends, acquaintances, colleagues and even strangers in the street and wondered what it would be like to have sex with them. In some cases this might only be a few seconds of 'never in a million years,' or it might be something that is more lasting and more thought out. It might even be something that we have followed up on and made happen. I don't know if women have felt the same way about the guys they have come across. I suspect not, but I can't be sure because I can't ask them. The reason why I can't ask them links into the third point about sex.

Whenever you ask anyone about sex, in whatever capacity, whether it's mates chatting in a pub or an officially approved survey – *everyone* lies about sex. It's a well-known adage that those that are the most vocal about it and boast about their conquests are probably the ones who are not actually getting it at all. There also seems to be a competition nowadays to see who can lose their virginity the earliest. Somewhere along the line, we have got our morals a bit mixed up.

When I was growing up I used to watch Noel Edmonds on that Saturday morning television show, *Swap Shop*. Saturday morning television was very important to us kids at the time. It seemed that everyone was divided into two groups. You were either a *Swap Shop* fan, which was the establishment and to an extent a more prestigious and accepted programme, very BBC in other words; or you watched *Tiswas,* which was the more anarchic, dangerous, anything could happen kind of show. The formulation of your television in one of these camps would end up later in life on whether you bought the *Radio Times* or the *TV Times; The Times* or *The News of the World.* I was always more the kind to come down on the side of safety, so I was firmly in the Edmonds camp.

Strange how memory can play tricks on you all these years later. I can't remember some things that I did last week and yet thirty-odd years later, I can still remember the *Swap Shop* phone number. I couldn't tell you the number of my own mobile phone if you were to ask me now, but I can remember a telephone number from thirty or more years ago. In fact, aside from my parent's phone number when I was growing up, it's probably the only number I know. There are some funny things that go on in our heads. I never actually telephoned the number, but I just got used to them repeating it all the time. Anyway, the point is, if you know the answers to any of this, then as they used to say on *Swap Shop* – answers on a postcard and send them in.

Oh, and the phone number was 01 811 8055.

Two

Secondary school was always something that seemed to loom large in the scope of things when I was growing up. Leaving the comfort of the primary school that you have been in for the majority of your life in order to go to 'the big school' seems to be a gigantic moment that pails to insignificance when looked back on later.

I was never someone that particularly had any aggressive emotions about school; it was simply something that had to be endured. In many respects, this is perfect training for later in life when your endurance of certain things can be tested to the limit. In this regard, it was much like having to work for a living. It's something that the majority of us would not choose to do if we could get away with it, but something that we feel we have to do – particularly if we have any ambition towards living in our own home, and being able to eat, drink and buy the things that we like, for instance.

There was always the talk about:

'When you go to high school, the bigger kids will flush your head down the toilet.'

I can't remember who said this to me, but it was probably some sadistic git. I can't say it was the kind of comment that was particularly designed to fill you with much confidence, but then I suspect that was the point. If head flushing actually happened, then it was certainly not something that ever happened to me and not something that happened to anyone else that I know. If you were a sensitive child then it was sufficient as a rumour to make you fret and worry about it though. I would like to think that I was sensitive when growing up and I probably still am, although other people may not agree with this. I can't remember worrying too much about it at the time, but it was a long time ago and the things that worry us in our youth are insignificant when we get older. I try to apply this philosophy to my current way of thinking; things that worry me today probably will appear as insignificant in the years that come when you look back on them. I can't say that it works.

Four years I spent at high school, which at the time seemed like a lifetime, but now seems to be a blink of an eye. Looking back on it now, it also seems to be a big long blur and there is some difficulty working out individual incidents and isolating specific moments. Lessons blend into one incomprehensible mass. I remember the good teachers and I remember the bad teachers, but I have no memory of the majority of the mediocre that are now lost. You lose touch with all of these people, of course, so I have no idea where these teachers are any longer, or even if they are still alive. I messed about in school a lot and probably made their lives more difficult than it needed to be. Sometimes I wish I knew where these people were so that I could apologise and thank them for what they tried to do. I couldn't see what they were trying to do back then, but I understand it so much better now. It is always rather too late. Kids are never interested in education, so it is completely wasted on them when you think about it.

I do have some vivid memories of these early teenage years. I remember how the teachers wanted us to cover our exercise books for some reason. I don't know whether this was done to make them more durable or whether it was done to allow us to personalise things. It seems unusual to me now that any institution run by the government would want you to have any form of individuality. I remember in the earlier years, my parents covering my books with offcuts of wallpaper, which gave the books a frankly very bizarre appearance, particularly the year that they decided to decorate with that God-awful wallpaper that contained woodchips. Later on, we would take the lead ourselves and cover the exercise books in film posters taken from movie magazines. I do remember getting into trouble with these exercise books in my religious studies class when I covered the book with an advert for vodka and labelled it 'the Holy Spirit'. It was returned to me, covered in copious amounts of red ink and crossings out which showed that my religious studies teacher did not have a sense of humour. He was a devout Christian.

In many regards, whilst I was at high school I was in a total wilderness with respects to girls. This is partially due to the fact that I was then and to a large extent still am, very shy. It's also connected to the fact that I did not really ever put myself in the way of girls. It may also have a lot to do with the fact that many girls perhaps just did not find me attractive. I remember a girl called Natalie who I believe was attracted to me as she spent a lot of time hanging around and teasing me, which is a pretty obvious clue in this day and age. By teasing me all of the time, she was clearly flirting her arse off which was about as effective as trying to nail fog to a brick wall. I am not sure that I would have been all that interested in any case. To an extent, I saw her as a pain in the arse. She eventually gave up and went away.

I also remember taking part in school plays. This was not an activity that everyone really enjoyed, but I took to it a great deal. I have heard, over the years, numerous professional actors giving interviews and stating that they got into acting because they joined local groups to meet girls. Let me tell you why I got into acting.

To meet girls.

It was as simple as that really. Acting enabled you to get close to girls. In some cases, you might even see them in their underwear during quick costume changes and, joy of joy, if the script required it, and from time to time it did, you might get to kiss them. How easy was that? I was not often given the chance to play the romantic male lead, but it did crop up now and again.

There was a girl who was involved in the acting scene called Dominique, and I have to tell you she was gorgeous. Everyone wanted to know her and if possible, have some kind of intimate relationship with her. I admired her a great deal from afar. She was so stunningly attractive that I felt that I never stood the remotest of chances in getting anywhere with her so being the pleb that I am, I never even bothered to try. She was too bright a star for my orbit. I haven't thought about

Dominique for years now, but at the time of knowing her I hardly thought about anyone or anything else. She was, for a time, my number one wank fantasy. I am not ashamed to say that; I have had rather a few over the years and I am sure I am not alone in that.

After high school, I never saw her again, I went on to college and I have no idea where she went. About twenty years after I had last seen her, I bumped into her at a petrol station whilst filling my car up. She still looked good although she was starting to get into her late 30s by this time. You could easily recognise her as the girl that she had once been, only she looked tired now and drained, as if life had taken everything out of her. She told me that she was divorced and had four kids, all of whom had different fathers – no wonder she looked tired. I would never have predicted that future for her. For some time after I had known her, I wondered what it would have been like if I had managed to have the courage and the confidence to ask her out and we had become 'an item'. Looking at her in that petrol station, I wondered if there would have been any difference in her life if we had got together. Probably not. Perhaps there are some things that you just can't change. We all had such bright ambitions for the future and how our lives were not going to be mundane and ordinary and how we were all going to be rich and famous. As far as I can tell, none of us achieved this goal.

***

Back in those days, if you were 'going out' with someone then it probably literally meant just that, you would go out with them and hang about with them. It didn't mean that you were having sex and it didn't mean that you were in any conventional sense, lovers. You might hold each other's hands and you might even do some kissing; it was doubtful whether there would be tongues involved and was not entirely certain that there would be anything else going on.

The first girl that I was serious about was a girl called Juliet. We were fifteen at the time and somehow, we got together and I suppose she was my first real girlfriend. We ended up being together for a while. It wasn't a particularly long while. To begin with, we only used to hang out together and she introduced me to MTV which I had never seen before because my family didn't have satellite television. It was something that my parents really couldn't see the point of. Television in general wasn't something that featured hugely heavy in my parents' lives, that was mainly dominated by books. Having watched a little bit of it myself, I started to fast come to the conclusion that I couldn't see much point in it either.

Juliet and I would hang around together, usually chatting and going on things that were not dates, but really were. We used to do the usual thing and hold hands and do the things that you feel you are meant to do at this stage. She is famous (in my mind at least) for being the first girl that I ever kissed. We had been hanging out somewhere one day, which my memory tells me was during the summer, but in reality, could have been any time of the year. We had walked home and I am not sure now if it was my home or her home. I would like to think that I had done the gentlemanly thing and walked her home as it was certainly the kind of thing that I have always tried to do. We were at that stage where we had not kissed and we were approaching the subject of should we kiss. It seems amazing looking back at it that there was almost a logical debate about whether we should engage in it or not, rather than just doing it. I certainly would say that with later girls and women it was something that just either happened or it didn't happen. I suppose the debate at this point was really just because of the fact that it was the first time, so we didn't know what we were doing. We sat on the wall outside her house, or my house.

'So?'

'So?' she returned whilst looking about her very casually as far as I could see, but probably she was just as confused and with as many butterflies in her stomach as I had. It annoys me now that in our immaturity, we were unable to articulate properly and yet this is the way that it is meant to be. From time to time in the future, even as a mature adult, I would surprise myself by still getting this giddy teenage feeling every now and then.

'Had a nice day?'

It wasn't the most brilliant thing that I could have said, but I think my brain was rather disconnected from the rest of me at this point. I am not sure if it has ever come back to me.

'Yes, it's been good,' she replied whilst turning to look at me. As she turned, her hair fell over her face slightly and it made my heart leap at how attractive she looked. This was probably the first time in my life that I lost my breath. I struggled hard to control my penis which has always been the thing that most betrays us men. It can either betray us by coming up when we don't want it to, causing all sorts of embarrassment; usually as a teenager when you are not used to being close to girls so end up trying to hide your hard-on at the slow dance at the school disco. It betrays you later in life, by refusing to get hard when you need it to. Although I have never had this problem, of course.

'So, what do you think we should do now?' I knew exactly what I wanted to do, which was to kiss her, in case you were thinking about something else (I wanted to do that as well, of course). Juliet and myself had spoken about kissing already, but mainly in the third person as if we were talking in the abstract about general things.

'I was just thinking –'

'Yes?'

'I was just thinking about how I would like to kiss you.'

This appeared to be the result that I was looking for, but rather than seizing the moment, I tried to look even cooler and for some reason I assumed a facial expression which I had once seen Bruce Willis do in some film. I probably assumed that this was an expression that girls would find attractive. Bit of an idiot really. That is the thing about being young though; always trying to be someone else.

'I suppose you should then,' I replied in what I hoped was the right tone and still maintained my air of coolness. It was probably doubtful about how cool I actually looked. I am sure if you were able to contact Juliet today she would probably tell you I looked like I was constipated; that is, assuming that she even remembers this incident. They say that you never forget your first kiss, but I am not sure I made it all that memorable for her. She was probably just the first in a long line of women that I was able to make things forgettable for.

We leaned forward and our lips touched together. My first kiss. As is usual with memories, there are things that I remember and things that I really don't remember. I remember that her lips tasted sweet which I suppose could have been some kind of lip gloss or something, or maybe this was how girls tasted. I do know that I was hooked on the taste from that point onwards. I still am. What I am ashamed to say I don't remember is whether this was the only way we kissed or whether we became more passionate. I don't even remember if this was the only time that we kissed or whether we made a habit of it from that point.

I was always perfectly well behaved and a gentleman, although God alone knows how, as I was running with hormones at the time. The relationship was somewhat flawed though. Juliet had a lot of anxieties and worries or what we would perhaps refer to in this day and age as low grade mental-health issues. I suppose she suffered from a certain amount of depression that caused a lot of strain on things and I believe that this caused a block on the relationship developing any further than it did really. I think it was something to do with the fact that, at the time that she was seeing me, her parents were going through a rather messy divorce that was anything but amicable and I believe, although I may be wrong, that her mother may have had a breakdown, or it might have been her father, or maybe it was someone else.

I remember that we didn't last all that long together and it was not too long after this that we split up and stopped seeing each other. I don't remember why, I don't know if it was due to the issues that she had and I felt incapable of dealing with that as an immature fifteen-year-old. Looking back, I think we just did a microcosm of a relationship in super quick time. We expressed interest in each other, we got together, we became intimate (as far as it went in this context) and then we drifted apart until it was time to go our separate ways. This would usually take a lot longer in the future. No, I don't know where Juliet is now or what she is doing, but I hope that she is happy wherever she is. My regret with regards to her is that I wasn't there for her when she needed me. She probably did better later on to be honest. She certainly deserved to.

***

And then there was Tina.

I suppose this was a couple of years later. I would have been seventeen and she was sixteen, I think. I had not really been with anyone since Juliet. I had poured myself into my studies when I had moved into college, concentrating on my A Levels as it was expected that I would go to university, which would mean I would have to study as they weren't going to give me something for nothing.

Tina was the one that approached me and asked me to go out with her. She was from my acting class and we had done a couple of plays together although I don't remember us having any particular scenes together and I probably didn't notice her all that much before we ended up speaking. Asking me out was a curious thing. She rang me up one day, and by rang me up, I mean she rang my parents' house. Nowadays every kid from the age of five has a mobile phone, but back then mobile phones had only just been made commercially available and they had a handset the size of a normal house phone that was attached by your standard telephone cord to the battery which was slightly bigger than your average house brick. You then had a handle and had to carry this around with you everywhere you went. It seems bloody ludicrous now when these days you can lose your phone in your pockets. No, I did not have one of these contraptions. If you wanted to talk to your friends in those days then you used what we now call a landline, but what we then called a telephone, as landline suggests an alternative, which there wasn't. My parents' telephone was a big monstrosity that would have made the perfect murder weapon as you could have easily brained someone with it. It also had a ring dial and for those of you too young to remember, this is where the numbers were arranged in a circle and you put your finger in the hole of the number you wanted and then dialled the whole thing round and let it reset before dialling the next number. Dialling long numbers could

28

easily result in you forgetting where you were and what it was you were dialling half way through and having to start all over again.

At any rate, the point is, she rang me up and we had a general chit chat. I can't remember how she got my number, whether it was something that I gave her or something she looked up in the phone book, which was an easy enough thing to do then. I don't get a phone book anymore; they used to send them to me all the time. Nowadays I suppose they expect you to do everything online. I remember my uncle at a Christmas or birthday party, when he was particularly drunk, demonstrating his ability to tear the phone book in half. Why he felt he needed this particular talent I have no idea.

'So, do you fancy going out then?' she asked me at some point in the conversation. This was something of a surprise as there had been nothing in the conversation thus far to suggest that this was what she was building up to. I was at a loss for a moment; I had probably just woken up. Being a teenager I kept very irregular hours.

'Where?'

'You know, go out?'

'You mean on a date?'

'Yeah.'

'So, are you asking me out?' The penny was beginning to drop.

'Yeah.'

'What, like to be your boyfriend?'

Okay, so I wasn't demonstrating any intelligence here, but upon reflection what I was probably doing was giving myself time to think.

'Yeah.'

'Okay, then.'

I thought, well, why not? It seemed to be an answer that pleased her so I guess that was good. I hung up the telephone with the strange feeling that I had somehow managed to acquire a girlfriend whilst standing in my boxer shorts in the hallway without leaving my house. All seemed a bit unreal.

Three

I remember more about the time that I spent with Tina for reasons that will become obvious. The kissing was definitely much more passionate than it had been with Juliet. There was definitely a lot of activity going on there. There was a lot more intimacy as well. I would walk her home from wherever it was that we happened to have been and as it was night, we would slip into a garage block area and lean against the wall, kissing passionately. It was then that I think I first made my attempts of 'feeling her up' for want of a better phrase. Nothing particularly spectacular, just slipping my hands into the back of her trousers whilst we were kissing and feeling her bottom.

'Do you mind?' I asked, as I was always very polite.

'Do you?' she replied.

She obviously didn't mind it all that much as she did the same to me, but neither of us made a move round to the front. I don't know why we didn't, but perhaps extending the touching up to include what we kept in front of us was a step too far for either of us at this stage. It must have been winter when we dated because I remember she wore tights under her jeans as I had to fight my way through three layers to get to her flesh. Maybe it wasn't winter, maybe this was just how she liked to dress, who knows? I don't remember her having the greatest of fashion sense, but I was hardly an expert in female clothing, then or now.

I would imagine that I cupped her breasts as well, although this would have been strangely pointless as it was probably through her bra and outer clothing at this stage so I might as well have not bothered for the amount of information that it gave me. It was not particularly glamorous and there was all the usual fumbling and oafish behaviour that one will come to expect from a seventeen-year-old boy who doesn't know what he is doing. The trick at that time of my life was to pretend that you did know what you were doing and make out like this was not the first time that you had ever done it. It was an illusion that fooled nobody, but it was exactly the kind of macho bullshit that we went in for at that age.

We both wanted things to go a little further, but the problem at that age is that you don't really have anywhere you can go and do these things. You don't have your own home, there are usually others in your parent's house and you can hardly go to a hotel. The first time we got a little raunchier was in the boiler room at the college. Yeah, romantic, huh? I know how to treat a girl. I guess the kissing and arse feeling had got the better of us and we wanted a little more so we snuck in there one afternoon and the passionate kissing turned into some stripping of clothing. We had probably been going out for about four months by this point. I remember laying on the floor (which was bloody freezing by the way and if I hadn't been a raging hormonal teenager, I would never have been able to get erect, given the circumstances), she was stripping me of clothing and the moment was slightly destroyed by the fact that she couldn't undo the buttons on my Levi jeans so I had to do it myself which wasn't perhaps ideal either. I then remember her pulling my jeans down, revealing my pants which I had decided to wear that day. Unfortunately, as I had no idea how this day was going to turn out when I had got dressed that morning, I had slipped on some old unexciting briefs instead of my usual boxers, so I can't imagine that she was overly impressed. I suppose I learnt a valuable lesson about my underwear choices that day.

Our entire relationship up until this point had been progression by slow stages as we made an advance, like the military across a battlefield, with an equal amount of time spent dug in, moving nowhere. I had assumed that she was planning on continuing to take things in stages so I thought the jeans would come off followed by some more kissing and then the pants. I was wrong. With the jeans around my ankles she then pulled my pants down really quickly, revealing me in all my teenage wonder (I can dream). Now it is possible that she wanted to remove my pants really quickly because she hated the look of them, but I like to think that it had something to do with wanting to see my penis. I assume that it was the first penis that she had ever seen, but I may have been wrong. It seems strange if that is the case, that having revealed it, she then left it alone and didn't approach it. We returned to kissing for a while without any further attempt being made for things to happen and with my trousers and pants around my ankles making it unromantic and difficult to move at the same time. Perhaps she had seen all she wanted to see and was not very impressed by it.

It was a short while after this whilst in a passionate, if uncomfortable, embrace that we heard voices outside and for a moment I thought we were about to be discovered. We quickly, but quietly scurried to our clothing and waited to see if anyone was going to come in. I had pulled up my pants but not my jeans and then I decided to pull them down again with the very vivid thought:

'It's taken her four months to get into my pants, if I pull them up now it could take her that long to get into them again.'

You can see what a caring person I was. What can I say in my defence?

Not a lot; I was a teenager and most of the day was preoccupied with thoughts of sex and this was as close as I had ever got to being naked with a girl. It would seem to be the culmination of a lot of wank desires up until that point and I was not prepared to let the moment slip away again. The voices ultimately went away and as Tina had decided that she was going to get dressed, she consented to give me the wank that I sorely needed after that. My first sexual experience, therefore, consisted of a hand job in a boiler house. It wasn't how I had imagined it was going to be in my head, but that is life for you. I could have made something up for you, but you might as well hear how things really were.

After that we decided if we wanted to do other things, then we had better do it somewhere safer. As luck would have it, my parents and brother went away on holiday to Wales shortly afterwards and I had the place to myself so I invited her round to stay the night. It is a fair assumption that her father would have gone mental if he had known that his sixteen-year-old daughter was sleeping around her boyfriend's house with nobody else present and that they were going to have sex. So she probably told him that she was doing a sleepover with a friend or something; after all, that is what friends are for.

Yes, we had decided before she came around that we would be having sex. Again, rather than the spontaneous happening, it had all been planned out in advance. After the boiler room hand job, we had discussed what it was that she wanted to do and whether she wanted matters to progress. I was at least considerate from that point of view, rather than just assuming that she would want to have me.

I am not going to go into the details of this first sexual experience as I don't intend this to be a pornographic account of my life. Suffice to say, that I will only tell you a few things that troubled me or amuse me when looking back on them. I think the first thing that surprised me was how hairy she was in the pubic area which was something that I obviously had no experience of. Not a good thing when it's your first time because you don't have a road map for where you are going and that just makes it like you are driving a car when thick fog has come down.

I was reasonably confident in knowing how to put a condom on as I had made sure that I had loads of practice – on my own, obviously. There would be nothing worse than looking a complete dick whilst trying to put that on your, well, on your dick. Due to the massive AIDS scare that was going on at this point, our school had ultimately decided that some kind of sex education, although obviously distasteful, might actually be required. Indeed, in some regards, it was their moral duty to provide us with the information that we needed to ensure that we would all be responsible. It was around this time that a lot of bananas were subjected to forcible condom wearing.

Unlike in the boiler room, I did actually get more of a chance to play with her whilst kissing her and whilst doing this she took a sharp intake of breath.

'Sorry,' I said thinking that maybe I had been a bit rough or cut her or something.

I know now, of course, that what happened was I brushed her clitoris and she was responding to the first time that someone other than herself had touched it, much in the same way I had when she had touched me. I know that *now*, of course, I didn't know it then. Back then I thought clitoris was a small village in Spain.

We had sex and it was wonderful and everything was perfect. Both of us did everything right and we came together as if we were meant to be and as if it was something that we had been doing all our lives. It was the best sex that either of us would ever experience.

No; of course, it wasn't.

It was the first time that either of us had done anything like that and we didn't know what we were doing. It was very much a case of trial and error really. Neither of us really knew what we could do to make each other respond more and there was a lot of fumbling and grunted apologies. I have no idea whether she enjoyed herself or not. I think our relationship started to fizzle out after this point. It was almost as if we had gone out with each other because we both wanted to experience what sex was like and having experienced it, started to lose interest in each other. Or to be brutally honest the way I promised I would be, it seemed to be the case that having had my way with her I was beginning to lose interest in her.

It was not a particularly good relationship and the deciding factor for this was that although I was very interested to be having a sexual relationship for the first time, on the intellectual level, we were just not compatible. I don't mean to sound harsh or big-headed, but that was the way things were. One of the biggest aphrodisiacs for me is intellect. Yes, I have a very high sex drive and I like to be satisfied in that department, but from a long-lasting relationship point of view it has to be intellect that is the biggest turn on. I could probably blame my parents for this, for raising me around a lot of books and with high expectations.

It became clear to me that Tina was becoming a little obsessed as well and one of the teachers approached me to talk about her as he felt that her studies were suffering from the fact that she was becoming a little obsessed with my dick. I would like to think that the teacher probably put it a little more diplomatically than that. I suppose at this time I was looking for a reason to get out of this relationship in a dignified way. There wasn't going to be a long-term future for us, we just would not have been able to get on in order to be together for a long period. I don't know if she realised this or whether she had planned a future for us that included marriage and children. I am sorry to say that this was something that never appeared on my radar.

I was looking for a reason to get out of the relationship in a dignified way. Is that what I just said? I don't think that there are any dignified ways of getting out of relationships. Even the most amicable split leaves you feeling like you have been in the boxing ring for a few rounds. Some relationships, you are lucky to get out without your genitals being carried in a bag. However, seizing the lifeline that I had been thrown, I took the opportunity to break up with her.

Break ups are very difficult things to do. I have been on both sides of the decision to break up and it's not nice being on either side really. I am not proud of the way that I broke things up with Tina. I know that I hurt her a great deal and what goes around comes around, as others were to hurt me in the future. We broke up whilst standing in a cloakroom in the college somewhere.

'I don't think we should see each other anymore,' I said, whilst standing over her as she sat on one of the benches and unsuccessfully fought back the tears.

'Is it because of what we did together?' she asked, meaning the sex.

'No, not at all,' I replied, trying to be comforting whilst at the same time not doing anything that might give her an idea that I had changed my mind and now felt that we should be together forever.

Yes, to an extent it was about what we had done together. Would I have broken up with her if we had not yet had sex and I thought that there was still a chance that we might have it in the near future? Let's be honest, of course I wouldn't. I was aware of the fact that I was cutting off my access to sex, but I wasn't interested any longer. It was not my greatest hour or something that I am particular proud of when I look back on it. My actions at this time led Tina to show me how someone could go from loving you to hating you in a very short space of time.

Her emotional state since the breakup was like a rollercoaster and I believe that she suffered a great deal from it and was subsequently even less likely to be able to concentrate on her studies than she had been when she had been obsessed with my cock; which just went to show you what bollocks the teacher was talking.

***

With the beginning of sex, I think it is fair to say that my childhood was truly over and I had moved into a different chapter in my life. I continued at college with my studies and I seemed to be playing the role of the typical angry young man at this stage. I was angry about everything and spent a lot of the time walking around dressed in black with a scowl on my face being angry about things. I don't remember what it was that I was angry about now, but I suspect that it wasn't really all that important, no matter how much it may have seemed to have been at the time.

I had decided that I would study history. I am not sure what it was that attracted me to this subject. Maybe because I liked to see how things were and I judged that you had to know where you had come from in order to know where you are going. I think I got hooked on it when I was younger. When I started to study history, we were taught it in chronological order. I remember early lessons at school where we learnt about Ur and Mesopotamia, before moving on to the legends of ancient Greece, which I am not entirely sure would class as history, so much as mythology, and then onto the Egyptians with a certain amount of emphasis on Tutankhamen. Now this was *real* history. Moving on to England, we mainly studied the monarchy. I know that a lot of people will show derision for this and say that it is not true history and it is far more interesting to learn about what the peasants were doing than the king; but the fact of the matter is that I loved hearing about monarchs going about declaring war, killing each other and in general acting like selfish children. You could still study social history because it is a simple fact that in the majority of cases, what happens at the top is going to affect what happens at the bottom. People like Wat Tyler and Jack Cade are perhaps the exception to this rule, but then look what became of them. The people sitting on the top of the tree nearly always win and Cade and Tyler were only doing what they were doing because of what was going on at the top in the first place.

History became more boring the further I got into the study of it. I think there were a couple of reasons for this. The first reason is because when I was at school I had a history teacher that could talk to you about something as mundane as the history of the paving slab, for example, and at the same time make it sound like it was the most fascinating and exciting thing that you had ever heard in your life. She was an amazing woman and she certainly was responsible for getting me interested in history.

When I moved higher up in the study of history, we ended up with a different teacher. She was a useless bitch and worse, she was a fraud. She used to have a folder that she would read 'notes that she had made' about whatever the subject was that we were meant to be learning. This she did to make herself look learned and important to the rest of us. Being bored with her monotone one lesson, I picked up the history text that we had all been allocated which was something on European Social and Economic History, and began to flit through the pages of the book looking for the section on Bismarck that she was currently rambling on about. I found the section and was staggered to see that the words she was saying were literally word for word copied from the text book that I was holding in my hands. So, she was so lazy she copied directly from a text book that she was then passing off as notes that she had made of her own thoughts. She was also so brain dead stupid, that the text book she had chosen to plagiarise was the same one that she had given us as a set text. I could go on and talk more about her, but she was a bitch and I will not dignify her with anymore words as it is a waste of print. If she is alive and reads this then she knows who she is, and that is more than enough said.

The second reason my study of history changed is because, as the title of the set text reveals, it all became social and economic which is fine if that is the kind of thing that you are into, but I have to admit that anything that becomes about mathematics and tables of figures makes my brain switch off and wander off somewhere else. I was still more interested in learning about which king was doing over which other king in order to play pass the crown. I think to a certain extent a lot more kids would be interested in history if it was taught like that. Too many people see it as a dead subject and they are just unable to get excited about things that happened hundreds of years ago to people that turned to dust generations before. This is a shame as history is something that is all around us. We are surrounded by it in our everyday lives and we can't really get away from it no matter how we try. I love visiting a place and looking for the telltale signs of history that are embedded in the infrastructure. Place names, street names and the like are an obvious example.

All of this is very interesting when you consider that I became a history lecturer myself.

***

The second year of my A Level study was taking up with the obsession of one person. In this instance, it was me that was being obsessive rather than the other way around. This is a story of unrequited love. It probably happens to each of us at some point in life that we probably fall for someone that just isn't interested in us in return. I suppose if you are a super attractive Brad Pitt look-alike or something like that then maybe you have never experienced unrequited love, but the majority of the rest of us that live on Planet Earth probably have. If you haven't, well then, I guess you are just lucky.

In some regards I think of this next person as a girlfriend, but it is an entirely inaccurate term as we never really came close to it. We were friends and had been through the last couple of years of high school and into college together, but we had never really considered the possibility of being together as 'an item'. Well, she probably never thought about us being together in that way, but if the truth is known I probably did. In fact, I thought of little else.

Her name was Lisa and I think she was the first woman that I was ever really in love with. She was an amazing woman and she definitely took my breath away for the majority of the time that I was around her or thinking about her. It was a developing obsession with Lisa and it went on for a fair amount of time. Too long.

We never did anything above kissing and that on only one night, but there was a time when I was easily able to convince myself that I was deeply in love with her. Perhaps for a period of time I was; but unrequited love can wear you down after a while and it isn't long before you find it all very depressing. If there is any hope left for you then you will stay clinging for years, but when it becomes obvious that you are doing something so futile, you have to give up for the sake of your own sanity. My hope, or obsession lasted for a long time and I seriously did feel like I was living in a Thomas Hardy novel. I suppose I felt like this because unrequited love features a lot in Hardy's novels and at this point I was just getting into reading his novels for the first time so it all seemed to click into place for me.

For the time that I was caught up with my obsession with Lisa, I never dated anybody else and at such a key time in my adolescence, that was quite a significant thing to do. I missed out on a lot during that period. A lot of development and a lot of experience that could have changed the course of my life significantly. Was it all a waste of time now looking back on it? I don't think so. I don't really think that there is any experience that can truly be classed as a waste of time as we will learn from everything that we do and have done. If we are sensible and intelligent we will realize this and not waste time mulling over mistakes and past experiences, but attempt to learn from them and grow. I think I can say that I learnt from the experience of Lisa.

So, how did we end up with this night of kissing you may ask yourself, when it was so clear that she was not interested in me? Well, it was all rather confusing really. Because we had been friendly from about the age of fifteen, we had spent a lot of time together and had developed a friendship. By the time we were eighteen and it was getting near the end of our college days and we were due to separate and go off to different universities, we were still friends and I had developed feelings for her deeper than just friendship. I told her how I felt towards her one night when we had gone out for a drink in one of the local pubs.

'You see, the thing is, Lisa, well, I think I love you.'

It was a definite breath being taken away moment for me as I sat there with my heart in my mouth, feeling that my entire future rested on what would happen in the next few moments. I can only describe her as looking at me as if I had just thrown a bucket of vomit all over her. I now knew what it was like to feel as if you had just been crumpled up like a piece of paper and thrown away, like a used condom. Perhaps I could have chosen my moment better, but then I am not sure that it would have really changed the outcome.

Oh, she was nice about it, but she made it clear that she wasn't interested in me in that regard and she would much prefer it if we remained friends. To her credit, she did remain friends with me and didn't try and distance herself as far away from me as it was possible to be. I don't know what it was that she didn't like about me, whether it was that she valued a friendship with me more than a relationship, or whether it was that she just found me repulsive. I don't know, and I don't imagine that I will ever know now.

The kissing came about because a few months later, I walked her home from the same pub and when we arrived at her darkened house and were preparing to say good night, she turned to me unexpectedly.

'I wonder what it would be like to kiss you?'

I had developed a little since I had dated Juliet and without any speech or hesitation, I moved in and we kissed very passionately and for a fair amount of time. I put everything I had into that kiss because I felt that a lot rested on it.

'Well, you certainly know how to kiss,' she said slightly breathlessly. So, we did it again.

This time she broke the clinch and pushed me away slightly.

'No. It's not fair on you.'

I was a little confused by this, but felt that as far as things were going, it was all pretty fair at the moment and definitely something that I was prepared to live with. We moved away from each other.

'Besides which,' she continued, 'I'm a lousy lay.'

I really wanted the chance to find this out for myself, but it was pretty obvious that this was not going to happen.

And that was it. Nothing else happened, then or ever since. She made it clear the following day that it had been the alcohol that she had drunk at the pub that had made her make the approach and that she was not doing it as a prelude to wanting to date each other. She had used me and thrown me aside and I had loved it. It took me a long time to get over her though and learn to move on. All for two kisses.

Is there any reflection that I can add on after all of these years? I don't really think that there is. My one regret, perhaps, is that I spent so much time on Lisa rather than really enjoying my time. Perhaps what I have learnt from this is to be cautious, to tread more carefully in the future and not make yourself look a total prat by throwing yourself at people at the risk of sacrificing everything else.

For a long time though, Lisa remained the only girl that I had ever kissed and meant it.

Four

My obsession with Lisa continued throughout the remaining time that I was in college and then for a little while into my first year in university. Hell, to be honest it continued for a lot longer than that. When I did have a couple of relationships, my heart wasn't really in it because I was thinking about Lisa all of the time. There is nothing more likely to put the dampeners on a relationship than the fact that you are spending all of the time thinking about someone else; I have found that women don't like you doing this. It took a bigger love to come along that took over things for me, but that is getting slightly ahead of myself.

Lisa was the first girl that I ever loved and she took my breath away. Because of the fact that it was unrequited love, when I look back on it now I wonder if it truly was love. I think it was. I have experienced a lot of lust and a fair amount of love over the years; it isn't always that easy to be able to tell the difference. I discussed this on a drunken night out with my college friend, David.

'What's the difference?' he had asked me, which was how the conversation had started. We had never really discussed matters of intimacy, despite our friendship. I suppose this was because of the fact that we were, in some regards, typical stiff-upper-lip, middle-class English guys who would probably rather have our eyelids glued shut than talk about emotion or intimacy together. I had no idea, therefore, how experienced or inexperienced David might have been when it came to women.

'It's a fine line,' I replied, finding it a little difficult to articulate through the alcohol. 'I think lust is reasonably self-explanatory. We can all lust after someone because of the desire for sex, because we find someone attractive.'

'I see it as a conquest.'

'Animalistic, but natural.'

'I have often found,' he continued, 'that the old cliché of the thrill being in the chase is the best part of it for me.'

'I think I know what you mean.'

'The pursuit of someone is full of adrenaline pumping through my body. It's excitement. It makes me feel like a giddy teenager. The thrill of chasing after someone to get their interest is almost like living on a knife's edge, unsure of which way matters are going to fall. I suppose, it's an addiction in the same way that some people get that buzz from drugs, drink or gambling.'

'Perhaps sex is an addiction.'

'The problem is that when the chase is over and the conquest has been made, I lose interest.'

'How do you mean?'

'I have sex and then almost from the second that I have come, I just lose interest.'

'Lose interest in what?'

'The person that I have been chasing after, of course. It's like I have achieved what I wanted and now the interest has gone and I move onto the next conquest, not thinking or caring any longer about the person I have been with, or having any desire to continue with them.'

'That sounds pretty harsh,' I said. Though I think to an extent I understood a little about where he was coming from, if you will excuse the expression.

'It's harsh; but there doesn't seem to be anything that I can do about it. I feel almost like a bee pollinating a flower and then moving onto the next one. It's almost as if it is something that I'm driven to do.'

'And you don't want to go back to the last flower because it's something you have already experienced?'

'Yeah, that's right. Sounds terrible, doesn't it?'

I was non-committal at this because if I was honest with myself, there had been moments when I had felt like this with Tina. Whilst the desire was there then all was attention, but when the desire exited it took the interest with it. I always concluded that the reason for this was because of the fact that, besides the sex, Tina and myself had absolutely nothing in common.

'The thing is,' David continued, 'with an attitude like that, how is it ever going to be possible to keep down any meaningful relationship when you are going to want to be bed hopping all of the time?'

I was surprised by the level of intimacy that he was revealing. Many of you might not think that this was particularly intimate, but I can assure you that for us, it was. I am sure you girls probably talk about things in much more graphic detail. We men assume that you do this when you go to the toilet which is why you so often seem to go off in groups.

'So, I'm not sure I really understand love,' he concluded. The long pause suggested that he might be expecting me to fill it with some kind of answer. I had told him already about Lisa and the predicament that I had found myself in. Now I was being asked to sum up what love was; well, what it was in my limited experience at any rate.

'I think,' I tentatively started, 'love is something where you have a similar obsession to lust, but it's less sexually orientated. With love, you just want to be with the person that you love. To sit with them, holding hands, walking along the beach, watching a film, curled up on the sofa – you name it, any one of a hundred different things that just means that you are with the person that you love regardless of what you are doing.'

'And not having sex?'

'Sex is secondary. Of course, you would like to have sex, but it's the presence of the person. Listening to the sound of their voice, the smell of their hair, their clothes, anything that reminds you of them.'

'I see.'

'I suppose the bottom line is that, taking what you describe when it comes to lusting after someone, it's exactly the same as that, only the desire continues afterwards. This is the person that you are not going to get bored with, but are going to want to stay with and keep coming back to. Ultimately the person that you want to spend the rest of your life with.' There was a silence for a while after this whilst David seemed to be digesting this information.

'I'm not sure I can imagine what it must be like to want to spend the rest of your life only wanting to have sex with one person. There are too many possibilities out there.' There was a glint in his eye as he said this as he looked forward to the prospect of what the future held. All those women and hardly enough time to explore all of the different varieties that were out there for him. He seemed excited.

***

David never got to find out how he would have coped with a long-term relationship or how he would have felt with love and having sex with only one person.

A couple of years after this conversation, when I was at university I heard the news that David, who was at another university, had died in a car crash. His parents had bought him a Mini Cooper when he had passed his driving test and to help him out with being away at university. The problem with David was that he drove it like he did everything in life, fast, and with little regard for others. He paid the price for that. In all honesty, I doubt he would have had it any other way.

***

Whilst I was in the wilderness of hanging around for Lisa to eventually not get together with me (yeah, I know, bit of a spoiler for things to come, or rather for things not to come), I was forced to take care of matters by other means; yes, of course, it's more masturbation.

It is a mystery to me why so many people are hung up about this, but who am I to judge? If it is something that bothers you that much then skip along to the next section as I shall be revealing some of the masturbation secrets that the teenage boys of this world probably would prefer you not to know about. It's like an exclusive wanking club really. When you join the Freemasons, you are told lots of secrets and then sworn to secrecy about them and told that you must never tell them to anyone. Actually, thinking about it, it's the other way around, you are sworn to secrecy *then* they tell you the secrets. It's the same with masturbation really. Teenage boys, presumably independently of each other (although I can't speak for boarding schools), discover the secrets of Mrs Palm and her five daughters and are then never likely to divulge those secrets to another for the rest of their lives. I am not going to tell you the mysteries of all of this. Why should I ruin the fun that comes with personal discovery? All I want to mention here is the two things that featured heavily for me during these wilderness years. The Wank Bank and the Wank Sock.

The Wank Bank was something that I actually overheard a friend of mine talking about one day. I can't remember the circumstances now, whether he was talking about a memory of sex with someone or was fantasising about a celebrity or someone that he had seen in the street, but he suddenly declared:

'That's one for the Wank Bank.'

I came to discover that what he meant by this, was storing a memory away in his mind somewhere (presumably in the section dedicated Wank Bank) and then retrieving it for when he wanted the solo pleasure. Chances are, we all do this; you just might not have such a formal name for it.

During this period of my life there was a lot of drain put on the Wank Bank. I even spent a lot of time going over my time with Tina. Not because I wanted to get back together with her or anything like that, but primarily because she was the only real sexual experience that I'd had. I very much doubt she ever thought of me in the same way. I think she was too busy hating me still for that and playing the martyr to all of her friends. I was overdrawn at the Wank Bank by then.

Talking of celebrities, I have to say that I don't think I have ever had a wanking fantasy about a celebrity. To me there is a falseness about them, not only because the pictures of them you see everywhere are probably doctored and they have spent thousands of pounds, if not more, on changing their appearance and altering themselves in such a way that they hardly resemble what a normal person looks like any longer; but also because of the fact that they seem distant and unreal in the sense that they are not really part of this world or walk among us. Perhaps they feel that they don't. I have just never been interested in them as someone that would excite me. I much rather prefer real people that I have met and in some cases, been with. This view, though, has caused me some minor embarrassment.

'What celebrity would you most like to shag?'

A question from a friend at some point during my teenage years. The reason for the question was double edged, firstly because of the fact that apparently you had to be into shagging celebrities and secondly, because it was the covert and subtle way that people had of finding out whether or not you were gay. If you answered 'Tom Cruise' then they might have a pretty good idea of where you were planning on planting your flag.

'Erm…'

I racked my brain as quickly as I could to try and remember any vaguely attractive female celebrity that would pass the test without making it look like I was gay or in some way a freak in their eyes. Ask me the same question these days and I would answer it honestly, without a toss what you thought about me. That is maturity for you. Instead, as a fifteen-year-old, I replied, 'Meg Ryan.' There was almost a question mark at the end of it.

'Ah, well, who wouldn't?' It seemed to be a satisfactory answer and had got me off the hook temporarily.

It's a fine line when it comes to celebrities, even as a fifteen-year-old I knew that Margaret Thatcher was the wrong answer to give.

At any rate, getting back to the point, that is what the Wank Bank is. The Wank Sock is reasonably self-explanatory, I would have thought, but I will explain it anyway just to clear up the merest suggestion of ambiguity.

One of the problems that face your average dedicated teenage wanker is what to do when the moment is over and all that is left is a bit of a mess. Now that I have written that about masturbation, I find it ironic to think that if you apply it to relationships as a whole then it is equally as true. With relationships when the moment is over, all that is left is a bit of a mess. There are many solutions to the masturbatory problem, most of which are sensible and hygienic. Somewhere along the line though came the idea of a Wank Sock. Yeah, it does exactly what it says on the tin. Being teenagers, most of us were too lazy to move all that much so it was necessary to come up with a design for something that would self-contain the problem and at the same time remove it from being an issue any longer, leaving the wearer reasonably clean, bearing in mind they are a teenager. The Wank Sock also had the ability to be used some times over, in theory.

The Wank Sock did present one problem though. Being teenagers it was unusual, if not unheard of, that you would do your own washing. This meant that you faced the possibility of having to put the Wank Sock in the wash and risk it being discovered. Obviously, this was not an ideal situation. Being teenagers though who didn't want to apply much thought to the problem, the Wank Sock would probably just be left under the bed, but within easy reach of course, until it is next required. When it becomes impossible to use any longer then it would perhaps be quietly disposed of. At that point, of course, you had the other one in the pair to start using. Ask a teenager about the Wank Sock and if they deny it, then there are really only two reasons why. The first is that they are lying to you and the second is that they have probably just as easily found another answer to the issue and it is something alternative to a sock.

Why do I tell you this? Well, it's a word of warning really to any mother who has a tendency to want to tidy up the bedroom of their teenage son. If you happen to be cleaning up the clothes on the floor and you come across a sock that appears to be made of cardboard, well you have been warned.

***

I suppose something I really should talk about that is something of an elephant in the room, is the topic of pornography. I know that opinion is somewhat divided on this subject. On the one side, you have the people who think it is harmless and on the other there is the camp that is firmly on the side of the opinion that pornography is female exploitation and dangerous sexist trash that is designed to raise boys into men with a poor attitude to women, seeing them as nothing more than a sexual object. I do see this argument and I understand it fully. I am not going to get into the argument of pornography right or wrong at the moment as that isn't really why I brought it up. I will let you make up your own mind about it.

My name is Max and I have used pornography.

That is my confession. I still do use it from time to time if I am honest. The issue for me was that, at the time that I was at college and university and really digging pornography during my wilderness years, it was pretty boring stuff. This was the early to mid-nineties and computers were not as common as they are now. Pornography on the World Wide Web was not so easy to come by and if you did manage to find some then it would take an age to download. Nowadays, it's wide spread and easy to get hold of and that is not necessarily a good thing. When I was growing up and into my teens it was Wank Mags that were the primary source for pornography and in truth, compared to what you can find on the Net these days, they were pretty harmless. Sadly, it seems online now you can find whatever you want no matter how extreme it may be. The younger generation behind me are open to a wealth of pornography that my little wanking chums and I would never have believed was possible.

During my time in the wilderness, it was my imagination and some pretty mundane top shelf magazines that fuelled my desire and most of the time I only got those because of the stories that were in them which in many ways were more erotic than the pictures. Of course, there was still a massive stigma involved in going into a newsagent and buying one of these magazines. You suspected that everyone in the shop, including the shopkeeper, was looking at you as if you were a pervert and the worst kind of sexual deviant that had

49

walked the face of the planet. Some people would argue that you were. It amazes me now that these magazines are still made and sold when the internet must surely have surpassed them in every degree.

Buying a dirty magazine was a trial by fire for most of us at the time and it was no less of an issue than the time you wanted to buy condoms. Why it should be that we got so worked up and ashamed of buying condoms, I don't really know. What should be the shame in going into a chemist and buying condoms? Nowadays you can buy them in supermarkets along with your weekly groceries. The times have certainly changed. It's all a mystery to me why it seemed so shameful to buy condoms. I do remember the first time I bought some, and probably for some time afterwards, I crept around the shop and must have given the appearance of acting like a shoplifter. Why we didn't walk round the shop waving them above our head shouting loudly, 'Yes, I am going to have sex!' I don't know. We were obviously bred to believe that there was something shameful in having sex. Perhaps the shop assistants thought that we were only buying condoms as an alternative to the Wank Sock. In some cases, there is probably some truth in that. It made you paranoid and if you got that paranoid, then just buying socks for legitimate reasons made you think that the shopkeepers all thought you were going to stick them on the end of your cock rather than your feet.

***

I have called this my time in the wilderness, but it was not a completely barren time. Whilst I was hovering around waiting for things to not happen with Lisa, I did have two brief encounters with other women.

The first of these two girls was called Maxine. I think if I remember correctly, she was a couple of years older than me. If you take a moral standard on masturbation and pornography then one night stands are probably also on your list. I know there is something morally indefensible about a one night stand, but they happen and I have had a few of them over the years. Maxine and I were destined not to last longer than a one night stand, can you imagine what it would

50

have been like if we had got into a long-term relationship and both being called Max? It was because of our first names that we started talking to each other in the first place. It was at a wedding.

'Hi, I'm Max,' she said extending a hand in an elegant manner that left me confused as to whether she was expecting me to shake it or kiss it.

'Hi, I'm Max,' I returned. This caused her to have some confusion as she looked at me as if trying to work out which of us was the biggest idiot.

'That's what I said,' she settled on, having finally decided that I was obviously the idiot for repeating back to her what she had just said.

'Yes, I know. I'm Max.'

'What's your name?' she said, leaning forwards slightly and stressing each word as she had obviously come to the conclusion that she was talking to an idiot; or in the same cute way that the English have when speaking to foreigners. I leant forward to meet her half way between us and matched her in stressing each word.

'My name is Max, *as well.*'

'Oh, my God,' she said her hand flying to her mouth as if she was afraid that her teeth were about to fall out. 'That is *so* funny.'

I didn't think it was that funny; mildly amusing perhaps, but hardly side-splitting. This might not seem to be a good start and you might wonder why it was that we ended up getting together, even for a one night stand. I can't say what the attraction was from her side, but from my side she was stunning. Extremely attractive, in a wedding outfit that left very little to the imagination and must have seriously pissed off the bride for distracting from her, as it is fair to say that more heads turned at Max walking by than when the bride did. I call that bad etiquette to upstage the bride.

Did we have a night of passion and romance? No, we had a quick shag in the rose garden of the hotel between the reception and the evening disco. Despite the fact that at heart I considered myself to be something of a hopeless romantic, I accept that all of the evidence so far is going heavily against romance. First the boiler room and then a quick hitching up of the skirt and against a hedge in a rose garden. I am almost ashamed of the memory now, particularly as I know that the only reason I remember her name is the fact she had a name that even I would find hard to forget.

I can't even remember the name of the second girl that I met around this time. Now you may think that this is terrible that I have forgotten the name of a woman I slept with, but I am pretty certain that if you were to track her down and ask her, she wouldn't be able to tell you my name either. She was a fellow student and we had not seen each other on campus before and come to think of it, I don't remember seeing her on campus afterwards either, so maybe she was not a student at all. We met at some kind of dinner and dance one night. I am not sure what this was, some kind of charity ball or something perhaps. One of those annoying black-tie occasions though which did give, whatever her name was, a chance to show herself off in an elegant blacksatin ballgown. We were introduced, we danced, we had a few drinks and then we spent the rest of the evening chatting.

One thing pretty much led to another. We had become absorbed with each other to the point where everything else and everyone else not only no longer mattered, but no longer existed really. Like most of these things it started with some pretty intense kissing.

'Maybe you should show me your rooms,' she all but purred at me.

'Seems like a good idea. We aren't meant to have people of the opposite sex in our rooms after dinner though,' I said between passionate, breathless kisses.

As you can imagine, this was a rule that we all vigorously adhered to. It also always amused me that you were not allowed someone of the opposite sex in your rooms, which struck me as unfair as it gave gay people the advantage.

'I won't tell anyone if you don't,' she replied as she ran her hand over my chest.

Anyway, it all went the way that you would expect it to and then that was the end of it. The next morning, I woke up and she was gone, not even a note or anything. Not a word. Off she went and I never saw or heard from her again, which I have always regarded as a shame as she was someone that I would have been very happy to have tried to make a go of it with.

Five

Everything always seems different in childhood. I have heard reference time and again to 'the innocence of childhood' and I think that this is something that can be taken a number of ways. In some ways, it is used in a rather upsetting way when linked with sex. I shudder at the thought of it to be honest. I am in the camp that believes that when it comes to paedophiles we should bring back public castration.

When I think of the innocence of childhood, I think of the fact that things were simpler and in many regards better. Think about it; as kids, we didn't have any responsibility, we didn't have to work, our food was always provided for us without us having to go out and buy it. We didn't really have to buy anything and anything we did buy was because it was something that we wanted and we bought it with money that someone would give us for doing nothing. When you become an adult, you have all the stresses and strains that you were just not told about as a kid. You have to work for a living. People stop giving you things for nothing. You have to provide your own food. The sharp wake-up call is just how expensive everything is when you suddenly have to spend all of your money on bills and essentials rather than going around and buying whatever you want with your money. It seems rather strange, therefore, that as children we seem to spend so much time wanting to be grown up and adult. Any adult in their right mind wants to be a child again.

Of course, there are a lot of things that come as benefits for adults that you don't get as children. Sex is one, of course, but there is also freedom. As an adult, you can pretty much do what you like within certain constraints. As a child, you are always being restrained and told what to do. You don't like your job as an adult? Quit and go do something else, it is your decision, and nobody is making you do it; whereas they are certainly making you go to school. I suppose, upon reflection, it is a matter for debate whether it is better to be a child, oblivious to the way that the world really is; or an adult who has all the perks that come with that title.

Memories are what I am all about. I remember my grandparents' house in the suburbs of London. I remember that the house was always very cold, this being many years before it was so common to have double-glazed windows and central heating as part of the very basic standard of what we expected in our homes. Come to think of it, it wasn't just their house that was cold; during the winter our house was cold as well. I remember that we used to have a bath on a Sunday evening before going to bed. A bath only once a week. Now I bath or shower pretty much every day. I think money was tighter in those days though. The 1970s were bleak, but as kids I don't think we realised just how bleak it really was.

I have a younger brother so when it came to baths, my mum would put an electric radiator in the room of whichever one of us was in the bath so that when we came out, we would be walking into a slightly warmer room. I can still to this day remember the smell that the electric radiator gave off and how it really did make the room so much warmer. We also used to wear vests as well which went out of fashion extremely quickly. You had to wear them in those days because it was just so cold without them. If we had a cold, then I remember my mother would rub our chests with vapour rub before sending us off to bed. This gave off a terrible smell and then made the vest stick to your chest. I used to hate it, but my mother always used to say that she knew what was best for us. So, off to bed you would be sent with a hot water bottle as well, which might be in the shape of some comical children's character to somehow make it more acceptable. Not a very attractive picture of making our way to bed, but a lot better than the routine I go through every night these days.

Usually, this traditional bath time would take place during the time when the Top 40 chart would be playing on the radio and you waited with a real eagerness to find out what the number one single was going to be. It seemed to really matter in those days; there wasn't one of us that didn't know what was number one in the Top 40 or the 'hit parade' as you would call it if you were from the generation before. These days I can never tell you who is at the number one slot and to be honest, I don't care. I know for a fact you could name everyone in the top forty and I would be amazed if I could recognise three of them. Each Sunday, we would religiously record the songs that we wanted from the Top 40 as we never had the money to actually buy them legally. The big attraction was the Christmas edition of *Top of the Pops,* where they would have the best records of the previous year playing along with the much-coveted Christmas number one slot.

You young people reading this now who didn't live through all of this will probably think that we all lived in poverty. To you, DVDs have always been there, you know nothing of VHS, let alone Betamax. CDs have always been the way, although now it's all streamed or downloaded or whatever it is. We had vinyl and had to remove the fluff from the needle so that we could listen to the track and then you had to turn it over to listen to the other side – go figure. For you of the technological age, a stylus is something that you prod your iPad with. For me, a stylus was something that you had on a record player. I don't consider myself to be all that old, and yet I can see that in the time since I was a child, until thirty years later, there have been so many advancements. I think that when it comes time to finally write the history for this period, the latter half of the twentieth century will be known as the technological revolution.

And now we have the really bizarre situation where time has regressed and vinyl is making a comeback. The only difference is that the albums on vinyl now are exorbitantly expensive, which makes me wish that I had kept my vinyl collection rather than consigning it to a charity shop, in the certain knowledge that I would never need it again now that technology had progressed so much. What does this portend? Are flares going to make a comeback as well?

Things may have been more difficult for us and they may seem very strange to you now, but we did grow up in harder times I think. We had the Three-Day Week going on, although I didn't know anything about this at the time. If money was tight, then my parents never mentioned it in front of me. They later would say how they always tried to make sure that us kids got what we needed and what we wanted even if it meant going without themselves. There would be the odd Christmas where we would never notice that as we opened our presents there were none, or far less, for our parents. This is the sacrifice that you make for your children. These days it seems to me that half the parents would never forgo their cigarettes, bottle of cheap alcohol and widescreen television, no matter what their kids needed. I remember once having a strip-wash in front of the fire in the living room, probably because they couldn't afford to heat the whole house or heat the water that would be needed for baths. Then again, it might have been because of power cuts.

There were a lot of power cuts in the seventies as the government realised that there was no way they had enough energy to keep things going because everyone was on strike. I knew nothing about politics at the time, of course. I remember being really annoyed if the power cut happened during *Doctor Who* or *Sapphire and Steel* because I would never get to know what happened. I also remember that my dad would keep various candles in convenient places, dotted about, as you never knew when the power was going to go off. Hard to imagine living like that now, but we did and we accepted it as the norm.

In a very short space of time, technology has moved very far, very quickly; some might argue too quickly. I remember how exciting it was getting the first television with *Teletext* and *Ceefax*. I would spend hours trawling *Ceefax* looking for something interesting and marvelling at the graphics and thinking how amazing it was that we lived in such times. You kids today can go on about your Xboxes or whatever it's trendy to have now. We had *Pong*. Now for those of you who don't know or don't remember, *Pong* was a state of the art video game. In essence, it was two-dimensional tennis where you moved a line up and down the screen to send a ball (which was a dot) back across the screen to your opponent. Thought of as pretty rubbish now compared to everything you can get forty years later, but at the time this was as good as it got and you couldn't imagine that it was something that was going to get any better.

It's only when I look back now that I can see the things that took place years ago and put them in a context that I can relate to things that were actually going on in my own life. The 70s is a decade that I remember as being drab, but I don't know if that is how it was or if that is just the way that I look back on it now. My memory of this decade is sepia-like, as it comes from faded Polaroid photographs which were the technological revolution that replaced the slides that you used to get. I still can't imagine why it was that so many photographs were put onto slides. There is hardly a Christmas or a family gathering that I can think of when someone or other (depending on whose house we were at) would not go and get the box of slides out and then the slide screen would be slid into place at one end of a room whilst we were all sent down to the other end of the room where we would crowd around the projector, which would steadily increase in heat and we would all watch photographs of recent or long ago memories. It may come as a shock to you now, but this was considered to be entertainment in those days. I remember a lot of dull colours, a lot of browns, dull yellows and the like. I know this entire glam rock thing was meant to be going on, but it wasn't going on anywhere near where I lived or to anyone I knew; probably just as well really.

***

When I was eight, or thereabouts, my best friend was a boy called Isaac, who came from a very religious family and had to suffer the indignity of being named after a character from the Bible.

'I might have blended in more if they had chosen a more common name,' he woefully told me one day.

'What would you have wanted?'

'Dunno. Already got brothers called Joseph, Daniel, Benjamin and Joshua. Feels like they took all the good names.'

'Could be worse. Could've called you Issachar.'

'True,' he looked at me with his big brown eyes as if to tell me that even this wouldn't have been as bad as Isaac.

We ended up floating together I think because we both hated our names and felt that we could never forgive our parents for their choice, which they ultimately would never have to live with. I had already started to demand mine shortened to 'Max', but there was nothing that Isaac really liked that he could put up with.

'What about Ike?'

He looked at me as if to say that this was somehow too American for his tastes, even at that young an age.

We used to spend a lot of time together and for a number of years we seemed to go everywhere together and do everything together. We were in each other's pockets all of the time. It will not be any surprise to you to learn, therefore, that I have absolutely no idea where he is now and what he is doing. I don't even know if he is still alive. So many people fall by the wayside as we go through life, it's truly amazing that we get through so many people from the cradle to the grave.

Isaac and I would go off and explore in the woods near where we lived. Now, I grew up in a reasonably large town that was in the countryside, so walk a couple of miles away from the centre of the town and you found yourself out in country lanes and woods. I should point out, though, that despite living in a situation like this, to this day I know nothing about the countryside. I took a girlfriend from the city back to the country one day.

'What are these flowers called?' she asked.

'I dunno.'

'They must have a name.'

'They're blue.'

'What type of tree is that?' she refused to give up.

'I dunno. A tree is a tree, isn't it?'

I think she was disappointed in my lack of rustic knowledge. I cannot identify a cry from a particular wild creature. I just have no knowledge of the countryside despite having grown up with it all around me. I am afraid I lacked the kind of Enid Blyton childhood that meant I ran about in shorts all the time and ran home for jam sandwiches and ginger pop after discovering something frightfully exciting in the woods. We did come in contact with Nature though, which included looking in stagnant ponds and at frogspawn or tadpoles or whatever it might have been, I don't know.

***

This period is when I also developed my interest in movies which was to stay with me for the rest of my life. The first film I saw in the cinema was, unbelievably now, *Star Wars*. My father came home from work one day and was talking about how it was that he had heard about this fantastic film from colleagues who had seen it. He then packed us all off into the clapped out Mini Cooper and took us all off to the cinema. Did I enjoy it? I was four years old. What the hell did I know about it? I remember going to see it and I remember the opening titles and thinking that it was silly that words could float in space and then I promptly fell asleep until later on I woke up and saw some people crowded into the cockpit of a spaceship and then strapping themselves in to fire some guns. I know that now, but I didn't know it then. So back then I asked my mother.

'What are they doing?'

'They're going for a haircut,' she declared with total confidence.

Now, either one of two things were happening here. It's possible that my mother was trying to shut me up so she could get on and watch the film without probing questions from a four year old that couldn't be bothered to stay awake; or it's possible that my mother had been so unable to follow the plot of this science fiction marvel, that she genuinely didn't have a clue as to what was happening. I suppose it is also possible that somewhere off in her own mind, she genuinely did think that they were going for a haircut.

Star Wars has its accepted place in the history of film now, but it is hard to believe just how revolutionary it was at the time. This was

60

the first science fiction film that had been made with a budget that enabled fantastic special effects, the like of which had never been seen before. It took a lot of people's breath away. These days, with computer technology, we just expect it to be spectacular.

The second film that I saw in the cinema was, I believe, *The Muppet Movie*. Fortunately, I don't remember anything about that film at all. My mother did later drag me off to see *ET* as it was something that she really wanted to see. Unusual really as she never really wanted to see that many things in the cinema; she just wasn't that interested in films. I suppose that must have been about 1982.

Films were an important part of my growing up. The *Carry On* films were as close as any of us got to pornography. Pornography was a very difficult thing to get hold of when I was growing up. Most of the time you gained what you could from watching *Carry On* films, which were not exactly the ideal role model for a young guy to grow up watching and to form his opinion of women over. I can't speak for my contemporaries that were exposed in the same way as I was, but I would like to think that maybe I was successful in growing up to not be like Syd James's character.

Now I should point out that we were not really being encouraged to watch *Carry On* films, it was illicit material that we tried our best to sneakily watch without anyone knowing. However, now I think back at it my parents may have allowed me to watch them as it was a simple way of introducing me to sex without having to explain it all directly to me. People steered away from talking about sex when I was growing up. There was no talk about it from the parents and there was nothing said about it at school. This is going to sound weird, but my knowledge of sex came about in a strange way. I had discovered masturbation by the age of eleven, maybe even earlier, and it fast became a favourite hobby of mine that sure beat the hell out of a lot of other hobbies. Nobody had explained, however, about sex. Nobody had mentioned what you had to do. I can't remember if it was before or after I had discovered the delights of Mrs Palm, but the way I remember it now, my knowledge of sex was almost a revelation. It was not so much something that I discovered as something that I *remembered*. I was dreaming one night and I suppose it would have been a wet dream if I hadn't been knocking a few out each day. In the dream, the various components of the male and female anatomy just came together and it all made sense. I suppose it was a bit like woodwork really and working out what fits where. It probably makes no sense to you, but that's how I remember it. Sex being something remembered, rather than discovered.

Maybe it's not so strange. Perhaps we have all been here before and we pick up trace memories from previous lives. That might be a fantastical statement to make, but all I do know is that if it hadn't been revealed to me in a dream, then I wouldn't have found out any other way until much later on. Nobody was telling us about how to go about it. I don't know why. I have spoken about nature and there really isn't anything that is more natural than sex when it comes down to it.

The other illicit films that we were not meant to watch when I was growing up were the *Hammer House of Horror* films. These were the films that were meant to be so terrifying that only adults were allowed to watch them. To a certain extent, I found them as camp and as comical as the *Carry On* films. That is not to say that I thought they were rubbish, because I thought they were great and I was a particular fan of Peter Cushing and Christopher Lee. It wasn't real, that's why I was not really frightened by them I think. I knew it was all staged and a film. Even the blood didn't look real. It was all a game and we were encouraged to go along with it and enjoy ourselves. I never got nightmares from watching those films. I don't remember having nightmares, but it stands to reason that I must have had nightmares about something. Everyone has nightmares about something.

The point is, that this is where my obsession with film developed from. I remember lying in bed one night thinking about a film that I had seen, I don't remember what one now, and thinking how good it would be if you could store all the films that you had seen in some kind of library so that you could watch your favourite ones whenever you wanted. Now, this was pretty forward thinking for the time, considering that VHS tapes were not really in widespread circulation at this stage and video recorders in the home were only just starting to come in. All in all, therefore, it goes a long way to explain why it is that I now have over a thousand Blu Rays and DVDs in my collection. I am a prolific hoarder of films and have accumulated a lot of movies and a lot of knowledge over the years. What I really get annoyed at though is the people who have no concept of the history of film. I met a girl at a party once and the subject got onto films.

'What sort of films do you like?' I asked her.

'Oh, I like anything,' she replied as she sipped her chardonnay.

I have always found this to not be the case. Whenever anyone tells you they like anything, when you start going for more extreme or obscure examples, it suddenly transpires that their tastes are very mainstream. It did turn out that she didn't like foreign language films, for example. After the debate, she finally said: 'Oh, I like old films best, you know?'

This was a better gambit. I liked old films. I had a collection of Chaplin films and most of the early Universal horror movies that had been made in the 1930s.

'Yah,' she continued. 'My favourite is probably *The Godfather Part III.*'

Now there was a problem that I had with this. *The Godfather Part III* is considered by many people to be the least successful of the trilogy of films, and they are probably right; however, it is a film that I have always liked and a film that I have always enjoyed watching. In some regards, it is actually my favourite of the three films. This was not the problem that I had with her comment though.

'*The Godfather Part III?*'

'Yah.'

'*The Godfather Part III?*'

'Yah, I just love old movies.'

'*The Godfather Part III* was made in 1990 for fucksake, it's not an old movie. Christ on a stick, I've got socks older than that film.'

It might surprise you to learn that this was not a successful collaboration and we didn't see each other after that.

***

The 70s were a very strange decade and I don't think it can really be fully understood unless you had the excitement of living through it the way that we had to. Friends of mine who were born after 1979 have, from time to time, asked me what it was like in the 70s. The answer to this question will very much depend on your own individual experiences, but to me the answer would always be: bland. It was the decade that fashion forgot as far as I was concerned. It was like the 60s and all that flower power shit had just drained the pallet dry and all we were left with were the dull colours, poor taste, flares and sandals with socks.

And then came the 80s which was an explosion of colour. Glam rock was replaced by the New Romantics and suddenly men were wearing make-up and everyone, men and women, had suits that had such big shoulder pads that you could successfully land a small plane across someone's shoulders. It didn't get much better from there if the truth were told. By the 90s we had shellsuits. God, I hated the idea of them and I always resisted the idea of owning one, let alone wearing one. I have always been suspicious of people, usually men, but not exclusively, who feel that it is acceptable to wear tracksuits as part of their everyday clothing. For me, a tracksuit is something that you wear in the gym, or when you are running on the street or in some way partaking of some form of exercise. For others, it is like a badge that they wear. I am a chav, it screams out at the uninitiated. The only time that I wear a tracksuit when I am not in the gym is when I know that I have a day of lounging around at home ahead of me and no one is coming to visit. During my wilderness years of no regular sex, tracksuit bottoms when at home also enabled easier access for Mrs Palm.

What? Like you haven't done it?

Fashion is a very strange thing. Each generation will always find something weird to look at in the next generation or the one before. Aside from tracksuits, I always found the tendency that old men have to wear trousers that come half way up their chest to be very bizarre. My grandfather used to do this all of the time; I mean, where do you

64

get trousers like that? Not that I want any you understand, I am more than happy with the way my trousers are, thank you very much.

***

I have mentioned how music was a great part of my life at this time. It still is if I am honest, although I have still never learnt how to play any form of instrument. That hasn't stopped me from having the odd try over the years. The problem with technology is, you build yourself up a great collection of films or music and then they change the technology and then you have to buy them all over again. I had a huge vinyl collection, which then transferred onto CD and which now I have bought all over again to use on my iPod. I dread to think what they will come up with next that will require me to start all over again. I have had to do the same with my movie collection. VHS to DVD to BluRay and God knows what the next thing will be like. Streamed directly into your brain, probably.

There were some great bands and artists in the 70s and 80s. Everything seems to have changed since then. I think to a certain extent I felt that music had died in 1991 with Freddie Mercury and then it took me a huge amount of time to get back into it again and to discover new bands and solo artists. Everyone was doing the Brit Pop thing and you were either in the Oasis or Blur camp, when I was in neither and would sorrowfully wander around with my Queen albums, bemoaning the death of music.

When I was at university it was considered very unpopular to like Queen and similar bands. I suppose it was just not trendy to like such a band. Despite the fact that they were a hugely successful act and probably one of the greatest bands that walked the earth, you were considered strange to like them. As a student, you were trendy if you liked obscure bands that nobody had ever heard of and who couldn't have held their own against Queen. All this proved was that the students were pretentious. From my experience, I can tell you that students still are pretentious and the reason why they didn't like Queen was probably because of the fact that it was just not considered "in" to like success.

You can't blame me for thinking that music had died when at the time, all that seemed to be dominating the charts were manufactured boy and girl bands that had never seen a musical instrument half the time, but were only successful for one reason, and one reason only. Yes, you've got it.

Sex.

Sex sells.

You see it all comes back down to sex at the end of the day. Deny it as much as you like, be as prudish as much as you like, but that is what it is all about; that is what this story is all about I suppose, in a roundabout sort of a way.

Six

Despite the one night stands, I still was obsessed with the idea of being with Lisa. I would have given anything at this point to have been with her as her partner. It's this which makes me think that I was still in love with her.

I think it was love, although to be honest when I look back at it, although I can see that the traces of love are there, they are diminished over the passage of time. Time is an amazing perspective. At the time that my thoughts were obsessed with Lisa, I would have told you that my love for her was a passion that burned so brightly that it could never be extinguished. Looking back at it all these years later, I wonder what the fuss was all about. Funny how something that once seemed so important can seem trivial after so many other things have taken place.

Towards the end of my first year at university I developed another relationship which was more substantial than my previous two encounters. Let's face it, after the fleeting one night stands that I had gone through, a couple of days would have been an improvement. As it happens, it was a relationship that lasted a couple of weeks. Her name was Sarah and we met because of a blind date that had been set up by a mutual friend.

Although the relationship was not long lasting, I did develop my experience with women with regards to Sarah. To be honest, she was the first blow job that I had truly experienced as for some reason it had never happened up until that point. That was an experience that I was very happy to discover and looked to have repeated whenever I could in the future. I have discovered that it is not something that every girl is really interested in doing and for others it is something that they can hardly get enough of. We all have our different tastes.

Other than that, I found my relationship with Sarah to be rather too restricting. Sarah placed strong regulations on the relationship and there were certain things that could not be done or said that placed a strain on matters and inevitably led to its downfall. You are going to ask me what these were now, but I am sorry, I can't remember what these actually were; I just remember that they were there. To Sarah, this was nothing more than a fling. To me, at the time I was hoping that it would be something more than just a fling. I think the reason for this was that at the time I was starting to become desperate for a relationship that was substantial and lasted because I probably felt that I was destined to spend my life alone. Rather stupid really when you think of how young I was at the time and how many more years there were ahead of me to experience a number of different things. As far as Sarah was concerned, there was never any intention that this could have developed into anything more serious.

I was probably frustrated by this attitude at the time, but with hindsight I can afford to be a lot more generous. I think the problem was that she was in love with someone else who was not really interested in her; something of a role reversal of my situation with Lisa really. She was hopeful that the situation would change and he would become interested in her. I think she probably had about as much hope as I did with Lisa. The blame is not all one sided, therefore, as to why this failed. With her having eyes elsewhere and me having my eyes elsewhere, it was doomed to failure before it had started. The relationship could not be anything but casual as we would both meet up and spend a few hours pretending that the other person was someone else. Our eyes were always looking at where the other person wasn't.

The separation when it did come, was with no ill feeling on either side and we wished each other all the best for the future. For about two years afterwards, I would receive a card from her at Christmas, but then this, which had become the only contact between us, eventually died out and then there was nothing but silence. Our mutual friend then told me a few years after that, that she was getting married, and not to the person that she had been in love with so I suppose she either got over him or found a substitute. I was extremely happy for her. I know a lot of people say that kind of thing in circumstances like this when it's usually the last thing that is on their mind. In my case, I can put my hand on my heart and say that I wished her nothing but the best. I can say that about Sarah, it is not something that I can say with total conviction about some of the others that were to follow her.

***

Although I was still clinging to the hope that Lisa would eventually come to her senses (as I saw it), Sarah did kick start me on a course of dates and exploration. The next girl that I was having dealings with was a girl called Justine.

Justine was elegant, attractive and overall a very nice person – she was just weird; a little too weird for my tastes. I think she genuinely believed that she was a witch. I don't mean that she was green or covered in warts and went everywhere on a broomstick, cackling. Credit me with some taste. No, she thought she was a white witch and apparently, the colour makes all the difference. Maybe she was a witch – who knows? I think I can lay claim to meeting a few later on in life.

Justine was a witch, sorry, a white witch, in the sense that she believed in the supernatural and would cast spells and in general feel that she had some ability with these. All harmless I suppose and it wasn't as if she had a cauldron or anything although I did look around for one as best as I could (discreetly, of course). It was at university and when you are young you believe in a lot of shit and act in a way that later in life you ridicule. Why does this happen? Partly, it is because university is a chance to stamp your individuality on your life in a way that you have not been able to previously because of the restrictions of school and the control of your parents. In its mildest form, this will represent itself in the clothing that you choose to wear, which is why students always look to be strangely dressed to older generations. You do have a habit of going somewhat to the extreme though, which usually is reined in a few years later, although in some cases it's a life thing. I don't know now which of us made the decision to part, but at the time I put it down to another disastrous relationship and started to think that this was the way that things were always going to go with me. We had a brief conversation when we broke up.

'I wish you all the best,' she said 'and to ensure that everything works out for you I will cast a good luck spell, so you will find true happiness.'

'Thank you.'

It was all I could really think to say in return for that. I was later to consider that as far as her being a witch was concerned, there were three options. In the light of what was to come later in my life, either:

a) witchcraft and everything associated with it is a load of bollocks;

b) she was actually a bad witch rather than a good one; or

c) she was really shit at this spell business.

***

I am sure that the more conservative tax payers amongst you will be delighted to learn that my time at university was not entirely spent on sex and the pursuit of sex along with unrequited love. A lot of my time was spent in this occupation don't get me wrong, but I did also work at my studies. I am aware that among certain groups there is a prevailing belief that you should not study at university. Either you should be naturally gifted without having to work at it and then walk away with no effort with a First-class honours; or you should lounge around doing the minimum that you can do not to be sent down and scrape through in the end with a Third. I suppose this was most seen by those that had been accepted at university not because of any academic talent, but because they were good at sport. There were some people amongst the university hierarchy that felt that they could accept certain students if they were academically useless, providing that they could row or excelled in some sport which would bring credibility to the university at the expense of the rivals.

I have never really agreed with this point of view. When I was at school I did waste a lot of time running after girls, exploring alcohol and dedicating a lot of time to wanking. At college, this was heightened slightly at the expense of some of my studies and it was not helped by my evil cow of a history teacher (remember her?) that conflicted with me over almost every single thing that I did. Regardless of her though, I did manage to score good enough grades to secure me a decent shot at a university place. When I got to university my studies, in history became interesting again. They had suffered a serious blow at A Level thanks to the bitch of a teacher who frankly should have been removed from any classroom before she could cause any further damage. At university, some of the same subjects that had bored the tits off of me at college suddenly became interesting again. More than ever I became aware that it is often not the subject, but the teacher and the way that it is taught which is most important. I remember the introduction that was given to the group by the first history lecturer that I had.

'History is something that you probably have never understood before in your studies,' he said.

We looked at him in expectation as he stood by the window of his rooms looking out into the quad with a mild look of distaste on his face. He couldn't have been more of a stereotypical lecturer if he tried. I actually do feel that he still felt that it was the 1950s or possibly even earlier. He favoured a lot of cardigans and tweed jackets as well as pipes which he smoked in his rooms whilst listening to students recanting their essays to him. I am not sure if smoking in the room was against university rules by this time or not, but I am pretty certain that he was the kind of person that could not have cared less. I remember him favouring a pocket watch and he kept it in the top pocket of his jacket with the chain threaded through the button hole. His room was lined with books not only on the shelves which were numerous, but also on every conceivable surface including the floor. I remember thinking that my father would have fallen in love with this room and probably never wanted to leave it again for the rest of his life.

'When you were at school,' he continued after a pause during which he had obviously spent tracking the progress of some undesirable across the quad. 'You were taught a certain view of history and then when you studied your O Levels you were taught that everything you had learnt thus far had been wrong and you had to relearn it.'

None of us bothered to correct him that the O Level system had been replaced by GCSE by the time that we studied. If the truth were known, he probably had no knowledge of the change at all.

'Doubtlessly, you experienced the same thing when you went to college.' He paused and sighed again as if he had the fate of the world upon his shoulders. I think upon reflection it was worse than that, he carried the weight of the Middle Ages on his shoulders. 'It is my painful task to tell you that it is something that I will now have to correct and teach you it all again.'

We all looked a little put off by this. Some of us had studied rather hard to be sitting where we were now sitting.

'What is history?'

We waited for a while as we were by no means certain if this was a rhetorical question or not.

'Well?'

Apparently, it was not rhetorical.

'History is the past. Things that have happened.'

This was a rather broken, inarticulate sentence that had been pronounced falteringly by a rather nervous student who just happened to be in the line of sight of the lecturer when he had turned from the window to see why nobody had answered his question. I don't remember that student's name and I am not entirely sure that I saw much of him again after this brief tutorial.

'Wrong,' he stated in a rather harsh way that left the student with no doubt at all as to what the lecturer expected from them in the future. The lecturer gave him the same kind of look that I imagine he would have given him if he had come into his rooms and presented him with a fresh dog turd. This was a university that could leave you intellectually quivering by the roadside in the remains of your once firmly held beliefs.

'History is not the past,' he eventually continued. 'Things that have happened in the past are *the past*. What you had for breakfast this morning is the past, but it is not *history*. People have a habit of saying things like "that's history" referring to things that they have done in the past, or God forbid, people that they have been involved in, or with. This is not the case. History is only history when you *write down* what has happened in the past and analyse it. History is the study of what has happened in the past, not the actual past events themselves. Your breakfast is the past, but thankfully it is not history.'

This was a fundamental change from most of the things that we had been taught so far. It was rather obvious when you put it the way that he had and I remember feeling a little short changed that this had never been explained to me like this before. It seemed to be a fundamental requirement. I actually got on well with this lecturer who had a rather unique view on the world.

'The world is divided into two groups of people,' he confided in me once. 'There are those who have a degree who are obviously graduates, and then there are those who do not have a degree and these are undergraduates.'

In his definition, if you did not have a degree then you were an undergraduate, whether or not you were actually studying for a degree was immaterial. You could argue that in his book-lined room above the quad in college, he was not living in the real world and did not venture out into it. You would be right about this. His speciality was mediaeval history and as far as he was concerned, nothing interesting had happened since and there was nothing at all that the modern world could offer him that would be in anyway beneficial or useful. It is probably also worth keeping in mind that he would have considered the Civil War involving King Charles I and Oliver Cromwell as being an event of the modern world. Talking of which, I had also seen him become rather annoyed on this subject when people referred to that period as *the* civil war. If a student in his presence ever mentioned the

73

Civil War he would assume they were referring to Stephen and Matilda in the 12th century. He could then advance the Wars of the Roses as another civil war, all of which could be used as evidence to suggest that *the* Civil War didn't deserve the title that it had.

I studied hard at university partly because I wanted to do well, but also because I actually enjoyed the study that I was doing. I felt that you needed to understand the past if you had any chance of understanding the present and if there was any hope for the future. Sadly, the study of history has proven that nobody ever learns anything from the past and that humanity is simply destined to keep repeating the same old mistakes again. I am not entirely sure I have ever come to a satisfactory conclusion as to why this might be. Possibly humanity is just stupid.

***

In my third year of university my life changed a great deal. I am sure you would like me to say that it was because my studies took off and I became a well-rounded person and was destined to make great waves in the academic world. The actual reason is because I met a girl that changed my life forever.

'Hi, my name's Susie.' Simple words, but I knew that she was the most wonderful person that I had ever met from the moment she said this.

She was truly staggering and there really was no doubt that she took my breath away. I had always dismissed love at first sight before as a fallacy, but when I met Susie I truly believe that I fell head over heels in love instantly. I would say this without a shadow of a doubt. I thought that I had been in love with Lisa, but Lisa couldn't hold her own against Susie. The most remarkable thing about Susie was that she fell for me as well. I was besotted with her and there was nothing that I would not do for her.

We moved into a little flat together and although it was a period of squalor to a certain extent and the place was hardly that great, it was the most wonderful period of my life. I couldn't get enough of her and wanted to spend every single moment that I could in her company, whether I was awake or asleep. We had a lot of laughs and a lot of good times together and to be honest the sex was fantastic and like nothing I had ever been exposed to before; not that I had been exposed to a huge track record at this point in my life.

Susie had declared that she was a nymphomaniac. She certainly had a very healthy sex life and liked to have sex three times a day. At the age that I was, it was easier to rise to this task than it would be later in life. She was pretty fantastic though and gave me a life-long love for seeing women in thongs. She looked pretty good in whatever she was wearing to be honest.

I apologise if this reminiscence of mine has made some of you go rushing off to the toilet to be sick. I know there is nothing worse than listening to someone else waxing lyrical about someone that you don't know. Nobody else can really understand the way that you feel, regardless of whether they have been there themselves or not. You are in love and you can't understand why the rest of the world doesn't feel the same way that you do. At this time, I probably spent a little too much time gushing to people about Susie and how much I loved her. There is no more certain a way of losing friendship than being obsessively in love with someone. It is a given fact that there is nothing more boring to people than someone else's love affair.

Whilst a lot of other students were holding out together in their dingy flats with no furniture, smoking cannabis, sitting on the floor getting slowly drunk, I was living in a world where I felt like a grown-up for the first time in my life. I never really liked the no furniture, cannabis life. In my second year, I had shared a multi-student accommodation house where all you had to sleep on was a sleeping bag on the floor, whilst living on Pot Noodles. One of my fellow students who was across the hall from me had even less space in his room than I did. This was chiefly because he had chosen to put a motorbike in the middle of his room. I have no idea why. It was obviously something that he felt he had a need to do. I suspect that he spent the majority of his time taking the thing apart and putting it back together again, rather than actually studying, or riding it for that matter. I hated that period in my life. I suppose this was because I had moved into the wrong group and these guys were not at university for the same reason that I was. I hasten to point out that not everyone at university slept on the floor or with motorbikes.

The flat I shared with Susie was very different from all of that. I can't remember all of the details about it now, other than the fact that it was up three flights of stairs in an old Victorian house that suffered from dry rot and mice. In the summer, it was one of the hottest places that you could ever find yourself in and in the winter, it was colder than Siberia. I loved the place. Outside my parental home, it was the first home that I ever had and it will always have a special place in my heart. The main reason for this, of course, had more to do with Susie than it did the actual building itself.

The one bedroom that we had was actually rather a large room considering the shit hole that I had been in before. This room always seemed to be warm and smelt of incense burners and candles from Susie's addiction that she had to such things. The walls were painted a dark red and we were fortunate enough to have been able to get hold of a large double bed that we had a great need for. I remember numerous times lying in this bed next to Susie as we were both face down leaning against pillows looking out the window that was at the head of the bed. I loved the view from this window that looked out over the rooftops to the distant spires of churches, cathedral and colleges. It is a view that I can bring back to my mind's eye now if I close my eyes. It's something that I don't think I will ever forget. There is much that I doubt I will ever forget from those days that were somehow more innocent and pure.

'I love everything about you,' I told her as we lay on the bed looking out the window.

'Everything?'

'Everything. I love the way that you smell. I love the way that you look at me. I love the way that you laugh. I love the way that you look when you sit at the desk, studying with your glasses on the end of your nose.'

'I don't like wearing my glasses.'

'You shouldn't worry. You look incredibly sexy with them on. I love the way that you look.'

'And you love the sex?'

'Of course.' Which was a cue to indulge in some more.

I tried my best to rise to her nymphomaniac tendencies which was not all that hard to do back in your early 20s when I was basically a walking hard-on. There is little that she could have done which would have made her less attractive to me. Our love had an intense passion about it that never seemed to die. We had baths together, candlelit dinners, would sit curled up together on our tiny sofa watching our hugely antique television that we had picked up from a junk shop somewhere.

'I've finally arrived,' I told a friend of mine at the time.

'Arrived where?'

'I feel my whole life has been leading to this moment. My entire life has building up to this moment. All of these years of hunting and being interested in girls and now I have found the one for me.'

'Sounds wonderful,' he replied without commitment.

I had finally arrived at where I wanted to be in life and there didn't seem to be a single thing that could have made it any better and there didn't seem to be any way that it could be spoilt. It was something that was going to last forever as far as I was concerned. The naivety of youth is something that is truly wondrous to behold. We learn from experience and probably become bitterer with it.

I had fallen so heavily in love that there was really nothing that I could do about it. I was in a hopeless situation. When you are this much in love, everything else takes a back seat and it was a struggle to keep up with my studies. Due to the distraction that I had when I graduated, I graduated with an Upper Second class honours degree.

'An Upper Second, Mr Durant?' my tutor had asked with a look of disapproval in his voice as if he had just caught him in bed with his daughter.

'Nothing too wrong with that, is there? Rather respectful result as far as these things go.'

'But you were on course for a First. What went wrong?'

I fell in love is what went wrong, but I doubted that it was something that I could have told him that would have made all that much sense to him.

I have in the past stated that I consider myself to be something of a hopeless romantic. It is possible with the evidence of the boiler room and the rose garden you might find this a little hard to believe; I maintain that I am a hopeless romantic and my passionate love affair with Susie was something that I would put forward as an example of the romantic side of me. I had been accepted to study for my Master's degree and everything was going so well. I therefore, took the next step that was entirely logical as far as I was concerned. Money was not hugely in abundance at this time, but I had started to get a small amount of money from assisting with the tutoring of undergraduates, now that I was a graduate. I saved up some of this money and then one night took Susie to the most expensive restaurant that we knew and, over a romantic candlelit dinner, I asked her to marry me.

Seven

Memories of holidays were much greater as a child. I look back now and although I know that it is completely implausible, I remember winters as being cold and snow covered and I remember summers as being dominated by bright sunshine and heatwaves. I suspect that it wasn't like that at all – it's just a trick that my memory plays on me - but this is how I feel that the weather should be. I do think that it should be blisteringly hot in the summer and we should be up to our knees in snow in the winter. I have always been an admirer of extreme weather. I love looking out and watching a torrential downpour of rain or a massive thunderstorm that seems to suggest that the end of the world is approaching fast.

The weather is something that we can't beat. People talk a lot about global warming and coastal erosion. I know that we have caused a lot of damage to this planet and humanity is without a doubt my least favourite of the species. However, we have lived through extreme weather changes before. Places that are deserts to us now were once pelted with rain and had rivers running through them. The continents have shifted over millennia. All of this is an ongoing thing. The difference is that we are the first generation that is trying to put a hold on nature and prevent it from evolving. We want things to remain exactly as they are regardless. It will never work.

I mention all of this because my thoughts are on holidays at the moment. As a family, we used to go to a variety of different locations for our holidays. One of my least favourite locations was to holiday camps. I have absolutely no idea if these places are still going now or whether they have long since vanished into memory. In all honesty, they were probably not as bad as my memory tries to convince me that they were. It is probably just part of the bleakness that I feel when I think back to the 70s. I suppose I just think that there is something a little depressing when I remember the lines of accommodation that reminded me of army barracks. The loudspeakers that were dotted about didn't help either as various announcements were made. I don't know, maybe I am confusing part of my memory with episodes of *Hide-Hi*.

Memory is something that has a habit of playing a lot of tricks on you. As time passes by, memories become clouded and it is difficult to remember fact from fiction. It has always amused me how some people can be absolutely certain that something has actually happened when in reality it is nothing but a figment of their imagination. If someone is so utterly convinced of a memory that is false, does it become a genuine memory? It just goes to convince you that the brain is something that we shall probably never completely understand, no matter how clever we may think we are.

I remember visiting my grandparents' house in London. It must have been somewhere in Middlesex now that I come to think about it. It is probably no coincidence that I remember it as Middle*sex*. You see sex is everywhere; there is no getting away from it.

I have already mentioned how cold it was in their house, but I should probably mention some of my other memories. I remember the house as a big old house that was probably built in the 1930s, but maybe it was a lot earlier. It had big bay windows and lead piping on the guttering. These days everything is made of plastic. I remember a long drive that went down the side of the house and in between the next house. This was a lengthy driveway that ended in a large garage. My grandparents did not have a car; as a matter of fact, I don't think they ever owned a car. I am not certain that either of them could actually drive. When you lived in London, or at least that close to London, you didn't really need a car, you could travel everywhere on the bus. I remember travelling with my grandfather on top of a big red bus, right at the front looking out the window.

Because they didn't own a car, my grandfather had converted the garage into his workshop. I was fascinated by this place. There were tools and jam jars containing all kinds of nails and screws and God alone knows what else. The entire place smelt of wood shavings and turpentine. I used to love looking at the mysterious instruments in there. The vice that was screwed to the work bench and the planers. I was never allowed to be unsupervised in this place as there was far too much harm that a young child could come to.

I would love to say that I developed an interest in woodwork from this childhood experience, but the truth is that I am totally useless when it comes to this kind of thing. My grandparents were of the generation that if something went wrong or if you needed something repaired, then unless it was an impossible task you did it yourself. They had the knowledge and they had the tools. Nowadays we just pick up the phone and call someone else to come and do it for us. This is probably due to the fact that a lot of skills of that generation have been lost on subsequent generations and it might also be due to the fact that we have more of a disposable income now than ever before. Even people of my parents' generation did not have the extra cash to spend on frivolities the way that we do now. It might also have something to do with the fact that we are just plain lazy these days.

Beyond the garage was the garden which I don't remember too much about, other than that there was a little grass area and then it went into a raised area where there was a greenhouse where my grandfather used to grow his own vegetables. Now I come to think about it, the older generation seemed to do so much more than we ever did. It amazes me how he managed to find the time to do everything that he was doing, but then I suppose that was because he didn't sit on his arse watching television all day.

Past the greenhouse and his vegetable patch there was an area of wilderness that had been left to overgrow. This, as you can imagine, was a fantastic place for a young kid like me to explore. I remember the sound of birds making cuckoo noises that you really wouldn't have associated with somewhere so close to London. I suppose they were cuckoos. It seemed a simpler age when you remember it, but there are certain things that I would not like to go back to. Like my grandmother's giant cooker. I have no idea what this actually was; some kind of stove, a monstrously huge black thing it was that really must have taken hours and hours to cook something that by today's standards could probably be done in minutes. Times have changed.

We used to use this house as a base when we visited London for holidays during the summer. I went back there a few years ago and on that visit, I found out something very important: you can never visit the past. That house and garden I used to play in so much is now somewhere deep underneath a supermarket car park. They call it progress.

***

'What is it that you would most like to see in London?'

This was from my mother who was trying to make conversation as my father was driving us down to London to stay at my grandparents'. She may have been making conversation to distract me from my father's driving which could best be described as erratic. I have no idea how old I was at the time. It probably wasn't my first trip to London, but it was obviously one of the first trips that I would actually remember what we were doing and have a say in. I had given a fair amount of thought to this question before it was asked so was able to provide an answer.

'I want to see Big Ben and a London taxi.'

My needs were simple in those days. You may think that these were strange choices, so I should probably explain it a little. Firstly, in those days a London taxi was pretty much exclusively the black cab that is famous all over the world. Back then, you could only find these cabs in London; today they seem to be everywhere. When I was a child, it was something more exotic than it is seen as today.

As to Big Ben; well, I know what you are going to say. Big Ben is the bell; the clock tower that everyone calls Big Ben is actually St Stephen's Tower. From that point of view, I have seen the clock tower numerous times, but to this day I have never actually seen Big Ben. I don't imagine there are all that many people who actually have seen it.

'That's nice, dear,' my mother said in an abstract kind of way.

My mother was often distracted and appeared to have other things on her mind. I think this was because my mother was distracted and had other things on her mind. She was a part-time lecturer in philosophy at the Open University, and seemed to spend the rest of her time reading books and thinking about things that most of the rest of us couldn't actually understand. From that point of view, she always seemed to be a little distant, as if all the weight of the world was on her shoulders. She, like a lot of philosophers, spent a great deal of time thinking about complex issues and trying to make sense of it all. She did this in the hope that maybe she would find the answers to all the questions that we had been asking since the beginning of time. It did make things a little difficult at times, as by the time that you answered a question she had asked, her thought processes had moved on and she was thinking of something else and had completely forgotten what it was that she had asked you. This was if you were lucky, if you were unlucky, then by the time that you answered she may have forgotten entirely who it was that you were.

My father was a librarian. Not a particularly famous librarian in a big library; I mean we are not talking Philip Larkin here. He worked in a university library because he could not stand working in a public library. I asked him about this once.

'Public libraries are so depressing, don't you think?' he had asked.

'I haven't really thought about it,' I replied on account of the fact that I hadn't.

'The problem with public libraries,' he continued whilst pouring himself a generous quantity of coffee, 'is that the books are designed for boring plebs.'

My father was never one to hold back on his opinion about anything. 'You see, the thing is,' he continued, 'the people that tend to use public libraries tend to be old age pensioners, who are the kind of readers who tend to want to read the likes of Mills and Boon and other pulp romantic bollocks.'

A rambling communication you might think. You might also glean from it that my father was someone who had started work in a library for the pure and simple reason that he wanted to work his way through the books that were there for loan.

'I've never been one for romantic novels, or trashy novels, or sex novels if the truth were known.'

'You want to read something a little deeper?' I asked.

'Exactly. I never excelled at education, at least not in the paper qualification sense of the word anyway.'

'You're one of the most educated and well-read people that I know.'

'Well, that's very kind, but let's not confuse well-read with intelligence. It annoys me that there is such a gap in people that use libraries though.'

'How do you mean?'

'You seem to be started out at a young age and encouraged to read and use libraries and then I suppose life just gets in the way of it all and you don't return until you are an OAP. You only return then because there isn't anything else to do.'

As you can imagine, I grew up in a house that was full of books. We had books everywhere. Every single room had books in it. We had books in the toilet and we had books in the bathroom. We had books piled up on each step of the stairs. Windowsills, bookcases, on the mantelpiece; you name it there were books placed absolutely everywhere. There were reasons for this. Partially, it was because my parents had more books than they actually had space to put them in; and partially it was because of the fact that very often my mother would forget where she was reading, and in fact what she was reading, and would leave it lying wherever she happened to be at the time. My father would occasionally do this as well, but nowhere near as often as my mother who had been known to leave books in the garden and the fridge. I don't mean by that for you to think that she used to read in the fridge, she was probably just looking in it.

It was inevitable that I would develop the same love of books that my parents had. During the course of growing up, either my mother or my father would read me stories at bedtime, it would more often than not be my father as my mother would either forget where she had left the book or forget that she was meant to be reading to me that night. This fuelled in me a lifelong love and passion for reading and the printed word. Lying there in my small bed with a quilt that might have been *Mr Men* inspired, paid testament to my interest in literature before I even knew the meaning of the word.

As I became older, I ended up being hooked on the various *Doctor Who* novels which I would read frequently. In an age of today where DVDs are everywhere and at the push a button you can watch television programmes that you have missed on iPlayer and download from the internet clips of television programmes from all ages, it is hard to remember a time when you watched something on television and then it was gone forever. Programmes were hardly ever repeated and then only at the whim of a television controller. Before the age of video, yet alone Blu Ray, the only way to recapture, remember and relive your favourite television shows was to read them. *Doctor Who* stories gave you the chance to capture shows that you had never seen, let alone ones that you had and were now gone. Later, of course, they would start to be released on video and then DVD. The problem with this was the realisation of the gap between the imagination and the reality that had been created in a BBC studio on a budget.

When I eventually grew out of these, I had moments where I drifted away from reading for a great deal of time. I had moved onto the *Biggles* books for a time and they were just as fascinating and good for the imagination. Old hardback copies from the 1950s in red covers where the dust jackets had been lost decades ago. Copies that had belonged to my uncles and were curiously and strangely marked '*To Timothy, Happy Birthday, 1954.*' Curious because I didn't have any uncles called Timothy.

By the time I was in high school there wasn't really anything that I was reading on a regular basis. Videos were developing their own individual art form and were taking up far more of the time of a teenager than reading books. Nevertheless, I remained a faithful, if infrequent visitor to the printed word. I would read the set texts that we were required to read for English, with few of them really doing anything to capture the imagination. It was then that something amazing happened. That something amazing was – Shakespeare.

At the age of twelve, I read *The Taming of the Shrew*. I say that I read it, but it was not as if I chose to read it, I was made to read it as part of my English class. I didn't really take to it; the correct pathways in the brain had not correctly aligned at the time. At the age of fourteen, I had reached *Macbeth* which captured my imagination a little better. *Twelfth Night* followed at the age of fifteen, but then at sixteen, I read *King Lear* and it set fire to my brain in a way that nothing had ever done before. From here, I found my way to *Hamlet* at which point there was no stopping me. I am still fascinated by this play and I can read it time and time again and not be bored with it. Each time I read it, I can see something different in it and a new way in which it can be interpreted.

It is without a doubt that Shakespeare led me back to a passion for reading. Ultimately, I ended reading every single Shakespeare play. I then went back to the A Level texts that I hadn't enjoyed when forced to read them, but when reading for your own leisure, became far more pleasurable. This was most pronounced with *Wuthering Heights*. Shortly afterwards I read *Dracula* for the first time and from that time onwards I never looked back and have read every day since. I now always have a book on the go. These two classic gothic tales were very instrumental in developing a library which, from humble beginnings in the early 1990s, now stands at a colossal 2000-3000 books. It's nothing compared to my parents' collection of course. I doubt that they could give you a figure on the number of books that they have.

People talk to me about print being dead and electronic books the coming thing, but I am old fashioned and I like to not only hold a book of real paper in my hand, but also to be able to see it on the shelf, sitting there expectant at some future reread. I asked my dad if he would like one of these electronic books for one of his birthdays recently. He replied in his usual characteristic manner,

'What the bloody hell would I want one of those things for?'

Reading is a runaway art though and one thing frequently leads to another. The uninitiated will not understand the magical power of books. Indeed, my friend Michael, when I was nineteen, told me with proud acclaim:

'I have never voluntarily read a book in my life.'

He seemed to say this as if this were some revelation to be proud of. We were never destined to be friends all that long, given how we were so diametrically opposed. I tried to explain it to him once.

'Books are alive, Mike. They are magical and have the ability to change the world. The ability to enter into minds and change your ability to continue life the way that you had so far carried on.'

He denied all of this and looked at me in a foolish manner.

'That's bollocks. Books cannot change anything, they are dead and only words,' he said.

To which I could only reply: 'Karl Marx, *The Bible, The Torah, The Koran, Mein Kampf.*'

All of which meant little to him, of course. I told my father about this conversation shortly after it had taken place.

'Ignorant little shit,' he had scoffed. 'Will probably end up as prime minister one of these days, or Education Secretary. They always seem to put the most useless of people in the roles that really matter.'

***

I did get to see my London taxi and Big Ben/St Stephen's Tower and that was something that I was very pleased about. Another memory of around this time is the London Underground trains. At my young age, the idea of a train that travelled under the ground was just fantastic, if not implausible. I used to love standing on the platform looking into the tunnel where the train would be coming from and listening out for it. I remember first of all there was a rush of wind along the tunnel onto the platform as the air in front of the train was pushed forwards in front of it. Then there might be a clattering on the tracks and then there would be the soft moan of the train itself as it approached and then arrived. To me, it was magical. I think of the thousands of people who use these trains every day and think nothing of them. They have become mundane and forgotten to them. I also remember the machines on the platform where you could buy chocolate. You put your money in and then had to pull the metal drawer out with all your force to get to the chocolate. I wonder if those chocolate dispensing machines are still there, or if the vending machine has taken over.

My main memories of holidays whilst growing up were of the times spent in Wales which has always been a favourite holiday location of mine ever since. The weather wasn't always great, I grant you and in fact, there were times when it was downright terrible. There were also times when it was lovely, though, and the sun shone across the mountains and the valleys. I fell in love with the place then and there and I don't think I have ever been out of love with it since.

As a matter of fact, I didn't just fall in love with Wales, but I fell in love with everything Welsh as well, particularly the culture. I read Dylan Thomas, R. S. Thomas, and Gwyn Thomas – I am sure that I probably read other people that were not surnamed Thomas. I am sure my dad was very pleased as he loved Welsh literature a great deal. Hell, he loved all literature.

'There is something very special about the Celtic spirit,' he told me one year after we had climbed Mount Snowdon. 'It's the triumph over adversity. Life is shit and has dealt you some hard cards, so you take them and you make something special and truly wonderful from it.'

'A bit like the Jews,' I stated.

'Yes, I suppose you're right there,' he said as he thought about it for a moment and poured himself another mug of coffee. (Yes, he was really doing this on top of a mountain.) 'I would say that they have a lot to write about.'

I remember these literature chats on holiday with my father with a great deal of affection. He may not have had a degree in the subject, but he really didn't need one.

'It's really just a piece of paper,' he said. 'Doesn't prove anything. What really matters is what you've got in here.' With this he would tap his temple as if it was Masonic code and only I would understand what it was that he meant.

With such a love for literature I wonder if he was ever disappointed that when I came to go to university, I opted to study history. I wonder if he had been looking forward to the concept of me coming home with an extensive reading list and then discussing the books with me, or maybe he imagined me ringing him up to ask for his opinion on some nuance of *Madame Bovary* that I was working on for some assignment or other.

Sadly, it never happened.

Eight

Some of you will undoubtedly feel that I was a bit of an idiot for asking someone to marry me when I was so young. You might be forgiven in thinking that we couldn't possibly have known our own minds in something as serious as this. Having a passionate love affair is one thing, but to marry was a step into something far different. To an extent, I can understand why you might feel like this. Twenty years on from the event if I were to learn today of someone wanting to marry at this age, I would urge them to caution and think that they were insane in much the same way that everyone cautioned us and thought that we were insane. If I were to be foolish enough to caution a young couple like that today, then I expect that they would do the decent thing and ignore me in the same way that we ignored everyone who said it to us.

Marriage was something that I had always wanted to do. I had always seen myself as someone that would marry and have children. This view doesn't seem to be so popular these days for reasons that I am not entirely sure that I understand. In these 'modern times' it is almost seen as a backward step going down such a traditional route. Some see it as a hopeless thing to do as so many marriages now end in divorce. Easy to marry and easy to divorce seems to be the thing these days, so many people just don't see the point of bothering. There is a tendency to want to just live together without getting married.

'What difference would getting married make?' a friend had asked me once. 'It's just a piece of paper.'

I suppose in many regards, not getting married just makes it easier to walk away when things don't go the way that you want. I can't really see the sense of all of the argument though. Yes, some marriages do end in divorce. However, some car journeys end in a crash, but that hardly stops you from wanting to get into the car in case your journey is one of them. Nobody enters into marriage with the expectation that it will end in divorce. You marry because you expect to spend the rest of your life with that person and then if it ends in divorce, it ends because something went wrong along the way.

I don't know what the statistics say about this. I don't know if marriage is on the decline and divorce is on the rise. I still feel that despite what the modern world might teach us or what we may feel now, that there is still a large contingent of people that do want to marry because they do feel that they have met the person that they want to spend the rest of their life with and that the best way to do this is to marry.

All I can tell you for sure is that I had found the person who was the one that I wanted to spend my life with. I knew that we were young and that in many regards we were still growing and developing and I knew that our characters and personalities might change in the future. However, all of that taken into consideration I also felt that beyond any doubt, Susie was the one for me. I couldn't imagine being with anyone else. How did Susie feel about all of this? Well, as far as I could see she felt the same way as I did. She certainly accepted my proposal of marriage and although money was still a little tight, we took the first opportunity that we could to go out and get her an engagement ring. It was the most wonderful time and we were so wrapped up in our own little world that we knew nothing of anything or anyone else. We would walk down the street, arm in arm, lost in each other's eyes and laughing at our own private jokes, oblivious to any outside influence. I make no apologies for the way that we were. I hope that at some point in your life you have felt the same way as we did then. It is never too late if you haven't though.

Experience has shown me that it is the case that when you are least looking for it, the unexpected can explode in your life. However, experience has often also shown me that no matter how good life seems to be and no matter how wonderful things are going, life is always prepared to turn the tables on you and suddenly give you an unexpected slap in the face that you really did not see coming. This can cause people to always believe that whenever they are on an up and everything is wonderful, it is only a matter of time before things come crashing down around you. It's a rather depressing way to look at life, but I suppose if you are always expecting to get a kick in the teeth then you will be pleasantly surprised when it doesn't happen. The real pessimist, of course, will just say that because it hasn't happened now doesn't mean that it isn't going to happen eventually. Every up must, by definition, have a down at some point.

Whether we like to admit it or not, every single relationship that we have has a timer attached to it. In some cases, relationships run their course because you drift apart, become different people and no longer are compatible with each other. In some cases, you might just wake up one morning and realise that you don't love each other anymore. In other cases, as the period of discovery grows into familiarity, you might just start to realise that the person that you are with is not the person that you thought that they were when you got together. In other cases, if all else is going well and you remain happy together, you do not escape the timer because it is inevitable that the relationship will end when one or the other of you dies. Given the pain that will be inevitable, some people will ask why bother to get into it in the first place?

What is the alternative though? Do you say that you will avoid relationships because of the fact that you cannot stand the pain that will follow at the end of it? What would that achieve? Is it better to spend a life alone, not knowing the joys of a relationship because of the fact that you are scared that one day the timer will leave you on your own anyway? Where is the logic of that? I suppose some would argue it is better to be on their own by choice rather than because of the death of the person that they love. I don't buy that, though. I still maintain that nobody really wants to be on their own if they had the choice.

How do you deal with the pain, though, of the loss of a loved one? If you really love someone and they dump you then the level of pain that you feel can be as equal to that of a period of mourning. As far as you are concerned, it's as if that person *has* died. Once they were in your life and the next moment they have gone. How do you deal with the pain that comes with loss, whether due to death or being dumped? I wish I had some great pearls of wisdom that I could offer you that would give you some guidance and consolation in this matter, but I am afraid that I can't. I just don't know. All I can really say is that the pain that may come is part of the deal if you want to feel the happiness at the time of the relationship.

That's the deal people, I am afraid. That is life and that is death. You can hide your head in the sand and avoid contact with people to try and prevent yourself being hurt; if that is the path that you really want to follow, then good luck to you. I just hope that when the inevitable end comes and you are on your death bed, you don't look back on your rather lonely life and ask yourself the question 'what if...?' For me, that has always been the driving force in my life. I never want to look back on my life and regret lost opportunities.

***

I have always had a better relationship with my father than my mother. I suppose the reason for this is that my mother always seemed to distance herself from me. I don't think this was because of any dislike or anything like that. She was just the kind of person that, because of her work and interests, distanced herself from everyone around her. She seemed to go through life being terribly distanced from it all.

I am not sure of the relationship that she had with my father and how he coped with the distance. I think it was probably something that he didn't mind all that much. I am sure that they loved each other a great deal, but the slight distance gave them the opportunities to follow their own interests. My father, I am sure, enjoyed the undisturbed time that he got to slowly read his way through two and a half thousand years of literature whilst his wife was off wrestling with some of the biggest problems that philosophy could offer.

They also had the advantage of living in a big enough house to have their own space without getting under each other's feet all of the time. They each had their own study, for example, which was a luxury for them both. I am probably painting a picture that makes it seem like they were hopelessly apart from each other, but this wasn't the case. It perhaps wasn't the most conventional of relationships, but I believe that they were happy with their love and wouldn't have wanted it any other way.

I was never really allowed into my mother's study which she kept as her own private sanctum where she spent most of the time thinking. When we were kids, we were always told to keep away from the study when our mother was in it because it was one of the worst crimes that could ever be committed to interrupt our mother when she was thinking. The problem was that she spent most of her time thinking, or so it seemed to my brother and I when we were growing up. Time moves differently for children than it does for adults so perhaps it was not nearly as much time as I thought it was.

My father's study was one that I loved and one that he never minded us being in and was more than happy for us to be quietly playing in the corner. He had more books in this one room than most libraries had, or so it seemed to me as a child. He had books everywhere and his study was less of a study and more of a reading room or library, as his desk was almost entirely unusable due to the large number of books that were piled up several feet high like a series of towers. A small paper city that he had constructed containing not people, but thought. Most, if not all of his books were paperback copies that had been well thumbed and probably read numerous times. As I got older I loved being in this room which always seemed warm and generated the smell of books, as you would expect. I loved looking through the spines and reading all the titles that seemed so exotic as a child. Many of them I have now read myself. I always loved the fact that I grew up in a household of books and I can't imagine those that haven't.

Despite the number of books that there were in the room and the seemingly chaotic nature that there seemed to be for the filing system, my father actually knew exactly where every book was. There must have been somewhere near 3000 books in that room and when I was in my adolescence and my father was trying to teach me about literature, we developed a game. I would say the title of a book and my father would point out where it was in the room without being allowed to get up from the sofa which was in the middle.

'*Great Expectations?*' I would state and he would point towards a corner of the room and off I would trot to find and locate the said book.

'*The Return of the Native?*' A finger would point to an opposing corner and I would disappear off in the direction.

'*The Mill on the Floss?*' Off I would go to the window.

From time to time I would invent the title of a non-existent book and try and catch him out, but he would just look at me chuckle, and say, 'You're making it up.' I was never able to catch him out. From time to time as I got to know where things were, he would test my memory and he would call out the name of a book and I would have to say where it was.

It may not seem like the most exciting game that you could play as a child, but as I could not catch him out with my made-up titles, I relished in the idea of being able to catch him out one day by finding that he had got the direction wrong. It also improved my knowledge of literature and I got to develop a detailed knowledge of who wrote what. I even read some of them as well. It never occurred to me to cheat and remove a book from its place and put it somewhere else to catch him out. That would just not have been the right thing to have done and I suspect that he would have known that I had done it and I wouldn't have been able to live with the shame.

Probably due to my mother's distance and faraway look in her eyes, my father was always more approachable. It didn't matter how busy he was reading, he would always have the time for us. We would come into his study and he would put his book to one side and take off his reading glasses and give us his full attention before returning to his book once we had gone again.

**

I went to visit my parents to break the news about my forthcoming marriage. Susie and I had decided that we didn't want to have a long engagement, but wanted to get married as quickly as possible. This wasn't because she was pregnant, as you might have imagined. It was simply because of the fact that we loved each other and wanted to formalise that arrangement as soon as we could.

When I came home, my mother was nowhere to be seen and I assumed that she was in her study so I made straight for my father's study. I was rather surprised upon entering to find him pacing up and down rather than lounging on the sofa reading like he normally was whenever I had entered before. He was so preoccupied that he did not notice me for a few moments and continued to walk up and down on the threadbare carpet, staring at the floor as if he was trying to see through it.

'Oh, Max, hi,' he said when he finally noticed me. He came over to me and there was a brief awkward moment as we were not the kind of family that hugged each other, so there was always a void that followed any meeting as each of us tried to work out the best way to greet each other. It was something that was never really satisfactorily decided.

'How's things?' I asked, noticing for the first time that he appeared to be so much older than he had been the last time that I had seen him. I suddenly became aware of the march of time and how the world was still going on around me.

'Oh, you know. Can't complain, trotting along.' He seemed to be lost deep in thought for a moment before finally coming up with the next question. 'How's university?'

'Pretty good. Going well.'

'Excellent. That's very good,' he seemed to lose focus for a moment and seemed to be distracted by something as he lapsed once again into silence. 'Oh,' he suddenly exclaimed as if he had just remembered something important. 'How's your girl? Susie, isn't it?' I had taken Susie to meet my parents a few months previously and they had seemed to get on very well although Susie felt that my mother didn't like her. I had to explain that to a certain extent most mothers feel that there isn't a woman walking the face of the planet that is good enough for their son. And the fact that she was so engaged in her own pursuits that half the time she had trouble noticing me, so any distance that Susie felt had come from her was not something that should be take as a personal slight.

'She's good, better than good, great in fact.' This would have been the ideal opportunity for me to tell him my news, but something held me back. Instinct, I suppose. I felt that something was bothering him, but that he was either not going to tell me or was trying to find the best way to do it.

'How's Mum?'

'Oh, you know Mum, she's the way that she is. Well, actually, I suppose that isn't entirely true.'

'What do you mean?'

'Look, perhaps you'd better sit down.'

I didn't like the sound of this or the way that it was going. I sat on the sofa and there was another period of silence whilst he seemed to be gathering his thoughts during which time I decided that it was probably best to leave him to it rather than trying to force the issue. I knew that when he found the route to tell me what he had to, then he would.

'You know how Mum has always been, somewhat- well, abstract I suppose?'

'Yeah, well, that's Mum.'

'Yeah, well it turns out that that isn't Mum.'

'I'm not sure I follow.'

I suddenly had the mental image that the person who I had always thought of as my mother was suddenly an imposter.

'No? Well you see, the thing is, all that slightly abstract nature that we always put down to her just being deep in philosophical

97

thought all of the time isn't actually the case. Those moments when she always appeared to be so distracted that she didn't know who we were half the time. Well, it turns out that she didn't actually know who we were.'

I had never seen my father look so at a loss and confused before, he really didn't seem to know what to do.

'I don't follow you.'

'No? Well, okay. How can I put it?'

He had not joined me on sitting down and had continued to pace the room but now came to a stop with one hand on his hip and the other moving slightly as if he was trying to pluck the words that he needed out of the air. For someone that had spent most of his life around books and words he certainly seemed to be struggling to find the ones that he wanted now.

'Thing is Max, that Mum's not very well.'

'Not very well?'

'No.'

'Flu? There's a lot of it about at the moment.'

'No. No, it's not flu. Would that it was. No, I'm afraid that it's altogether more serious than that.'

'How serious?' I was starting to get worried and had a very uneasy feeling in the pit of my stomach.

'Erm, pretty serious.'

'Pretty serious?'

'Yeah, pretty serious.'

'How serious?' I asked again.

'About as serious as it can get.'

'What is it?'

'Well, it turns out that all that abstract distanced stuff that we so know and love your Mother for, isn't because of the fact that she is just scatty, but because she has a, well, a brain tumour.'

'Oh fuck.'

'Yeah, oh fuck. That's pretty much what I thought. Sums it up rather nicely.'

We lapsed into silence for a moment, each to our own thoughts. My father awkwardly standing there and looking like he had turned up in fancy dress at a funeral and me staring into space trying to make sense of the words that he was telling me.

'How long have you known?'

'Well, not that long really. Turns out she has known for a lot longer than any of us, but chose not to tell anyone. Didn't want to tell me about it. Thought it might upset me, I suppose. Bit of a pisser really as I didn't think we had any secrets.'

'She's known a while?'

'Years, I would guess. It's testimony of your mother's intellect that she has been able to hold it together for so long without anyone really guessing the truth. I'm afraid that the medical science is a bit beyond my ability. You mention medical terms to me and it goes in one ear and out the other. You really need to give me the Ladybird book of diagnosis for me to make any sense of it all, though. From what I can understand, from what I've been told, it's something that you can live with for a long period of time without it really causing all that much harm.'

'So, she's going to be alright then?'

'Well, no; not really. You see, it turns out that she has been living with it for a long period of time without it really causing all that much harm already.'

'So, what's changed?'

'Well, it has always had the potential to grow and if it does it can then eat up parts of the brain, which explain the memory loss and distraction most of the time. It would seem that it has been doing it for some time. To a greater or lesser extent, it's a little bit difficult to know for certain.'

'Fuck.'

'Yeah, well maybe. I don't know, maybe I've got all that wrong, but I am pretty sure that's what they said the problem was. It's a little difficult to concentrate on someone telling you something so serious when they must realise that you are not taking it in because the bottom of your world has just fallen out.'

'So, what's happening now?'

'Well, it seems it has been progressively growing and causing more and more problems, little cancerous, parasitic prick. Seems that it has reached a point now where it's only a matter of time.'

'How long?'

'Don't think they like to commit themselves to useful things like that. We only found out because of the fact that I thought there was something wrong so insisted on taking her to a doctor. Turns out that the doctor thought I already knew about it. Would have made life easier if I had. Ironically, it turns out that it's attacking the memory so much that she forgot she even had it.'

'What do we do now?'

'Well, the most logical thing is to carry on as if nothing has changed. I was just debating on whether I should tell you boys when you came in. I hadn't really made my mind up, but your arrival was fortuitous. I guess you have the right to prepare yourself for the inevitable.'

'Fuck.'

'Yeah, I couldn't really put it any better myself. Trouble is, I can't really imagine life without her. I can't imagine what it will be like. I'm not entirely sure that I have the courage to even go on without her. My entire life has been about her.'

'You don't mean suicide?'

'No, I'm rather too much of a coward, like Hamlet, to be able to do that kind of thing.'

I nodded my head and struggled to think of what I could say that would bring comfort to him or in any way make a difference and I am sorry to say that I fell short when the moment was required of me.

'Anyway,' he said, seemingly pulling himself together. 'What brings you here today?'

'I came to tell you that Susie and I are going to get married.' I hadn't meant to say it, but in my shock the truth just slipped from my mouth.

He nodded his head at this and seemed to think about it for a few seconds.

'I think that's a bloody good idea.'

Nine

I thought that only love could take my breath away up until this point, but the news of my mother's illness hit me like I had been punched in the stomach. You never expect to lose your parents. Logic tells you that it is something that is bound to happen, has to happen, in fact, and yet a little part of your mind doesn't believe it because they have always been there. How can you imagine someone who has always been there, who has been the rock and stability throughout your life, suddenly not being there any longer?

When I look back on it now, the news that I was very likely to soon be losing one of my parents came as a big shock to me, but I realise that it must have been a thousand times worse for my father. Losing a parent, in most cases, is a big traumatic experience, but how can it compare to losing the person that you have chosen to spend your life with, to be your companion. I shudder to think of it and yet I know it is a possibility for many of us to have to face. We can't choose who our parents are and it's all down to luck whether we get on or not and how we go through life with them; but our partner is someone that we have chosen to be with from all the other possibilities that we might have gone with.

My father was more open and honest about this than he had been about a lot of other things in life. I don't mean to make that sound like he was a liar, he wasn't. He wasn't someone that went in for displaying his emotions; he was very old fashioned in that regard. As I have already said, we were not really a hugging family that went in for displaying emotions openly. Typical of our background, I would think.

That being said, I had never seen him hit as hard as he was by this. Maybe it was because of the fact that he had not been expecting my visit so he had not had time to prepare his face for meeting me.

'The thing is, I just can't imagine what it will be like without having her around,' he said to me as we sipped some coffee that he had poured us from a small coffee pot that he kept in one of the corners of his study. For my father, coffee had probably as much importance in his life as books. I am sure he survived on a diet of caffeine and literature.

'It is almost incomprehensible to come to terms with the concept of not having her there. I mean, even when she is locked away in her study marking papers and doing whatever it is that she's doing, I'm aware of her presence and the fact that she is there. I just can't imagine what it's likely to be like not being able to feel that any longer.'

I made sympathetic noises because I couldn't really think of something to say in response to this. I didn't really need to though because he carried on without waiting for me to say anything.

'I know she has always been a bit scatty and maybe I should have picked up on that earlier and done something about it. The problem is that this is part of her character and I should have known when the character ended and the tumour took over.'

'You can't blame yourself.'

'No, but I will. I know she has been to see doctors and there is nothing that could have been done to have changed anything, but that will not stop me from thinking that maybe if things had just been slightly different then this might not have happened.'

I tried to find words that I could offer that might be of comfort, but despite being from such a well-read family I found it very difficult to find the words that I thought might be of help. I suppose there is some truth in the fact that there are no words that would have helped. Some customs have it that when visiting someone who is mourning, it is better to say nothing, but to sit in silence rather than offer empty words of comfort that do no help and are probably not listened to at any rate. I have to admit that I could see the sense of this.

All of this makes it sound like my mother was already dead. Of course, she wasn't, but the news seemed to hit both of us as if we had learnt that she had just died. Even now, I find it hard to find the words to describe what was going on here and how we were both feeling. I suppose that this has something to do with my suppressed upbringing and the culture that I had become accustomed to.

'Where's Mum now?'

'She's in her study marking some university assignments.'

'Should we go and talk to her?'

'I'm not sure that's a brilliant idea. The thing is, she wants to carry on as normal; well, as best she can and for as long as she can. I haven't actually spoken to her about letting you kids know what is going on at the moment and I'm not sure how she will react to knowing that I've told you.' He lapsed into thought for a moment. 'Probably best to keep it to yourself that you know. It might upset her further if she knows that. Might bring on some extra worry for her, you know?'

I could see the logic of this to an extent.

'What about Jerry?'

'Ah, well, yes, good point.'

'It hardly seems fair to keep him in the dark when I know about it.'

'True, but you know what Jerry is like.'

I should probably explain at this point that Jerry is my younger brother. I have not mentioned him all that much up until this point, I am not entirely sure why, but probably because he has just not featured all that heavily in the events that I have described. Jerry owed his name to my father's fandom of Jack Lemmon once again and he had been named after the character that Lemmon played in the classic film *Some Like It Hot*. At least in Jerry's case, he had actually been named after a Jack Lemmon character. I still wonder about that and whether my naming was a mistake due to lack of attention to detail.

Jerry is a couple of years younger than me and was something of a tearaway as far as the family were concerned. He had rejected the more academic life with the pursuit of knowledge and learning, to go his own way. He had left school with minimal qualifications and had jumped from job to job with no formal training in what it was that he was doing and where he was going in life. He was, in essence, directionless and wandering around in the quiet confidence that it really didn't matter because it would all work out in the end. This appears to be a talent that is most exercised in the young as it seems to be something increasingly more difficult to do the older you get. He was the most relaxed person not only out of everyone in my family, but out of anyone I ever met, I think. He was so laid back that he truly was horizontal. He really did aspire to the philosophy of going with the flow and would turn his hand at anything that came along until such a time as he became bored with it and would then wander off in a different direction. He lacked stability which probably caused my parents a fair amount of worry. His fickle nature made him someone that was difficult to pin down to anything.

I wouldn't say that I didn't get on with Jerry, we just saw things very differently and I suppose we didn't really have all that much in common. I was not sure that I wanted 'the big family secret' to be one that was known to everyone apart from him, though. To an extent, I knew that it was my father's decision to tell who he wanted to about what was going on with mother. I was painfully aware of the fact that if I had not chosen that day to return home to tell my news to my parents, then it was highly likely that I would not have found the news out myself until much later on. I was not sure how I felt about that.

'So, marriage then?'

'Yeah.'

'Wow. You don't think that you're...'

'What?'

'Well, too young?'

'I don't think you can put an age on something when it's the right thing to do and you know you're in love.'

'True. When are you thinking of doing it?'

'As soon as possible.'

'She's not -?'

'Oh God, no.'

'Well, that's something. Not that there would be anything wrong if it were the case that she was – you know?'

'Yes.'

'You do feel you are doing the right thing, though?'

'Yes.'

'Only I wouldn't be much of a parent if I didn't urge you to some degree of caution.'

'How so?'

'Well, you have to be sure about these things. Rushing into something that you haven't thought out properly can result in a disaster that's a lot more difficult to get out of than it was to get into. You don't feel you want to wait a little while longer?'

'No, Dad. I'm sure that Susie is the one for me and I want to be with her and spend the rest of my life with her.'

'Well, if you're sure then that's fine. We had better make some preparations then and sort some things out.'

So, we did and that was the end of what he had to say on caution and making sure that I was doing the right thing.

***

Susie and I had talked about it a little already and we had decided that we wanted a low-key wedding. We didn't want all of the fuss, but more importantly, we didn't want the expense that would come with a big wedding. We didn't expect our parents to pay for the wedding. We anticipated that we would pay our own way and that was fine as it meant we could have some kind of control over what was done and how it was done. It's a little difficult to dictate your big day when someone else is picking up the bill.

We decided on a registry office wedding because neither of us was particularly religious and getting married in a registry office was bound to be a lot cheaper than getting married in a church. We were of the opinion that if you got married in church that would mean a lot of added expenses including hiring an organist and then there would probably be a choir plus you could not help but turn up to the church in a limo. The expenses just spiralled and we were of the opinion that the Church knew how to fleece people for a huge amount of money; after all, it was something that they had been doing successfully for hundreds of years. A registry office wedding followed by a reception at a local hotel would probably cost us £2000 whereas a church wedding could easily end up nearer £10,000, if not more. Marriage in a registry office came with different stipulations.

'There cannot be anything within the ceremony that is of a religious nature,' the registrar had told us.

'I understand that,' I replied, a little impatient to get out of the room.

'No religious jewellery is permitted.'

'This won't be a problem.'

'Your vows will not be able to contain any reference to God, or any other religious deity or representative.'

'Of course.'

'The music that you choose to play during the ceremony will also be vetted as well to ensure that there are no religious references.'

'I see.'

'*Angels* by Robbie Williams, is however acceptable.'

'Not to me it isn't.'

I know it is considered to be the big day of your life and in some regards a once in a lifetime experience so it should be special, but we were of the opinion at the time that you made the day special in your own way rather than because of the venue that you had chosen. A friend of mine got married recently and told me that due to the expense they were keeping the wedding small and would be working to a budget.

'Working to a budget is a good thing,' I replied.

'Yes. We have had to limit a number of things that are not really essential.'

'Well, there are a lot of extra add-ons that people do for weddings which are not really necessary when you get down to it.'

'Still, we've got the budget down to £8000 now, so that's good.'

'What the hell do you deem essential for it to cost £8000?' I was rather amazed by what she considered to be cost cutting.

'Well, we simply had to have the vintage Rolls Royce, naturally.'

'Naturally.'

'Plus, my dress has cost over £1000.'

'Over a £1000 for a dress?'

'Yes?'

'Why?'

'Well, dear boy, it has to be a special dress. I simply couldn't turn up in any old frock now, could I?'

'A £1000 for a dress that you are only going to wear once?'

'Well, I might wear it more than once, Max.'

'More than once?'

'Of course.'

'I'm not sure that you're entering into the true spirit of what marriage is meant to be.'

Perhaps you will agree with her and you think that I am being rather too harsh about it. We all have our own ways of doing things I suppose.

Our wedding was a very low key affair; we only invited close family and friends. I discovered that one of the most stressful things about getting married was the guest list. People came out of the woodwork that you had probably not spoken to for years who wanted an invite, in some cases they saw an invite as their God-given right because they happened to be a cousin that you probably only saw and spoke to at Christmas. Tempers would run high over this which all seems so trivial as far as I am concerned. It was my wedding and I should be allowed to invite whoever I damn well liked and leave out people if I didn't want them there, particularly as we were trying to keep it small and only had space in the registry office for forty people. We invited no cousins from either side, invite one and there is an expectation that you should invite them all. People can become very selfish when it comes to weddings.

Once you have decided who you want to alienate by not inviting, you can decide who will get annoyed by where they sit. I found all of this the most stressful thing about getting married. I really couldn't be dealing with it all. The way things were going I was tempted to elope to Gretna Green and get married secretly and just come back and tell people that we had done it. Now that would have seriously pissed off everyone involved. Sometimes I wish I had done just that.

We got married in April on a day that was a little blustery with spring winds and showers. It didn't matter as we had not arranged to have a wedding photographer so the dark skies didn't really inflict on the permanent image of the day. Instead, friends and family brought their own cameras and took snap shots whenever they felt like it. We didn't go overboard on the outfits either, Susie opted for a simple dress and I went to the expense of buying myself a new suit that I could wear for the day, but would also be able to use afterwards for everything from other weddings, job interviews and funerals.

'You look lovely, dear,' my mother had told me when she arrived at the registry office. I am not sure if she meant it or whether it was something that she had felt that she had to say to fill the awkwardness of not really being too aware of what was going on. This was confirmed a moment later. 'Where are we going?'

'I'm getting married, Mum.' She looked at me in surprise.

'Don't be ridiculous, you're far too young, you haven't left school yet.'

'I'm twenty-two, Mum.'

'I don't know where you get these ideas from, Maximillian, but I should think that as your mother *I* should be the one to know *exactly* how old you are.' With this, she marched off in a different direction to find some long forgotten relative that she could annoy. Sadly, at this point in her life, some long forgotten relative could, in her mind, relate to almost any of us.

Since the revelation from my father, it was evident that things had started to go downhill for my mother. My father looked a little uncomfortable with an uneasy grin on his face, but I suspect that this may have something to do with the suit that he was wearing, which was at least twenty-five years old. Like his suit, he was looking very tired and I thought that things at home were not going that easily for him.

I didn't really have any male friends that I was particularly close to at this time in my life so I had asked Jerry to be my best man. It would have been good if he had worn a suit but he didn't own one and I doubt that he would have worn it if he had. He did make the effort of trousers and a shirt instead of the jeans that he normally slumped round in so there is always that I suppose. Actually, aside from his appearance he did make a good job of things. He seemed to have at least half a tub of gel in his hair and had used it to some amazing creative ability. Naturally, he told lots of embarrassing stories in the pub afterwards about our childhood growing up together which was clearly something that he felt was part of the bestman role.

And then the day was over. If I was asked to give one bit of advice to a couple getting married, it would be to stop and look around you every now and then on your wedding day. The day is long, but paradoxically it goes really quickly and you have to take the time to remind yourself that this is your wedding day or it will pass so quickly. The ceremony took less than twenty minutes. I walked in a bachelor and within the time that it takes to watch an episode of your typical sitcom, I walked out a married man.

I was married. I had a wife. I could hardly believe it. I had married the woman of my dreams and things could not have been any better for me.

***

There are a lot of horror stories told by people that are divorced that they like to tell to make the unmarried wary. It is however, also possible to have a perfect thing going for you. Thinking about my marriage to Susie, I cannot help but wonder if it was the happiest time of my life. It might be that I feel this way because it was possibly the first time in my life that I had ever been truly happy, and whereas I have been happy since then, the original memory of what it was like has stayed with me. These things can make a lasting impact on us and shape the way that we view things in the future.

I had a very contented married life and there were those that said that marriage agreed with me. We moved into a small flat not too far away from where I was working at the university. I had by this stage, completed my Master's degree and was hoping to start off on a PhD. I had always liked the idea of a doctorate, probably because of my awareness of the Indiana Jones films when I was growing up. I doubt that I would have been allowed to have been a doctor like Doctor Jones though. I was still making a bit of money from tutoring the undergraduates and there was a suggestion that this might translate into full-time. Susie had stayed to complete a teaching qualification as she felt that this was the direction that she wanted to go into. Her preference was towards school age, however, whereas I rather preferred to have students that could wipe their own arses and in theory, could at least string a sentence together.

I came to love the smaller things in life that are so often forgotten when the distractions of everyday life get in the way. One of the things that I was very proud of was wearing a ring on my finger which seemed to signal to everyone that I was married, though the truth probably was that the majority of people didn't notice it and probably wouldn't have cared if they had. To me it was a beacon that shone from my finger in a light of gold for all to see. I was very proud of being married. I was very proud of having a wife and a home to go to when I had finished work.

The one downside that happened was that I was starting to get really tired. I was plagued with insomnia for a lot of the time, and completely unable to switch my brain off. One of the curses of the academic life, perhaps?

We were struggling to live in a tiny little flat that we were renting that was always the wrong temperature for the time of the year, was infested with rodents, had archaic plumbing and wiring, a place where hardly anything appeared to work; and yet, it was the one place on the face of the planet that I wanted to be. It was Susie, of course, that made me feel like this. I could have lived in an underground cave drinking rainwater and living off morsels so long as I was allowed to be with her. I would have followed her to the ends of the earth.

As it happened, there was a far closer distance that she had in mind.

Ten

I have vivid memories of childhood in the 70s and growing up through the 80s and then when it comes to the 90s, it's just a blur that I don't really have all that many memories about. I suppose to an extent it was because I was far busier in the 90s than I was in the earlier two decades. I was at university and then I was completely taken up with Susie. We got married, of course, and then from then onwards it was all married life and working to sustain the home. I felt like I had achieved something for the first time in my life. In other words, I was not in touch with popular culture.

When most of my contemporaries were out clubbing and raving, I had settled down into something that was fast approaching middle age. I just did what I felt it was the right thing to do and that I was happy about doing at the time. Being with Susie and getting married just seemed to be the most natural thing to do in the world.

Due to the amount of work that I was doing, I didn't get to go home to see my parents as much as I would have liked. Unfortunately, life just got in the way of things and I wasn't able to put everything to one side. I realise now that these were just excuses. Nothing is more important than family and there is very little that can't be put to one side for the sake of it. I am not sure why it is that I made the excuse of being too busy. I suppose, looking back on it now I see it as some kind of denial as to what was going on and burying myself in my work and my marriage was a coping mechanism. They are all clichés now when I look back on it. No excuse is good enough. I feel ashamed about it now and wonder why it was that I did not spend every single moment of my time with them. I made telephone calls regularly to dad.

'How's Mum?'

'Oh, well, you know? Not so good today. Good days and bad days, but not so good today.'

'Sorry to hear that.'

'Yes, well the university have not renewed her contract.'

'Really?'

'Yes, well, it makes sense, I suppose. She's not really able to lecture and mark papers so I suppose she isn't really going to be all that good to them.'

'She's worked for them for years; you think they would show a little compassion.'

'Well, yes, but no. No compassion in the academic world, Max, you should know that. It's a cut-throat business. I don't suppose you can really continue to pay someone for not being able to do anything.'

'You should get a solicitor,' I seemed angrier about my mum giving up work than my father was. I later came to the conclusion that the fight had gone out of my father. He was just so tired now and was trying to make things as easy as he could for my mother, for all of us really; including himself. I suppose he had also come to accept the fact that mum not being able to work was something that was really inevitable.

'Really? I mean, seriously? Seems a lot of hassle as far as I'm concerned. It's just a bit Cnut-like, isn't it?'

'Cnut?'

'Yeah, trying to delay the inevitable.'

'I think the point that he was trying to make was not that he could stop the tide coming in, but rather than he was only human and nobody, not even a king, could stop the tide.'

'Ever the historian,' my father chuckled down the line. 'The analogy still stands though, even with that interpretation.'

'Yeah well, take the letters in Cnut and rearrange them and I think you're more likely to come up with the true nature of the situation.'

'Yes, well, probably.'

'Do you want me to speak to Mum?'

'Better not; no, not a good idea.'

'Why?'

'She's developed a phobia for the telephone.'

'A phobia for the telephone?'

'Yes. Hates it. Despises it with a passion. I think she has forgotten what it is, so she gets confused when she hears the voice at the other end and can't work out what is going on.'

'That's terrible.'

'True, but on the plus side I do get less people ringing now. Always hated the phone myself. Seems like a bloody good idea to get rid of the awful thing really. Might stop people ringing up and trying to sell me things that I don't want.'

'Well, look, I will try and get up and see you both sometime soon.'

'That would be good.'

'I will see what I can do, bye, Dad.'

Life all around me was changing from what it used to be into something entirely different. I had no idea at the time just how much the world was changing around me and how much more of a change there was yet to come. Life is an evolution of change though. The thing with the telephone should have been a warning bell for me to get my act together and it is to my eternal shame that I didn't.

Shame on me.

***

'I always seem to ache all of the time,' it was a complaint that was coming from me whilst sipping coffee in a café in town.

Seemingly out of nowhere, these American 'coffee houses', for want of a better phrase, had sprung up all over the country. First, there had been the invasion of the burger bars and now the Americans were flooding us with coffee as if they were trying to eradicate the English necessity for tea. They were vastly expensive places to buy a cup of coffee in, but I was always very fond of coffee so couldn't resist the temptation to sample what they had to offer. You know what these

114

places are, but I am unable to name them for legal reasons. Name one of them and I have to name them all, so just pick your favourite one and imagine that this is where this particular scene was taking place.

'Oh?'

This was from my friend, Nat, who was also into coffee as much as I was. Nat was someone that for as long as I knew him, was so thin that you felt that he could successfully win at hide and seek by standing behind a lamppost. He also always wore black clothing as he seemed to despise colour. Further to this, he always seemed to be wearing the same clothing, but I later found out that he had a wardrobe of near identical clothing which he kept so as to save time not having to think about what he was wearing. Nat was someone that firmly believed that you had to channel your thoughts to what was necessary and choosing clothing was not something that he wanted to waste so much as a second on doing. I suppose when you think about it there is a certain logic to this. I certainly remember the wasted hours waiting whilst Susie went through everything that she had in the wardrobe trying to choose the right outfit to wear for a night out and then ending it all saying that she 'simply had nothing to wear', despite the evidence of the huge pile of clothing thrown on the bed which would seem to belie that information. The most difficult thing for me to decide about an outfit was what tie I was going to wear.

'Yes, I'm always aching in my limbs. So, irritating. Don't you find that?'

'No, I can't say that I ache at all. Unless I have done some heinous manual task, which was probably quite unnecessary in the first place and then I might ache.'

Nat didn't believe in physical exercise and I came to the conclusion that he only managed to maintain his thin frame by sheer mind power. We were both young tutors trying to make it in the world of academia but it is a mystery to me now how it was that Nat and I became friends. We were both completely different from each other. I was a history graduate and Nat was a physicist. He always used to say that he got into physics because when he was younger he had fallen into trouble with the law; the law of physics. It was an old quotation

115

and not original to him, but he nevertheless enjoyed using it whenever he could. We couldn't have been more separated academically if we had tried, and yet somehow, we had gelled. Perhaps it was the camaraderie that came with both being at the bottom of the chain and trying to make a go of it in the world.

'I have been feeling very tired lately,' I continued, drinking my coffee with its double shot in it which I was hoping would peel my eyelids back and enable me to get through an afternoon of marking.

'Not sleeping?' Nat was leafing through some complicated text book whilst we were drinking and chatting. The text book was thick and looked complicated, it exhaled complexity just by looking at it and yet Nat was reading it in the same way that I would read a pulp novel.

'Insomnia.'

'Oh, really?'

'Yes, I've been a sufferer since I was sixteen. I've come to the conclusion that I'll eventually have lived twice as long as anyone else on account of sleeping less than they have.'

'Not good. Sleep is essential to function.'

'Yes, I know, thanks for that. I'm not saying it's something that I've a choice over. It's something that I'm afflicted with.'

'Not good.'

'Naturally it makes you debilitated and you also get fluctuations of feeling ill at the same time.'

'I suppose that's largely to do with the fact that your immune system is run low due to lack of sleep so there's more chance of you heading face down into illness.'

'Eloquently put, Nat.'

'Have you tried to do anything about it?'

'Yes, of course I have. I've tried everything from sleeping pills to alternative medicine; reading books, listening to music; everything. You name it I've tried it. What amazes me the most is whenever I meet anyone new and tell them I have insomnia, they all immediately have a surefire cure that I must try. Invariably, this cure of theirs is a load of bollocks.'

'So, what do you do?'

'Smile politely and compliment them on being the first person to have come up with an idea that I've heard a hundred times before.'

'Ok; but I meant what do you do about having insomnia without finding the right cure for you?'

'Live with it, I suppose, it's just one of those things.'

'I take it you have been to a doctor.'

'I was prescribed sleeping tablets which didn't work. The wonders of modern medicine, I suppose. I have come to believe that if doctors cannot easily shoehorn you into a category in their medical text books then they tend to give up on you. Probably think that you are making up your symptoms to spite them.'

'So, you're aching all of the time because you're not sleeping. You're not getting the charge into your body to be able to regenerate it.'

'Bugger, isn't it? It's funny all the things that you think of when you can't sleep. Personally, I don't know why I bother with sleep, well I do, but it would be nice if someone could invent a way of getting rid of the need for it.'

'I think there are some people who would be very stressed by not being able to sleep. I have to confess to quite enjoying my bed.'

'Spoken like someone who has never suffered with trying to sleep. Time is short though and after all we haven't got very long lives and it doesn't help when we sleep through half of it.'

'How would you plan to regenerate and give your body rest then if that were the case?'

'Oh, I don't know, perhaps they will develop a way where we can be plugged into a light socket or something whilst watching television.'

'Interesting idea, not entirely convinced of the practical applications involved though.'

'There are drawbacks to everything. An insomniac lives in an isolated world. Secluded. There's nobody else around at 2 am, or so it seems. All you can hear is their persistent snoring.'

'Susie, you mean?'

'Well yes, but not just her. Living in a flat you can hear the people around you just as easily as if they were in the same room. It's highly irritating.'

'Your parents aren't exactly poor. How comes you have never asked them to help out on the old housing front? I'm sure they could help you get somewhere a little better to live in.'

'I prefer to make my own way in the world without having to rely on others for favours.'

'How are things with Susie?'

'Great, although things are a little tiring.'

'How do you mean?'

'I'm finding it rather difficult to keep up.'

'Do I want to know more about what that means?'

'Probably not,' the trouble is that it had been worrying me and I had to tell someone. 'When we got together though, things were pretty intense. They still are, but I am finding with the insomnia and the tiredness, it is something that requires a lot more effort and only results in making me more tired.'

'We're talking pretty regularly then?'

'Daily, often more than once.'

'Bloody hell. No wonder you are knackered.'

We lapsed into silence for a while, each to our own thoughts and each of us sipping on our overpriced coffee that we were fast becoming addicted to. I know that many of you will probably tut and shake your head that someone moaning about insomnia should drink coffee, but the simple truth of the matter is that I stopped drinking it in the early afternoon and it was one of the few things that I really enjoyed in life. If I cut it out then there wouldn't be much point in carrying on. You have to have some pleasures and indulgences in life or there really is no point in living. It's the difference between living and merely existing.

Strange thoughts can invade an insomniac. It's even possible to become paranoid; in fact, it's almost compulsory, along with depression. 'Why am I the only one to suffer?' you ask yourself. I see

118

nobody else in this house that can't sleep. All the other lights in the other houses in the street are all turned off. Insomnia distorts reality.

I have spent a lot of time over the years trying to unravel what it is about me that makes me prone to insomnia. I think it is probably a number of different things. Someone once said that insomnia was caused by an overly active mind which I would like to think of as a compliment and I can see the issue that you will be tortured if your body is worn out and your mind is still running at full speed and refuses to shut down; however, it does seem a little arrogant to me. At times, I'm far too restless to sleep. I can feel the insomnia at the edges of my mind, just waiting to leap into action the moment I try to go to sleep. It is like a black demon that lurks in the darkness, you can't always see it, but you know that it is there and just biding its time until it can be most unhelpful to you. The amount of time that I have crawled into bed with my eyes heavy and hurting because I am *so* tired, only to have my head hit the pillow and my insomnia kick in and find myself instantly wide awake. If you have never experienced it then I don't think I can really fully explain it to you.

Some say conscience plays a large part in it. Does it? I don't know. Do I dwell on my past too much? It's possible. I do spend time thinking about when I turned left when I should have turned right. When I said 'yes' when 'no' should have been preferred. Most of the time I think about the people that have fallen into the mists of time. Friends, enemies and lovers. I watch them all disappearing from my present into my past, never to be heard of again. In some cases, this is a good thing, in others not so good.

I do spend time considering the future as well. I may be a historian, but whereas I work in the past, I don't live in the past. When it comes to the future I dwell on all kinds of questions, both philosophical and practical. Which path do I take now? What happens next? I'm a man that likes to know what's happening. I don't like always being in the dark, and when it comes to insomnia you are in the dark in so many ways.

I looked up at Nat who was still working his way through his complex book with all the outward appearance of reading a gossip magazine. I think I envied his natural intellect at that point. I would say that I am intelligent, but it is something that I have had to work at. It doesn't come naturally for me. I still have to work at it to this day. I have never had that big idea that I have been chasing after for so long. That wondrous idea that will make everything fall into place for those involved in academic history. I always felt that Nat could set the world on fire if he could only be bothered to do so. His most common fault was that he couldn't understand when others didn't get what to him seemed obvious. He tried hard to disguise it, but when he encountered moments like this I could see him kick up a gear in patience and begin to explain whatever it might have been as if he was speaking to a child that had failed to grasp the basics of arithmetic.

'Ah, what the hell' I said, causing him to look up from his book for a moment. 'There'll be time enough to sleep when I'm dead'

***

If you have never suffered from insomnia then you won't understand any of this. You will not understand the frustration that insomniacs suffer from or the annoyance when we are with someone else who falls asleep the moment their head hits the pillow. Oh, how we envy you if you are one of the people that fits into this category. Envy and to a degree, admire you.

And yes, the sexual Olympics were becoming a little difficult to keep up with. Nat was the first and only person that I voiced this to, but it was something that I found deeply frustrating that I often felt too tired to be able to perform my duties as a husband. I am not sure if Susie understood this. I hadn't really been able to explain things to her without feeling guilty that I was not pulling my own; so to speak.

Susie could pretty much fall asleep anywhere and at the drop of a hat with no discomfort or fidgeting at all. Seemingly, she was able to do it without the slightest bit of effort. I would often lay awake tossing and turning whilst she was several hours into a good sleep. I feel agitated that I can't sleep. Every part of my body seems to want to move and won't lie still. I feel that I have to get up and run about or whatever, just so long as I'm doing something rather than suffer from insomnia. I don't look forward to nights very much and would sometimes reach a point where I would dread going to bed. What I didn't know back in those days was just how lucky I was and how later in life I really would learn what it was like to dread going to bed.

I considered that part of my conflict with insomnia was due to the fact that I found lying down in bed to sleep so boring that if I didn't fall asleep instantly I couldn't wait around. I have maintained this point of view for most of my life. I suppose to an extent I see sleeping as such a waste of all the other things that I could be doing, that I want to be doing or would rather be doing. I then have to get up and do something in the hope that as I work, I will grow more tired so that the next attempt at sleep will come quickly and easily. This doesn't always work. I think that so much time is wasted on sleep when I could be doing other things.

It used to be the case that you should really just get on with it and 'man-up' for want of a better phrase.

'Thatcher used to cope with running the country on four hours sleep,' Nat said in a manner that I supposed was him trying to be helpful.

'That explains a lot. What is your point though?'

'I don't know. Makes you wonder though, if Thatcher can do it why it is that the rest of us can't cope.'

'With six hours sleep a night, the latest research states that you have the same reaction times, concentration and thought processes as someone who is drunk. In fact, you would probably be better drunk than sleep deprived.'

'Not sure the police would agree with that.'

'It's true though. I really should try to give in to sleep more, but it is something that continues to elude me. Look at my eyes.'

'What about them?'

'They look sunken. The skin is yellow and they are speckled with red to form a bloodshot appearance. I've got those deep uneven ridges down each side of my nose and bags under my eyes.'

'You look okay to me, but if you don't mind I'm not going to sit here and stare into your eyes.'

Fortunately, this appearance is not everlasting, and on the rare occurrence when I am actually able to sleep the night in full, I find that this ghastly appearance slowly disappears – but only in order so that it may reappear at a later date. It is the haunted look of an insomniac that makes you look older than you really are. I have always been mistaken as being older than I really am and I attribute this entirely to my struggle with insomnia.

I spoke to my father about it once as well and he confirmed for me that he had struggled with insomnia for most of his life.

'Maybe it's hereditary,' he said as we sat in his study which is where the majority of our conversations took place.

'I'm not sure if it can be,' I replied.

'I have found that insomnia has its advantages.'

'Oh really?' This should be good. It would be ironic if the answer to all my sleep problems had been held by my father all these years and I had never known.

'Yes, well, whenever I have suffered from it I have used the extra time to my advantage.'

'By doing what?'

'Reading, of course. So many thousands of years of literature to catch up on, there simply isn't enough waking hours to do it all in so I make the most of every sleepless night that comes my way.'

'Not ideal.'

'Insomnia has given me the chance to read extensively. I simply won't let the bastard beat me. One of the worst things that you can do with insomnia is lie in bed and toss and turn, trying to force yourself to sleep. It just won't work. You need to get up and engage in something and not give in to it.'

'Sometimes I feel like I've got the answer to it all, or I am using the time to do something constructive, but it's just beyond my grasp.'

'A bit like the Great Gatsby then?'

'You've lost me there, Dad. Never really been a Fitzgerald fan.'

'Gatsby, looking across the water at the green light in the distance. The green light that we reach for because we think that it's our future and then one day, with a shock we realise that all along it's been our past – slowly, but consistently moving further and further away from us.'

'Very profound.'

'Yeah, but not very practical advice, I admit.'

'No.'

'It's the second shelf, third bookcase, over there.'

'What is?'

'*The Great Gatsby,*'

'Oh.'

I didn't bother checking; I knew that he would be right.

Eleven

Sometimes I wonder if I chose to study history because I want to in some way recapture the past. I have been thinking about this a lot lately.

I had a good childhood, it wasn't traumatised. It was just a standard childhood with its ups and downs, I suppose. There are so many advantages to being an adult, but when you get down to the root of it all, there is something so special about childhood. Childhood for me brings back memories of when life seemed simpler, when it always was either a glorious summer full of sunshine; or it was Christmas and there was excitement that shone in our eyes brighter than the tinsel that we draped around the tree. Things were not complicated, they just *were*. No problems or worries to concern us, and if there were, then they were really very minor problems that our undeveloped brains had made mountains out of. Wouldn't it be great to be able to get back to those simpler times when the choices were less difficult?

The truth of the matter is that life has never really been like that. It is an illusion. To the mind of a child it is simpler and easier; but when I was growing up and I was remembering the wonderful excitement of Christmas and lazy summer days with no school, the adults were suffering just as much as we do as adults now – maybe more so. As children, we were oblivious to all of that, of course. Perhaps the children of today feel the same way as we did back then. Perhaps they will look back with equal nostalgia and wonder where these hedonistic days have gone to that we are now living.

The bottom line is, we can't recapture what has gone before. When it has gone, it has gone and there is nothing that we can do to bring it back. It took me a little while to get this idea firmly in my head, but I got it in the end.

***

Susie was responsible for changing my life. I was never really truly happy in my life until I met her, at least that is what I think when I look back at it. It does sound a bit ungrateful when I remember my life up until that point, but I just can't find the words to describe how she changed everything for me. You will just have to take my word for it that she was someone that lifted me up and gave me the very reason for living that I had been longing for. I must have been walking around with a permanent smile on my face all of the time from the day I met her onwards.

Ours was a very passionate love affair that burnt like fire. We could hardly keep our hands off of each other and we frequently didn't bother to try. It was an all-consuming passion, the like of which can only be experienced and can rarely be explained. Take Richard Burton and Elizabeth Taylor; now they were a couple who were madly, passionately, in love with each other – why else would they marry, get divorced, remarry and then redivorce. Rumour has it that if Burton had not died then there was a chance of them trying again for the third time. Why?

The answer is simple, they had a very rare thing in a love that burned so brightly that it was dangerous and they simply couldn't live with it. They couldn't live with each other because their passion was burning them, but they couldn't live without each other because the passion and desire was too strong to be kept apart. That is a passion that comes along once in a lifetime, if you are lucky. Most of us will not be that lucky. On the other hand, you might count it as unlucky, as with Burton-Taylor it is something that is all-consuming and dangerous to be involved with.

Susie and I had a burning passion and I loved it. It was like nothing I had ever experienced before and probably ever would again. The problem that I did not realise at the time was that fires eventually will burn themselves out. The more quickly they burn, the more quickly they are likely to burn out; then all you are left with are ashes, burnt fingers and a rather horrible smell.

Susie was responsible for changing my life. She changed it by coming into my life and then she changed it by going out of my life once again.

***

The way that it happened was almost clichéd in itself. You can't make these things up though, sometimes in life this is the way that it happens and then what can you do? Pretend that it didn't happen that way because it seems to be something out of a movie?

I was now twenty-four-years-old and we had been married for two years. I have said it before and I will say it again, they were the happiest years of my life. I had no idea of the huge car crash that I was about to walk into that would leave my life in tatters.

I had gone off to work and left Susie at home. She had still not qualified as a teacher. I got half way towards the college when I remembered that I had promised a student that I would bring a book in on the Anglo-Saxon Chronicle that he was keen to borrow. I retraced my steps and headed back to the flat. I went in and that was when I walked in on Susie and some guy, whose name I still do not know, who was bending her over and fucking her as hard as possible from behind.

There is no other polite way of putting it. Those were the facts of the situation. This lover of hers must have been waiting around the corner for me to leave so that he could get inside as quickly as possible – in more ways than one. I was devastated. For a moment, none of us said anything. The man (to be honest I have never wanted to know his name) stood there looking guilty, which under the circumstances was the least he could do. He tried for an indignant look as well which is actually something that is very difficult to do when you are standing naked with a rapidly deflating penis in front of the husband of the woman you have just been screwing. To be fair, I don't think that words needed to be said at that point. The situation was summed up pretty well and at least I was not subjected to something along the lines of, 'It's not what you think it is.'

'How long has this been going on?' I asked, trying to keep the trembling note out of my voice.

'With him? Not long.'

'Two things occurred to me at that stage,' I later told Nat. 'First, the fact that this guy was not the first.'

'And the second?'

'I wondered if she actually knew his name in the first place.'

'Must have been difficult.'

How do you explain how difficult it is when your world has fallen apart? I was in shock about what had happened, I was disappointed, I was heartbroken and I was indignant. I was indignant partly because of the situation, but I was also indignant because I happened to notice that my wife's lover did not appear to be wearing a condom. Now, I suppose it is possible that the shock of seeing the husband arrive home meant that he pulled out so quickly that it came off inside her, but I think it more likely that she was having unprotected sex, possibly with someone that she didn't even know the name of. This was probably the point that upset me the most. Susie and myself had not had unprotected sex because she didn't feel that the time was right for us to have a child. I had respected her wishes on this and yet it seems that she was stringing me out all of the time so that she could have unprotected sex with anyone else that she felt like. It should also be remembered that the AIDS scare was still a recent memory. Although advancements were being made and it was slowly becoming possible to prolong people's lives to make it less of a death sentence, it was still only seven years since Freddie Mercury had died. The potential for pregnancy was one thing, but the potential for a sexually transmitted disease was unforgivable, particularly as one of those sexually transmitted diseases could still kill you.

127

'She has had the decency to move out,' I told Nat.

'That's the least she could do I would have thought.'

'Well, she always did the least that she could do.'

***

'Thanks for not saying the obvious,' I said to my dad while I sat on his sofa and he fiddled with the coffee machine.

'What's obvious?'

'Saying "I told you so."'

'Why would I say that?'

'Because you did tell me so.'

'No, I don't think so. Don't remember that.'

'You warned me before I got married and asked me if I thought that I was doing the right thing.'

'Ah well,' he bought some coffee over to me, 'that's not the same as telling you it would end like this.'

'True.'

'And is it the end?'

'Oh, I think so, don't you?' I had told my father everything.

'Well, it does seem to be a situation that would be rather difficult to come back from. However, if I cautioned you before you got married to check to see if you were sure that you were doing the right thing, then it is only fair that I do the same now.'

'How do you mean?'

'Well,' he rearranged his cardigan slightly and sat down. 'Marriage is something that is serious and not to be taken lightly, you know that. The same is true of divorce.'

'Go on.'

'Divorce is so permanent. You have to be sure that it's what you want to do. A lot of people seem to get divorced today simply because it's an easier option to actually sitting down and sorting out your problems. Talking it over, you know?'

'Do you think this is a situation where talking would help sort the problems out?'

'Well, probably not. This does seem to be a rather permanent fuck up, if you will excuse the expression. The only reason I am urging you not to be rash at this point is that you were so in love with Susie, so certain that she was the one that you wanted to be with that you have to be certain that ending it is what you want to do.'

'I don't think I have much choice. From what I can gather she wants to end it just as much. Turns out that she is really not ready to settle down yet and wants to be off having a lot of sex with a lot of different people before she finally decides that she has had enough. If she ever does.'

'Well, quite.'

'You're right though, she was the one for me. We had a lot of laughs and a lot of good times and to be honest the sex was pretty good.'

I am not sure why I felt compelled to tell my father this, but he took it in his stride and made some kind of gesture as if to say that this was no more than was expected. It is true, though, that I had learnt a lot from Susie and she had opened my eyes to what was sexually possible. The price, though, was costly. It was costly in both the money that I was shelling out whilst she was not working and it was far costlier in the emotional heartache that it caused me. I was taken for a ride really. I wonder at times whether she actually really loved me or whether she was just after some form of financial stability and a good cover to give her the opportunity to continue with her quest to shag everything on campus. If that is the case, then she really saw me coming. It broke my heart without a shadow of a doubt.

We had to meet several times since I caught her with her lover (if that is even the right term for him) and they were strained, difficult affairs that were always in public, in some café, coffee shop or something. It was like I was the monster. I was the evil one and she only felt safe meeting me where there were other people around so that she had some form of protection. This was just one of the many injustices that I felt at the time. Why was I being painted to be the one that was in the wrong? What had I done other than discover her infidelity?

'Well, I did tell you I was a nymphomaniac,' she said, taking a drag on a cigarette as we sat outside a café one day. She made this statement as if it explained everything and clearly it was my fault for not taking her seriously with regards to her sexual desires.

Even though I know that I was badly treated, my feelings were so strong towards her and remained in residual amount that I cannot look back at that period with hate or anger. I forgave her for the way she treated me many years ago and I have always looked back at that period in my life with great affection mixed with a certain degree of regret. Regret that it ended? Regret that I found out what she was like? I don't know.

'I suppose it turned out that she was not the person that I thought she was,' I told my dad as we sat there talking things over.

'Well, that can happen to any of us. Very rarely do we actually know people as well as we think we do.'

This was true in so many ways.

'Love is a very strange thing,' he continued.

'I suppose so.'

This was also something that was true in many ways.

'Do you remember this?' he flapped a battered copy of *Far from the Madding Crowd* at me that he was obviously reading at the time, or more accurately rereading, or re-rereading; it was hard to say.

'Yes, of course.'

'Love really screws this plot up, doesn't it?'

'How so?'

'Well, Bathsheba sends Farmer Boldwood a Valentine card, as a joke if you remember?'

'Yes, even though she doesn't actually have any feelings for him.' I remembered the novel well, it had been one of my favourites and for a time I felt that I had been living it because of my unrequited love situation.

'Well, it makes him fall in love with her even though he had never looked twice at a woman before that. Because she rejects his advances due to never having been interested in the first place, he is virtually driven insane with desire for her and ends up shooting her husband, when she does marry, and spending the rest of his life in prison.'

'Doesn't sound brilliant, does it?'

'And all because of a silly Valentine prank. If she had never done that then he would have had a life left to lead, instead his life is ruined because of her. I often feel that the point of that is missed out by people that read this book.'

'Dad, I am not sure what it is you are trying to tell me.' He thought about this for a moment.

'No, neither am I.'

***

Susie may have turned out to not be the person that I thought she was and upon reflection, it may be that there was a lot of lust mixed up in what I thought was love. I have said before that it is not that easy to always be able to tell the difference between the two. Looking back now I still can't work out the difference between the two, but I would be an idiot if I were not to recognise that when it came to Susie, a lot of it was driven by lust. It would be foolish to think anything different really.

We both agreed as we sat in that café, where I was made to feel like a wife-beater, that a separation was really the best thing that we could do.

'I think it's for the best,' she told me.

'Divorce?'

'Yes.'

'It's something that I don't want to rush into.'

'I think it's inevitable.'

Okay, it was something that I was less willing to jump into. Maybe because even after the devastating revelation that I had uncovered, I still had some forlorn hope that we would sort it out and life would be able to carry on as it had done before.

'Stupid, I know,' I told Nat later.

'Well, I suppose you are entitled to feel a bit stupid about it all.'

'I feel like a drowning man, trying to cling to whatever wreckage comes my way.'

'Perhaps that isn't for the best.'

'I don't think that she can argue that I have excellent grounds for divorce.'

'No, I don't think she can.'

'I don't want to label her a slut though.'

'I think you worry about these things too much.'

'Perhaps.'

'If you love her so much,' said Nat as he stirred his coffee, 'why don't you forgive her?'

'I'm not sure that I can ever think of her in the same way again.'

'Plenty of people have forgiven their partners for having affairs and continue with their relationships.'

'Maybe so. I'm just not all that certain as to how many affairs she has actually had.'

'Have you asked her?'

'I daren't and if I did, could I be certain that she was telling me the truth?'

One affair I might have been able to forgive, but several? It also became evident that Susie had no intention of mending her ways. She clearly intended to continue to sleep with as many people as she could. I don't think that we could have survived that. No, I don't think that I could have survived that. We didn't enter into our marriage truthfully. We didn't discuss an open marriage when we entered into it and we couldn't now try and fit a round peg into a square hole.

In the end, the easiest option was to wait for two years. The law with regards to divorce states that you need sufficient grounds to be able to get a judge to agree the divorce. If the judge doesn't feel that the grounds are sufficient, then you can't have one. As previously discussed I think even the most liberal judge would agree that discovering your wife being screwed over the back of the sofa probably amounted to sufficient grounds. However, two years of separation can be deemed to be sufficient grounds on their own without the need to bring in any other elements such as:

(1) I don't like the way she leaves the cap off the toothpaste,

(2) I don't like how she doesn't put the washing in the wash basket; or

(3) I don't like the way that she takes it from strangers over my furniture without using a condom.

You get the idea.

Two years of separation and providing that both parties are in agreement, then it is pretty much sorted and agreed. You might think it a little harsh that I would have to wait two years, but I wasn't in any hurry. I knew in my heart that things with Susie were over and there was no real chance of getting back together again because I knew that I would never be able to trust her. I still did not know how long she had been unfaithful to me, at what point in our marriage did it start, and if I am honest, I don't think I wanted to know. After what had happened, I was in no great desire to rush off and find someone else to be with. I had indulged in a lot of sex over the last few years and I could do without some for a while.

A few months before the two years were up, I applied to the court for the divorce to take place. We had agreed that we would go for an absolute break so that neither of us would be trying to take the other for everything that they had got. This was probably because of the fact that Susie didn't have anything and I didn't have all that much more. She could have tried, I suppose to take something from me, but she had the decency to realise that she was really the one in the wrong and if she did try and take me for any money then I would probably change the grounds to adultery. If she had thought about this more logically, then she probably would have come to the conclusion that it becoming common knowledge that she liked to sleep around would probably go a long way to help increase her chances of making it happen more often; although from what I had gathered, she didn't really need to advertise.

At any rate, she didn't contest the divorce and it went through without any issues. It probably, nevertheless, must have cost me about the same as the wedding had. Jointly, there was a few thousand pounds that I would never see again. We didn't really see all that much of each other during the two years whilst we waited to get divorced. We kept in touch only enough to be able to know where each of us was and to be able to pass on anything that was necessary to do in order to ensure that we would be able to go to the court easily enough when the time came. On the few occasions when we did meet, there was still a frosty atmosphere and she was doing her best to paint herself as the one who was being hard done by. Perhaps in her own head she felt that she was. Perhaps she felt that she should not be penalised for her interest and pursuit in cock. My final papers came through a few weeks before the end of 1999. One final touch that I added was ensuring that she got the sofa in the divorce. There was no way that I was ever going to sit on it again.

1999. This was going to be the big millennium. There had been much talk about the world ending and the Millennium Bug shutting down all of the computers and we would all end up back in the Dark Ages. As far as I can recall nothing of this kind happened at all, but I can't say that it was entirely accurate that my world had not ended. I suppose it was fitting that one particular chapter of my life should die with the old century.

I had always liked that scene in the film where Laurence Olivier plays Nelson and Vivien Leigh plays Emma Hamilton, I can't remember the name of the film now. Anyway, the reason why I mention it is because there is a scene in the film where Nelson and Lady Em are heavily into their affair and it is New Year's Eve 1799. As the bells strike to show that it is now 1800, they kiss so that Larry can then say that he has now kissed her across two centuries. This is not something that you can do very often, every one hundred years to be precise. I had the opportunity to do this as 1999 became 2000.

I didn't do it because I was alone on that night.

On that night when nothing else happened at all.

Twelve

There are different kinds of people in the world. Some will just go to pieces when something like this happens and they will not cope with it at all and others will pick themselves up, dust themselves down, lick their wounds (if appropriate) and start all over again. Everybody has their own way with dealing, or not dealing, with things and I am not here to tell you who is right. You have to follow your own path on that one and work out for yourself what is the most sensible. What I will say is that negativity will breed negativity. If you constantly think that everything is going to go wrong for you then the chances are that everything *will* go wrong for you. This is chiefly because of the fact that you will subconsciously make it happen so that you don't disappoint yourself. I am not saying that if you conversely are positive about everything then only positive things will happen. A lot of it does depend on attitude though. Go into something believing it is doomed to failure and it probably will.

I wasn't really in the mood to start another relationship after Susie. I hardly had a brilliant track record before Susie. Nothing in my past suggested that things were going to get any better. I left my wedding ring on for some time in the hope that it might deter a lot of women from even asking so I didn't have to go through the annoyance of having to reject someone who really didn't deserve to be rejected. Unfortunately, I discovered that there were a lot of women who found the appearance of a wedding ring a huge turn on and seemed to target me because I was married.

A lot of women try to make out that they are not like men when it comes to sex and are not into one night stands and extra marital affairs and the like, but I have discovered over the years that men and women are essentially the same. Some women are like this, some men are like it. Some of either sex will be the 'mate for life' type and some will shag anything that moves. Stop trying to make differences between the sexes where there aren't any. There are enough problems in the world without making more.

I entered the year 2000 as a newly divorced male that was now in a position where I could perhaps pick up the pieces of my life from where they had been scattered. I didn't really have all that much time as, not very far into the New Year when I was preparing myself to return for another term at university, I received the telephone call from my father that I had been expecting for the last four years.

Mother had died.

***

There are two ways of looking at someone dying. There are two reactions to hearing that someone has died.

There is the death which is unexpected. This is something which is probably not good for anyone involved. The person who dies does so quickly (perhaps), so they do not have to suffer a long drawn-out demise, but they have no time to put their affairs in order or to say goodbye. My father always hated the idea of dying this way.

'Knowing my luck,' he said once. 'I shall die halfway through reading a really good book and will spend the rest of eternity being really pissed off that I don't know how it ends.' I pointed out to him that the afterlife, if there were such a thing, would almost certainly come with a well-stocked library. That was probably his idea of Heaven. A library that not only contained every book that had been published, but also contained every book that ever would be published.

The other way for people to die is the long drawn-out illness. I know that having someone die suddenly without being able to tell them what you think and saying what you want to say is hard for those left behind. I can't imagine the grief that was felt by those phone calls that were made from the aeroplanes before they hit the World Trade Center. The grief felt by those making the call and the grief felt by those receiving the calls, or worse, picking it up on the answerphone later knowing that you were not there at the time when you could have said goodbye.

The problem with the long drawn-out illness is that the person dying goes through a hell of a lot of suffering and those who are left behind go through a hell of a lot of suffering watching their loved one slowly disintegrate before their eyes.

Which is the best way?

There is no best way. With regards to having someone die without saying the things that you want to say to them, well the answer to that is simple. Tell them today. Why bother waiting until the last minute? Life is short and any one of us could go at a second's notice, so live each day as if it is your last and you probably can't go too wrong.

'Dying is an inevitable part of life,' said Nat. 'There's nothing we can do to get away from it.'

'I can't remember when I became aware of my own mortality. There must have been a point when I realised that one day I was going to die. I cannot remember for the life of me where I was, when it was, or how old I was.'

'Neither can I. I don't think there are that many of us that probably can.'

I suppose it could have been around the age of about ten when my grandfather died. I was annoyed about this as it was decided that because I was so young, they would keep the information about his death from me. Quite what they hoped to achieve by this, I don't know. It's not as if they could cover up his absence forever, I mean, eventually I might have noticed even if I was only ten years old. The reason for this deception was largely down to one of my aunts who was an atrocious woman who felt that she knew better than everyone else and she felt that as a ten-year-old child, I should be shielded from death.

My father was furious when he found out and made a point of telling me immediately.

'Max may only be ten years old,' he said, virtually bursting with anger as he spoke to my aunt, 'but we do not keep from him things like this.'

Aunt Violet sniffed in a very 1930s way and spent the rest of her life ignoring my father. I don't think he was all that bothered. I am not even sure if he noticed.

'It must have been around that time,' I told Nat. 'I just can't remember though. You might think that something as earth shattering as that would have been something that stuck in the memory and traumatised me, but it has completely gone.'

'Death is a very strange thing. People who say they are frightened of death are really being irrational. Dying is not something to be worried about.'

'How do you mean?'

'If there is an afterlife then depending on how it is made up, you may have some questions to answer depending on the kind of life that you led.'

'My aunt will probably have some questions to answer.'

My aunt was someone that was very publicly a Christian. She would fawn over the vicar and make sure that everyone knew about the large donations that she had made to the church. The vicar would describe her as 'a good Christian', chiefly because he was getting a fair amount of money out of her and that was clearly how he liked to define what a good Christian was. Her Christianity was of the very public variety.

Away from the prying eyes of the church, she was a total bitch. To her own family, she was a right cow who wouldn't do anything to help. She was all about taking and looking good in the community when behind doors she wouldn't have given you the time of day. People like her would be the kind of people that put me off of religion for life. I can't say that the Church has ever done anything to redeem itself in my eyes.

'If there is an afterlife then things will continue,' stated Nat. 'So, what is there to worry about?'

'Not much, I suppose.'

'If there isn't an afterlife and we just fall into oblivion then we're not going to know anything about it. So there really isn't anything to worry about.'

'It's the process of dying that people are worried about. Not death itself. The long drawn-out, painful process. Death at the end of that will probably be a relief, whichever way it falls.'

I am not sure that it was for my mother, but I would like to think that it was.

***

'She wasn't really the same person any longer,' my father said as he stood in the same suit that he had worn for my wedding four years before.

'I wish I could've got over to see you both more often, you know, what with the divorce and everything, it hasn't been easy.'

'No, that's fine. I know you have your own affairs to sort out.'

It was the day of my mother's funeral.

She had gone downhill rapidly over the last few years. I had not seen her as much as I had wanted to. I had been busy being married and shagging my heart out with a woman that clearly wasn't getting enough from me; I had been working hard as well at trying to get my PhD sorted. After the separation, it was just too difficult, I suppose. I was on a low and I didn't think a visit to see my mother, who probably wouldn't remember me anyway, would actually do all that much to make me feel any better.

'I think the worst thing was,' my father continued, 'that she started to forget words. Isn't that a terrible thing for someone who has lived their life by letters so much?'

'Yes, it is.' It was. There was no denying it. Horrible thing. 'Do you think she knew?'

'Knew that she was losing it?'

'Yes.'

'In the early days, she knew. She knew what was happening and what was going to happen and I think it scared the shit out of her. She also knew that there would come a time when she wouldn't care any longer. She would be too far gone to realise what her life had once been like and what it was like now. "Frank," she said to me one day, "there is going to come a time when I won't remember you any longer." She wanted me to be prepared for it.'

I nodded my head and thought about all the suffering my father had gone through without me being there to help him.

'How the hell can you prepare yourself for the fact that one day you will wake up and the woman you have lived with, loved with, cried with, and had children with for the last thirty years simply doesn't know you any longer?'

It was a fair question and I really didn't have the answer to it. I can't imagine how terrible that must be. Not only knowing that you would lose your wife, but also knowing that by the time the end came she would have no memory of your time together.

***

Funerals are a very strange affair. I am not entirely sure that I understand what they are all about. By that I mean I am not sure who is meant to benefit from it. People talk about 'giving them a good send off', and 'paying respects'. Is it really about doing what is right for the deceased or is it a form of self-indulgence for the mourners?

We sat in the pews in the cold church, we listened dumbly to the vicar talking in a monotone voice about someone that he had never met, saying words that he had probably said a thousand times before. This is what annoys me the most about funerals. The impersonal nature of it all.

What also annoys me is the expense of it all. If they fleece you to marry you, they absolutely screw you over when you are dead. When I die, I don't want the expense of a huge funeral. I would like things to be as basic as possible. Firstly, no vicar, please. Let people that actually knew me stand up and say things about me. Not some textbook rambling from someone who hasn't even seen me dead, yet alone alive. I also don't want flowers, or any waste of money like that. I don't understand the expense of a coffin. They are so bloody expensive for something that you are, in theory, only going to use once and then either set fire to or bury in a hole. If I had my way, I would settle for a bin bag. It can be biodegradable if that makes it easier.

The thing that I probably object to the most is the fact that when it comes to Christianity and funerals, the standard method of preaching seems to be that if you believe in Christ then you will be saved after death, whereas if you don't believe then you are pretty much screwed. If this is your belief then fair enough, but as far as I am concerned any afterlife that excludes people unless they believe certain things is not something that I want to be part of. I don't think any religion has the right to claim exclusivity.

The funeral service continued and we sang hymns that I suspected had been chosen by the vicar as I can't imagine them ever being anything that my mother would have specifically chosen to want played. She wasn't really a big church-goer. I don't imagine that my father would have chosen them either, he wasn't really into all of that. As my mother's coffin was lifted from the church, the Beatles song *My Life* echoed through the marble surroundings. Finally, there was something about the funeral that I believed my mother might have actually had some say over. This was the first hint of the personal in the whole affair.

We followed the coffin out to the hearse and then slowly followed it as it made its way to the newer part of the church cemetery on what was to be my mother's final journey. We walked behind and nothing was heard but the sound of our shoes crunching on the gravel beneath our feet. We were silent out of respect and we were silent because we didn't really have anything that we wanted to say. God alone knows what was going through my father's mind. He seemed to be staring into space and had gone noticeably greyer since I had last seen him. He looked older than his fifty years.

'The problem with her dying so young,' he had told me 'is that I face the possibility of living for so many more years without her. I mean it could be another thirty years before my time comes. I can't imagine another thirty years without her being about.'

More words were said at the graveside that I didn't listen to. I was numb to it all by then and when the earth was thrown onto the coffin and all the words were said, I manipulated myself so that I did not have to shake hands with the vicar. I really didn't agree with what he was preaching. Not his fault, he had been brainwashed into believing it more than anyone else.

I moved to the graveside and looked into the final resting place of my mother. It all seemed to be so surreal really. I found it so hard to believe that they had put my mother in that box and then lowered it all the way into the ground like that and that we were then about to walk off and leave her there, forever.

***

'I'm not sure what I'm expected to do now,' my father said. He was uncomfortable but that was probably because we were standing in the living room whereas he didn't really like coming out of his study if he could help it. Since my mother's progressive illness, I think he had spent even more time in there.

'What do you want to do?'

'I don't know,' he just shook his head and looked at the floor, the untasted glass of wine, or whatever it was in his hand. 'Someone actually said to me that I was still young enough to find someone else. Can you believe that? My wife has just died and someone already is suggesting that I look for someone else.'

I did find it pretty hard to believe and it wouldn't have surprised me if it was one of my aunts that had said it. It sounded like the kind of heartless thing that one of them would say when they think that they are doing good.

'I can't believe that anyone would think that,' he said still shaking his head. 'My entire life is over. My very reason for getting up every morning has gone; and some *fuck* says something like that as if I they are talking about buying some television set that if you don't like you can take back to the shop and upgrade it.'

'People are wankers, that's why,' said Jerry coming up. 'Especially Aunt Violet, she is a complete wanker.' He raised his glass in the direction of where the said aunt was sitting in a chair. Jerry had a way with words that I often lacked. Whilst I was at a loss for words to say, he just waded in.

'Well, yes, I suppose that's true,' my father said with the ghost of a smile on his lips, which was the first time I had seen him smile in ages. 'Oh, what's the point?'

'The point is,' Jerry said taking my father by the arm, 'that Mum wouldn't want you to just give up. As a matter of fact, she would kick your arse.'

'You're probably right.'

'Come on; let's get you off to have some rest.'

'What about everyone?' he looked around at the room full of people.

'Fuck them,' Jerry said. He said it loud enough to ensure that everyone had got the message as well. 'They aren't important.'

My father nodded his head and then Jerry moved my father slowly, but firmly out of the room and away towards his study. I don't think he was ready for the bedroom that he shared with my mother and Jerry appeared to be aware of that by instinct. Not for the first time in my life, I felt that Jerry knew far more than I did.

'Well, I think that was a trifle uncalled for.' This was from Aunt Violet who now looked as if she had moulded herself into a chair. I looked at her and I looked at the other people present. I suddenly realised that I didn't care about any of them. I then saw the vicar standing there stuffing his face with the sandwiches that had been put out on the buffet. I suddenly started to get angry. I have no idea how much my father had paid for him to say the meaningless crap that he had said at the funeral, but having received his hefty fee he was now making off with as much of the free food as he could get. I turned back to Violet.

'There's absolutely no sense in talking like that to people that have never done him any harm in the world,' she continued.

'Why don't you fuck off, you horrible old bitch.'

I hadn't been planning to say it, but it was something that just came out. I guess I had been suffering from a lot of tension over the last couple of years and it all came out directed at her. She looked as if I had physically walked up to her and slapped her in the face. I don't think anyone had said anything like this to her before in all of her life. It must have been a shock. I think all the talking in the room had already stopped by this point, but if it hadn't then my comment had certainly made sure that the conversation was over. The vicar obviously felt that he had to intervene at this point. Being a man of God, he seemed to think that he had the God-given right to interfere in everything.

'Now look here, your aunt –'

I turned on him and raised a finger which I hovered centimetres from his face. Whether it was the finger or the look on my face that did it I don't know, but he stopped in mid-stride and mid-sentence.

'I had the decency to come to your house and keep my mouth shut whilst you spoke bollocks about my mother,' I told him, my finger shaking with rage. 'You have the decency to shut up now that you're in my house.'

He had the decency to close his mouth but I imagined this was because he was as shocked as my Aunt Violet was. I turned back to her.

'Now get your arse out of that chair and get out of this house,' I turned back to the vicar. 'And take this charlatan parasite with you.'

I then looked in the faces of all of those that were in the room, every single one of which was silent now watching what was going on as if a great performance was taking place. I was aware that in many cases I would be looking into these faces for the last time, but I didn't really care as none of them really cared about any of us. They were the hangers on that every family seems to attract. I took a final look and then ignoring the spluttering that was coming from the corner where my aunt was sitting, I walked out of the room and after the only two people that really mattered to me in the world any longer.

Thirteen

It will probably come as a surprise to no one that I suffered my worst period of insomnia in the months that followed. I estimate that at this period in my life I was probably sleeping three hours in every thirty. During my insomnia, I searched from book to book trying to find the answers, but I didn't know what I was looking for. I was driven by something in my soul that I did not understand.

The quest for knowledge overtook my being and became dangerous in its obsessive nature. The more knowledge you gain; the more sorrow you gain as well. For what worries do the ignorant have? The more you know, the more you are going to worry about it. We are fighting a hopeless battle. We have questions, so we gain knowledge that we may answer the questions, but knowledge does not bring answers; it creates even more questions that we are unable to answer. But once the quest has started it is almost impossible to stop. It is a drug that we are addicted to that drives us for the rest of our lives.

I roamed the night. A lone figure looking for answers to questions that I didn't yet know. I searched forwards and backwards in every genre. I searched the history texts to see if I could understand my ancestors. Did they have any hidden messages for me? I sought a task that I knew I would never finish. I will never find the ultimate answers. I wasn't setting out to solve the questions of the entire universe. I expected that I was really trying to calm my own self. Trying to find out the reasons why my life was the way that it was. I found that at this period in my life I was often restless without knowing why. I felt that somehow, if I were to succeed on my quest, I would find the answers that would allow me to be at peace with myself. I don't think the government want people to be too intelligent. There are certain questions that they just don't want asked, let alone answered.

You might think that this was the perfect time for me to be studying for my PhD, but my study in that area had become neglected and I found myself abandoning it for the other avenues that were being presented to me. Learning for the sake of learning, knowledge for knowledge. I am not sure that it has amounted to anything over the years.

***

Needless to say, my work was suffering. I had been cut rather a lot of slack by 'the powers that be' as they knew about the separation and the divorce followed by the death of my mother. They were prepared to be tolerant to an extent because it was fashionable to be so. There is only so far that they were prepared to allow their compassion to stretch though. I don't think we can really come to expect all that much compassion from those who pay our wages. They think because they pay our wages that they can control us and that they own us and that they have some degree of right over our private lives as well as our work lives. Whilst I am at work I will do all that is required of me, but you don't own me and you don't control my life. What I do outside of work is up to me.

I was finding it difficult to put everything together in my life. I suppose to an extent I just didn't care about such trivial things as work. I felt that I had more important things to do than the mundane things that made up everyday existence. It is the smaller things in life that actually make up what it is that living is all about. I spent some time visiting my father as well. I had spoken to Jerry shortly after the funeral and we both agreed that we would have to keep an eye on him. He was alone now in a house that was far too big for him and there was a real danger that he might come to some harm.

'Have you thought about selling?' I asked him on a visit one day sometime after the funeral had taken place.

Despite the vastness of the house, he still spent most of his time in the study. It was a splendidly large house with a fantastic garden. I had grown up in the house as we were not a family to move around from place to place. I had a lot of memories in the house, most of them were happy. I would hate to see it fall into neglect. I didn't really want to see him sell the place either. It was my family home. These days we seem to have got out of the habit of passing property on from generation to generation. Instead, an older generation dies out and their property is sold off. I think there is something nostalgic about the idea of a property passing down through the generations.

'Selling what?' he replied, looking over his reading glasses at me as he held a copy of *Tom Jones* in his hands.

'The house.'

'Never. This was our home and it's where I intend to stay until the day I die. When I am dead, you and Jerry can do what you like with it.'

'I wouldn't want to see it go, but I thought that there might be too many memories for you here.'

'I don't need a house to remind me of your mother. I see her everywhere I go. I see her in this house, in the garden, I see her in the street, I even see her in the frozen food aisle of Tesco.'

I nodded my head in understanding. I had felt the same way about Susie for some time and was always expecting to see her appear out of a crowd when she wasn't there. It is the nature of us that we look for the familiarity I suppose. My father eventually fell asleep with his glasses hanging off his nose and his book across his chest. He looked tired and I suspected that he had not been sleeping as much as he probably should have done.

Whilst he slept in the study, I crept around the house like a naughty child doing things that he knows he shouldn't be doing. I explored downstairs, walking across the tiled entrance hall area from my father's study across the corridor to the dining room that was hardly ever used. I don't remember using it all that much as a child. I think it was somewhere that we only ever used when we had guests or when it was Christmas or something. It had a very unused look about it as I just poked my head in at the door and did not bother to venture any further in. From the door, I could see that the silver in the cabinet needed to be cleaned.

I walked back out and down the hallway passed the staircase and to the small cupboard that was under the stairs and looked in at all the raincoats and Wellington boots that were stacked inside. I had no idea who these belonged to. They just seemed to congregate together from the four corners of the planet. Perhaps this is where such items came to die. There was a room opposite the cupboard which I chose to ignore for the time being. Instead, I walked down to the kitchen which was at the end of the hall. I have never been a great fan of cooking, much preferring to dine out, or get a takeaway. I blame my school as I was never taught to cook anything other than an egg. The one useful thing I know about cooking is how to prevent hard boiled eggs from getting that grey tint to them when you cook them. My mother had enjoyed cooking, though, although she was adventurous in her planning and didn't really follow any known recipes. She adopted the method of hearing about something, liking the sound of it and then cooking it from the ingredients that she thought should be in it.

The kitchen was still neat and tidy and I wondered how much of it was being used by my father, or was he just microwaving things or getting takeaways himself. It was a large cook's kitchen with plenty of work surfaces and just about every cooking implement that you could get, including some that I had no idea what they were for. I walked past the breakfast area where we would normally take most of our meals as children and out to the conservatory that my parents had added at some point in the 1980s. This was where my parents would often be found reading the papers on a weekend. I don't remember them reading the papers for the rest of the week, but they seemed to read them at the weekend. There was a small pile of discarded newspapers, next to the chair where my mother usually sat.

Beyond the conservatory was the garden which had been a paradise to us as children. A large garden was an excellent place for a child to grow up in. So much to explore and so many games that you could play. I looked out and thought that the grass was in desperate need of cutting. I didn't venture out into the garden today, but instead turned back and walked down the hall again, past the door that I had still not opened and up the stairs to the rooms above.

The first door was to my parent's bedroom which was reasonably anonymous compared to the rest of the house. I didn't explore in here as there was still something forbidden about this room. I went across and opened my brother's door which opened out into one of the messiest rooms that I have ever seen. Jerry was someone that was incapable of putting something back when he had taken it out. The result was that his room was scattered with items all over the place.

I smiled and closed the door before moving onto my own room which was exactly as it had been the day that I left for university. This was where I still slept when I came to stay over. The only concession that had been made was that the old single bed had been replaced with a double bed. My room was considerably tidier than Jerry kept his. There were still a number of items from my youth dotted about. I smiled at the *Biggles* books that were still sitting on one of the shelves, untouched for a decade. I sat in this room for probably about half an hour pretending that it was 1990 once again and that the last decade had not happened.

It was not something that was to be though, so eventually I had to come out and return to the 21st century. 2000; a year that still sounded to me like something that was obscenely futuristic and should have been reserved for science fiction only. Obviously, science fiction and science fact were out of sync with each other. *Space 1999* had been something that had been shown to be widely different from the truth, which is something that disappoints me even to this day. Here we were in the year 2000 and I suspected that the following year would be nothing like Arthur C Clarke or Stanley Kubrick had imagined that it would be. Growing up in a period where space exploration was supposed to jump forward exponentially, we all have a right to feel grievously wronged as we slowly slumber our way into the opening decades of a new century that has not lived up to fiction.

One unusual thing about the upper floor of the house was that this was where the living room was located. My parents spent most of their time in their own rooms which were, as shown, located on the ground floor. They had dominance in the house and the living room was something that they only spent a little time in, usually to read or for dad to watch his vast collection of VHS films; mainly adaptations from novels, it has to be said. This room was hardly used all that much and for a living room did not have much of a lived-in look. There was nothing for me to see here, so I turned away and closed the door behind me.

The other rooms were bathrooms and a couple of guest rooms which had not been used for some time either. I didn't bother with looking into these rooms as I doubted that they would provide me with anything of interest to actually look at. Instead, I turned away and worked my way down the stairs once again.

I eventually found myself standing outside the door that was opposite the cupboard under the stairs. I took a deep breath and opened the door. This was my mother's study. There was a hint of danger about venturing into the forbidden area. My mother had been dead for six months now and looking in, it was like she had just popped out to make a cup of coffee for a moment. The desk was still littered with paperwork she had been working on. There was an out-of-date wall chart calendar with lots of stickers and markings on it. She'd have known what they meant, of course, but to everyone else it would have been like trying to decode the Rosetta Stone.

I sat in the chair before the desk, something that I had never done before in my life. I could probably count on the fingers of one hand the amount of times that I had actually been in this room. I had the sense that the chair had somehow moulded itself to my mother's frame and it resented my unusual and unknown shape trying to force the contours to fit. I know the personalisation of a chair is not to everyone's tastes, but I think that there are certain inanimate objects that somehow get to know their users.

I looked across the desk which, to my eye, looked like a bomb had hit it. Papers were all over the place and the odd philosophy text and novel was scattered around as well. On top of the pile of work that was in the middle of the desk were her reading glasses which were casually thrown onto the top of the papers as if she had left the room and was intending to come back to complete what it was that she had been working on. I picked up her glasses and held them up before my face, looking through the lenses which showed me a world that was blurred and out of focus. I wondered how blurred life had seemed to her as she slowly drew towards the end of it all.

I sat there holding the glasses in my hand and staring into space and for the first time since I had been told the news of her illness, I cried. I don't know if I was crying for my mother or crying for myself, but the tears flowed down my face for the first time.

***

I said that I can't remember the time when I realised my own mortality, which is true. What I am conscious of though is the passage of time. I write this now in my forties, looking back at things that happened twenty years ago and they are as fresh as if they had happened yesterday. I really don't know where the years have gone. What I am aware of though is that I must be at a point now where, assuming I live out towards my natural life, there must be less years ahead of me now then there are years behind me. That is my awareness of my own mortality.

I had tried to put my life back together. I had been divorced for over six months, my mother had been dead for six months and I had been separated for two and a half years, during which time I had not had a relationship. I began to consider that it might be time to start things off again if I could meet the right person. The trouble, of course, was finding the right person. That is never the easiest of things to do.

One tip that I would have for you is if you are waiting for the perfect person to share your life with then you will be waiting a hell of a long time. There is no such thing as the perfect person. The only question is: are you perfect for each other? If you are, then despite any faults or flaws that may exist on either side then the chances are you will be able to make a fair go of it.

I had been out of the dating game for some time by this point and I was a bit rusty about the idea of getting back into it again. I considered the possibility of going to nightclubs and the usual sort of places where I supposed that you could pick up women. I didn't really want any one night stands at this point, though; I presume I was looking for someone to replace Susie.

Despite not really wanting flings and one night stands, I had a few flings and one night stands at the start of getting back into the dating game. None of them are particularly memorable and are probably not worth commenting on. All that I can really say about them is that each one of them served as a reminder that the person in front of me was not Susie. As you can see, I was still pretty hung up on her. Almost three years down the line since I had caught her with another man and I was still thinking about her and comparing other women to her. I have no doubt at all that she had completely forgotten me and was off doing what she really wanted to do without so much as a backwards glance in my direction.

I was reaching a stage where I thought that things were hopeless and I might as well settle into the way that things had been outlined for me by a fate that I had no control over. I didn't think that it was likely that I would enter into another long-term relationship again. That is assuming you can refer to my two-year marriage as long term; by some people's standards it was a one-night stand.

I had developed a taste for alcohol at this point. I wasn't an alcoholic, but I had got into the habit of spending a lot of time in bars and pubs in the hope that I might meet someone vaguely interesting. Due to the inevitable closeness of alcohol, I decided to try the various drinks that were available to me to see where they would take me. I would often take a bar stool at the bar, smoke cigarettes (which I had started to do by this stage) and drink my alcohol whilst starring into the mirror at the back of the optics and in some way, try and make myself feel like I was Richard Burton.

My interest in films had led me to try and order some drinks that I had seen ordered in films. *Highlander* led me to order –

'Double Glenmorangie on the rocks.'

The pained expression that I got from the bartender left me in no doubt at all that he knew exactly where this reference had come from. I tried to up the stakes on another occasion.

'Vodka Martini,' I said when I sat down on my stool.

'What's in that then?' the female behind the bar asked me. I gave up at that point and decided to stick to Guinness.

The thing is that I never really liked the taste of alcohol. Most of the spirits, for instance, were drinks that just tasted bloody horrible to me. I can't imagine why anyone would like the taste. I could never have taken alcohol all that seriously. My idea for hanging around in bars, drinking things that I didn't really like and waiting to meet the love of my life that would never show up, didn't appear to be coming to anything and as I sipped the last of my pint, I reached the conclusion that I was wasting my time and I should put all of this behind me and just get on with what I was meant to be doing; working, for instance.

It was whilst I was thinking about all of this and bemoaning my fate in life that Gina walked into the room and things changed for me once again.

Fourteen

Picking someone up in a pub or a bar is not necessarily something which is the bedrock to a great relationship. I think it is difficult to know the best place to pick someone up that you can be sure will be a soul mate. I could have spent ages hanging around the library waiting for someone to come in that would prove to be the perfect wife; with a few exceptions, I don't think there are many women who go to libraries with the specific intention of picking up men.

Gina walked into the bar that night and she was clearly looking for someone to be with. What I don't know is whether she was looking for someone to be with for a drink, someone to be with for a one night stand or someone to be with for a long-term relationship. As it happened, we were together for two years. Two years seemed to be my limit for a relationship at this point. After that things started to go wrong, one way or the other. I am not sure I can say why, it was probably a different reason each time.

Gina and I had a very strange relationship now I come to think of it. I am not sure why it was that we got together in the first place; nor am I sure why it was that we stayed together. I suppose that there was a certain degree of desperation on each side and the feeling that it was better to be with someone than to be alone. The older I get the less I think this is true. When I was younger, I used to think that you couldn't go to the cinema or the theatre on your own; nor could you go out for a meal in a restaurant on your own without everyone thinking you were sad. When I became older, I looked back at it and realised that I could do these things on my own and I didn't care if anyone did think

I was sad. Chances are that the truth of the matter is, that for the majority of the time we, as humans, are too busy being self-absorbed in our own issues and lives without paying too much attention to what other people are doing.

We fall into conventions of how we think we should act, and they are not always right by any stretch of the imagination. I see no reason why you shouldn't go to places because you want to, because they are things that you enjoy doing and it shouldn't matter if there is someone else there to do these things with you or not. Back in the day when I met Gina, these things did matter. I am glad that I have grown out of them now.

Gina and I got together and started to date, to put it quaintly, in the sense of dating each other's brains out. We made no effort to move in with each other and there was never any talk of marriage in the two years that we were together. It was as if we both valued our independence and neither of us felt that the other person was really someone that was suitable marriage material, or for anything more serious than what we were already involved in. At least, I assume we both felt this. If I am honest, I know for a fact that it was something that I felt with regards to Gina. The relationship was tempestuous at the best of times. There were perhaps moments of real love every now and then (I cannot say all the time), but there were also a lot of moments when things were too claustrophobic and depressing. For the two years that we were together, I did suffer from an overabundance of headaches. I suppose that should say something. I know now that they were stress-related headaches. Thinking back on it, I am not sure why I decided to stay around for as long as I did with Gina if the relationship was causing me such headaches and migraines for the first time in my life.

What you have to understand though, is that all of this is said with hindsight. The relationship with Gina wasn't bad to start with, otherwise I would never have gotten into it. Things developed and there were good times. Times when we laughed and revelled in each other's company. If there hadn't been times like this then I really would have been a fool to have got into it in the first place.

Why do we stay in relationships that we know are not 'the one?' I suppose it is because of loneliness or because of fear. So many of us will stay in imperfect, even abusive relationships because it is better than being on our own. It hardly makes all that much sense when you really think about it.

Let me talk for a little while about migraines, because it is a point that I do feel really strongly about. A migraine is not just a headache. You get a headache which is the worst headache that you can ever imagine in a thousand years, but there is more to it than that. You can't tolerate the merest glimpse of light, or sound. You want to lie still and wait for the world to end. You can't talk which makes it really difficult to tell people to be quiet because you want to die. I make these points because I have seen people state that they have a migraine and yet they are still standing upright, walking, talking, and driving their car. Do not confuse a mild headache with a migraine. The two are entirely different things that should never be confused.

***

'Have you ever read Thucydides?' This from my father who was lying on his sofa with a small leather-bound volume in his hands which I assumed was *The History of the Peloponnesian War.*

'Briefly, once, whilst at university. We used to annoy the lecturer by deliberately pronouncing his name "fuck-he-did-heeze".'

'I used to think he was as dry as papyrus, but looking back there are some fantastic stories in here. Fantastic funeral speech,' he looked off into the middle distance as he said this.

'What made you want to read him?' I asked, as I didn't imagine that he was the top of many people's reading list.

'Just fancied broadening out a bit. Lots of books to read and they don't all have to be novels. I'm open to anything that captures the imagination and allows escapism really.'

I knew people at university who had made a career out of doing just that. These were the people that never retired; otherwise they would have to face the real world. Instead the faculty quietly ignored their advancing age, gave them less tutorials to do, handing the bulk over to the younger staff (say those under seventy), whilst quietly sidelining the aging professor who would continue in their own little world without a clue as to what was going on in the world outside of the college walls. They lived, ate, slept, read and if they had the decency to do so, died, in college. They managed to go through their entire life with no real knowledge of reality. They studied as undergraduates and then went straight in as tutors where they remained safely behind college walls until the day they died. As a widower, it was a life that I think my father would have embraced with both hands if they had only let him.

'So,' he said putting Thucydides to one side and taking his reading glasses off. 'What's the problem?'

'What makes you think that there's a problem?'

'Because you're here. You nearly always come here when there is a problem, Max.'

I blushed as I suspected that this had an element of the truth in it.

'I wouldn't say that –'

'Don't worry,' he interrupted, waving my objection to one side. 'That's what being a parent is all about. Helping out when it is needed. So, what's on your mind?'

I sat down in one of the other chairs that he had dotted about and gathered my thoughts together. I realised that I probably had come to see him because of things that were bothering me more than because I felt that I was doing my duty as a son.

'How did you know that mum was the one for you?' It was a question that I had never asked him before, I don't know why. He smiled and thought about it for a moment.

'I knew she was the one for me because I could not think about anyone else other than her from the moment that I met her. She swept me off my feet. It took me a little while to realise what was happening, but when I finally got things together, there was no stopping us.'

'Where did you meet?'

'University.'

'I didn't think you went to university.'

'I went. It was 1970 when we met. There were so many political groups at the time. Mostly left wing, of course. They always thought that they were the most important groups that existed and that they were changing the world, Trotsky, Lenin, Mao –all ridiculous really.'

'They're still around today.'

'Which is proof that no matter how important they think they are, they are really no more important than anything, or anyone else. The reason why they are so useless is because of the fact that they used to spend all of their time fighting amongst themselves. Rather than being united together against the far right, they would splinter off in their desire to be the purest group that they could be. The result being that they would spend all of their time attacking the other groups that were not as pure as they were.'

'So many students seem to fall in love with the far left and indulge in a love affair with Communism, or the like.'

'And they usually grow out of it when they realise that Communism has never worked. The only place it probably has been successful is in a kibbutz. I couldn't hold with it all. A lot of poncing about pretending to be so self-important. Pretending to screw over the establishment and being anti-everything without actually realising or being intelligent enough to realise, that by being at university they were already in the establishment and part of it. The self-importance frankly bored the arse off of me; the obsession with a load of Trotsky bollocks; thinking that they can change the world by revolution when they were nothing but children, unable to live their lives without help from mummy and daddy. Your mother felt the same way so we ended up discovering each other in coffee houses whilst we listened to Bob Dylan.'

'Special times?'

'In many ways the best that there could have been. Don't get me wrong, we were no fans of the Government, but we were not taking part in all of the groups that wanted to bring the Government down. It seems to me that there is nothing that can be done to improve government. If my life has taught me anything it has taught me that no matter who is in power, they are just as bad as the ones before them.'

'I can't argue with that, but you were talking about Mother.'

'Sorry, I'm easily distracted. Yes, your mother. Well, we realised that there was no point in wasting our energy in pursuits that we thought of as a waste of time. We decided to be radical students and concentrate on our studies. We then spent a fair amount of time concentrating on each other. I later dropped out. It was too regimented for me.'

He got up from the sofa putting his book to one side and walked over to the coffee pot in the corner of the room. 'Coffee?'

'Please.'

'To answer your question though,' he said whilst pouring coffee. 'How did I know she was the one for me? Hard to answer that. I just did. I was only twenty and so was she. Neither of us had spent a lot of time and experience in getting to know the opposite sex, despite having lived through the summer of love, as it was amusingly referred to. We just didn't come from that kind of family. I doubt anyone in my family, or hers, would have been able to tell you what Woodstock was. We only discovered Dylan at university, even The Beatles were a little too radical.' He handed me my coffee and sat down once again.

'So, you just knew you were right for each other?'

'Yeah, pretty much so. She was beautiful. She always was, I always thought so; even to the end. She took my breath away without even knowing that she was doing it. She made me feel so happy inside. I guess I knew that she was the one for me from that point onwards. Nobody had even come close to making me feel the way that she made me feel. Nobody ever will again.'

'They might,' I said it more because I felt that I should say something rather than because it was something that I actually believed.

'Well, that's your Aunt Violet talking again. I believe that there is only one person like that in your life. If you are lucky, you can only ever find one true love. One soul mate. Most people are unlucky enough to go through their life without finding anything that comes even close. I was lucky and I was even luckier that it was someone that I found pretty much from the beginning.'

'Sounds logical. I'm not sure that I will be so lucky though.'

'There's still time,' he sipped his coffee. 'I was just so lucky to find my ideal person from an early age. For others, it may take longer.'

'Or, it may never be at all.'

'Well, that's true. I won't lie to you about that.'

'The thing is, that I can't help but feel that Susie was my soul mate. She was the one for me.'

'I doubt it.'

'How can you be so sure?'

'Because if she was the one for you then you would still be together. You may have felt that she was the one for you, but the way things turned out proves that it wasn't the case. If you had been destined to be together then you would be together still.'

'I suppose you're right, but maybe she was the one for me, but I was just not the one for her.'

'There's someone new in your life?' It was framed as a question, but it was more of a statement really.

'Yeah.'

'What's her name?'

'Gina.'

'Good name. What's she like?'

'She's nice enough.'

'Not a very ringing endorsement, Max. You have doubts?'

'Oh, I don't know. She is fun to be with and I like her a lot, but there is something that I just can't put my finger on. Something that makes me think that I can't see a long-term commitment taking place.'

'You feel that she's not the one for you?'

'I guess. You think I should stop it before it goes too far?'

'I wouldn't presume. It's not for me to say who you should be with. Your mother and I came to the conclusion a long time ago that when it comes to you and Jerry, we will let you make your own choices and even if we don't like the choices that you make, it doesn't matter because they are *your* choices, not ours.'

'Must be difficult though.'

'What?'

'Knowing that your children are about to make a mistake, but knowing that you can't interfere.'

'Well, they're your mistakes to make. You would hardly develop as good characters if we were constantly telling you what you should and should not do. Plus, you would really resent it and then go out of your way to do whatever it was that we didn't want you to do anyway.'

'And would therefore do the opposite of what you were telling us to do.'

'Exactly, and I can't say that I would have been any different with my parents if they had tried to tell me what to do. I'm not sure that they approved of your mother and I getting married.'

'Really? Why?'

'They thought that we were too young and that we were making a mistake.'

'Is that why you tried to caution me about marrying Susie?'

'I didn't think you were making a mistake, but I had to be sure that it was what you wanted to do. It was, so that was all right.'

'But it was a mistake.'

'Only if you think it was. Nothing's a mistake if you can put it down to experience. Yes, your experience with Susie is something that has cost you a fair amount, both in monetary terms and in emotion, but it is an experience that you need to get in life.'

'So, no matter how painful the experience, you wouldn't change it for any reason.'

'Not in an instant.' He put his coffee cup to one side and got up and put his book back in its own special place on the shelf. 'You might think that I would regret being with your mother because of the pain that she caused when she got ill and died.'

'It had crossed my mind.'

'I wouldn't have changed a second of it. To lose the thirty years of our life together to avoid the pain that follows? It makes no sense to me at all. I could have avoided being with her so that I wouldn't be in pain now, but if I'd done that then I would not have spent thirty years of being happy and I wouldn't have you and Jerry now. I wouldn't have the pain, but I would have the emptiness inside. You can't second guess the choices that you make in life.'

I thought about this for a second. 'So, I could get worked up about the fact that things with Susie did not work out?'

'But it won't achieve anything. Yes, of course, you can second guess what might have happened if you had a future together and where that future would have taken you and in which direction away from where you are now; but that really is no more valid than saying what would the world be like if Hitler had won the war.'

I finished my coffee and thought about what he was telling me. 'I might go in a different direction to the one that I'm going in now, but I'll never know what that direction will be, or would have been.'

'So, make the best of the direction that you *are* going in, rather than worrying about a direction that you are not going in.'

'Makes sense.'

'This has something to do with Gina?'

'I'm just not sure about her. Whether she is the one for me.'

'Then why don't you just have a little bit of fun? Not every girl that you date has to be the one that will turn your life upside down. It would be nice if they did, but it simply doesn't work out that way. Just relax and enjoy yourself a little. I think you deserve it after Susie, don't you?'

'I guess you're right.'

'I'm pretty sure that your Mum would agree with me if she were here as well. She may have lost it towards the end, but she did have her lucid moments when it appeared as if everything was fine and there was nothing wrong with her at all.'

'That must have been good.'

'It was very good. It was like the old days before we knew that there was anything wrong. She was weak, but she had more control over her mind on those days than any other towards the end of her life. Rather amazing really how she could float in and out of awareness. It was difficult though because in those brief moments she knew what was happening and where she was going. She received less moments like that as it progressed towards the inevitable.'

162

'It must have been difficult having her drift in and out like that. Not knowing if she was going to be aware of you or not.'

'Difficult, but that is what we had come to expect. I still would not have changed it for a million pounds. I consider myself to be a very lucky man. She wanted me to look after you boys though. It was one of the last things that she asked of me before she lost it completely.'

I smiled weakly, feeling a lot of emotion welling up inside of me. There were a lot of things about my mother that I had not known whilst she was alive and I was finding out that it was a little too late to be finding out about them now.

'It's something that I intend to do and I take the obligation very seriously. So, if you want to talk at any time about anything; well then, you know where to find me.'

I nodded my head. I didn't trust myself to speak at this point. Life has an interesting way of pointing you off in directions that you are not always that sure about.

Fifteen

So, then there was Gina.

Everything that I have said about her so far probably makes you wonder why it was that I wanted to be with her. I have painted a rather poor image of her and I apologise for that. Yes, our relationship was, somewhat fraught, shall we say. It was a phase of my life where I had some pretty intense headaches and suffering from a neurological point of view. It is possible that Gina was the direct cause of that. We did have a lot of arguments, particularly towards the end of our relationship.

I remember when I first met Gina. It was 2001 and it was February. I was feeling pretty shit with a raging cold and not feeling particularly good about myself. I was after a lot of sympathy. I had lost a lot of my loyalty for work, for reasons that I am not entirely certain of now and rather than carrying on like I would normally have chosen to do, I decided to take the time off instead and curl up on the sofa under my duvet. I probably would have been better off going to work, but I wasn't in the mood for it.

Thoughts of my mother had made me realise that I had missed out on a lot of what she had studied throughout her life. I was taking a lot of the time off to read some of the philosophy books that were in her library. I particularly found philosophy that had some practical use of interest rather than the more abstract style. I only mention all of this because I was attracted by a line somewhere in Schopenhauer. If I remember correctly it said something like: "To be shocked at how deeply rejection hurts is to ignore what acceptance involves." This made a lot of sense to me and enabled me to put my own life into some kind of perspective as well as my father and the thoughts that he had about living without my mother now that she had died.

I don't know why I remember this so vividly now, but it is something that remains stuck in my memory as clear as anything else that I remember. I started to feel a little better after my study of philosophy and that was the night that I decided to take myself out to the pub and prop the bar up and see what the night brought me. As it happens, it brought me Gina.

'So, you alone then?' she had asked me as she had sat next to me at the bar.

'Does that seem strange?'

'Seems strange tonight for a lot of people.'

'I'm not sure I follow you.'

'Wow,' she looked at me as if seeing me for the first time. 'You really are a dedicated bachelor, aren't you?'

'Divorcee, actually.'

'Ah, well that might explain it a little. Wow, when did you get married, when you were sixteen or something?'

'I was a little young. What should that explain?'

'Explain why you don't know what day it is today.' I thought about this for a moment. It is true that I didn't know what day it was. My illness and deep study of philosophy had detached me somewhat from the goings on in the normal world. I thought as hard as I could, trying to work things out in my still hazy brain.

'It's Wednesday, isn't it?'

'Yes, well done. It also happens to be February 14th. You know, St Valentine's Day? You have heard of it I assume, or is that why you are divorced?'

'No, that's not why I'm divorced and I've heard of it, yes.'

'Good, so are you going to buy me a drink then or do I have to wait here all night on the off chance that you eventually get with the picture?'

She was rather forthright, I suppose. She later told me that the reason she had approached me was because of the fact that we were apparently the only two single people in the place; I had not noticed this, but then I hadn't even known the date so it wouldn't have made any difference to me. Being St Valentine's Day, it appeared that all the single people had hidden themselves away. Probably staying at home watching films that would make them depressed and result in them crying into their pillows at the end of the night. Neither Gina nor I appeared to be the kind of people that were inclined to do that. That was the reason why she had told me she had approached me. What she later told me was that she had stayed with me because she found it fascinating that for someone who was under thirty years old, to be divorced was something unique. Looking back at it now, it seems rather ridiculous that you would want to establish a relationship with someone that you had learnt was such a young divorcee.

St Valentine's Day has never meant all that much to me. It obviously meant little during my years of being single, but even when I was with someone it was not such a big event. I could never see the point of it. It is all commercialisation. Why do I need a special day to tell the person that I love that I love them on this one day of the year? A lot of couples seem to push the boat out on this one day of the year and spend a great deal of time ignoring each other the rest of the time. If you love someone, truly love someone, then you should show that love every day of the year and not just on the one day when everything has been pushed up in price so you are paying a huge amount to make the gesture.

We very soon realised that we were relaxed in each other's company. I was aware of the fact that this was potentially the first serious relationship that I had become engaged in since Susie and I refused to allow my memories of her to get in the way of the future. I was becoming aware of the fact that Susie was more than capable of casting a huge ghost of a shadow over my life, even though I had not seen her for a long time. I was not going to allow that to happen as I was almost certain that she didn't think of me at all. Things may have been one way in the past, the present may be something else and the future may be something entirely different altogether. There was no sense in dwelling on what might have been. I had learnt my lesson that the best course of action that can be taken was to take one day at a time and see where it takes us.

Whilst we sat drinking at the bar that night, I had no idea where it was leading to and I had no intention of thinking too deeply about where it was going to end. I really was trying my best to live for the moment.

We did not spend the night together as you might have imagined. Instead, we parted company when it was closing time and agreed that we would meet up the following day and spend some time together in a more congenial atmosphere and see where things went. I was meant to be back at work, but I really didn't care having decided that there were simply some things that were more important than others. It has taken me a long while to realise that.

We spent the entire day together. Most of it was spent just talking and getting to know each other. We took a walk in the park and a look around the bookshops. We had lunch in one of the little restaurants that was in the park that was mainly aimed at tourists, but seemed to suit us just as well. As I started to get to know her, I began to realise that I really liked this woman. I was twenty-seven-years-old at this time and Gina was twenty-five. She worked as a chemist in one of the pharmacies and was fortunate to have a day off today, rather than escaping from work in the manner that I was doing. One of the biggest fundamental differences between Gina and Susie seemed to be that Gina appeared to care a hell of a lot more than Susie had ever done. At the time, I had felt that Susie did care, but experience showed me that the only thing she really cared about was cock. Crude, I know, but that was the fact of the matter as far as I could see. I suppose that it was only natural that there would be a certain amount of comparison between Gina and Susie. It will be obvious to anyone that Susie was more interested in sex than anything else. Finding her bent over the sofa should mean that this would not come as much of a surprise to anyone. Gina seemed to be interested in more than just a physical relationship. As a matter of fact, she was the complete opposite to Susie in this regard, not really being interested in sex at all, after a brief initial period.

167

I suppose you might think this strange. She started out interested in sex and we had a lot of quite good sex together. After a couple of months, though, she began to lose interest. Maybe it was because of the fact that she had grown bored with me; maybe she was getting it elsewhere. Perhaps she was just one of these people that liked to have sex when it was new and fresh, but then became pretty bored with it rather quickly. I never did find out the reasons why. I don't suppose that it really matters all that much.

We had spent a good day together and it amazed me how quickly the time had flown by. I found myself wondering at the end of the day where things were going to go, we had both decided after having spent the day together that we would make a go of it and start dating. Sometimes things would be easier if we had the ability to see the future, at other times it is better if it is a surprise, or a shock. I suppose that deep down inside I was still a little insecure about relationships and what it is that I actually wanted out of all of this. I don't think I could be blamed for the damage that had been caused by Susie.

'It's been three years,' said Nat. 'Don't you think that it is time to move on and forget about Susie?'

'I'm not sure that I can just forget about her.'

'Well, the least you can do is stop comparing every other female to her.'

'Gina is one of the nicest people that I have ever met.'

'I'll try not to be offended.'

'You know what I mean. I'm determined to give this a go and hopefully will have learnt from the lessons of the past.'

'Well, you can hope.'

***

Lisa was the one that finally concluded matters for me with regards to Gina. Remember Lisa? All that time I spent chasing her to no avail and a feeling of unrequited love that lingered for ages. How did she make up my mind for me? Well, she really just turned up out of the blue one day.

I bumped into her briefly whilst I was sitting in a café reading a book that was supposed to have been something to help me gain my PhD, which I had still not managed to finish. The conversation was really not that important and it was rather strained, but what it did do was give me the confidence that I needed to take a step back into the dating game. The chief reason for this was not because of anything that she did or said, but just because it was her. I knew that I had wasted a lot of time waiting for her to make up her mind and I felt that she had strung me along like a puppet for her amusement whenever she felt like playing. It made me decide to take a chance with Gina as I was not going to be caught hanging around again.

It occurs to me when I read those words back that my view of Lisa is somewhat tainted. It is hardly her fault that I wasted my time on her. She probably didn't string me along at all; it is just the way that my warped brain remembers things when it is distorted by love and lust. We always tend to remember things the way that we want to remember them, rather than the way that they actually are.

On saying that, it took me some time to get Gina to agree to go out with me again. We had agreed to start dating on the first full day that we spent together, but then she disappeared for a while and we were only able to stay in touch by texting, which was something that I was reasonably new at, only recently having discovered it. I soon found out that it was something that was addictive, but did nothing to improve my phone bill which soon became rather large.

I found that I was very relaxed in Gina's company, probably because she didn't seem to be making all that many demands on me. Things were moving more slowly and at a more natural pace than the explosion that had been Susie. I felt that we had a lot to offer each other and if things worked out the way that I wanted them to, then I thought that we were going to be very good for each other.

Things seemed to be going very well with us and I suppose that should have given me a warning signal that things were about to go wrong. History had taught me so far in my life that things were never going to continue to be perfect for me. From time to time, I would notice the odd signal that I chose to ignore at the time, but that should probably have been a warning to me that should have been taken more seriously.

***

Things would be moving along rather normally when Gina would show signs of becoming distant from time to time. I had no idea why it was that she would do this. I tried not to read too much into it at the time. I didn't know all that much about her past and the kind of relationships that she had. It was distinctly possible that there was someone lurking in her past that had hurt her just as much as I had been hurt. Perhaps she wanted to take things slowly and not push things too quickly.

'I think you could do better than me,' she told me out of the blue one night.

'What do you mean?'

'I'm sure that there are better girls out there that you could be with?. Better than me.'

This was not the first time that she had voiced an opinion like this, it wouldn't be the last either.

'Don't you think that is a choice that is rather up to me?'

'You would say if you didn't want to be with me though, wouldn't you?'

'Yes, I would say if I didn't want to be with you. As a matter of fact, if I didn't want to be with you then I wouldn't be here now.'

'Are you happy?'

'Yes, I'm happy. Are you?'

'Yes.'

When we were together she very rarely seemed to get paranoid about whether or not I would be better off with someone else. It was really only when we were apart that her doubts about her suitability would come into force; force was the perfect word for it. I realised that this was something that would have to be sorted out if we were to have any kind of future together. Perhaps the lack of any attempt to live together or formalise our relationship was an indication that we were not destined for a lengthy period of time together.

The bizarre thing was that her moods could swing backwards and forwards. We could go out and have a lovely, romantic meal together and then when we got back to my place or her place, the arguments would start. Without a shadow of a doubt, there were moments when Gina could be hard work. She had the ability to be very 'off' with me from time to time for no apparent reason.

'Perhaps it's just the time of the month,' Nat suggested when I told him about the problem over one of our many coffees together.

'Ignoring the very obvious sexist nature of that comment,' I replied, whilst working at demolishing my latte, 'it would also mean that she has a period about four times a month.'

'Well, that would make life a bit difficult for all involved if that were the case, wouldn't it?'

'More than likely. The thing is that in the aftermath of the argument, I have to admit that I've no real idea as to the cause of the argument in the first place, or indeed what it was even about.'

'So, you're saying that you have arguments when you don't even know what they're about?'

'That would probably be a fair assessment of the situation, yes. The problem is, the more she says that she thinks I can do better than her, the more likely I am to start believing her.'

For the first time, having voiced all of this to someone else, I was beginning to realise how bizarre this must look to an outsider. It looked pretty bizarre to me now that I thought about it.

***

I tried to involve Gina in some of my thoughts on my work. It was something that she had not shown previous interest in, and indeed showed little interest in at that time either. During this period, I was working on a paper regarding Aeschylus and in particular, his play, *Prometheus Bound.* I know this was more literature than history, but I was of the opinion that if you wanted to know about the culture of the

171

people of a given period then the literature was always a good place to start. I had explained all of this to Gina.

'Who's Aeschylus?' she had asked after I had finished explaining to her who Aeschylus was. Her lack of attention might have had something to do with the magazine that she was leafing through. Gina was always reading magazines. Before meeting her, I had no idea that there were so many magazines in circulation. I dread to think how much she must have spent on magazines each month. At times, she would do puzzles in them, or enter competitions or read scandalous stories which I sometimes found hard to believe could be true. Stories like "My best friend married my brother, slept with me and then turned out to be a nun" or "I fell in love with Elvis and kept his secret about where he has been all of these years". Presumably, faithfully keeping his secret until offered enough fame and money to reveal it. I couldn't see the point of all of these, and it explained a big gap that existed between the two of us. Gina prolifically read magazines, but she never picked up a book in all the time I knew her.

'He was a playwright from ancient Greece, some two and a half thousand years ago. I'm looking at what can best be described as the ways of God to Man.' She nodded her head for a moment.

'Why?'

'Why what?'

'Why are you doing this?'

This actually threw me for a moment. I knew why, it was my job, it was what we did in academia. We studied things, drew conclusions and wrote papers about them so that other people could study them. The advancement of learning would probably be the way that Nat would have looked on it. Suddenly trying to explain it to a lay person who didn't seem to move in the same circles as I did, I found that I couldn't see what the point was. At least I couldn't see what the point was from a perspective that Gina would have understood.

I explained it all to her as best as I could.

'But seriously, Max, who but you really cares?'

That seemed a bit harsh to me, but then she was entitled to this opinion. It just happened that her opinion happened to be the wrong one.

'I find it fascinating.'

'But does anyone else?'

'Yes, I think so. I have only been looking at it briefly, but it raises a lot of questions.'

'Oh, really? Like what?'

'For instance, a question that puzzles me at the moment is why doesn't Zeus destroy the human race? We are told that when Zeus achieves his power from Cronos, he intended to have the human race destroyed and replace us with a more superior race with fewer faults. He is frustrated in his plan by Prometheus' actions and is so angry that he treats Prometheus the way that he does.'

'Well, yes that is something that puzzles a lot of people, I suppose.'

'My question, however, is why doesn't Zeus continue with his plan to create a superior race? What difference does Prometheus' intervention make? Surely, Zeus has it within his power to destroy the human race whenever he so wishes, regardless of any actions of the lesser gods? Is the reason perhaps, that Zeus realises that now that humanity has fire they have the ability to destroy themselves without intervention from him?'

I looked up and saw that Gina had a glazed look on her face. I may as well have been speaking in Greek to her for all that it was worth.

'I don't know,' I continued, having decided that I was not ahead so there obviously seemed little point in quitting. 'There's the possibility, of course, that this is just a flaw in the text. Perhaps Aeschylus was just rather too busy to notice this particular question.'

'You know what I think?' she replied after a few seconds of silence whilst she twirled her hair around in her fingers.

'No; what?'

'I think I should dye my hair blonde.'

Now, you might think that the recall of this particular memory is designed to deliberately paint Gina as someone that was stupid. If this is the impression that I have given then I should correct it now. She wasn't stupid in the least. She was intelligent and she was happy in her world with what she was doing. It was just that when it came down to it, she wasn't all that interested in the things that I liked. Thinking about it now I wasn't all that interested in the things that she liked. You would get a similar reaction from me when she was talking about something that she was equally as passionate about. We just didn't seem to have all that much in common; that was probably the thing that would bring us down the most, out of all of the things that would bring us down in the end.

We were engrossed in our own world though and we were still happy with each other for the majority of the time although the arguments were still there. We didn't really discuss much about what was going on in the big world. She wasn't all that interested in current affairs and I spent most of my time in the past rather than the present anyway. We existed in our own little bubble.

And then one day, some mad men decided to fly some aeroplanes into some buildings and from then on nothing was the same again.

Sixteen

September 11, 2001; a date which will live in infamy.

Okay, well that is what they should have said, if President Roosevelt had not already decided to use those words to describe the Japanese attack on Pearl Harbor. They are words that could equally apply to either of the two events if the truth be known. Most people of my age would be hard pushed to tell you the date of Pearl Harbor though. The generation before mine would often talk about 'Where were you when you heard that Kennedy was shot?' It became apparent that for my generation it would become 'Where were you when you heard about the twin towers?'

The answer to that question was easy for me. I was at work. In some circles of the closeted world of academia where they never branched off into the real world, if you asked them about the Twin Towers they would assume that you were in some way talking about Tolkien. On the other hand, I had just finished a lecture and I noticed that a lot of students were flocking to the common room and there was something of a big buzz going around as if there was something major going on. I didn't pay that much attention to it to be honest, as despite the fact that I was not so very far from them in age, the goings on of undergraduates were really not of any interest to me at all. I made my way to the staff area and walked in to find a number of members of staff crowding around the television, apparently watching some kind of film; something that was a little unusual for that time of the day.

'What's going on?' I asked Nat, curious as to why so many people had so much time on their hands to watch television in the middle of the day.

'Some mad fool has flown a couple of planes into the World Trade Center.'

'What?' I sat down in shock, realising for the first time that I was watching the news and not some Hollywood afternoon movie. I had arrived late so had missed the actual footage of both planes going into the buildings. I sat there watching the smoke pouring from both buildings. 'My God, those poor people.'

Being a historian, I realised the significance of the events that were unfolding on the screen in front of me. I was sure that this was a day that would enter into history with the events taking place being much talked about, written about and analysed.

'It seems they hijacked an aeroplane,' said Nat, filling me in on what I had missed. 'Then flew it into one of the towers of the World Trade Center. A few minutes later a second hijacked plane flew into the second tower.'

We watched in shocked horror as live in front of us, beamed to television screens throughout the world, first one and then the second tower collapsed. As someone who had been raised on fiction, as someone who took part in a culture that involved television and film, it was hard to equate what was happening on the screen in front of us as reality. It flashed through my mind that people were dying, right there in front of me as I watched, powerless to do anything thousands of miles away; but then what difference would it have made if I had been there. I wasn't Superman and if ever America needed Superman it was now. Nobody could stop what was unravelling on the screen in front of us.

We then later learnt that a third hijacked plane had been flown into the Pentagon, collapsing one of its walls. There had been further talk of a fourth plane crashed in Pittsburgh.

'Well, there can be little doubt about it,' Nat said. 'America is under attack.' I nodded my head as I continued to watch the news. The afternoon lectures had been cancelled as everyone remained glued to the television sets.

'America has had terrorism brought home to it,' he continued. 'I imagine that it will be a big shock for them when they realise that their world has changed forever.'

'How do you mean?'

'Think about it. America has always been so insular. They don't really understand the global position of the world. Some of them even think that England is a state in America somewhere.'

'Judging from the way that Blair acts with Bush, I'm not entirely sure that they are wrong on that front.'

'Now things have changed. We have lived with it for years with the IRA. The way they will start feeling now isn't alien to us. Some Americans have spent a lot of money funding the IRA; I wonder if they will feel the same about terrorist groups now. All that stuff about one man's terrorist group is another man's freedom fighter is all very well until the time when they start killing you on your own soil.'

'Something tells me that they are not going to be all that tolerant about it now.'

'Think of all the times that they have been critical about acts or retaliation against Palestinian terrorism by the Israelis. I wonder if the Americans will show moderation now. It's okay to urge it to another society, but a different thing altogether when you are required to actually do it yourself.'

'I rather suspect not, Nat.'

'This is war, you know that, don't you? The world has just plummeted itself into war. God knows when and where it might end.'

Later on we saw the division of the Arab world. Whilst Arafat joined world leaders in offering condolences for the attack on America on behalf of the Palestinian people, news crews showed the Palestinian people dancing in the streets. Cheering, firing their weapons and burning the American flag. They did themselves no favours or their cause by being seen on the world news to be celebrating the murder of so many innocent people. It destroyed any of the small credibility that

Arafat might have been trying to obtain by aligning himself with other world leaders.

It would take the world some time to recover from the shock that had taken place. The live feed footage on the television was something that will remain in the memories of everybody that has seen it for the rest of their lives. The images are haunting and devastating.

I remember my father telling me of the shock when John Lennon was killed. It was a great loss, but what I remembered the most was him saying that for the first time celebrities all over the world realised that it could have been them. They realised that they were targets. On September 11, many Americans realised they were targets and it was probably a shock to realise that not everybody in the world liked them. Nothing was sacred any longer.

***

At the time that the world was recovering from the shock of what was happening in America, things on the domestic front were clouded by arguments with Gina once again. Shortly after the news of the terrorist attack, she responded to what had happened by getting into a major row with me. In hindsight, it is difficult to work out exactly what the argument was about, or why indeed it even started in the first place. It almost felt as if she was arguing with me for the attack that took place in America, although that would make no rational sense at all. I think most of these arguments stemmed from a level of insecurity. It is going to sound like I am blaming Gina for all of the arguments that we had but it wasn't always her fault. The difference is perhaps that whereas we both had problems in life, with her problems, she projected them on to the entire relationship until her problems seemed to define the relationship.

Gina could get very moody from time to time and she was quick to tears at almost any situation regardless of what it was. I am sorry to say that I found myself quite unable to deal with the situation. It worried me that at the age of twenty-five, she had not yet come to the realisation that life is going to deliver her some hard knocks if she doesn't learn to toughen up a little.

It was probably around about this time that I began to realise that, with regards to this relationship, perhaps things didn't need to be like this all of the time. I did begin to wonder if I was cut out to be with Gina. I thought back to my relationship with Susie, something that I had tried not to do as I could hardly see it being productive. I indulged myself though because I wanted to see if there were any lessons that I could learn. I didn't want my relationship with Gina to become just another love affair that didn't work. We seemed to be in danger of destroying ourselves. Perhaps that is what love is all about – living close to destruction without actually ever falling off the edge. It is a very delicate balance. I had already fallen off once and went burning all the way down to the bottom. I had no desire to fall off again, but nor did I have any intention to submit to a life that would make me miserable.

Around this time was the first time that I remember waking up in the night and gagging for breath, being unable to breathe. I assumed that I had suffered a nightmare and had taken it badly. My heart was racing and I ached with the strain of gasping for oxygen. Eventually it settled down and I thought that was the end of it. Little did I know then that this wasn't the end of it and that it wasn't a nightmare; not in the conventional sense of the word at any rate.

It was around about now that I began to think of Gina as someone who was a manic-depressive. It wasn't a sudden thought; it was something that had been festering at the back of my head for a long time. Over the course of the year that I had been spending with her, it was something that had grown in intensity. Sometimes, for no apparent reason whatsoever, I would find that she had slipped into a depressive mood; sometimes this would result in an argument. We would disappear off in different directions and then within a couple of hours she would be back and would be her usual happy self once again. It was quite inexplicable really. I hadn't had much experience of this kind of thing so I might be forgiven for being a bit out of my depth

179

and not sure what it was that I was meant to do. The situation with Gina continued to escalate into more arguments and problems.

'If things continue like this, then it's obvious to me that there's no future for us at all,' I told my father one day when I was back in his study for a form of therapy.

'Well, yes, I can see your point,' he replied.

'Everything hinges on Gina owning up to her responsibilities and not acting like a spoilt child when she can't get her own way.'

'Does she do that a lot?'

'Almost every day; I have been working like crazy to try and keep this relationship together.'

'Perhaps you shouldn't be trying so hard.'

'How do you mean?'

'Well, this is just me thinking out loud and you don't have to take it as advice or anything like that, but it seems to me that if you have to work so hard at keeping this relationship afloat then the chances are it isn't worth it.'

'I think I agree with you.'

'Some things are worth fighting for, and other things are often just a waste of energy. What you have to decide is which category Gina falls into.'

'That's easier said than done.'

'Nobody said that it would be easy.'

***

My headaches were not getting any better so I decided to be logical about it and take myself off to the local optician to see if I needed glasses. It had been some time since I had last had my eyes tested and they could just as easily have been the cause of my headaches as much as Gina might have been. I had been experiencing a lot of eye strain as well as the headaches so it was just as likely that it was medical rather than psychological. Spend all your days bent over manuscripts and books and there is bound to be a price that must be paid somewhere down the line.

'You seem to have very healthy eyes, Mr Durant,' said the young and rather attractive optician. 'I certainly can't see any reason for why you are getting eye strain or headaches.' I guess that answered my question. 'Have you seen a doctor about your headaches?'

'Yes, he said that it was stress related.'

'Well, that would seem to be the conclusion that I would come to as well. I think the medication you need is a reduction in the stress in your life. Is there anything particular that is stressful in your life at the moment?'

'I can think of one or two things,' I said as I squirmed slightly in my chair. It was at this point that things started to become complicated.

It was clear that the chief problem at the moment was that I was getting a lot of stress from my continued relationship with Gina. Gina suffered a great deal from paranoia. One of the things that she was paranoid about was my friendship with someone that worked in my department, Karen. Now Karen was very attractive, young and intelligent. I won't deny that for a minute, it would be wrong to do so. Gina thought if I spent any time with Karen that meant I was having an affair with her. If Karen and I had lunch together and Gina found out about it then she would be paranoid that I had chosen to have lunch with her. If I kept it a secret that I had met Karen in order to stop the arguments that would develop from finding out, well then, you can imagine how paranoid she would get because I had met a female friend for lunch and then kept it from her. I don't think she was actually all that paranoid about Karen, I think she was paranoid about any woman that I came in contact with – no matter who it was.

Gina was no doubt jealous of Karen and I am sure that she was of the opinion that I would run off with her to have an affair at the first opportunity that I had. Therefore, the thought of us having lunch together was more than enough to make Gina go into one of her moods. It was self-defeating behaviour really because if Gina didn't behave the way that she did half the time then we wouldn't have been in the position that we often found ourselves in and she probably wouldn't suspect that I wanted to run off with Karen.

I think by this time in our relationship we had reached a point where if I thought that Karen was even slightly interested in me in that manner, then I wouldn't have hesitated in running off with her. Sadly, however, I suspected that Karen wasn't interested in me in that way at all.

And then one day it all came to a head. As these things have a habit of doing.

***

Where do I start to explain what happened next? It was a bad time. I thought that the way my relationship with Susie ended was bad, but it was nothing to how my relationship ended with Gina.

Well, I suppose it started with an uncommonly long day at work. Sixteen hours as I was rushed off my feet to get some presentation or other ready for some kind of visiting dignitaries. As you might expect, I was really very tired by the time that I got home. The moment I got home, Gina was waiting there for me to start an argument.

'I suppose you have been spending all of your time with that Karen?' she challenged me almost as soon as I had sat down.

'Well, yes, in a way. She does work in my department after all.'

'If you love someone else, and you don't want this relationship, then perhaps you should just go and save us both from the lies and misery,' she flung at me.

This was not a new theme for her. This was something that she used at some point in almost every argument. Each time she had mentioned it previously, I had assured her that there wasn't anyone else and that she was only being paranoid. Accusing her of being paranoid was not something that helped the situation, of course, no matter how true an accusation it was.

'Max, did you just fall asleep?' she virtually shouted at me. There was a possibility that I had fallen asleep. The sofa was comfortable and it had been a long day, plus I had been sleeping badly once again.

'I can't believe that you would fall asleep whilst I'm talking to you about something so important. Clearly it isn't important to you.'

'Perhaps you're right,' I said resignedly.

'What?'

'There isn't anyone else, but things clearly are not working, so perhaps it would be better if we had a break. Perhaps take two months and get some space between us and see where we are in two months.'

'I beg your pardon?'

'I think we need some space.'

'You want some space? Get a rocket and shove it up your arse and blast yourself off into all the space that you want.'

If I had not been so tired, then I would probably have found this to be a funny line. However, if I'd have laughed at this, then it would have only made things worse and she would probably have stuck a knife in my head.

'You don't think we should have a trial separation?'

'What's the point? You think I should give you two months to go off and shag whoever you want so that you can eventually decide after two months that you don't want to be with me any longer?'

It was a point; although it hadn't been in my mind when I had walked into the room, I was not going to allow that to stop me.

'In that case, I suggest we split completely. We gave it a chance, Gina, and it hasn't worked. It's time to call it a day. We will both be happier if we are free to run our own lives again.' I stopped because I was aware of the clichés that were spilling from my mouth. She stood there in silence for a few moments and I swear I could see the anger bubbling up inside her.

It was rather curious really because she had spent so long in her paranoia believing that this was about to happen or that I was shagging someone else that you would have thought that there would be a degree of relief from her now that she had finally been proven to have been right all along and what she had so often predicted and worried about had finally happened. Apparently, getting what she wanted was not what she wanted after all.

'Get out!' she screamed at me. 'Get out of here at once and never come back.'

'Well I would, but this is my flat.'

It would have been so comical if it had not have been so tragic. When the vibrations of the door having slammed shut had died down, I settled down on the sofa and tried my best to get some sleep. Dinner would have to wait.

***

I was woken, I don't know how much later, by the incessant blaring of the telephone that broke through the first peaceful sleep that I had had for months. I fumbled for the phone.

'Yes?'

'Mr. Durant?'

'Yes.'

'This is Doctor Dalby from the Infirmary. I'm sorry to tell you that I have someone here that I think you know.'

For a moment, I thought that it was my father or perhaps something had happened to Jerry. It was Gina of course.

'She's taken a quantity of tablets,' the doctor told me.

She had then panicked about it and called for an ambulance. She had taken sixteen pills – I didn't find out what they were.

'She wants to know if you will be visiting?'

'I don't think that's a good idea.'

'Okay, well she just wanted you to know.'

I thanked the doctor and put the phone down. She would be all right; there was no chance that she would die from what she had done. She would certainly be getting the psychiatric help now that she needed so much.

My first instinct, combined with her request that I visit, was that I should go to her and make up with her. I almost did, but then stopped myself and sat back down again. I had to think this through.

It hadn't been a really a serious attempt, but more of an attention grabber. A form of emotional blackmail. Or, if you want another cliché, it was a cry for help. She was a chemist after all so if she really had wanted to take something that would have killed her, she would have known exactly what to do. Too much damage had been done to

184

hope to recover anything from this. If you really love someone then you don't do a thing like this to them.

The sad thing was that I had been living with the belief that we were heading this way for some months now. I had not imagined that it was likely to be a suicide attempt, but it was clear that things could not last all that much longer. Something that had started off so well and given us both such good times, had now collapsed and left us with nothing but tragedy.

You may think me heartless for not going to her and I wouldn't blame you if you felt that way, but I knew that if I went to her now then I would be trapped for the rest of my life and that I would never be able to leave her. It would do us no good to be together. We each had to go our separate ways. I was not immune to what had happened. I am not that heartless. There were periods just after the news and for a short while afterwards, when I would just collapse and break down over it all. I had to force myself to see the bigger picture though. I did have a lot of support from my family and from friends like Nat.

I knew that it was time to look to the future for the both of us. It was time to move on and put both the bad times and the good times that we had experienced behind us. I sincerely hoped that she would be able to overcome her problems and realise that she would be better off without me in the future and making her own path.

I received a lot of texts and missed phone calls from her in the time after her 'accident'. I had decided that the best course of action was to cut all connection with her. This may sound harsh, but I knew that if I opened the door again then there was a chance that I would be giving her some kind of false hope that we could get back together, when as far as I was concerned there was no hope of that at all. On my side, I was also concerned that being in contact with her would cause me a lot of guilt that would result in me collapsing and agreeing to get back together again. That would be disastrous for the pair of us.

It was a bloody awful mess and I acted like a coward by taking a leave of absence, turning off my phone and going to stay with my father until I felt that the dust had settled and it was safe for me to return to my life once again.

***

By the magic of writing, I now want to bring things right up to date as something has recently happened in my life that has had a massive impact on things. I could wait and tell you about this in chronological order, but you will have to forgive me for wanting to get it out of my system now.

'I think you should go and see a doctor,' this was from Ellie and was out of the blue one morning when we were having breakfast on one of the days when neither of us had to go to work.

'You're not the first person to say that,' I said lowering my coffee cup and looking at her strangely, wondering why it was that she had suddenly come out with this. 'Is there any particular reason why?'

'You have some very strange sleeping habits.'

'Oh?'

'You've a very disturbed and restless sleep each night and you wake up every few minutes.'

'No I don't.'

'Yes, you do. You just don't realise that you're doing it. '

'Don't you think I would remember if I were waking up throughout the night?'

'Not necessarily. Not if it were so quick that it was happening so fast that you didn't even realise it; probably because of the fact that you are not fully awake when it happens.'

'Why would I wake up throughout the night?'

'Probably because you stop breathing.'

'I what?'

'You stop breathing. Regularly throughout the night. I know; I watch you do it. It's actually rather off-putting. Fortunately, you wake up and start breathing again before then falling back to sleep and starting the whole thing off once again.'

This was disturbing news and several things hit me at once. I suppose the first thing that hit me was that if this were true, then it might explain why it was that I felt crap all of the time and why it was that I kept needing to go to sleep in the afternoon. It stands to reason that if I were waking up throughout the night like this then I wouldn't really have been all that rested when I did wake up. If this were true, then my body was not getting the chance to regenerate. It made absolute perfect sense as to why it was that I would be feeling crap all of the time.

The second thing that occurred to me was the fact that if this had been going on for some time, which I believe that it had, then how come nobody else had picked up on it? Maybe it hadn't been going on when I was married to Susie, so I probably couldn't have blamed her for not noticing it, but then it could have gone back that far in my past. Others should have picked up on it though.

'I think you should go and see a doctor about it and find out what is going on. There might be something that they can do about it.'

It was a suggestion that had been mentioned by a number of people over the years, most notably Nat, but it took the woman that I was in love with and had total trust for, to finally get me into the surgery.

***

It had been some time since I had last visited my surgery, but I was sure that the magazines in the waiting area were the same as the ones that had been there the last time I had leafed through them. I looked around and found the place rather depressing, but then I suppose it hadn't been designed with the intention of making you feel happy.

'Do you think these walls are painted green so that it doesn't show up as much if you vomit or leak pus all over them?' I asked Ellie as I leant into her as she sat there reading some magazine that she had picked up from the table.

'It's psychological, Max,' she said flicking through the pages in boredom. 'Green is meant to be soothing. They are obviously designed to calm down people who are anxious about seeing a doctor or worried about what it is that's wrong with them.'

'It isn't working.' Looking around the room, it wasn't just me that was failing to appreciate the subtleties of decorative medicine. 'They look a miserable lot in here.'

'Well, they would be, Max. They are all sick with one thing or another. That's presumably why they are here.'

'Mr Durant?' This was the doctor. It was time to face the music.

'What seems to be the trouble,' he asked when we were settled in his consultant room. The colours were not all that much better in here either. We explained to him what the problem was and he asked me a series of questions.

'Do you ever fall asleep in meetings?'

'Yes. I always assumed that was because they were boring.'

'Do you ever fall asleep as a passenger in a car?

'Almost always.'

'Do you feel the need to sleep in the afternoon?'

'Daily.'

'Do you become tired in theatres and cinemas?'

'Yes.'

The questioning went on for some time and then he fiddled with some notes for a moment.

'Mr Durant, it seems clear to me that there is every likelihood that from the answers to your questions and the information that you have provided me with that you are suffering from sleep apnoea.'

'Sleep apnoea? I've never heard of it.'

'Yes, we will need to refer you to the local hospital for further tests before we can be absolutely certain, but from everything that you have told me I would say that is the most likely diagnosis. We will know more after the tests have been run. In the meantime, try not to worry too much and don't go rushing off to the internet and Google it. Googling your symptoms and illnesses just scares the shit out of people.'

I could see where he was coming from. Naturally as soon as we got home we Googled it.

Well you would, wouldn't you?

Seventeen

In the months that would follow 2001, we came to learn new household words that would be as familiar to us as if we had known them forever; Osama Bin Laden, Al Qaeda, Weapons of Mass Destruction. If you needed any proof that the politicians were prepared to lie about things, then these words would be the proof that would be required; along with the word 'expenses'. Nat was right when he had spoken about the lengthy conflict that was to follow that was to damage the reputation of a president and pretty much destroy the reputation of a prime minister. We were living with war each day and it had become as uniform to us as anything else in our daily lives.

Gradually, my contact with Gina stopped and she seemed to grow wise to the situation. We have not seen each other since although I have heard that she married a few years ago and has somehow managed to raise a family. All I can say is her mental health must have improved since the time that I knew her, or maybe it is just that her husband is a better man to her than I could ever have been. I can only wish her all the luck in the world whilst being glad that it was not me that ended up being trapped with her. I felt guilty when I thought about her; not because of the fact that I had arguably driven her to attempt suicide, but because I did not feel guilty about this. My lack of guilt made me feel guilty, if that makes sense?

***

'I think that the best thing that I can do is completely back off for a little while,' I said to Nat as we sat in our usual place for coffee.

Nat was very used to the idea of me talking about my love life to him. Over the years, he had become a sounding board for bouncing ideas off. I would have returned the favour, but Nat never seemed to be all that interested in relationships. For him, it was all about work. I had asked him about this once.

'Ah, well, when I was younger I fell in love with knowing things and nothing else seemed all that interesting. Physics was just too big a mistress for anyone else to be able to even come close.'

It was one way of running your life, but I don't think that it was a path that I could have walked down.

'Back off?' he asked as he flicked through his customary text book.

'Yes.'

'But I was under the impression that you hadn't actually done anything to be backing off from?'

'Well, that's true.'

'Why do you feel you need to be in a relationship?'

'How do you mean?'

'Well, forgive me for saying it, but ever since I have known you, you have either been in a relationship, just come out of a relationship, or are trying to get into a relationship. You seem to be rather driven to want to be with someone.'

'Isn't that a human thing?'

'It's never bothered me all that much.'

'Well, that's because you are in a long-term relationship with Einstein and Newton.'

'Touché.'

'I do take your point though,' I said as I sipped my coffee. 'I know that I'm driven to be with someone and it's probably true that I don't feel all that complete without being with someone else. Probably makes me seem rather sad.'

'Makes you seem rather human.'

'I suppose I'm driven by the desire to be with someone. It isn't just sex, although that's a rather powerful reason for wanting a relationship.'

'There are worse things to be driven by, but you don't need a relationship to have sex.'

'I don't know, maybe it's all a waste of time and I'm being very foolish about it.'

'Life can be so much simpler when you don't have to bother with crap like this.'

It was a fair point. I didn't believe that it would be all that much better if you were a monk though. You could suppress desires if you wanted to, but that didn't mean that you didn't still have them.

'I've always lived by two premises,' I said as I munched on a muffin. 'The first is that if something is important then you will always find the time to do it.'

'And your second premise?'

'Don't bother with those that can't be bothered.'

'An interesting philosophy.'

'Undoubtedly. It would be easier if there weren't always so many games and rules involved.'

'That's life, I suppose.'

***

As I had been accused of having an affair with Karen, I decided that I would ask her out to dinner and see if there was any possibility that she might be interested in me. Thought I might as well try my luck with the situation.

I enjoyed being in her company and she seemed to enjoy herself as well. As we reached coffee and dessert, I decided to broach the subject of whether she wanted to go out with me in a more formal sense. I asked the question and she looked at me with her head on one side.

'You didn't really ever think that was a possibility, did you?'

'No, not at all. Just a bit of fun really.'

We finished dinner and I picked up my heart and left the restaurant. I was getting more than a little tired of all of this kind of thing by now if I am honest. It's hard to be a romantic if other people are not prepared to play ball.

***

'To cut a long story short, she made it clear in no uncertain terms that she has no interest in that kind of thing at all,' I said to Nat as I sat in his therapy session once again. 'As a matter of fact, I get the impression that she might have thought it rather funny that I would even have seriously considered the possibility in the first place.'

'Well, that does seem a little harsh.'

I have no idea why it was that Nat had become such a confidant in my love life. Perhaps I just felt the need to share it with him. He didn't seem to be bothered by it all that much and I suppose that it was a measure of how mature we were in our relationship now that we could talk about this sort of thing without being awkward. Well, to be more precise I talked about these things, it wasn't something that Nat talked about. It occurred to me that I was becoming less English in my ability to keep my emotions buttoned up. Perhaps it was the march into the 21st century that was doing it. Outdated views and opinions no longer seemed to matter.

I have to admit that although I never did seriously consider that this was ever likely to be a true possibility, to have it put so bluntly to me caused me a certain amount of pain. It was time to move on, therefore, and think on other things. I seemed to be doing this a lot in my life.

'Now that I have had time to think about it and reflect upon it I, don't like the way that she told me that she had no interest.'

'Would you rather she had clouded it in ambiguity so that you felt you had some kind of false hope?'

'It might have been better if I had been given the opportunity to climb down gently from the height that I had climbed rather than plummet as I actually did.'

192

I had been hurt once again. It wasn't so much the rejection that had hurt me, but the way that I had been rejected. Rather it was the comment, *"You didn't really ever think that was a possibility, did you?"* Oh yes, how foolish of me. Oh, indeed I am fortune's fool. How naive of me to even think such a thing for even the shortest length of time.

'You have been involved with more than a few girls, Max. Why does this bother you so much compared to some of the others?'

'Because it matters. This is somebody that I thought liked me and enjoyed being with me.'

'I like you, Max, and I like being with you; but I don't want to go to bed with you. Isn't it possible that she just wants to be a friend?'

'Hmm.'

'In many regards, friendships can be just as important. In some cases, more so.'

'Well, I won't deny that.'

***

I suppose this would be a really good point for me to give anyone out there who needs it some helpful tips on how you can deal with rejection.

It might be a useful thing for me to be able to do and someone out there might benefit from it, but to be honest, I really can't think of anything that might be remotely useful. Being rejected is all part of life and something that you really have to go through. If you don't experience it then there is a real danger that you are just going to be a big-headed, arrogant, prick who thinks that the entire world can't resist him, or her; let's be equal about this.

Rejection is not something that it is easy to cope with. It isn't meant to be easy. I have never sought out rejection although I understand it is part of what you have to go through to be a more rounded person; at least, that is what I tell myself when I am rejected. What I have never understood are those that seek out rejection.

As I said at the start of all of this, I have had my share of rejecting as well as the one being rejected. It isn't particularly nice on either side of the rejection. When I think about it now though, I cannot be certain that there has ever been a time when I have knowingly rejected an offer from a woman. I might have inadvertently failed to pick up on the signs in the past.

'I'm not sure I understand women,' I told my father as we sat in his study one day, surrounded by the heavy tomes of literature.

'I don't think you're meant to.'

'I think I've got it all sussed and then it's like the goalposts have been moved and the rules that have been established and laid down have suddenly changed, but nobody has bothered to tell me.'

'That's life, Max. That's the way that we all go through life.'

'It doesn't seem the most productive way to go about business. It's amazing to me that the human race has not died out years ago, with all of the strange dating rituals that seem to exist.'

'Well, you're the historian. You'll be best placed to work out, given our wonderful track record so far, whether the human race should have been allowed to die out.'

'We could have handed over to someone who could've made a better go at it without messing it up so much.'

'Monkeys, perhaps. They always seemed to be inoffensive whenever I went to see them. Look like complete lazy bastards in the zoo, though. Mind you, I don't suppose there's all that much that you can do in a zoo, aside from lounge around scratching your nuts all day waiting for something better to come along.'

'It's something that we have been doing on a far more dangerous scale for a great number of years.'

My father looked into his coffee mug, as if he thought that the answers to all of the great, big questions would be hidden within its depths. If he had not found the answers in this room of knowledge lined with the best of human thought for two and a half millennia then there probably wasn't much hope of finding it in a half-drunk cup of coffee.

'You say you don't understand women,' he said after a while. 'I say again, I don't think that you're meant to.'

'Perhaps it is also true that they do not understand us either,' I said.

'Oh no,' my father chuckled to himself. 'I think the problem that exists there is that they understand us only too well. There's not such a mystery to solve when it comes to us. I think we're pretty straight forward, almost two dimensional in fact. But women, they are the real mystery. Probably because of the fact that they confuse us.'

'That's why we are driven to seek them out?'

'Possibly. Who knows? Perhaps it is possible to look at these things a little too deeply when there really is no need and everything is much simpler than we first think.'

'It doesn't feel like that.'

'The only question that really matters is what are you going to do now?'

I thought about this for a little while. What was I going to do? I had received more knock backs in one form or another than I had believed it was possible to receive. What I needed now was something a little more encouraging.

'I think one of the problems is that I have been trying too hard. I think I would benefit from going with the flow for a while. Getting on with life and just seeing what happens.'

'Well, as the great John Lennon said, "Life is what happens to you, whilst you're busy making other plans." I think that's very true, certainly seems to have been in my experience.'

'I will just pick myself up and carry on then; see what happens.'

'It really is the only thing that you can do.'

Once again it was sound advice from my father. We don't always listen and that is a fault that we will regret later in life.

Eighteen

I would like to think that I am not the kind of person that dwells on things and becomes moody and mopey about what has happened to me. I would like to think this, but I know that it isn't true. I am very much someone that dwells and reflects on things. I always have been. I suppose it means that I might actually learn from my mistakes because I dwell on them so much, beat myself up about them to such a degree that when it comes to it, I will never allow myself to forget when I have done something wrong, or when I have screwed up.

Surprisingly, Karen was more of a blow to my self-esteem than even Susie had been. Years later, I had still not forgotten Susie and I still used to think about her a great deal, I probably always will do if I am honest. You can't really be married to someone, be so in love with them and then walk away and forget all about them. If you can, then the chances are that you never were in love with them in the first place.

You never know what is waiting for you around the corner. Sometimes it is a bloody good idea that you don't know what is waiting for you, if you did, then there is a high chance that you would do your best to make sure you never turned the corner ever again. I have been caught out in my life a number of times by the unexpected happening. At times this has been a pleasant surprise and at other times it has been less of a surprise, more of a shock and with precious little about it that was pleasant in any degree. I was about to enter a new phase of my life once again; I did not know this at the time. I will leave it to you to discover if you think things were finally on the up or not.

***

Her name was Beatrice, because, yes, any turn of events in my life would always revolve around a female. Beatrice, a name which sounded somewhat alien to me, like it belonged in a Shakespeare play. It wasn't the kind of name that you imagined someone who grew up in the middle of a council estate in an inner city somewhere deciding to call their child.

Beatrice was actually from a pretty wealthy family. I suspect that her family probably owned Kent or something. They certainly were not short of a few pounds to rub together. I think her father was someone that had been pretty high up in the Royal Air Force, or something like that; I am not entirely sure, I don't think I was ever told. A lot of things when it came to her family were vague. It just wasn't seen as the polite thing to ask and was certainly not the done thing to talk about in polite conversation. Try and talk business at an inappropriate manner and you would be met with a stony silence that left you in little doubt that your topic of conversation was not approved of. That is what I hated about the well-bred, they never actually told you when they disapproved. They just made it clear from their silence that they disapproved and you were meant to take their lead from that.

I suspected that Beatrice's family were perhaps not as well-bred as she liked people to think they were. Real aristocracy are relaxed in their own skins and don't need to worry about their status. Beatrice's family seemed to try too hard. I suspect that they were more upper middle class with pretentions to lower upper class. The belief that you might deserve to be treated as upper class just because you happened to have shed loads of money, was not an automatic right.

I met Beatrice at a university faculty function. I thankfully didn't have to go to this kind of event all that much. My supervisor at the university was of the opinion that I needed to be kept away from these events as much as possible as it tended to lead to me meeting members of the public and then telling them the truth. I have learnt over the years that most big organisations don't want the truth told to people. They all have their guilty little secrets and things that they like to hide firmly under the carpet. I can't be doing with all that kind of bullshit.

I know it has hardly made me popular amongst those that like to think of themselves as my superiors, but that is just tough luck.

Beatrice was easily the centre of attention in the room, which probably had something to do with the fact that she was wearing more jewellery than the Queen. To a certain extent, I found there to be something distasteful about this. And this explains my opinion of the classes, I suppose. Beatrice was decked out in jewellery that made her look like a walking Christmas tree, whereas if the Queen had turned up she would have been subtler. She wouldn't have needed to plaster diamonds and precious jewels all over herself. She would have been more discreet because people know that she is the Queen, regardless of the decorations. Pretentious people don't seem to realise this distinction.

As she seemed to be spending a lot of her time being fêted by everyone else in the room I decided that the best policy that I could adopt was to steer clear of her. I didn't really fancy the idea of being treated as a servant by anyone. I spent the majority of the time hovering around the fringes of the room and the conversation whilst holding a lukewarm glass of wine that I found extremely unsatisfying and was doing my best to not drink. Unbeknown to me, this lack of interest in Beatrice was exactly the kind of thing that made her interested in me. All of the fawning that the other faculty members seemed to be doing didn't seem to be having all that much success.

'You seem to be avoiding me,' she said when she eventually negotiated the room so that she was able to corner me. I suppose she had some talent at being able to spot this in a room full of people.

'I wouldn't say that.'

'Well, you do seem to be doing your best at keeping away.'

'It's nothing personal to you. I have been keeping away from the entire event. It isn't really aimed at you.' I looked around the room and caught the very distinct, worried frown of one of my supervisors who clearly didn't like me talking to the person that he was trying to screw some money out of.

'You don't approve of these events?'

'Let's just say it wasn't why I got into academia.'

'Why did you?'

'Why did I what?'

'Get into all of this.'

'Because I love history. I love uncovering why things happened in the past in order to perhaps explain where we are now. I love knowledge and I love seeing how other people lived and despite the fact that it might be hundreds of years ago, they don't seem all that dissimilar to us. They have the same problems that we have today.'

'And what might they be?'

'The same basic emotions and drives. Money, jealousy, ambition, greed, desire, love.' I had paused on the last word and suddenly realised that I had somehow started to flirt with her, which had certainly not been my intention from what I had seen about her so far.

'And which of those would you say is the most important?'

'Well, I suppose that depends on the individual and what matters the most to them.' I was aware of the fact that she seemed to be standing unnecessarily close to me. I was suddenly very confused about what was happening here and where this was going. Unfortunately, I have found out that once this kind of thing gets started with me it is like a rollercoaster that I am unable to stop. You just have to run along the tracks and hold on for dear life hoping for the best.

'Yes, but what I was asking was, which of them is the most important to *you*?'

'I would like to say that it's love. It certainly seems to occupy a lot of my time. Sadly, life as we live it these days does mean that the pursuit of baser necessities like money takes a priority.'

She nodded at this. 'A sensible answer. We have to eat, drink, pay the bills and we can't do that by love alone.'

I wondered exactly how much of a worry money was to her considering that the jewels that she had draped about her person would probably be at least ten years' wages for me to buy. It was my perception of the rich, though, that they were rich because they tended to be tight with money and save as much of it as they could. I tended to have little money because I tended to spend as much of it as I could. I always adopted a policy of spending money as if I were rich. I always thought it was important to act like you had lots of money, especially when you never had any.

'Would be nice if it was possible, but you're right,' I concluded.

'My name is Beatrice,' she said extending a hand to me in an awkward fashion that somehow made me think that she was offering me a snake. 'You may call me Bea.'

'My name is Max,' I took her hand and shook it slightly. I suspected that she had meant for me to kiss it as she seemed a little surprised. 'You may call me Max.'

'What do you do here, Max?

'History lecturer.'

'Ah yes, well you did say you liked history. History is very important to my family. My family goes back generations.'

I think I knew what she actually meant by this.

'And tell me Max, are you single?'

'I'm divorced,' I replied. Immediately I didn't know why it was that I had said this. Was I still so hung up on Susie that I was unable to admit that I was single without having to in some way invoke her spirit?

'Divorced? Forgive me, but how old are you?'

'I will be thirty in a few months.'

'Married and divorced all within your 20s. You seem to be a fast worker.'

'The divorce was not really something that I had hoped for or planned for. It was something that I was left little choice over.' She didn't ask me to expand on this, which I was rather pleased about as I didn't want to have to go into any further detail about how my marriage had come to an end.

'And you're not currently with someone since your divorce?'

'I have been with people, but I'm not with anyone at the moment.' I had absolutely no idea why it was that I was telling her all of this.

'I am not with anyone myself at the moment,' she said.

'I find that hard to believe.' I was very much aware of my supervisor giving me the evil eye from across the room. He was obviously of the opinion that I was messing up any chance that the faculty had of getting an endowment from her or her family. She smiled at me, fully aware of the game that we both appeared to be playing.

'Well, in that case, why don't we skip away from this place that you are as obviously uncomfortable at as I am and go and have some dinner?'

'Together?'

'That would be the most appropriate way for us to have dinner.'

'I'm not entirely sure that my supervisors would approve of us walking out of this event that they have arranged in your honour, particularly as they might see the chance of the endowment walking out with me.'

'You would say that the driving emotion of your supervisors was more to do with money and greed than love?'

'I'm sure; that is, it's not really for me to say.'

'Well let me worry about that. Assuming you do wish to have dinner with me?'

'I would be delighted.'

'Then wait there,' she walked off in the direction of the huddled group of people that were trying to get as much money as they could from her and her family.

I found that I actually would be delighted to have dinner with her. I could feel that there were the tell-tale butterflies in my stomach which always made me feel like a teenager when I found myself in situations such as this. I had to stop and remind myself that this was only an offer of dinner. The questions about my being single were probably just diplomatic so that there were no issues with her inviting an otherwise attached man to dinner. It was possible that she was interested in me, but it was more likely that she just wanted to find out a little bit about the faculty before deciding on an endowment or not. She had obviously decided that it would be better to find this information out in a more relaxed atmosphere than in the formal manner in which we were currently. That made perfect sense when you thought about it. She was coming across the room to me.

'That's all sorted then, they have their endowment, so there really is no further reason that they would want me to hang around. Let's go and have dinner.'

Or, maybe not.

***

Dinner, as I could have expected, was to take place in a rather expensive restaurant. I felt my heart sink as we approached it as I knew that the chances of me being able to pay the bill for the smallest of items on the menu would be impossible.

'Don't worry,' Bea said as we walked through the door. 'I invited you to dinner, this one is on me.'

The restaurant seemed to be pretty full and I suspected that there was no way that we were going to get a table so the debate on who should pay the bill was probably going to be a moot point. The maître d', however, clearly knew Beatrice and cleared the way to a table that had suddenly become vacant, probably by having some lesser mortals taken out into the kitchen and shot. Certainly, it seems that money is something that can buy you a lot of things. Quite clearly, she was known in the establishment and deemed a valued customer. She also appeared to want to impress me. To a certain extent, it was working.

My food requirements have always been somewhat simplistic. As a student, I spent a fair amount of time eating beans on toast, cheese on toast, peanut butter on toast, and well, most things on toast really. If I were feeling particularly adventurous then I would explore takeaways ranging from burgers, through kebabs to pizza. A little while afterwards when I was working for a living, I enjoyed the standard French and Italian meals that could be picked up in chain restaurants that had sprung up all over the place. This restaurant was different. For starters, the menu was written in another language which made it slightly unclear as to what it was that you were actually being offered. Furthermore, it was one of those restaurants that offered minute portions of food decoratively arranged on a plate and then lightly sprayed with some sauce that always made me think that someone with a serious health problem had just jizzed all over it. The point being that I failed to understand how anyone would be able to eat a meal in a place like this and then walk away with a full stomach afterwards. No wonder that so many of the rich seemed to be thin all the time, if this was how they eat then the poor bastards were starving themselves to death.

I tried to keep my choices from the menu as simple and, above all, as cheap as possible, whilst Bea seemed to splash out in different directions, ordering the most expensive of everything. I have to confess that her choice of wine was pretty spectacular and not something that I had ever tasted before as my previous experience of wine tended to be limited to what I could buy cheaply in the local supermarket. From time to time there were some pretty good offerings on High Table, but I rarely indulged myself in that department. I have a feeling that the wine we drunk at this dinner was older than I was.

I can't really remember what it was that we talked about. Most of that evening is a blur when I look back on it. I do remember some of the conversation though, particularly when I asked her what it was that she did for a living.

'Well, I don't really do anything, I suppose. Not in the sense that you mean at any rate.'

'How do you mean?'

'Well, it will be no surprise to you that my family are rather, well shall we say, well off? The faculty event that we have mercifully escaped from will be evidence of that I should imagine.'

'I had gathered as much.'

'I don't need to work to earn money, therefore.'

'That must be nice.'

'I don't think you are the kind of person, Max, who would enjoy that very much.'

'You don't?'

'No, I sense that you enjoy your work too much to want to give it up and not have to work.'

'That would be true. However, there is a big difference in working because you have to in order to pay the bills and working because you want to and not having to worry about the money.'

She titled her head slightly, as if acknowledging the truth of what I had said.

'So,' I continued. 'If you don't have to work to earn money, you imply that you are working in some other capacity?'

'Well, you know, charity work, worthy causes. Things that interest me.'

'Including the university?'

'I suspect that it is likely that Daddy will be given an honorary degree from the university because of his endowment. He seems to care about such things.'

'If that is so then why didn't he come tonight and speak to them himself, rather than you?'

'You would prefer to be having dinner with him?'

'Not really. No offence.'

'None taken. I would be worried if you had preferred to have dinner with him. However, to answer your question, he didn't come because although he is interested in getting his piece of paper, he is not so interested that he should actually have to come and work for it.'

'Hardly seems much like working to me.'

'We all have different definitions, but I wouldn't necessarily disagree with you.'

'What do you think about the university?'

'I hardly saw it so I wouldn't like to form an opinion just yet.' She started to twiddle the stem of her wine glass. 'Perhaps you should show me around it some time.'

'I'm sure that could be easily arranged, if it was something that you really wanted to do.'

'Well, there are certain aspects of the university that I would certainly like to get to know a lot better.'

'Really?'

'Yes, very well in fact, if the opportunity arises.'

'Oh, I'm sure it will arise.'

We finished dinner, which I have to admit was better than I had thought that it would be. True to her word, Bea paid the bill, despite my protestations that she should at least let me pay some of it. An offer that I made half-heartedly, I suppose, in the hope that it wouldn't be taken up. Having paid the bill which seemed to be put onto some kind of account, we then walked out into the night which was rather chilly compared to the warmth of the restaurant. We shared a taxi which dropped me off at my flat upon her insistence because she lived out of my way, so she told me. She told the taxi driver to wait, in the tone of someone who seemed to be used to giving servants orders, and accompanied me out onto the pavement.

'I would invite you in for coffee, but the place is a bit of a mess and I wasn't really anticipating any visitors. I'm not actually even sure that I have any coffee in.'

'I think I can forego the opportunity. Just this once though,' she said as she put her finger on my lips to prevent me from making any protest.

'I had better stock up on coffee then if you are likely to be swinging by this way at any point in the future.'

'I think that the issue there will depend on whether you want me to or not.' I moved a little closer to her.

'Oh, I think I would like that a great deal.' It was another one of those occasions when you end up kissing someone without really knowing how it was that it started in the first place. One of those magnetic moments when you are pulled towards each other by an unknown force. The kiss was not as passionate and as lengthy as it might have been as Bea controlled the level of how carried away we were going to get. She took a step back from me and reaching into her handbag, bought out a piece of paper and a pen which she scribbled on quickly.

'My number,' she said handing me the piece of paper. 'I hope to hear from you, very soon.'

'I don't think there's much doubt of that happening,' I smiled as I took the paper.

'Then we shall speak very soon, Max. Thank you for rescuing me from what promised to be a boring evening.'

'I hope it was less boring then you anticipated then.'

'Very much so.' She waved and got back into the taxi and drove off into the night, leaving me standing on the doorstep with the piece of paper in my hand.

It is funny how life has a habit of changing things when you least expect it. There are times when you can go looking for something and never find it. At other times when you are not looking for anything, it can come up and slap you in the face. I suppose, that was how I was feeling as I stood there, like I had been slapped in the face.

It felt good.

Nineteen

I waited until I was indoors before I sent my first text message. I know that there are a number of you that will no doubt feel that by texting so soon I was losing any attempt that I might have been able to get at ultra-coolness and was appearing as somewhat needy. I understand the logic of this argument and I see entirely where you are coming from. I have only one thing to say to this: I couldn't have given a toss.

I was feeling happy and as stupid and sickening as it may sound, I felt as if I was walking on a cloud. If you have never experienced this then it will be something that you dismiss as a cliché from poets and romantic novelists. If you have experienced it then you will know exactly what I am talking about, and you will know that this is no trick of a poet. I'm sorry if it is something that you have never experienced and therefore think I am just making it up or being lazy in my prose. For what it is worth, I got a text back straight away; this then leads me into another area that some people may find delicate.

I have spoken about masturbation and pornography so far in my story, but what I have to talk about now is a curious phenomenon that was developing in the 21st century – well, developing for me at any rate, I have no idea how long others might have engaged in it. Phone sex. The prudish of you will no doubt want to move on once again because you don't like hearing the truth. People have phone sex and they send intimate pictures of themselves via text message. It does happen. I have always found this to be a rather curious thing to do, given how texts can be intercepted and monitored as easily as sending mail. Sending your loved one, or perhaps lusted one, a picture of you in an intimate fashion, as far as I can understand is as equivalent of sticking the picture on a postcard and putting it in a letterbox. That might give a few people pause for thought in the future.

I would be lying if I denied ever sending such a picture myself; or receiving one for that matter. I would also be lying if I denied having phone sex or sending dirty text messages. I have done, I probably will do again. I would imagine that most people probably have. Like with masturbation though, they may not all admit that they have. Why do it? Because it is all part of the game of sex, I suppose. Texting dirty messages has a way of distancing you from what is going on. How can I explain it? Well, I suppose there are things that you can say over text that are a little more to the point that you wouldn't say in person because etiquette perhaps doesn't allow it. It removes your inhibitions.

I got my first mobile telephone in about 1998, if I remember correctly. I was flirting by text pretty much as soon as I got it. I know that I wasn't really dating all that much around that period as I was separated from Susie, but I still flirted from time to time and there were some friends who tried to set me up with people now and again. One memorable text message came from a girl, can't remember her name now, who sent me a text saying: I WANT 2 FUK U. Nothing in our texting up until that stage had justified this, so I assumed that she was drunk and told her so. She seemed to take some offence at this. With hindsight and the experience that I have gained since, it is clear that it was the prelude to what could have been an interesting sex text session, perhaps leading to other things. I can't stand the use of 'text speak' though.

What is the point of all of this, you may ask? Well, I told you I would be telling warts and all so nothing but the honest truth should be mentioned. It all leads me to Beatrice, of course. Beatrice and I had flirted all evening, but there had been nothing to suggest that we were doing anything other than having some harmless banter. When the inhibitions of being in person had been taken out of the equation, we quickly began to talk about what had really been on our minds, which was, of course, sex.

I don't remember how it started now and I don't remember who started it. Pretty soon though we were heavily into it. A lot of people have hang ups about sex, and most of the time they have it wrong. Take the Catholic Church, for instance. It spends ages going on about the fact that homosexuality is wrong, that you must not use contraception, and that masturbation is a sin. I examined these arguments with Nat.

'Homosexuality isn't wrong. It isn't abhorrent.'

'I know,' said Nat.

'I realise that it isn't everyone's cup of tea, but amongst consenting adults, does it really matter?'

'You're preaching to the converted.'

'The Catholics are against it and yet a lot of priests seem to have been at it, and not always with consenting adults, but with children. *That* is something that is wrong with sex.'

'I suppose that would upset a few people.'

'Then there is unprotected sex.'

'What about it?'

'Well, I know that life is sacred and that the Catholics take the view that life starts with semen, but is it really responsible to not allow people to wear condoms if they want to have sex and not get pregnant?'

'I suppose they stick to their guns about life being sacred.'

'Is it the sensible thing to do to not allow it with the threat of sexually transmitted diseases and HIV? I know, you are not meant to be having sex out of wedlock anyway so there should be less chance of disease, but even in wedlock is it necessary to have the chance of pregnancy every time you have sex?'

'I don't pretend to understand the ways of the Catholics. I'm not really on the side of any religion. I'm a scientist.'

'Has masturbation ever really hurt anyone?'

'I doubt it. Repetitive strain injury, perhaps?'

'Whenever I think about the Church, I think hypocrisy in the same breath.'

'I'm sure that will offend a few followers.'

'I'm entitled to my opinion just as they are. I'm not saying that they are not entitled to hold contrary views.'

'You can hold an opinion on anything in life but the moment you stray into religion, it suddenly changes and people are prepared to kill over it and spread hatred.'

How is that a message of any religion?

***

Naturally I had to go and see my father. Nat and my father were the two people that I confided in the most about these things. I started with Nat, probably because I had no choice.

'Rumours are all over campus,' Nat said to me on one of our regular coffee meetings.

'Rumours are always over campus. It's what the campus thrives on. Without rumour, it would shrivel and die.'

'These particular rumours are rather interesting.'

'Most rumours are. That's why people enjoy spreading them and hearing them so much,' I said as I continued with my latte.

'These rumours concern you.'

'I had a feeling they might.'

'Why's that?'

'Because in all the time that I have known you, you have not really been someone that's all that bothered about rumours. Logically it would seem that this particular rumour has to have something more personal of interest to you. It could be a rumour about you, but it is more likely to be someone else connected with you.'

'How very clinical of you.' He lapsed into drinking his coffee and flicking through the compulsory physics text book that he always brought along with him when we had coffee. There was silence for a few moments.

'So, are you going to tell me what the rumour is?'

'I'm not sure that I'm going to now, seeing as how clinical you were. Clearly, you're not all that interested in it.'

I slapped him with the history magazine that I had brought along with me.

'Very well,' he concluded. 'A little bird tells me that you disappeared off from the faculty dinner a few weeks ago with the guest of honour.'

'Well, I'm amazed it has taken that long to get around.'

'So, there's some truth in the rumour then?'

'No, there's a lot of truth in the rumour.'

'Interesting. So, what's that all about?'

'I don't know. Not yet. It's early days at the moment, but Bea and myself –.'

'Bea?'

'Yes, that's her name.'

'Sounds intimate.'

'Intimate to use someone's name?'

'Perhaps it's the way that you say it.'

'Stop talking crap, Nat. For what it's worth, we are somewhat intimate at the moment.'

'Thought so. So, where's it going?'

'I'm not sure at the moment. Early days you might say.'

'But you are hoping for things to develop?'

'I wouldn't say no.'

'That means yes. You're just trying not to sound too eager.'

'Maybe.'

'Sounds like it to me. You're not worried about getting yourself burnt again?'

'I don't really believe that you can go through life without giving these things a chance, to be fair. You fall off a bicycle they tell you to get back on again straight away. It isn't the greatest analogy, but it has some merit of similarity about it.'

'Well, I have got to admire you. I hope it works out for you and you get whatever you want.'

'Thank you.'

I am not entirely sure that I was aware of what it was that I wanted at that particular time in my life. I am not sure that I know what I want now. I do know that with regards to Beatrice, I didn't know what I wanted.

***

I was not too worried about letting my father know that I was getting serious with someone again. I had no idea how serious things were, but I thought that it was pretty serious. I thought my father would be likely to want to caution me again against rushing into something as I had done with Susie. He really didn't need to tell me about that. I was well aware of the situation that I was in with regards to my love life.

'Oh, jolly good show,' he said when I visited him and told him that I was dating someone.

'I was expecting you to say cautionary words of advice,' I replied having been somewhat taken aback by his answer. He put down his copy of *Vanity Fair* and looked at me over his glasses.

'Are you happy?'

I thought about this for a while. Thinking about the times that Bea and I had spent over the couple of months or so that we had been dating now.

'Yes, I think I am. Possibly for the first time in a long time.'

'Then that's all that matters,' he said lifting his book up once again. It was sound advice and something that I should really have expected from him. I think he trusted me enough by now to do what I thought was right. I had gone passed my 30th birthday by this stage and was certainly old enough to be able to do what I wanted to do and make the mistakes that I felt I should make. Hopefully, of course, I would not be making any mistakes at all, but you know what I mean?

'Do you think it's serious?' he asked after a while of reading.

'I think it's a little too early to say at the moment. I'm learning not to rush in as much as I used to when I was younger.'

'Younger,' my father snorted. 'You make it sound as if you are older than I am.'

'Well, you know what I mean.'

'There's nothing wrong with taking your time.'

212

'The thing is,' I said as I mulled things over. 'I'm not sure what to do.'

'How do you mean?'

'Well, I was sure that Susie was the one for me, so we got married and I was prepared to spend the rest of my life with her and we all know how that ended up. Now, I think about Bea and I find myself becoming confused.'

'In what way?'

'I was sure that Susie was the one for me and it turned out that she wasn't. Now, what happens if I'm sure that Bea is the one for me? How can I be sure when I was so sure before? I don't feel that I can really trust my feelings to know what it is that I want.'

'Perhaps you analyse things a little too much.'

'I can't really help myself on that front. I think it's probably something that I inherited from you guys.'

'Well, if that's the case it does seem to have bypassed your brother rather successfully.'

'How's he getting on?'

'Same old, same old. You know what Jerry is like. He does his own thing and goes his own way.'

'He usually seems happier than the rest of us.'

'If your Mother was here she would tell you that the unexamined life is not worth living. Not that she had a great habit of quoting philosophy at people. Jerry seems to be the exception to the rule when it comes to that.'

'There are times when I envy him.'

'There are times when he envies you.'

'Really?'

'Of course, sibling rivalry is hardly uncommon. There are times when he wants what you have and vice versa. The trick is learning to want what you have rather than harking on about something else.'

'Profound.'

'I learnt a long time ago, that there was no sense in trying to be something that I was not. It took me a while to get there, but I eventually learnt that the best thing for me was to be myself and not try to be either anyone else, or what other people expected me to be.'

I nodded my head. Perhaps there are times throughout our lives when all of us pretend to be something that we are not, probably because we want to fit in or because we want to impress someone, or maybe it is because it is just easier to keep the peace that way.

'To thine own self be true.' I quoted.

'Exactly. There's nothing that we can say that hasn't already been said better by Shakespeare. It's a travesty that he's taught so badly at school and it puts people off him for their rest of their lives.'

I knew that this was a particular bug-bear of my father. He hated the fact that Shakespeare was read in monotone, line by line in school with no attempt to understand what was being said. Often taught by teachers that didn't enjoy it themselves, who then passed on their lack of enthusiasm to the kids. Kids are not stupid. If a teacher is enthusiastic about a subject then it shows, it rubs off and maybe, just maybe it will inspire a child as well. Likewise, if you found the subject boring and you hated it, then that would become apparent to the class as well. My father was very much of the opinion that Shakespeare should be taken out of the English class and put into the Drama class. Perhaps if they watched it be performed and performed it themselves then they might just get to understand why it was that he was still being read, watched, performed and listened to four hundred years after he had died. People who say Shakespeare is shit are talking out of their own ignorance. Can something so shit really last four centuries and be more popular today than it was at the time that it was written?

My father was of the opinion that if you looked, you could find a line in Shakespeare that fitted every moment in contemporary life. The quotation from Polonius was a case in point.

***

Things have a habit of being very strange. I have noticed this a lot as I have gone through my life.

214

Despite the fact that I was engaged in what appeared to be the start of a new life with Bea, I still found myself from time to time thinking about Susie. I suppose to a certain extent this is inevitable. My memories of Susie became more prominent after I broke up with Gina. I didn't really think about her so vividly when I was with Gina, I suppose because I was otherwise preoccupied. Dwelling on the past a little, I looked at some old photographs of when Susie and I were together. It strikes me that I never knew what I had there. To a certain extent, I never made the most of her in a way that I would now. Things change with experience and moments are lost because of it. It is certainly a case that we often do not know what we have until it has gone. We are capable of becoming somewhat complacent about things. Familiarity takes over and we do not treasure the moments that we have, not thinking that one day they may no longer be there.

'I know that there are some people,' I said over the usual coffee to Nat, 'that regard my relationship with Bea as something that's happening too quickly.'

'Does it matter what they think?' Nat returned.

'No, it doesn't. I feel very strongly about her and I believe that there are moments when you meet someone that you are able to uncover very quickly whether you're likely to get on or not.'

'I assume you feel that you get on rather well with her?'

'Of course, and although we have not known each other all that long, it feels like we have known each other for a very long time. We are very relaxed in each other's company; which is great because I don't think that I was ever one hundred per cent relaxed in Gina's company.'

'No?'

'Chiefly due to the fact that Gina had a number of mood swings and I was never able to be totally sure of what kind of mood she could be in from one moment to the next.'

'I find myself being like that with a lot of people.'

'Living with something like that really puts you on the edge. We had a great deal of arguments as well and my increase in headaches whilst I was with Gina was astronomical.'

215

'I meant to ask you how they were these days.'

'Since breaking up with Gina I have hardly any headaches at all. Certainly, none that are worth mentioning.'

'That's interesting.'

'I thought so.'

'And how is the sleeping issues?'

'Well, sadly there's no change on that front.'

'No?'

'I still struggle with sleeping a great deal. I still wake up in the morning feeling like I've gone ten rounds with Mike Tyson.'

'Doesn't sound right to me.'

'I've also noticed that there are times when I wake up struggling to breathe.'

'An anxiety issue perhaps?'

'I suppose it could be a panic attack, but a panic attack in my sleep? I don't know what it is.'

'I think you should consider going to see a doctor.'

'Well, I'm not so sure about that.'

I didn't think that doctors would have all that much help that they could offer me. I had probably come to the conclusion that I was just stuck with it.

Twenty

Despite me telling my family and friends that I didn't spend all that much time thinking of Susie any longer, it was not entirely the case. I find myself thinking about her even to this day, many years since we last saw each other or spoke. I primarily wonder how she is getting along. She was not particularly good at dealing with certain situations and conditions. I wonder how she is coping and what state her life is in at the moment. From this step, it is easy to move on to a certain amount of reminiscences about the good times that we had. It is a peculiar trait of the break-up of certain relationships that after the break-up, when things have settled down again and are not so intense, you begin to reflect on the relationship, but strangely you only seem to remember the good times, or to be more precise, you remember the good times more predominantly. You find yourself having to think hard and remind yourself of the reasons why the break-up occurred in the first place. Regarding my previous relationships, most obviously, Gina and Susie, yes, there were some good times. To be honest there were some very good times, and if I am totally honest there is still a part of me that misses those good times and remembers with a smile some of the things that we had and some of the things that we did. However, there were too many bad times that ultimately clouded the issue and made it impossible to continue and eventually destroyed the relationship – despite my best efforts to save it.

I might now wander into an area that would best be suited to my mother as a philosopher than myself as a historian. That is the area of free will. It's something that I talk about now because it is possible to view my relationships from this stand point. It is best summed up in a conversation that I would have with Nat around this time.

'Do you believe in free will?' I asked him in our usual place under the usual set of circumstances.

'Of course, I do.'

'Really?'

'Yes, I believe in free will, we have to believe in free will. We have no choice.'

'I see what you did there.'

'If we didn't believe in free will, then we would have to accept the alternative. The alternative being that everything is pre-planned. Programmed into us from the very beginning. Placed on the cosmic agenda before the meeting began. Takes away some of what we like to think of as our independence.'

'We like to think we are making our own choices,' I said as I mulled over what he had said.

'Yes. We like to think that.'

'But is it true?'

'Who knows? It's one of those philosophical puzzles that we may never know the answer to, but nevertheless is something that we can tie ourselves up in knots over for generations.'

'I remember some very basics about it from my Mother. I never really paid as much attention as I probably should have done.'

'Is that regret?'

'It might well be.' I mulled on this for a moment. It was probably true that there was actually rather a lot of things that I regretted about my relationship with my mother.

'What was it your Mother said?'

'Well, I'm not entirely sure that I remember the argument correctly, but I think it went along the lines of the fact that if we believe that everything is laid down for us then we live in a universe that is determined.'

'Yes, I remember the deterministic philosophy.'

'Everything is determined. It does exactly what it says it does. Whenever we think we are making a choice it's actually an illusion.

The decision has been decided for us long before we ever came close to the thought process of it.'

'You have to admit it isn't appealing. If we turn left instead of right, we like to think that it's our choice rather than something that we never had any choice over at all.'

'Precisely. It might be an illusion.'

'Probably is, a lot of things seem to be. The alternative to determinism being free will?'

'Ah, well that is where my mother differed. She said that the opposite of determinism was not free will, but rather it was indeterminism.'

'Go on.'

'The opposite of a planned universe where everything is worked out in advance is where it's undetermined and everything is random.'

'And because it's random we therefore can't have any control over them?'

'I always said that you were cleverer than you look.'

'Too kind.'

'Basically, though, yes. You can't have free will over something that's random because it's still not something that you can have free will over.'

'So, in a nutshell your Mother believed that we don't have free will.'

'Pretty much.'

'What about you?'

'To an extent, I think the same thing. I think that things happen for a reason. We might not always know what the reason is, certainly not at the time, but there's a reason behind things that happen to us.'

'Is that wishful thinking rather than any rational thought?'

'I can't say that it isn't. It's perhaps something that I'm hopeful for. A belief without any scientific fact to support it.'

'Things controlled by God?'

'Well, let's leave God out of it shall we.'

'Suits me.'

'People always seem to use God as the answer when the question is too big. I have never been comfortable with the view that you can get away with any mumbo jumbo just because you can argue it away as having faith in it.'

'But isn't your belief that things happen for a reason, nothing more than faith in itself?'

'Perhaps, but it's not something that is linked to some supreme being that's all-powerful, all-knowing and sitting on a cloud somewhere throwing thunderbolts and passing judgement.'

'That's something at least.'

The thing is that I really did believe it. I look at my life and there are times when things happen and I can't imagine why they have happened. It seems too terrible and there can be no rational reason for it. Take Susie, for instance, as a case in point. When we broke up I could have just taken the attitude of 'shit happens', and pretty much left it at that. If I were religious I could have stood upon a blasted heath beating my chest crying, 'Why, God, why?' I didn't because I am not religious and it really wouldn't have done me the slightest good to have done that at any rate, even if I were.

I was rock bottom at this stage in my life. Didn't believe that I could go any lower than I had done. As it turns out, it all worked out for the best. I went through a few rocky patches after Susie, but then I met Bea and things were wonderful. Bea and myself had a fantastic relationship, full of hope, love and companionship, to name but three. I was more content, relaxed and peaceful when I was with her than at any point in the last few years.

I was more than happy in the life that I had created with Bea and had no desire to turn back the clock at all.

***

Bea and I had been together for quite some time by now and it was at the stage that we were really beginning to acknowledge the seriousness of the relationship that we were in when I got my first real test. Out of the blue, when I had not really given her all that much thought or consideration for a very long time, Lisa popped back into my life once again.

She didn't pop back in to tell me that all my years of unrequited love were about to be paid off as she had finally come to her senses and decided that I was the one for her after all. If she had have done, then it would have frankly been too late. There is only so much messing about that you can take. She didn't come back into my life because of that. She came back into my life in the strangest way that it was possible to imagine. Out of nowhere, having not seen or heard from her for years, she tracked me down and having found me told me that she was getting married.

I can't imagine why she felt she had to tell me this, other than she had decided that she was going to invite me to the wedding. That was probably the most surreal thing of all time and the last thing that I could expect to have heard her say.

It was something of a problem for me as I had very mixed emotions about the news that she was getting married, even though I knew I had no right to be, it nevertheless didn't stop me. I was rather rusty from my acting days, but I felt that I was giving the best performance of my life when I was told the news and I tried to keep my face from looking like she had just waved a dog turd under my nose. I thought that it was the best acting that I had ever done. I later realised that if I were to go to her wedding like she wanted me to then my greatest performance was yet to come.

You may wonder why it mattered to me so much if I was set upon being with Bea and everything was going so well with me? You may ask, and I can't tell you why. I just know that it *was* something that mattered a great deal. Please don't expect any form of logic from this at all. I think if I am honest, though, this was just a shock. A few years ago, I would have been devastated at the thought of Lisa getting married; now I was just miffed by it I suppose. Times change and people change with them and things that were once so important no longer seem as important as they used to. Perhaps they had not changed as much as I had thought, or wished.

The best thing about writing all of this now is that I can fast forward time and move things along at whatever pace I feel like. I can wipe months away in a paragraph or a line. Rid myself of long moments that are but fleeting when it comes to this account. I can use this power now to rip aside the months and move from the news of the wedding to the wedding day itself. It cuts out a lot of unnecessary waiting around.

I have to say that the church service was not as good as I imagined that Lisa was hoping that it would be. She might not have noticed in all honesty as I should think she was probably caught up in the moment. As far as I was concerned, the seams were a little too visible. For instance, the organ player kept playing bum notes that churned out music that would have had J. S. Bach turning in his grave. To top the harmony off you had a choir that were very under rehearsed by the sound of it, with one bloke singing louder and more off-key than anyone else. I would have asked for my money back to be honest. Maybe the reason for it was that they had not been paid enough in the first place.

All of this may sound like I am being a bit of a bitch or something, but it's just my true and accurate observations on the day, as far as I remember them at any rate. By the time of the wedding, I was genuinely able to wish Lisa and whatever her husband was called a very happy life together and mean it as well. You might think I am bitter and resentful, and I can understand you thinking that. I can only express the opinion that this is not the case. 'The lady doth protest too much' you might quote, but that is the way of things.

Am I bitter and resentful? Well, one of us might be, because when it came to my wedding, she never came. Draw your own conclusions.

***

Lisa's wedding and subsequent marriage probably did hit a nerve. Tina could have got married, she probably was for all I knew, and I wouldn't have batted an eyelid. I don't think I would have been all that bothered by Gina getting married; it would have been a wrench to an extent but I could even have been less moved by Susie getting married, again. What seemed to bother me the most was the idea of the likes of Lisa and Karen getting married. Why should that be? The ones that got away perhaps? The ones I never really fully had a chance with? Well, as I have said before, none of it really makes any sense to me. It was just the way of things.

Every action has its consequences. Whether it was free will or determinism depending on your belief, the one thing that I was pretty sure of was that life was a game.

'Some people will tell you life is like a game of chess,' I told Nat.

'Or dice, rolled by a supreme being.'

'I think that the most suitable analogy is that life is like dominos.'

'How so?'

'You do something, or in some cases don't do something and a chain is set in motion that knocks down one domino after another leading to somewhere that at times you can only guess at.'

'Interesting. The one flaw being that you don't play dominos like that.'

'Okay, if you want to be pedantic about it then life is like a proper game of dominos where you have to match the numbers up in order to progress through things. Satisfied now?'

'Much better, thank you.'

The point that I was trying to make was that Lisa had set things in motion and one thing led to another and before you knew it Bea and I were engaged. I know what you are thinking, why didn't I learn from the first time around? The answer to that is simple. Although my first marriage had been a disaster of Biblical proportions I still believed in the concept of marriage, not because I believed that living in sin was wrong. I had done more than my share of living in sin and several other things that were probably sins as well, but then so had half the clergy, so they weren't really in a place to moan at me for committing sin. No; I believed in marriage because I thought it was a nice idea. I thought it was the moral thing to do. If you really love someone then why wouldn't you want to share your life with them in marriage?

Apologies to all the other girls that I haven't married then, but I guess I just didn't love ya enough.

Should I have been put off by Susie and what went wrong there? I don't think you can really live your life by that kind of philosophy. If you fall off a bicycle, then the idea is to get back on it rather than never go near it again. I had been very young when I married Susie and I wasn't that much older when I divorced her. I had grown a few years in mentality and experience since then and although there were many things that I was sure that I wasn't sure about, one thing that I was sure about was that I was not prepared to live my life under the ghost of Susie any longer. It was time to move on and get on with my life. I was convinced that Bea was the person that I wanted to do it with.

'Marriage?' my father had asked with a slight look of confusion on his face over his copy of *The Pickwick Papers*.

'Yes, you know, where you stand up and say "I do".'

'I know what it is. You're sure it is something that you want to do again?'

I went over the same arguments that I have just outlined to you.

'Well, if you think that's the right thing to do.' He didn't sound too impressed by the notion and I realised that more than anything I wanted the approval of my father. I had never realised this before, but I suppose I had always sought his approval. It was a very strange thing to suddenly understand. I guess I had just never thought about it before. Perhaps it is the case that all sons seek the approval of their fathers whether they realise it or not. I don't know. Some sense of acknowledgement of achievement is nice.

'You don't think it's the right thing to do?'

'My dear, Max,' he put the book down and looked at me. 'It's entirely up to you what you do and how you do it. I have never tried to interfere in your life, at least I hope I haven't interfered in your life; never intentionally anyway, well, except when you were a kid, but that's what parents are supposed to do when you're growing up.' He looked a little confused for a moment as if he had lost the point, which I rather suspect that he had.

'The point is,' he continued, having regained it. 'All I want is for you to be happy and if marrying Bea makes you happy then you go ahead and do it. You know I am here as a sounding board for you. Sometimes I play advocate so you can make sure in your own head that you are sure of what you're doing. Even if you weren't sure though, I would still support you.'

And so, that was how I became engaged to be married for the second time.

Twenty-One

Leaving my reminiscences to one side for the moment, I am drawn back to write about the present once again and how I had been waiting for a hospital appointment to see if I had sleep apnoea.

The hospital appointment took a couple of months to come through, but eventually arrived. I don't like going to doctor's surgeries; I like hospitals even less. Hospitals have changed greatly over the years. These days they are like mini cities. They have food courts and shops. It is easy to get lost within the endless miles of corridors that the designers of *Doctor Who* would have been so proud of. It was easy enough to get fit just walking the corridors. It amazed me how vast the place was.

'I wonder how many people, patients, staff, visitors, are in this building at any given time,' I asked Ellie as we worked our way through the seemingly endless corridors trying to find where the Department of Respiratory Medicine was.

'I have no idea,' she replied as we took a turning that I was sure that we had been past already. Eventually, we found what we were looking for and having clocked in took a seat in the waiting area.

'Do you think all these people are here for the same reason?' I always found this to be a fascinating game.

'I should imagine they are here for all kinds of things related to breathing. Look, here's a jar of tar that shows you what smoking does to your lungs.'

'Charming little thing for the children to play with whilst they wait for their parents. Whatever happened to traditional toys?'

'The NHS is not what it used to be.'

'Mr Durant!' This last was screamed into the waiting room by a short, dumpy nurse that looked like she was having trouble breathing herself. Perhaps that was why she was in the respiratory department; the management felt it was the safest place for her to be in case she decided to collapse.

The none too subtle summons was so that I could be taken through to another area where I was weighed, measured and then asked to blow into a tube, presumably to check to see if my lungs were working or not. I was then bustled outside once again and told to wait until the consultant was ready to see me. Fortunately, this did not take too long.

'Well then,' said the consultant who was called Dr Black – a rather bleak name for a doctor I thought and momentarily reminded me of the name that you might expect out of *Carry on Doctor*. 'Well then,' he said again, having listened to all that I had said. 'Sleep apnoea is the most likely cause of the problems that you're having. However, we cannot take it for granted that this is the case, so I would like to run a number of tests before we settle on one diagnosis.'

This seemed to be a good response and looked like I was going to be getting a better service than I had anticipated. I had assumed that they would run with the first diagnosis in order to save money rather than checking to make sure that I was getting the right treatment.

'The first thing that we will do,' he continued, 'is send some machinery around to your home next week for you to wear whilst you sleep. This will record data and give us an indication of what your sleeping is like. We will then be able to have an informed opinion of what your sleep problems are; and what we can do about them, of course.'

'That sounds good.'

'I'm concerned about your weight though.'

'I thought you might be.'

'You can afford to lose a little, I don't think it will change the apnoea issue all that much as it appears more likely that it is an underlying genetic problem with the lining of the throat more than anything else, but it won't hurt your general level of health to lose a little.'

'I'll have to see what I can do.'

'I also want to run some other tests to rule out other possibilities. We will start with checking you for thyroid problems, Cushing's and cancer.'

I must have looked very alarmed. 'Don't worry, it's necessary to check these things out. Many of the symptoms can fit a multitude of offences. Increased tiredness, lack of sexual appetite, increased weight, increased thirst, increased passing of urine. All of this can fit sleep apnoea as there are a mixture of issues there. If it is Cushing's, then it could be caused be a tumour which we would naturally have to deal with.'

'Excuse me, but what is Cushing's?' I am glad that Ellie decided to ask it. Being an academic for too long I never liked to show my own ignorance so I would rather sit in silence than ask questions. I would then go and look it up later.

'Cushing's syndrome is prolonged exposure to inappropriately high levels of the hormone cortisol.'

'Oh, I see.'

'It's very common in dogs.'

'Well, that's reassuring.'

'Of course, there are a number of other things that it could be, so it's a bit early to be carried away with putting all our eggs in one basket. Let's just take one step at a time and see how we go, shall we?'

It seemed the most logical course of action to take. I have to admit that I was feeling somewhat less reassured than I might have hoped to have been. I was expecting to leave the hospital with some degree of reassurance that my issues would be over soon. As it turned out, it seemed like they were only just about to begin.

***

The materials that were promised were duly sent round by recorded delivery the following week. The delivery man informed me that he would be back to collect the machine the following day.

It wasn't what I was expecting, but then I wasn't entirely sure what it was that I had been expecting in the first place. I had to sleep with some minor tubing that fitted over my nose, probably to test what I was breathing like. I also had to sleep with a thing clipped on my finger which was the same as those things they put on when taking your blood pressure. The last element was something that was strapped to my chest which I then had to press every time that I was conscious of being awake during the night, whether it was because I was going to the toilet or just aware of the fact that I had woken. This presumably contained the computer chip or whatever it was that recorded all the data as well so that it could be looked at later.

I couldn't tell you what kind of night I had. It was the same as any other I suppose, with the added disadvantage that this time I had bits of machinery strapped to various parts of my body which hardly makes it a sensible means of getting a good night of rest. True to his word, the delivery guy was back the next day to collect the items and take them back. I would have to wait a few weeks until I got the results and found out what was going on.

The following day, I went down to the dreary surgery once again to see a nurse who took some blood to check for the thyroid issues that the consultant had talked about. I confess my ignorance when it came to this sort of thing. I had no idea what a thyroid was or what kind of issues I could have with it. I didn't even know where my thyroid was. Prior to this I didn't even know I had one.

***

'And then what happened?' Nat was always very curious about my medical side of things since I had finally gone to the doctor like he had been telling me to do for years.

'I had to go back to the hospital for further tests which were a bit harsh.'

'Why, what did they do to you?'

'I don't pretend to be a medical person so I'm not sure what it's all about; this last visit involved them taking some blood from me.'

'I thought the nurse did that when you went to see your doctor?'

'No, I mean this involved taking a lot of blood from me over a three-and-a-half-hour period.'

'Seriously?'

'They took enough blood from me to run a small child for a week.'

'Why?'

'I forget the reason now. I had to sit in this comfortable chair and every twenty minutes or so a nurse would come in and take some blood and then come back twenty minutes later. I had to drink this glucose mixture, which was frankly horrible, and they kept taking loads of samples. I suppose this will be the test to see if I have Cushing's or not.'

'Cushing's. Seems such a strange name. Makes me think that you are suffering from something that will make you turn into a Hammer House of Horror actor.'

'Sadly, the truth is far less exciting.'

'When do you get your hospital results?'

'I have to go back in a couple of weeks by which time they should be able to tell me the results for all the tests.'

'And then it will be time to move forwards and get on with your life.'

'I bloody well hope so.'

***

The same plump nurse was there that was there the first time that we went. She still looked out of breath and as if she was going to collapse at any moment. A simple task of walking across the room with some patient files seemed to be too much for her. 'I wonder if she would be better off being transferred to the cardiac unit?' I asked Ellie as we sat there again, looking at the same grim scene that there had been before.

'No, seriously, I have real concerns that she is going to keel over in a matter of seconds and I don't know CPR.'

'I think there are enough medical staff nearby, Max, to deal with an emergency should it arise. Don't you?'

'They might be busy.'

'I'm sure they can prioritise.'

The visit to the hospital was split into two parts. First of all, we were ushered into a room where I was to get some of the results back from the tests that they had carried out. The doctor in this particular room had me lie down on the examination couch which worried me slightly as I thought it must be bad news if they wanted me to lie down for it.

'Well, the good news, Mr Durant, is that you are actually extremely healthy,' the doctor said, having looked over my notes and looked over my body.

'I don't feel it.'

'No, I don't suppose you do. However, as far as the blood tests show us, you are healthy. You don't have diabetes, no issues with thyroids and no signs of any cancer.'

'Well, that's good news.'

'Yes, it is, isn't it?' The manner in which this was stated seemed to suggest the opposite. I felt that the doctor was disappointed that I had not presented with an interesting and challenging disease that she could really have got her teeth into. Leaving the vaguely disappointed doctor behind, we went back to the waiting room before it was time to see Dr Black.

When we entered the room, Dr Black spent a few minutes reading the notes that had been made about me. This was slightly off putting as he decided to do this out loud which made it rather difficult to concentrate as he mumbled a great deal and whereas I am sure that it made a great deal of sense to him, it was a completely different language as far as I was concerned.

'Yes, this is pretty much as we expected it would be,' he concluded with a slightly satisfying look on his face.

'And what is that?'

'Oh, you have severe obstructive sleep apnoea.'

'Okay.'

'I think we would like it broken down rather a lot,' Ellie put in, knowing that I wasn't about to.

'Oh, really?' He seemed to be somewhat surprised that anyone would need things explained more than this and rather put out that we were asking him to go into things in more detail. 'Well, okay. Firstly, as you know sleep apnoea is the temporary inability to breathe, for whatever reason. Primarily, this is because the throat relaxes during sleep and closes the airway. The natural result of this is that you stop breathing.'

'Yes?'

'So, the brain doesn't really like this so it wakes you up so that you start breathing again. The moment you wake, you start breathing; the brain then sends you back to sleep until the next time that it happens. It happens so fast that you're awake and asleep again that you don't even notice that it has happened.'

'Okay.'

'If this happens a few times in an hour, say ten times, or less, you probably won't suffer any issues from it. Each time you stop breathing it's called an apnoea. If you have fifteen or less apnoeas an hour then you would be diagnosed as mild. If you were suffering from fifteen to thirty apnoeas an hour then your condition would be moderate.'

'But, Max is suffering from severe apnoea?'

'Yes, our tests show that Max stops breathing on average thirty-nine times an hour.'

'That's a lot.' I was shocked.

'That's why we call it severe. Your apnoeas are also lasting a minimum of twenty-four seconds to a maximum of sixty seconds in duration.'

'So, each time I stop breathing, I stop breathing for anything from almost half a minute to a minute.'

'That's correct.'

'And I'm doing this up to thirty-nine times an hour?'

'On average.' He seemed pleased that I had grasped the basics of what it was that he was saying.

'And these apnoeas can last as long as a minute?'

'Yes.'

'So, in theory at my worst, I could be not breathing for thirty-nine minutes out of every sixty?'

'That's true. In theory, there is no difference between you being asleep and awake.' There was a pause whilst this fact was allowed to mellow. I couldn't believe that with that amount of non-breathing going on, the outcome was going to be even remotely healthy. After a moment, Black continued.

'This is why you are also aching a great deal. The oxygen circulation in your body is reduced by 20% as the oxygen circulates to the brain and the vital organs in your torso as a matter of priority. Your arms and legs are less important as far as your brain is concerned.'

'Which is why my limbs always ache?'

'Yes; the lack of oxygen is what we call hypoxemia, which is a complication from sleep apnoea, as indeed is sleep deprivation. You have already experienced this condition as well as some of the other common symptoms such as loud snoring, restless sleep and fatigue during the day.'

'So, I'm snoring because of this?'

'Yes. People snore for various reasons, but in essence the noise that you are making as you sleep, which we call snoring, is you trying to force the air down your throat to open the gap which has closed.'

'So, what treatment is there,' asked Ellie as she seemed to be taking a lot more of this in then I was.

'Some treatments involve lifestyle changes, such as avoiding alcohol or muscle relaxants, losing weight, and quitting smoking. I recommend that we give you a CPAP machine.'

'A what?'

'CPAP; it stands for Continuous Positive Airway Pressure.'

'Okay, and what's that?' He had explained what it stood for as if that were more than enough of an explanation.

'In essence, it is a mask that you wear strapped to your face. You can either have ones that only cover your nose, or ones that cover your nose and mouth depending on what you tend to breathe through the most when you're asleep. As you sleep, the machine will detect when an apnoea is about to happen and the intensity of the air being blown down your throat will increase and keep the air way open, thus preventing you from stopping breathing by keeping your air flow continuous. As a result, you won't be waking up all of the time, nor will you be suffering from moments of not breathing at all.'

'Okay.'

'I should point out to you that this is an extremely serious condition if not treated. Aside from how crap it makes you feel, the chances of a heart attack or stroke are increased a great deal each time that you stop breathing.'

'I understand.'

'It's an extremely common condition that most sufferers will have for years before a diagnosis takes place. In many cases, they will never be diagnosed. All of the time that you remain undiagnosed and untreated puts you at risk of high blood pressure and many forms of heart disease. You should be prepared for the fact that for many people CPAP takes a bit of getting used to. It is not the easiest of things to live with, but it is something that is essential to get to grips with.'

'For how long will I have to wear this machine?'

'Every time you sleep.'

'Yes, but for how long until I don't have to use it any longer?'

Dr Black looked at me over his glasses with the air of someone who was indulging someone who was considerably more stupid than he was.

'For the rest of your life, Mr Durant.'

'Shit.'

'But this CPAP thing is not a cure?'

'No, there is no cure as such; there are only ways that we can improve your condition to make it less difficult.' He smiled indulgently again. 'I'm sorry if this seems harsh. You should also be aware of the fact that untreated sleep apnoea can cause morning headaches, irritability and moodswings along with depression, learning or memory difficulties, and sexual dysfunction.'

'Memory difficulties?'

'Yes, it has been hypothesized that repeated drops in oxygen lead to brain injury. I cannot emphasise enough, therefore that you need to continue with this therapy by CPAP – no matter how discomforting you may at first believe it to be.'

I really didn't like the sound of that.

'Due to the levels of apnoea that you are suffering from and the issues that we can see in your specific case, I must also tell you that until you are successful in your treatment, you cannot drive. By rights, I should inform DVLA and get them to suspend your driving licence; however, you seem reasonably sensible, so my suggestion to you would be that you don't drive until you are successful with CPAP and then you can write and inform the DVLA that you suffer from sleep apnoea, but that it is being successfully treated. That shouldn't present any problems.'

'At what level would you say treatment was successful?' asked Ellie.

'He would need to have at least five hours of treated sleep a night to be regarded as successful. At the very least.'

It all seemed so easy, and yet I didn't know just how much difficulty was still waiting for me and that my troubles were far from over.

Twenty-Two

There is really no comparison between my engagement with Susie and my engagement with Bea. When Susie and I were engaged and indeed when we got married, we did everything on a shoestring and were carried away on our love, not caring for anything. My engagement to Bea was completely different; it was more of a social event or a business contract. That is really the best way that I can explain it. I was always uncomfortable around Bea's family as I really did feel like I didn't fit in. There was a reason for that; I didn't fit in. It was something that I was never entirely allowed to forget either.

Bea's family were obviously very well off and used to doing things a certain way. I am not sure that they approved of me in the least. They probably tolerated me when they thought that I was just Bea's bit of rough. They probably saw me as a phase that she was going through and it was necessary to allow her to get things out of her system before she settled down. She then seemed to betray what the family wanted when she turned out to want to marry me instead of throwing me aside when she was done with having her fun and marrying a duke or someone.

'Darling,' she said in that way that she had of saying it that made it sound like she was some kind of movie star. 'We really must not worry about what other people think.'

This was in response to the fact that I had been discussing matters with her and my feeling of inadequacy, I suppose.

'It's your family. I'm concerned about what they think about me, that's all.'

'Does it matter what they think about you? Surely, it is what I think about you that is important.'

'Well, yes.'

'There is one issue though.'

'Oh?' I had that sinking feeling that I was used to getting when it came to relationships.

'I have not told my parents that you are divorced. They wouldn't approve of me marrying someone who is divorced. If they knew, it might also mean that we couldn't have the church wedding that they want me to have so much.'

'Well, why don't we just get married outside of the Church?'

'Oh, darling, that just won't do at all. They would never allow me to get married in a registry office; such a thing would be far too common. We shall just have to keep it secret, that is all.'

'I'm pretty sure that would be illegal, Bea.'

'Oh, these things are easily fixed if you know what to do about it. Just leave all that to me. We will keep it secret from my family and I am sure we will be able to find a – sympathetic member of the clergy, that will be prepared to perform the service. I have found that they are usually prepared to do most things if they are given the right form of motivation.'

This was the kind of discussion that I had frequently had with Bea. It wasn't her fault I suppose, but she had obviously grown up in an environment where she had been taught that if you couldn't find the answer to a solution, then you would be able to wave some money about and the solution would present itself. The sad fact of the matter was that she was probably right. Bea was giving me a crash course in how her family liked to do things. Fortunately for me, her father was footing the bill which probably amounted to a vast amount of money. He may not have been happy that I was marrying his daughter, but he was certainly going to make sure that his daughter got the wedding that she deserved.

Naturally, all that mattered to him was that his little princess was happy and I got the distinct impression that he was standing in the background with his shotgun ready to make sure that I never did anything that would cause her to be upset. Bea obviously always got what she wanted as far as he was concerned.

With regards to the wedding, I was sidelined to a certain extent. The majority of the plans were discussed between Bea and her father with no involvement from me. My opinion was neither sort after or desired from either of them. All I was expected to do was to go along with the plans that they were putting in store for me. When we became engaged, it was Bea who went out and bought an engagement ring that must have been worth a couple of thousand pounds at the very least. There was no way on earth that I would have been able to afford to buy that for her. It was inconceivable that she should have to put up with something that was cheaper, the shame of it would have been too much. The problem had been simply solved, therefore, by her going out and buying herself the ring that she felt she deserved and that I should have bought for her if I had only had the money.

'Everything is going very well,' she told me on one of her regular updates.

'Do you think it's really necessary to go to all this expense?' Money was something that I was very worried about. When you never had any money, you worried about not having it and spending it. Bea had never had this as an issue so she was used to treating it like it was water.

'Well, Daddy has decided that he is going to limit the number of guests to two hundred, so –.'

'Two hundred!' I think there had been about twenty-five at my first wedding.

'Yes, darling, an intimate affair would be something nicer, don't you think? So, we will keep it limited to that amount.'

'We obviously have different definitions on what the word intimate means.'

'Darling, don't be difficult.'

'How many of these guests will be friends of mine then?'

'Well, probably about twenty or thirty.'

'I see, so I get to invite thirty people and you get to invite one hundren and seventy?'

'Don't be a bore about it, really. You know that there are people that I have to invite. I simply *have* to invite them. I don't want them there any more than you do, but you have to understand that it is just the done thing. You have no idea what a snub it would be to not invite some of these people. Besides, you know that there are more people that we know that need to be invited than people that you know.'

'Is this really what you want?'

'Darling, it is not a question of what I want, it is a question of what needs to be done. Really, there is no need to be so difficult about this.'

'I'm not being difficult.'

'Then just go along with what Daddy wants and there won't be any argument.' I wondered exactly how much of it was what 'Daddy' wanted and how much of it was what Bea wanted. 'Which reminds me; Daddy has made a list of people that he thinks are suitable for your best man.'

'He's done what?'

'Made a list.'

'No, no. Sorry, but no. That's too far. You can tell "Daddy" that I will be choosing my best man and it's my choice and my choice alone.'

She stuck her lip out in the pouting way that she did whenever she was not getting her own way. It probably worked under certain circumstances, but she had crossed the line now and was really taking the piss.

'Sorry, Bea, but that's the way that it has to be. I'm not going to have everything dictated to me. I can live with the fact that you have more guests than I do. I can live with the fact that you have bought your own ring, but what I cannot live with is the dictating going as far as deciding who my best man is going to be.'

'Sometimes I think you do not want to marry me at all.'

'Oh, don't start playing that one. You can't get your own way on everything. So, stop acting like a spoilt rich kid.'

I probably had not meant to say it like that, but I was annoyed. I had taken a lot of dictating over this wedding about how things were going to be and this was a step too far as far as I was concerned.

***

It was probably around this time that I first really started to take notice about how shit I was feeling. For some time, I had noticed that I was feeling tired and that I was aching a great deal.

'I always feel run down,' I told Nat.

'Well, you have been working hard, I suppose, and of course, you have had rather a hard time with regards to relationships.'

'What's that got to do with anything?'

'The emotional impact of your life can manifest itself in physical symptoms. If you abuse your brain, it can make your body shut down.'

'You mean that you don't ache all of the time as well.'

'No.'

'I thought it was an age thing.'

'You're hardly old.'

'No, but I just assumed that as you got older you became more achy and tired all of the time.'

'Well, probably you do, but at the end of the day you really shouldn't be feeling it when you are only, what thirty-one years old?'

'I suppose not, and if the truth is known I've felt like it for a lot longer than just recently.'

'Perhaps you should go and see a doctor.'

'I'm not sure that will help.'

'You won't know unless you try.'

'I suppose not.'

I was not really all that keen on doctors and hospitals. I am not sure why this was. There was no rational reason for it really. Perhaps I was afraid of finding out something that I really didn't want to know. I realise that this is even more illogical than anything else. Perhaps it was also something to do with the fact that they didn't seem to have done my mother all that much good.

'Perhaps the stress of the upcoming marriage is not helping matters either?'

'How do you mean?' Nat knew everything about the issues that I had been having as I had asked him to be my best man. It was a decision that had not gone down well with Bea and her family, but that was something that they would just have to learn to live with as far as I was concerned.

'Emotional strain. You know what they say about the most stressful things in life; marriage, divorce, moving home. You have been through a fair few of them.'

'True.'

We were talking in my office at work and at that point a female entered and said:

'Oh, hello, Dr Bingham. I've photocopied those reports for you, like you asked.'

'Thanks, Ellie.'

She looked at me and seemed to blush slightly. 'Is there anything I can do for you Dr Durant, whilst I'm here.'

'No, I don't think so. Thanks.' She nodded her head and left the room.

'Who was that?' I asked Nat.

'Ellie. She works in my office.'

'In your office?'

'Yes.'

'I thought she was part of this faculty.'

'Why?'

'It's not the first time she has been in and asked if there is anything that she can do for me.'

'Interesting.'

There wasn't all that much that I had left to do with regards to the marriage. Everything had been organised and planned at great expense. I suppose I stood back and allowed things to go the way that they were because planning the wedding was something that made her happy. As a matter of fact, I don't think I had seen her so happy for such a long time. How could I do something that would make the woman I love less happy? I went along with the ride that I was being taken on.

We were drawing closer to the wedding date and I started to suffer desperately as I tried to fight off the onset of a cold that was in danger of disrupting the entire day for me. It was a battle that I felt was being fought in vain as I couldn't seem to help but succumb to the cold that wanted to get a grip on me. I started taking every medication that I could get my hands on to try and stop the advances, but I think my immune system was near enough shot to pieces. I suppose I was just run down and not able to cope all that well. I suppose that one of the reasons for this was due to the lack of sleep that I was getting. The insomnia that I had struggled with for the majority of my life was causing even more of an issue on the lead up to the wedding. I assumed that the insomnia probably played a part for why it was that I was always feeling so run down and tired all of the time. Only to be expected really.

The lack of sleep, the work that I was still continuing to do and the stress of the upcoming wedding were leaving me feeling very run down and I was just not able to fight off the cold virus. I felt terrible, but all I could do was take as much medication as I was safely able to do and pray for the best. At times, I have found that this is the only thing that you can do, despite my lack of faith in there being anyone who actually hears the prayer.

***

And then the day in question arrived. The big day. Finally, here. Despite the fact that I had been through it all before it didn't really do all that much to stop me from feeling any less nervous. If anything, I felt more nervous this time around due to the larger event that had been planned. I knew that I would have been happy to have had another low-key affair, but there was really no chance of that.

I woke up at half past seven in the morning and began the preparations that are needed for getting dressed. I knew that there would be a lot of people there that I didn't know which would add to my level of nervousness. I was hoping that everything would go according to the plan that Bea and her family had concocted; chiefly because of the fact that if it didn't go according to plan, I imagined that her family would find some way to blame me for it, whether or not it was my fault.

Nat arrived at nine thirty and it was difficult to tell which of us looked more uncomfortable in our formal wear that Bea's father had insisted that we wear. We were both amused by the fact that he had insisted on us having top hats. It seemed rather pointless to me to have hats. Most of the time you would only wear them for one photograph and the rest of the time, if you did wear them, you would run the risk of having a hat mark on your forehead for the rest of the photographs which would just make you look stupid. So, because you couldn't wear it, you would spend most of the rest of the time carrying it around with you not knowing what to do with it. This obviously didn't seem to be a massive problem as far as Bea's side of the family were concerned. For my father, it made him look like he was being made to wear fancy dress. In a sense, of course, he was being made to wear fancy dress.

'I really don't see what the problem was with my old suit,' he complained to me at one of the fittings that we had all been made to suffer. I had to be grateful that the fancy dress didn't extend as far as Jerry.

'Neither do I, but it seems that we must be made to know what our place is in the pecking order.'

After Nat had arrived, we had a strong cup of coffee and then made our way over to the church where we picked up our button holes.

'Have you got the rings?' I asked for about the third time that day.

'No. Why? Do you think you might need them?'

'I could do with a drink.'

'Should have bought you a hip flask really. Sorry, didn't really give it that much thought. I could use a coffee.'

'We just had one.'

'I could use another one.'

'Feeling a bit nervous?'

'Aren't you?'

'A bit.'

Whilst waiting around, I tried to engage in conversation with some of the guests, but not knowing any of them it was rather difficult to talk to them. I searched the crowd that was beginning to mill around and tried to spot a face that I might actually recognise. It was a bit like playing *Where's Wally?*

Whilst the business of seating the guests started to take place, we were invited to overlook the register to make sure that it was all in order. I was so highly strung that anything could have been written in the book and I wouldn't have been able to tell. Thankfully, Nat seemed to think that everything was okay so we managed to get through that without looking like idiots. I was not entirely sure that we were going to be able to do that all day.

Now, I have probably made it clear by now that I am not a great fan of religion. I suppose the intellectual nature of my parents meant that I was raised with the view that religion was something of a superstition. Nevertheless, I have to admit that you couldn't help but admire the architecture and the work that must have gone into making such impressive structures with such limited tools and equipment. I was always impressed by the ability of humanity to do things when they really put their minds to it. Despite my admiration of the architecture and the skill of those that designed and built such places as this, I have to admit that I always found them to be cold, unwelcoming places. Also, slightly spooky I suppose. Perhaps that was the intention.

We weren't getting married in a church, of course. A church would have been far too common for the likes of Bea and her family. We were getting married in a *cathedral*. Makes perfect sense when you think about it. The only thing that surprised me was that they hadn't gone for something bigger.

'It is a sore point,' Bea had said to me when I had raised the issue.

'How so?' I had meant it to be a joke, but I was curious now to think that they may have actually tried to get the ceremony in a more prestige location.

'I was in favour of being married at St Pauls.'

'St Pauls?

'Yes.'

'As in big domed cathedral in London? Designed by Christopher Wren?'

'Yes, but apparently only members of certain orders can get married there and those with OBEs, of course.'

'And Daddy doesn't have an OBE?'

'He was offered one a few years ago, but really OBEs are awarded to anyone these days. He is holding out for a knighthood, but it does mean we can't get married there and of course Westminster Abbey is the same or you have to be royalty.'

So, we had to settle for a cathedral where you didn't have to be royalty. Bea entered as regally as I suppose her family had devised that she would do. We had organ music, a choir and lots of pomp and circumstance. I have no ideas what the hymns were and I just mouthed the words, glad that I was at the front and facing away from the rest of the congregation so that nobody else could see me. It was hardly my fault that I didn't know the words, not my upbringing.

And then that was it, before you knew it everything was over and we were married. Afterwards came the taking of the photographs which was a mind-numbingly tedious affair that went on for far too long. The trouble was having so many people to organise and take pictures of and I had to be in nearly all of them with a gormless smile on my face which made my face ache by the time that we had finished. I don't have a single photograph from my first marriage. Nothing to remind me of the day, other than memories.

After the photographs, there was a certain amount of time to mill about and to talk to some of the guests, mainly people that I did not know who came up to congratulate me on the marriage and welcome me to the family. Bea and I were then bundled off to the vintage Rolls Royce that her father had laid on for her and we were whisked away to the venue for where we would be having our wedding breakfast.

I had not had any choice in the venue and it had been decided to have the wedding breakfast at a nearby hotel which was frankly so far out of my pay range that I doubt I could have afforded the coffee without having to think twice about it. Fortunately, I was not all that hungry as the food that was served was of the small and expensive variety that is so favoured by people who have more money than actual sense. I suppose that I should really have been grateful that I had not been expected to pay any part of the costs of the actual day.

The meal sailed past and then it was time for the speeches. This was something that I was dreading. Partly because of the fact that I know that Bea's family did not approve of Nat as my choice for my best man, but also because of the fact that I had to stand up in front of a lot of people that I didn't know and talk. You might think that this was not a particularly difficult thing for me to do seeing as how I was a university lecturer and this kind of thing was really within my remit. What can I say? Some actors can stand up in front of a theatre audience of 2000 and deliver the greatest emotional acting that has ever been demanded of any actor, but ask them to be themselves and open a school fete and they shrink in terror.

As it happened, I thought that Nat was very good. He was both funny and sincere. He certainly managed to get a few laughs but I couldn't tell you entirely where in the room they came from. He did the usual character assassination which was probably only slightly marred by the fact that the vast majority of the audience had never actually met me until that day so had no idea about the references. Jerry seemed to try and compensate for this by laughing as loudly as he could. Jerry seemed determined to annoy someone that day anyway. He had point blank refused to wear the 'monkey suit' as he had termed it. Instead he had gone in the opposite direction as only Jerry can and had turned up in faded jeans. I had seen my father having a few choice words with him but I think we both understood that it was impossible to change the way that Jerry was. He was very clearly making a point.

I remember nothing of my speech, whatsoever. That's probably a good thing as I had taken advantage of the fact that the wedding breakfast involved alcohol.

And then the wedding breakfast was over and we were two thirds of the way through the day. It's amazing how quickly things go really. Bea's father had eventually succumbed to the idea of an evening disco. I am not sure what he thought we would have instead, as it is pretty traditional to have such a function at a wedding in the evening as far as I am concerned. He probably would have liked to have continued with the string quartet that had been booked to play throughout the wedding breakfast, which was a nice touch but also kind of weird as you had these four complete strangers who didn't know anyone sitting in the corner of the room for the whole meal. I was probably the only one who seemed to think this, everyone else seemed to think it was perfectly natural; but then the majority of the people present probably were used to having butlers and other staff hovering around whilst they ate anyway so didn't see anything strange in it at all.

The evening food looked expensive so that probably meant that it was expensive. Large selections of meat and pate were spread out on top of what appeared to be large ornamental mirrors.

'Perhaps they ran out of plates,' said Jerry as he scanned the buffet, desperately looking for crisps and a sausage roll.

And then it was all over. The day had gone by really quickly and before I knew it midnight had come and we were finished. Those of us that were left went into the lounge for a last drink and we finished at about one o'clock in the morning and eventually staggered off to bed. The debate had been had about us leaving earlier in the evening and going off to the honeymoon directly, but I have never really been one to want to leave a party early if there is no good cause and this was a party that was, in theory, 50 per cent for me at any rate.

I felt that it had been a really fantastic day, despite the odd feeling of discomfort that I always felt whenever I was around Bea's family; strange that I never felt it around her though, she was clearly very different to the rest of her family. There were some good moments of humour – from my side of the guests, of course; I suspect that Bea's side had not found anything funny since Richard II overcame the peasants. There had been some fond memories of the day though.

I went to bed that night, exhausted, but content. I know it's traditional to seal the marriage with conjugal rights, but frankly we were so tired that Bea wasn't really in the mood for it.

Twenty-Three

I woke up the next morning with a headache which couldn't have been a hangover as I did not really have a huge amount to drink the previous day; well, not by the standards that I could have drunk. Perhaps it was caused by a relief of stress and tension that the entire day had gone off with no major problems. It wasn't an easy night of sleep either, if I am honest. We had a really nice room at the hotel with a fantastic four-poster bed. Unfortunately, I did not sleep all that well in it due to the fact that I am unused to sleeping with blankets now after so many years of a duvet; so, I tossed and turned and became entangled a bit, but you can't really have a duvet on a four-poster bed and maintain the historical ambiance.

Talking of historical ambiance, it was around this time that Bea and I had one of those pointless arguments. We had been to see a film: *Troy*. It was something that I had been looking forward to as I love the history of the ancient Greeks and it was something that Bea had been looking forward to because she loves Brad Pitt. I should have known better. My expectations were not met. I apologise now if you are a fan of this film, or of Pitt, or anyone else connected with it. It was appalling.

'Well, I thought it was rather good,' returned Bea.

'It was terrible. Historically inaccurate.'

'It is Hollywood, Max, they are allowed to take some artistic licence, you know? It is a film. It is not Plato.'

'Homer.'

'Whatever.'

'Taking artistic licence is one thing; taking the piss is another.'

'Okay,' she said throwing down her fork. 'I can see I am not going to get any peace until you have had your say so tell me, what is so wrong with the film.'

'Well, the first thing that was really annoying was the pronunciation of Menelaus.'

'What about it?'

'I have always learnt that Menelaus is pronounced Men-a-*lay*-us; however, throughout this entire film the name is pronounced Men-*allow*-us.'

'So?'

'So, they are pronouncing it wrong and irritating me enormously.'

'Greek myths are not your speciality; is it possible that you just learnt the pronunciation wrong?'

'Possibly, but even if I had it doesn't stop it grating because that's what I have come to expect. I found it hugely irritating after a while.'

'Perfectly rational then. What else was so annoying then?'

'There are also two "historical facts" that are wrong; at least they are wrong as far as Homer is concerned at any rate.'

'Artistic licence.'

'The first of these,' I continued ignoring her, 'is the fact that Agamemnon is killed at the end of the film whilst they are burning Troy to the ground.'

'So?'

'It didn't happen! Agamemnon made it home and was killed by his wife who was shacked up with someone else. However, Brian Cox plays the part of Agamemnon so well as an evil bastard, that the film producers obviously decided that it wasn't right that he should be allowed to live.'

'Well, that is Hollywood.'

'Don't I know it. According to Hollywood, the Americans won the Second World War single handed. They should ban Hollywood from making history films; it gives kids the wrong impression of history.'

'Spoken like a historian.'

'I *am* a historian. The second inaccuracy that is glaringly obvious is the fact that in Homer, Achilles died before the entry to Troy took place. In this film, he dies at the very end of the film after the Greeks have captured Troy. They couldn't allow him to die when he was meant to though because Achilles is played by Brad Pitt and it's obviously impossible that Pitt should be allowed to die at any point other than the film's climax. Actually, come to think of it, I'm amazed that they even let him die at all.'

'Well, the more Brad Pitt the better as far as I am concerned.'

'Homer is spinning in his grave. It amazes me they didn't change the ending of *Titanic*.'

I suppose this is when the decision had been made that we were not going to see any historic films together any longer.

***

'You know they expected me to give up work, don't you?' I asked Nat.

'Who did?' Nat looked up from his physics book with a confused look on his face. It was often the way when he was trying to bring his thoughts back down to earth from wherever his text book had taken him.

'Bea's family.'

'They expected you to give up work?'

'They didn't think it seemly that someone married to her should continue to work in such a menial job as this.'

'What should you have been doing then?'

'Either charity work, or on some board of directors or something. I don't know. I don't pretend to understand it. It all makes sense to her family, but makes bugger all sense to me.'

'Perhaps you're not meant to make sense of it.'

'That sounds like a great idea.'

'I'm assuming from the fact that you're still here that it's something that you didn't take them up on?'

'Why the hell would I want to give up work?'

'I don't know, I think there are a lot of people that would have bitten your hand off there.'

'Not me. I enjoy doing what I do and I don't want to give it up for anyone. Besides, I would be bored without it and would miss the independence that it gives me.'

'Well, there are a lot of people that would envy you the choice.'

We lapsed into silence for a moment. Nat continued to read whatever physics text it was that he was reading today and I continued to read the work on Henry III that I was flicking through.

'It's Holocaust Memorial Day today,' Nat said out of the blue.

'Is it?'

'I thought, as a historian, you would know that.'

'I know a lot about the Holocaust; the Memorial Day is a current affairs thing. It's a chance for politicians to show us how much they care. Why else has it taken so many decades to get one started? If they really cared, it would have been something that they would have started decades ago, but it took a complete drop in popularity before they decided to mine the depth of depravity of trying to win approval out of the Holocaust.'

'You don't approve of the idea?'

'I'm not sure it will make a difference. Look at them all out there.' We were sitting in the window of the coffee shop and I was indicating the people that were walking by. 'How many of them know about Auschwitz? How many of them care? And if they have heard of Auschwitz, how many of heard of Dachau or Treblinka? So few people seem to care about anything other than themselves these days and in the cities this seems to be far more concentrated than in the country.'

'Well, that's a little gloomy a view.'

'Truth though, isn't it? Take the Royal Family.'

'What about them?'

'I'm a supporter of the monarchy. I have no problem with the majority of them. They are great for bringing in tourists to the country. When it comes to the Holocaust, though, they have become an embarrassment.'

'Are you referring to Harry going to that party dressed as a Nazi?'

'Not the most diplomatic and intelligent of things to have done you have to admit. Obviously, Harry is insanely stupid to do something like this; but then again, I always did suspect that he was pretty stupid.'

'Not your favourite member of the family?'

'Not at all, but it doesn't end there. Because of Holocaust Memorial Day, they send a member of the family to Auschwitz as a representative of the British monarchy. Who do they send?'

'Well I am hoping it wasn't Harry.'

'Prince Edward. I mean who the hell is he? All the other states are sending their topmost important people – presidents, prime ministers, kings and queens and we can't even be bothered to send even the second in line to the throne. I mean how does that look in front of the world media? Firstly, we have members of the Royal Family dressing as Nazis and then we practically shun the 60th anniversary of the liberation of Auschwitz.'

'Okay, so you feel a little stronger about this than I thought you did.'

'Sorry, it just pisses me off. Things are getting me down at the moment.'

'Anything you want to talk about?'

'No, I don't think so. Not yet at any rate. I just wish that we had sent someone more senior to represent us. It makes me feel that there is a general feeling out there that people just don't care any longer.'

'Well, Charles couldn't go. He is too busy planning for his forthcoming marriage. How do you feel about that? I know there's a lot of controversy about it.'

'I know it isn't a popular view, but I never liked Diana. I know we have all been brainwashed into thinking that the sun shone out of her arse, but that just isn't the way that she came across to me.'

'How did she come across to you?'

'Manipulative and very media aware. She knew how to play to the cameras and get things the way that she wanted.'

'There are people in this country that would lynch you for saying something like that.'

'I know there are. They are usually the people that are a few steps away from spending the rest of their life in a lunatic asylum somewhere. Having been married and divorced myself and then remarried I personally think that he deserves some happiness and he has obviously always been in love with Camilla, so why shouldn't he be entitled to that happiness. Beyond all that, who really cares?'

'You seem to be in the kind of mood today where you are not sure that anyone cares about anything?'

'I'm not sure that they do.'

'I would have thought that with your wife's family, you would have been going to the wedding.'

'I think her father is going.'

Clearly a registry office wedding was more acceptable to her family when you were first in line to the throne.

***

Sometimes, no matter how much you study and understand history, it never makes any sense when things happen that just throw you out of sync with the world. I was working late one night trying to get some papers sorted and getting the notes together for what I hoped might turn out to be a book that I wanted to publish. I worked long into the night and in the early hours of the morning I went to bed feeling tired and drained, both physically and emotionally.

I woke up the following morning to discover that a number of bombs had exploded in London in what was apparently a terrorist attack. As the day progressed, it became apparent that there had actually been four explosions. Three on the London Underground and one on a double-decker bus. I watched the news as it unfolded in shock and horror; the memories of 9/11 flooding back. Man's inhumanity to man was a common theme throughout history and it was as clear as anything that we had not learnt a single thing from all of the tragedies that had happened in our past.

253

'They don't know how many people have been killed,' my father said when I went to see him later in the day. It was one of the rare occasions when I saw him watching television. He probably only knew about it because someone must have told him. His television went days without being turned on. It was very unusual to find him somewhere else other than in his study.

'They are saying it could be more than thirty,' I replied.

'The worst terrorist attack on UK soil. All the years of the IRA and when you think that things are finally sorted, this starts.' He shook his head as disgusted with humanity as I was.

'Is Jerry okay?' My brother was often in London.

'He's fine. Rang up to complain about the fact that he was caught up in the aftermath and couldn't get anywhere. Typical Jerry really, but he's fine.'

'I don't suppose that this is something that should really be all that unexpected when you think about it.'

'I suppose the only thing that is unexpected about it is the fact that it has taken almost four years since September 11th before it actually happened here.'

We both stood in silence for a few minutes, watching the images that flicked over the television screen repeatedly. Newsreaders who were recurrent because of the lack of information that they were getting, but the need and drive that was required by twenty-four-hour news broadcasting to have to say something; *anything*. As the day grew towards the end, we watched the people quietly walking home because of the lack of transport that was available. The resolve of the British people is to get up and get on with it though. There was a lot of shock and confusion, but there was also a surprising amount of calm amongst the people of London as they went about their business. It actually made me feel proud.

The following day, the death count had reached over fifty and was expected to rise further. I had stayed with my father overnight and we watched the developments again through the next day.

'There are a lot of people that will be mourning today,' my father said after we had eaten breakfast. 'It doesn't end here though.'

'What do you mean?'

'There's going to be a backlash against the Muslim community now as people perceive what they think they have done and the threat that they think they pose.'

'It's only the fundamentalists. Fundamentalists of any religion are dangerous. They all think we should convert, or be killed as infidels. No different to Christianity during the Crusades really. I would genuinely like to think that the vast majority of Muslims in this country are as shocked by this terrorist attack as we are.'

'You might be right, but it is the fundamental English twats that worry me. They are the ones that will now prey on the innocent. The fundamentalists that are behind this attack have now changed the way that their own people will be perceived. A radical step in the wrong direction by the ignorant really.'

There didn't really seem to be all that much more that could be said. Some people found reading history depressing because of the bleak nature of it all. In my view, the future didn't really look all that much better. I began to understand why some historians that I knew tried their best to bury their heads in the sand and hide away in the past. History may be full of depressing events, but you can convince yourself that these are things that happened long ago and we have made a great deal of progress since then. Look out of your window and you will see that the same things are still going on today, and that is the more depressing of the two situations.

***

When I woke the following morning, I was extremely disturbed and felt claustrophobic and restless. I had a strange feeling that I was trapped and needed to break away but something was keeping me from being able to get away. It is possible that the bombings in the Underground station in London had played on my mind and worried me by making me have nightmares.

I told my father that I had to get back as there was work that I needed to do, but it was really because, despite how big the house was,

I was feeling very claustrophobic and just needed to get out as quickly as I could. I don't think that I have ever felt so disturbed in my life. I feared that it was a sign of things to come.

The reason for this was that Bea and I were not getting along that well. We had been married less than a year although it was not all that far away from our first anniversary now. At this stage of things, I should have still been in the honeymoon and happy stage of my marriage, but I wasn't.

It is very difficult for me now to look back and put my finger on exactly what the issue was. I suppose there were a number of them. These things rarely stem from only one problem. I think it is fair to say that my marriage to Bea was not what I had expected that it would be. I was very reluctant to admit that I had screwed things up again, but I was beginning to seriously believe that I had screwed things up again. There was now not a day that went by without us arguing about something, nothing, and anything. The usual, petty arguments that were designed purely so that we could snipe at each other and win points; in such a game, of course, there are no winners. For most of the time I doubt we even knew why we were doing it. It had just become a habit that we had fallen into.

Nat would tell me that each action must have an equal and opposite reaction. In the case of my marriage, he was right. The arguments increased and the sex decreased. It decreased to the point where it really stopped and there was no sex. This happened in a surprisingly quick period of time. I have heard people say that there is no sex after marriage, but bloody hell, it could have been written for my marriage. The lack of sex on my wedding night was the start of what was to follow for the remainder of my marriage. If I were lucky, we were having sex maybe once or twice a year. Bea just suddenly appeared to be not interested in it any longer. I tried to talk about it, but she simply wasn't open to discussion on the matter. It was one of the things that she didn't talk about and if Bea didn't talk about it then that was the end of the discussion.

Come to think of it, she didn't appear to be interested in me any longer. I have no idea what was going on here, but she had been wonderful before we got married and then almost immediately afterwards she just didn't want to know any longer. I am sure she had her own motives for what it was that she was doing but she was not about to share them with me. I was in the dark and I was very much alone.

***

'So, the four hundredth anniversary of the Gunpowder Plot. Doing anything special?' This was from Nat.

'I'm not going around with a Guy if that's what you mean.'

'I think it might suit you to do that. Get yourself a few pennies as well.'

'I bemoan, as I do every year, the fact that people have never worked out what it was really all about and how little it has to do with all this rubbish that they celebrate today.'

'You mean the general firework and burning of straw men thing?'

'Whilst subtly ignoring the fact that the Gunpowder Plot was just as much of a terrorist attack as what happened back in July?'

'Well, people do like to honour the last time that someone entered Parliament with open intentions.'

'Well, it's true that there probably wouldn't be all that much mourning for the fact that they would have killed a lot of politicians. Not to mention the monarch, of course. People tend to gloss over the fact that it was a Catholic plot as well. The Catholics rather like to forget that they once acted in the same way that they like to accuse some Muslims of acting now.'

'What I don't understand is why it is that you burn the Guy on a bonfire when in reality, he was hung drawn and quartered.'

'No, I have never really understood that either. I wonder if there would be less crime today if they were to bring back that as a punishment.'

'Probably not,' Nat sipped at his coffee. 'Despite what people would like us to think when we used to hang people, it never stopped people from still killing each other. Capital punishment was ultimately no deterrent. It just cut down heavily on the reoffending rates.'

Bea and I were now sleeping in separate bedrooms. The reason for this was because she complained about my snoring. It gave her the opportunity to side step the issue so that she didn't have to keep refusing me sex all of the time. I am not sure that the snoring was a reason, as I am not entirely sure that I did snore. I suspect that she was just making things up to try and get the sex out of the equation. Still, it did fit in with her belief that the upper class slept in separate bedrooms because it was the more aristocratic thing to do.

That night, snoring or not, I was unable to sleep, so at three o'clock in the morning I found myself sitting in my study at my desk, surrounded by the pool of light that was given off by my desk lamp. I thought about how my life had gone in a direction that I could not have anticipated in a million years. I thought about Gina. I still felt guilty about the lack of guilt that I felt about her. I began to come to the realisation that despite the problems that we had and the issues that clouded our relationship, even that was better than what I was living through with Bea.

Twenty-Four

'It's Dad.' The phone call was from Jerry.

'What about him?

'He's had a stroke. He's being taken to hospital.'

I am not sure what I said in response to this. I am not sure what it was that I could say in response to this. It had taken the wind out of my sails. This was the last thing that I had been expecting. I can't remember for the life of me what I said to Jerry, but I know that I was soon packing things up and getting ready to go to the hospital. It was probably about six o'clock in the evening or something like that. I went through to see Bea.

'My Dad has had a stroke; I'm going to the hospital.'

'Okay,' she hardly looked up from what it was that she was doing.

'Are you going to come with me?'

'I would love to, but I am too busy at the moment. You do understand, don't you?'

'Oh yes, I understand.' I walked out and slammed the door in a manner which I hoped would cause her the maximum of irritation.

I remember little of the trip to the hospital. I am probably just lucky that I managed to get there without killing myself or anyone else. I was in a trance. I met Jerry at the hospital and we both went in to see our father. We were only allowed to see him briefly and he didn't seem to be entirely with it although he was at least able to recognise who we were.

'This is a fucker.' His speech was slightly slurred and he seemed to struggle, but we didn't have all that much of a problem in understanding what it was that he had said. 'Try not to talk, Dad,' said Jerry as he fluffed a pillow in what he hoped was a caring and medical way.

'Bloody kind of thing always seems to happen when you're in the middle of a good book. If I don't get to finish it, I'm going to be extremely pissed.'

At this point a nurse arrived around the corner and gave us a look that seemed to say that we were as welcome on the ward as undertakers. She seemed to have one of those disapproving faces that suited her role perfectly. I have a lot of respect for the nursing profession, but there are some of them who seem to have mastered the art of disdain and spend all their time disapproving of everything and everybody. We decided to take the opportunity to leave before we really pissed her off.

Both of us were staying in our old family home whilst Dad was in hospital, but I don't think either of us had much sleep that night. It is very difficult to see someone that you have known all of your life to be strong, to appear to be so weak and helpless.

The following day we heard very little news. All we could get out of the hospital was that they were running a series of tests.

'I know there's such a thing as doctor-patient confidentiality, but you would like to think that as I'm part of that equation, they would tell me something.' My father hadn't lost his sense of humour at least.

'It would seem that we are not really going to know all that much until the tests are complete, Dad.' Jerry seemed to be trying to calm the situation. I had never seen him handle himself so well.

'The NHS are bloody useless to still be running all these,' I said looking around in frustration. 'I'm sure that if it had been private they would have sorted it all out by now.'

'Well, it isn't, so let's just work with what we've got, hey?' Jerry darted me a look that clearly told me to shut up.

'I really can't stand these places,' my father continued.

'I don't think that there are all that many people who do like them,' I replied, thinking of my own dislike for hospitals.

'I have tried to avoid hospitals all my life. I really can't stand them, I would happily dig a tunnel out of here if I could get away with it. Not sure what it is. Some sort of phobia I have about the places really. Don't ask me.' My father lapsed into silence and looked around him with a depressed look on his face.

I decided to leave the bedside and go and track down a doctor. Eventually after much hassle, I managed to find someone who was prepared to tell me what the hell was going on.

'The fact is, Mr Durant, we don't know,' said the young doctor that I eventually found who would talk to me. It troubled me slightly that he appeared to be younger than I was. I don't suppose there was any logical reason for this, but it was like policemen, the older you got the younger they appeared to be.

'What do you know?' I asked in return.

'It's possible that your father has had a stroke.'

'Possible? Not certain then?'

'No; it could be a number of things. It could be some kind of brain haemorrhage or it could be linked to a brain tumour. The possibilities are endless at the moment and it is very difficult to say what any outcome could be.'

A few days went by like this without any real diagnosis taking place. I had to return to work and what life I had with Bea. Jerry and I tried to spend as much time visiting father as we could whilst still trying to maintain some normality in our lives. He was particularly insistent that we get on with our lives. All that seemed to annoy him was that in his current state he was unable to read. I can understand this, it would probably have annoyed me as well and I didn't read half as much as he did. During this time he remained very weak, but that was probably more to do with the fact that he had not really eaten for a week by this stage. He boasted that he was going to market it as a new diet.

I might have been imagining it, but I felt that his speech was improving from the first night that we had seen him in hospital. He also appeared to have all of his mental faculties as it was easy to have a conversation with him still and he seemed perfectly aware of what was going on around him. All that seemed to be going on at the moment was that he was left in a limbo state where he hadn't been diagnosed and yet he was not well enough to be allowed to go home and get on with his life.

Eventually after a little more time, the information was shared with us that there had been a bleeding in the brain which had caused the problems with the right-hand side of the body linked to the stroke. From what we could all gather, there didn't appear to be all that much problem with the movement and control of this side of his body now and there appeared to be none of the severe signs of a stroke that you would expect.

'He can't walk at the moment,' the young doctor told me. 'This may have something to do with the lack of food and general weakness, or it may be directly linked to the stroke. We need to build his strength up and see where we go from there.'

It all seemed logical. One of the most disturbing things I saw was seeing the nurses attempting to fit a tube down my father's nose so that they could try and get some nourishment into him. I have no idea why it had taken such a long time for this to be done, but for whatever reason they were still attempting, and failing, to do this. It is a very disturbing sight and must be something that is far more painful and horrible to have to sit through. Personally, I think I would have been out of the window given the chance; or I would have laid out the nurse with a carefully aimed punched.

I found myself becoming rather selfish in my thoughts and hoping that I never had to go through such a thing in my life. I don't think I would handle it all that well. I detested hospitals as much as my father did and would do anything I could to keep out of them. I would like to hope that I never have an illness that puts me into this position and when it comes to the time when I am going to die, I can only hope that it is quick and leaves the minimal amount of suffering for myself or for the people that I leave behind me.

'He's getting there,' said Jerry as we sat in the hospital café. 'Slow and steady, but he seems to be making progress.'

'He's a fighter.'

***

262

'It's not good,' this was from Jerry. It was a few days later and I had received a phone call from him to get to the hospital as soon as I could. I had handed over my afternoon lectures and made my way to the hospital.

'What's happened?'

'They discovered that he has a blood clot in his pulmonary artery.'

'What does that mean?'

'It's caused problems in the oxygen level of the blood and the circulation of the blood to the lungs and the heart leading to myocardial infarction.'

I must have looked a little blank at this. I wondered where Jerry had managed to acquire such medical knowledge.

'He's had a heart attack, Max.'

'Jesus.'

'He's in critical condition. It's life threatening now.'

'He was doing so well.'

'I know.'

'What do we do now?'

'There's nothing that we can do. We just have to be here and wait. I think we need to prepare ourselves for the worst-case scenario.'

'That bad?'

'I firmly believe that you prepare for the worst and if it doesn't happen then it is a lot easier to back down from than it is to have it fall upon you unexpectedly.'

Jerry had his moments when he could be perfectly logical and calculating despite his overall appearance of being reckless and carefree. I felt that I was falling slowly to pieces whereas he was keeping it together. It was a role reversal.

The following day they were able to bring him back to consciousness and were able to remove all of the tubes that were helping him breathe. The next problem was going to be whether or not there had been any brain damage. I knew my father would be in a living hell if he survived this and was unable to read and continue his life as he had done so far. The nurses reported that he was fully aware of where he was and has been able to respond to questions put to him, which was pretty good news.

Hopefully this meant that things were going to be on the up and on the mend now. Jerry was trying not to be too optimistic as he maintained that it was still a good philosophy to prepare for the worst. He was slowly beginning to make improvements, but the road to recovery was going to be a long one. It was also very early on and it was not known if the recovery that he would make would be full or partial. Like so many things in life; only time would tell.

'You look tired. You should rest,' said Jerry. I was exhausted having hardly slept at all in the last few days.

'No more than you. We could both do with the break.'

'Max, don't think I'm prying or anything-'

'But?'

'Where's your wife?'

'Probably doing something that she thinks is more important than this.'

'What might that be?'

'Painting her nails, probably.'

'Things not going all that well?'

'You could say that.'

***

Dad was still in the neurological intensive care unit and probably would be for some time whilst they kept an eye on him. He had been through a great deal and I suspected that it was far from over yet. It was difficult to know at this stage what would happen next. He was in a weakened condition and his speech had become difficult to understand once again. This was probably more to do with the intense tiredness and having to wear an oxygen mask, than because of the stroke. He was on 40 per cent oxygen at the moment, which was probably a good thing as previously he had been on 100 per cent. Improvements were being made, but slowly. As slow as it might be though, it was clear that a recovery, of sorts, was taking place.

He seemed to be in and out of things most of the time. I would think that he was making a degree of progress and then it would seem that he had taken a backward step. There were times when he really did not know that we were there. He was in a very confused state and I wondered if he would miss us if we were not there. This was the argument that Bea used when I challenged her for why she was not coming to hospital with me.

'There really doesn't seem to be any point. From what you have told me, there seems a likely possibility that he would not know that I was there anyway; and if he did know I was there, he probably wouldn't know who I was.'

'*I* would know you were there.'

'Well, that is hardly the point now, is it?'

'It would have been nice to have had your support in this.'

'I am sorry you feel like that, but I really do not do hospitals. Far too many sick people for my liking. Makes me shiver at the very thought of it.'

'No that's right, I forgot.'

'Forgot what?'

'People like you only enter a hospital if you're there to open it.'

The arguments were becoming more intense and more frequent. I began to wonder if there was any hope for us. I simply didn't recognise in her the woman that I had fallen in love with and decided to marry. It was starting to become clear to me that marriage was not something that I was cut out to do.

I left and went back to the hospital where I was spending a great deal of my time at the moment. He seemed to be considerably better than he was the last time that I saw him and from what the doctors were telling me, he was making progress. It was going to be something of an uphill struggle, but it was going to happen. When I saw him this time around it was possible to hold a conversation with him and he was in a more comical state than he had been for a long time. At this particular moment in time, he had no idea what it was that he had gone through. It was a relief to be able to talk to him and to see that the indications seemed to point to the fact that he was on the mend.

'There's still a long way to go and a lot can happen,' explained the young doctor.

'But he's making some progress?'

'Yes, he is.'

'We can't ask for more.'

***

The situation with regards to my father had brought a number of things home to me that I had been aware of, but that I was refusing to face up to. The chief of them being, Bea.

I could no longer hide from the fact that there was a problem between Bea and me. The problem, aside from the arguments, was that we didn't seem to have all that much love and affection for each other any longer. Certainly, the sex was a thing of the past having completely dried up and was now non-existent to the point of no physical contact at all. I found this rather difficult to cope with as I had always considered myself to have a high sex drive and I was now back to the adolescent requirement to masturbate on a daily basis. Even if you took the sex out of the equation, there was still a desire to have some form of contact with another human being. Bea was offering nothing that could even be remotely considered as love.

I had tried to talk to her about the issues, but she just closed things up and refused to talk about it. She enjoyed hiding in her own world and hated the idea that anyone would intrude on it. As far as she was concerned there was nothing to talk about. She didn't want to do anything about the physical side of things because she was happy as she was. It was just not something that she wanted. What is there to a marriage if there is nothing but friendship, and even that is something that is distant. I had ceased to have a marriage in any sense that most people would have understood the term to mean. I began to realise that if things were to continue along these lines then there would be little point in carrying on. I had been married for two years and it was a disaster.

It was a painful subject to talk about and I kept it secret from everyone else. I hardly would admit to it myself. I felt that I could no longer ignore the coldness that existed between the two of us. We just didn't spend any time together. We didn't sleep in the same room and there always seemed to be good excuses to not spend any time together during the rest of the day. What kind of life is that?

I couldn't deny that it was all rather depressing and that there was no fun in it any longer. I still felt so embarrassed by it all that I didn't even confide in Nat. The continued unhappiness was beginning to have a toll on me and I wasn't sure how much longer it could last. In a moment of having had too much alcohol after a visit to my father, I told everything that I felt to Jerry.

'I dread to think that my marriage may have run the course of all my other relationships already and that it's time to start looking to leave it,' I concluded. He thought about this for a moment.

'It doesn't necessarily mean that,' he eventually said. 'I have to confess that I have never really gone in for long term relationships, certainly not in the way that you have, but don't all relationships go through rocky periods?'

'Yes, they do, but this is a rocky period that has really gone on since the day we were married. I really don't understand why.'

'You think it's over?'

'Most of the time things are either cold between us, or they just escalate into argument.'

'Well, I grant you, that doesn't sound all that good, Max.'

'Living with a cold wife who refuses to show any love of any kind whatsoever, it isn't easy. What really worries me is that I'm also very much conscious of the fact that I can walk away from this at any time that I like. That's not the problem.'

'What's the problem then?'

'The problem is that I just might find myself wanting to.'

Life has its ups and downs as does any relationship. I could set aside all the time in the world to try and sort it out, but it wouldn't make the slightest bit of difference if it was a one-way conversation.

***

My father was making a recovery that was truly amazing. I watched him coming away from the machines and out of intensive care and onto a normal ward. He had some progress that still needed to be made. He had little patience with the physiotherapy which most of the time he found to be intensely frustrating. I cannot imagine how this must have felt. Learning how to walk again and finding it so difficult to do what you would normally have done without even thinking about it. We take so much for granted that we find it difficult to cope with it when the basics are taken away from us and we are forced back to some kind of infant state. We are all so fragile; so easy to break, and yet we treat ourselves in ways that we would never treat our cars. If we treated our cars the way we treated our bodies they would be in pieces and never work properly. We never starve our cars of maintenance or fuel; we always look after them and make sure that they are running well, whilst we allow ourselves to fall to pieces.

Many weeks passed as my father moved on his slow road to recovery. We were now drawing close to 2007. As 2006 closed, my father was well enough to leave the hospital and return home.

'Bloody hated every minute of it,' he told me as we were leaving and he waved at the nurses with a slightly sick look on his face. 'If we're ever in a position where I am likely to die, then make sure it's something that happens to me at home amongst my books and not in those horrible sterile environments.'

'Consider it done,' I replied smiling slightly as we got into the car that would take him home.

We took him home and Jerry and I told him that we had arranged things so that for most of the time one of us would always be on hand. He was disgusted with the fact that we had fitted handrails and various other aids around the house to help him get upstairs and steps, as well as in and out of the bath.

'Bloody holes drilled in my walls all over the place. They're going to be a right pain in the arse to sort out when the things come down.'

Ultimately, he had regained nearly all of his mobility and speech. In fact, you could not have told that he had gone through the hell that he had. It was rather remarkable really. When I had seen him in the hospital bed linked to all the machines, I thought that he was going to die. I would never have imagined that he would one day be walking, near enough unaided, into his house again and heading once more for his beloved study. It just went to show you that you could never really tell.

***

'Why does it mean so much to you?' Bea asked one night as we sat in front of the log fire.

'I'm sorry?' I looked up from the book I was reading. It was one of those rare moments when we had decided to spend the evening in the same room as each other. We may have been in the same room, but for the majority of the time that we had spent in there so far, we had not said a word. Therefore, her question had taken me by surprise as it had come out of nowhere.

'I said, why does it mean so much to you?' she repeated.

'Why does what mean so much to me?'

'Sex.'

I sighed and put my book to one side, suddenly having the feeling that this was likely to be a long conversation and one that would probably end in an argument.

'It matters because it's a basic human need.'

'Well, I seem to manage perfectly well without it.' It was on the tip of my tongue to tell her that she was barely human.

'I suppose that it's just one of the basic parts of a marriage.'

'Well, Mummy told me that she and Daddy have not had sex for ages.' I could well believe and understand this.

'I suppose if I have to explain it,' I said 'then it's something that really you are not going to understand.'

'Are you saying I am thick?'

'No, I'm not saying that. I'm merely saying that it's something that you either get or you don't get, regardless of explanation.' She thought about this for a while and the only sound was of logs burning.

'Would it help if you had sex with someone else?'

'Excuse me?'

'Well, I am not interested in it really, but if it means so much to you why don't you have sex with someone else?'

'I'm not sure I'm following you?' The trouble was that I thought I was following her.

'I am saying if it means so much to you, I wouldn't object if you wanted to go off and have sex with others.'

'Are you telling me you want me to have an affair?'

'Well, I am saying that it wouldn't bother me if you felt that you had to; but if you want it in clear English, then yes, I am telling you that you can have an affair if you want to.

I remember it clearly. It was a cold winter night. The sky had been battleship grey all day long and come the night, the stars shone brightly in the clear sky as the frost settled everywhere. The fire burnt in the grate and cast an orange glow all over the room and slowly toasted the side of my face that was closest to it. I was reading Suetonius in an excellent leather-bound volume that felt good to the touch. Everything seemed so peaceful and calm. It was truly freezing outside, but inside there was the smugness of being able to stay in front of the fire with no place to go so you didn't have to worry about how cold and miserable it was outside.

I remember it all clearly. It was the night that my second marriage rolled over and died.

Twenty-Five

Now, I know there are some men out there who would probably have thought that all their Christmases had come at the same time. They got to be married and live a life that was pretty wealthy and not have to worry about all that much, plus they had permission from their wife to have sex with anyone they wanted. I know that for many, they would think this was paradise. It wasn't for me. I knew that things were over from that point. No matter how long we stayed married to each other, there was nothing there that was left to stay for.

I was increasingly tired. I would wake up in the morning and could barely stand on my feet for the pain that came up from my ankles. I always felt like I had not slept at all. Every bone in my body would be crying out in pain and aching like I was being stamped upon by something very big, very heavy and very angry. I would say that this was linked to the stress of my collapsing marriage, but I think it was more than that. Now I came to think of it, I had been feeling like this for a very long time indeed. Probably anything as close to a decade. The pain that I experienced though, seemed to be growing worse with each day and there appeared to be little that I could do about it.

'It probably is something to do with the way things are going with your marriage,' Jerry said when I spoke to him about it.

'I think it has been going on for a lot longer than that if I'm honest,' I replied.

'Perhaps you should go and see a doctor about it.'

'So that they can tell me that it's just a sign of age. I've been burning the candle at both ends for rather a large number of years, perhaps it's just all catching up with me.'

'Perhaps. You won't know unless you find out though.'

My old reluctance to go and see a doctor was not something that had left me; the situation with regards to my father had probably only added to that particularly irrationality.

Despite what other men might have felt about the situation, I was not other men. After what had happened between Susie and myself, I was not going to be the kind of person who cheated – either with or without permission. Frankly, I had never heard of anything so ridiculous in my life. I know that having been cheated on by Susie might have made a lot of guys turn into a regular adulterer themselves, but it just wasn't something that appealed to me in the least. No, it wasn't because of some Biblical commandment, but rather due to my own moral code. I had been well and truly shafted and hurt by what Susie had done to me and in all conscience, I couldn't put anyone else through the same thing.

I could have stayed and suffered through the situation, keeping up the pretence of a happy marriage and taking advantage of the wealth that came from her side of the family; but what kind of a person would that have made me? Aside from my job I had given up everything to be with Bea, my old flat had long since gone. Although I knew that things were pretty much over, I was still reluctant to walk away. If there were some way that the situation could be remedied and we could carry on then it had to be worth a try.

We were some months into 2007 when I eventually came to the conclusion that I was being rather optimistic in this view.

'You know,' I said to her one day when I found her in the garden. 'We should probably give consideration to the fact that if this is not going to work, we should just call it quits.'

She didn't reply to this but looked at me for a moment before nodding her head. And that was how it ended, not with a bang, but with a whimper. It just fizzled out and died.

***

We agreed to separate and I moved back in with my father as the most sensible option until I was able to get a place of my own sorted out. Here I was approaching thirty-four years old and living back in my parent's house. I had come full circle and I had pretty much nothing to show for it. Three years of marriage and it was over again. It would be nice if I could actually hold down a relationship, but I had reached a stage where I was proving that it was either the worst run of luck in history or I was just not genetically capable of holding down a relationship.

'I don't think it's genetic,' countered Nat when I told him about it. 'It isn't as if your parents couldn't hold down a relationship. I would say that you just have the rottenest luck in the universe.'

'The first thing I did when we split was to drink three bottles of wine.'

'Only three?'

'I ran out of wine.'

My marriage was over, again. It was a sham, and it had been for a long time. Married to a woman who was cold, with no compassion and no sex life at all. I don't know at the end whether she was just uninterested in sex with me or uninterested in sex, full stop. She could have been shagging her heart away behind my back without me knowing about it. If she had, then I think, added to what Susie had been doing, I would have the biggest complex in history. She might have been having affairs which was why she was so keen for me to have my own affairs.

For the last three years, I had been treated like shit. I had gone through a miserable time and I only realised within the last few dying weeks of the marriage exactly how unhappy I was. It is amazing how you can fool yourself most of the time as well as others. At least I thought that I had fooled others.

'Oh, we all knew that you were having a terrible time and that she was an absolute bitch to you,' said Nat over coffee, soon after I had left Bea.

'Why didn't you tell me?' I asked, looking at him in surprise.

'Oh, my dear fellow, it's not the sort of thing that you can do. I couldn't just come up to you and tell you something like that. If I had've done then the chances are that you would have turned against me and sided with her immediately. There are some things that friends can do and there are some things that friends can't do. In circumstances such as this, all we can do is watch hopelessly and pray that it will all work itself out in the end.'

'How long did you feel like this?'

'Frankly, before you were married I thought it was going to be a disaster and I gave it no more than a year. I'm amazed you lasted as long as you have to be honest.'

'Fucking hell.'

'That's what I thought.'

There were things that I needed to talk to Bea about. Things that needed to be arranged, but her phone was switched off. This was not unusual. Bea only liked talking about things when she wanted to do so, and if she was not ready then it didn't matter what I wanted. Frequently, whenever we had gotten into arguments in the past, she would turn her phone off so that she didn't have to talk to me; either it would be turned off or she would consistently cancel the calls that I made. I always thought that this was a little childish and just about suited the way that she was about everything really. You may ask why I didn't see her in person, but I would imagine that she had given orders that I was no longer to be admitted into her presence.

I packed up as many of my things as I could (mainly books) from the cold house that we had shared together and shipped them over to my father's house. A few sad trips back and forward and then it would all be done. It was sad how few trips it would actually take to remove all physical trace of myself from her life.

'How do you feel?' my father asked me as he watched the small stack of boxes appearing with what I imagined was a small amount of apprehension.

'It's not unexpected. Things have not been going well for some time now and it's been a long time since Bea was a wife to me in any sense of the word. I suppose you knew that along with everyone else though?'

'I had my suspicions, Max, but it was not my place to say and as I have told you before, you have to go your own way and find your own path in life, even if that does mean having your fingers burnt from time to time.'

'I'm not entirely sure that I have any fingers left to get burnt. It seems I have been something of a fool.'

'Actually,' said my father as he sat down next to me in the hall. 'I think it's her that has been the fool. I don't know what her motivation has been, but I suspect that one of these days she will regret what she has done.'

'I can't imagine that happening.'

'Time will tell.'

'Oh well, what does it all matter now? Marriage and I are not meant for each other, clearly.'

'I wouldn't say that. You're still young. There's still time to find the one for you. There's always hope. Look at me, a few months ago I bet you thought I was going to be dead, but now I'm fighting fit.'

'Are you looking for a new wife?'

'No. There's no one that can replace your Mother for me, but if there is ever an example of hope and triumph in the face of disaster then I'm it, and so are you.' He looked around the hallway at the large stacks of books that I had brought into his house. He picked one up from the pile nearest him and flicked through it. 'And do you really read this stuff?'

***

The university agreed to give me a couple of weeks off so that I could get my head together and sort myself out over what had happened. I don't think my supervisor was particularly pleased about what had happened as he saw the chance of the benefactress disappearing into the night. He didn't care in the slightest that my life and marriage had fallen to pieces; money that was all that mattered to him. Well, at least he was honest I suppose.

If I am honest I had known that it was coming for a long time, but the knowledge doesn't soften the blow when it finally does happen. It's rather like a plane crash. You know you are diving out of the sky, but that doesn't soften the impact when you eventually hit the ground. I needed the time to relax and get some strength back. The whole experience had left me feeling drained and tired. I felt like I had not slept in weeks. It didn't seem to make the slightest bit of difference how long I slept. I could sleep for ten hours, but still wake feeling like I had been kept awake all night long by having people jump up and down on me.

It may come as a surprise to some people, but I was far from feeling depressed at the collapse of the marriage. After everything that had gone on and the pretence that I had gone through, I felt a great sense of freedom. I felt as if a weight had been lifted from my shoulders and that I had been liberated from a miserable existence. The future was stretching out in front of me and rather than being depressed and scared by the thought of it, I embraced the possibilities that lay ahead and what was possible. Although I knew that there would be elements where I was now worse off, I also knew there were a number of opportunities that lay open to me and for the first time in years I might be able to make some progression.

Due to my time off and not really having all that much to do, I took myself out of the city, into the countryside and off for a long walk into the forest to clear my head and get my thoughts in order. I probably walked for about five or six miles, I don't know for sure. By the end of the walk I stopped at a pub and ordered myself an ice-cold lemonade and sat outside watching everyone else running about their business. I wondered what the individual stories were that each of them had. What were their lives about? Who were they and who did they care for? Questions that were impossible for me to ever know the answers to.

Did I feel bitter towards Bea? No, I don't believe that I did. I think I was so numbed by our marriage that I didn't feel any emotion for her at all. Not worth wasting the energy on, I suppose. That probably sounds harsh, but it's the truth. I have no doubt that if you were to speak to her she would give you a long list of all of the things that were wrong with me and perhaps the majority of them would be true. Her lack of compassion was the biggest accusation that I could level at her.

Separation and divorce is often about levelling accusations at each other about who is responsible for the split, and assigning blame. I didn't really want to fall into that trap if I could help it. I didn't think that there was really any way back from where we were. When some things are broken, with a little work it is possible to put them back together again, but when other things are broken there is simply nothing that you can do about it other than admit that they are broken, and throw it away and start all over again. This marriage was completely broken.

I say all of this because I want to make it clear that the matter was over. There was nothing that could be done and nothing to repair the damage that had been inflicted in such a short time. I know there are some among you who upon hearing this, will tut-tut and shake your head, believing that with one divorce under my belt and another one soon to join it I was just simply not trying hard enough. What do I say in response to these people? I say that I know all about the sanctity of marriage and how it is important to maintain it, but the point that I would like to raise is that there is no point in living an unhappy lie. If you are in a relationship that leaves you feeling miserable and you wake each morning unhappy and go to bed each night as equally unhappy, then get out of it. It's just not worth it; life is too short to be stuck with someone who makes you miserable.

***

So, here I was back to square one all over again. Apparently not having learnt a thing from my first marriage; I am sure that was what some people were saying. I had finally reached a stage where I didn't care what people were saying about me. I also had no intention of sitting at home and bemoaning my lot and wailing about how terrible life was. I was going to enjoy myself. I had no intention of getting into a relationship again; I thought it was probably best to steer clear of that. Instead I took myself off to the cinema and the theatre and would eat in restaurants if I felt like it. It didn't bother me if people thought I was a sad lonely fool that couldn't get a date. I didn't know what other people's stories were and they didn't know what mine was, so I just went about my business, enjoying myself as best I could and it wasn't a feint, I really was enjoying myself. My newfound freedom had liberated me in a way that I could never have imagined before.

I knew that I would eventually have to start to sort out a divorce. We were separated and there was no possibility of us getting back together. Neither of us seemed to be in much of a rush to formalise the situation though. I can't speak for why this might have been from her side of things; perhaps it was easier for her to keep the pretence up for a little longer or maybe it was because of her family. I don't know; I could easily develop a headache trying to work out Bea's motivation. As for my part? I wasn't in any rush. I wasn't planning on going off to date anyone else, let alone get married again, so there was no rush for me to get another sheet of paper that would tell me that I was divorced once again. Besides which I would have to go through all the grounds for divorce once again and the longer that we spent apart, the easier it was to add time separated as grounds for divorce.

It wasn't all easy. I was for the most part liberated and feeling so much better, but from time to time my black mood would swing in. I think the most depressing thing for me was being back in the family home. I would have dark moments where I would wonder where it was that I went wrong. It was 2008 and I was thirty-five years old, near enough. Twenty years before I had been full of optimism and bounce, excited to get on with life; twenty years later I was back living in my parent's house, no further forward than I had been before and feeling pretty shit for it.

***

I was getting tired for no reason that seemed logical. I would wake up and within a few hours, or sometimes less time, I would feel the need to go back to sleep and would often return for an afternoon nap if time allowed me to do so. I didn't even have to be doing anything strenuous, I was just going about things as normal, but I was feeling tired all of the time.

'Why do I feel so crap all of the time?' I asked Nat.

'I'm afraid that I don't know the answer to that. I'm not that kind of a doctor.'

'By the end of your typical day, every muscle of my body is aching and protesting. I'm going to bed in the evenings earlier most of the time than I was when I was twelve. When I wake up in the morning, I feel like I have not been asleep at all.'

'That does seem to be strange.'

'I just assumed that it was the way that everyone felt.'

'Not the way I feel.'

'Just me then. That's bollocks. Half the time I sleep all night but feel crap and the other half of the time my insomnia is back and making it impossible for me to sleep. Perhaps I am feeling crap because the insomnia of twenty years has finally caught up with me. After all I have been awake twice as long as the rest of you.'

'Well, that's a possibility. I still think you should go and see a doctor though.'

'I doubt that there is anything that they could do.'

'You don't know until you try. I forget how many times I've told you that.'

'Most of the time I long for the sleep that will bring me oblivion. Oblivion from having to think and oblivion from the pain that all the aching muscles causes.'

'And the rest of the time?'

'I dread going to sleep. It's like a monster waiting for me.'

'You're talking about your marriage again.'

'If Hell exists then I believe it is full of insomniacs. A place of eternal night. Tossing and turning with no respite.'

The levels of tiredness and exhaustion were higher than I could ever imagine at this stage. The thing about insomnia is how it entirely screws you up for the following day – or sometimes days – that follows. For someone who falls asleep the moment they hit the pillow, sleeps soundly throughout the night and wakes refreshed ready to face a new day, this is all a mystery to them. For most of the time now I ached all over my body.

I was finding it increasingly difficult to concentrate at work and more than once had found that I had fallen asleep at my desk; fortunately, nobody important had discovered this yet. I am pretty certain that since the separation between Bea and myself, the powers that be at the university were looking for any excuse that they could get to punish me. Obviously, as far as they were concerned, I should have put the needs of the university before my personal life.

I didn't know it then but things were starting to come to a critical point. Things that had been a mystery to me would begin to make sense, but before I realised this I was to discover that my life was about to change. Once again, the game was going to deal me a hand and it would change my life forever, in many ways; not all of them would be for the better.

Twenty-Six

I tried to continue in my life as best that I could, but things must have been dragging me down. I felt tired all the time and no amount of rest seemed to make that much difference. I was in my mid-30s and yet couldn't seem to make it through the day without feeling the need for a mid-afternoon sleep. When I did go to sleep in the evening it always seemed to be slightly restless and was either a conflict with insomnia or I managed to sleep fine, but woke up aching and tired as if I had not been asleep at all. Now I realise that this was something that had actually been going on for a long time and I probably should have gone to see a doctor. Surely there is something wrong to be feeling so shit at such a young age?

'How are things with you, Max?' my father asked me one morning when I wandered into the breakfast room. I was still living at home as I had not yet found the means to get my own place together. We had discussed the possibility of my father helping me out in that regard, but I was in no hurry to move out.

'Didn't sleep all that well to be honest.'

'Really?'

'No, I feel like crap.'

'You seemed to be sleeping okay from what I could tell.'

'How do you mean?'

'I could hear the snoring from across the house.'

I don't snore.'

'I beg to differ, Max. Either you were snoring rather heavily or you were doing some woodwork at three in the morning.'

I have never really been into woodwork so this wasn't a likely possibility that I was a somnambulist crafter. This presented an interesting problem. I had always believed that I did not snore at all. Bea had told me that I did, but I had always assumed that it was just an excuse that she was using so that she didn't have to sleep in the same bed as me. My father, however, had no reason to lie. It begged the question of how could I wake feeling so tired and unrested if I had been snoring my head off all night long. It is always difficult when the preconceptions that you have of yourself turn out to be not entirely true.

'Have you given any thought to what you want to do next?'

'In what way?' I had a feeling that he wanted me to move out again so that he could revert to his solitary life. I can't say that I would have blamed him if this had been the case.

'Well, you can't stay tied to someone forever. You're going to have to get divorced at some stage I would have thought; move on with your life.'

'I haven't really thought about it.' I hadn't. 'I could use some advice from you on that front.'

'From me?'

'Yes. Why not? You're the most intelligent person I know.'

'Don't confuse intelligence with being simply well read,' he laughed as he buttered himself some more toast. This was one of my father's favourite sayings. 'You know you have to follow your own path. You also know that this is your home for as long as you want it to be.'

'But you'd rather I left?'

'Not at all, I never said that. I merely think that the chances of you meeting girls and getting on with them is going to be seriously hampered by the fact that you can't bring them back home without bumping into your old man. I should imagine it will cramp your style somewhat.'

I had to admit that it wasn't an easy thing to get around. I wasn't exactly in the dating game once again, but I knew that both myself and my dad would find it difficult if I were bringing girls back to the house for some intimate moments. It did tend to cramp the style; he was right in that regard. I would have to look at my financial situation and see if I could get a flat of my own once again.

***

It took me a few more weeks, but I was eventually able to sort myself out once again and found myself a little flat not too far from college that would be more than suitable for my purposes. After living in the house that I had shared with Bea, it was like living in a shoebox of squalor once again, but I cannot deny that there was something spectacular about it. It was mine. It was me regaining my independence once again. I was free to be able to use the toilet without having to shut the door, if I chose to do so.

'So, how's the new place?' asked Nat. It was one of those very rare occasions when we had decided to have dinner rather than stick to our usual coffee. It always amused Nat as he had noticed that due to people's preoccupation with sex, they assumed that two men having dinner together must be gay. It is sad that the stereotypes mean that there are some who will think about this when they see two men having dinner and yet bizarrely the same thought will probably not cross their mind if they see two women having dinner. It didn't matter in the least to either of us what people thought of us.

'It's lovely,' I replied as I scanned the menu, although in truth there was little point as this was a regular dining place and I always tended to stick to the same tried and tested items each time.

'Is it?'

'Of course, it's my home and somewhere that I can actually be myself rather than living the lie that I was living for the three years, or whatever it was, with Bea.'

'I can understand how that would make you feel good then.' The waiter arrived and we placed our orders and he then weaved his way between the tables to the kitchen leaving us in peace once again.

'So, does a new pad mean that you are going to be dating once again?'

'It seems to be a question that everyone is intent on asking me. Perhaps people are not so happy with the idea of me being on my own.'

'You strike me as the kind of person who has to be with someone. You're not meant to live life on your own.'

'Do you think so?'

'Wouldn't have said it if I didn't think it.'

'I'm not so sure. My past relationships have hardly given me a cause for thinking that I was likely to be able to sustain a happy and meaningful relationship.'

'But you can't deny that amongst all the pain and suffering you have had some fun along the way.'

'Well, that's true. I give you that.'

'So, I think it unlikely that you will shun the attention of the fairer sex for the rest of your life.'

'Are you allowed to call them that any longer?'

'What?'

'The fairer sex?'

'Probably not. Good point, I hadn't thought about it.'

Our starters arrived and we lapsed into silence for a few moments whilst we enjoyed them. I do love eating out whenever I can and it is something that I would make a habit of if I had the opportunity and the money to do so. When I was with Bea we used to go to restaurants a lot, but they were not like this. They were the pretentious kind that those with money favour where you go to be seen not to satisfy your appetite. I learnt that if we were going out to one of these restaurants then I would grab myself a Big Mac before so that I wouldn't feel so hungry that I would try and eat the table decorations. It always amazes me that there are moments when pretention takes over from what is sensible. It seems to do this with the wealthy on a daily basis.

'You don't have anyone on your radar then?' He was persistent I will give him that.

'No, Nat. I don't have anyone on my radar, as you so eloquently put it. I think life has been complicated enough as it is recently without the need to make it any more complicated. Don't you?'

'Possibly; but I would be very wary about losing any opportunities that might come your way.'

'Do you know of any opportunities? Is that why you are asking?' I was naturally suspicious. I suppose given my previous relationships suspicion is something that I have come to take as a normal procedure for me.

'Well, I'm not sure that it's my place to say.'

'Rubbish, Nat, you know perfectly well that it's your place to say.' What else were friends for?

'Well, I hear a rumour that Ellen in my department has been interested in you for some time.'

'Ellen?'

'Yes, you know the one who used to hover around your office and ask if there was anything that she could do for you.'

'You know, now you mention it I always used to wonder why it was that she was in the arts faculty rather than science.'

'Well, yes, that's because of the fact that she was always very interested to see if there was anything that she could do for you.'

'Ellen.'

'That's the one.'

It set me thinking. I couldn't help it. It seems to be the way that I am built or wired or something like that. I can go merrily along without giving any thought to a relationship or to any form of sexual encounter, and then all of a sudden someone will say something like Nat had done, and then that is it from that moment onwards; there is nothing that I can do to get the thought out of my head. Rather shallow, isn't it? My father would no doubt remind me of the danger by invoking the memory of Farmer Boldwood from *Far From the Madding Crowd* as an example of this phenomenon of being able to plod along contentedly until someone puts something in your mind and then that is it – obsession from that time onwards.

There was nothing to say that there was any truth behind what Nat was saying about Ellen, but the sheer suggestion of the matter had been enough to stir the usual feelings within myself. The feelings that stir the loins as well as the butterflies that would flutter about in my stomach and make me feel like I was sixteen all over again. This was what the merest suggestion was able to do to me. Imagine what reality could have done.

You might ask why it was that I would feel this way after all the issues that I had experienced in the past. The simple answer to all of that is that I really don't know. Logic would suggest that the best thing to do was to hide myself away and have nothing more to do with any of it ever again; however, I suspect that it probably has something to do with that desire to not be alone that I have talked about previously. That drive we have to be with someone, no matter how much pain we may go through with each new encounter.

'What I can't get over is how much I still ache,' I stated when I dragged my thoughts back to the present moment.

'Still having problems then?'

'Just seems to always be the case that I am achy and tired, no matter what I try to do about it. I wake up and I feel terrible and I really can't make it through the day without wanting to go asleep again. I end up falling asleep when I am the passenger in cars no matter how short a journey it is.'

'That does seem rather strange, Max. I really think you should see a doctor about it. I'm pretty sure that isn't the natural way you should be.'

'Perhaps you're right.'

Naturally, I had no intention of going to see a doctor about it.

***

'Oh, hi,' I was acting like a teenager once again.

'Hi.' It was Ellen and she probably looked like she was acting more like a teenager than I was. We were in the quad and had just bumped into each other. It is strange, though, that before Nat had mentioned it I would have previously walked passed her without so much more than a brief greeting whilst we both went about our business. Now that I had the intelligence from Nat – true or not – I was giddy and acting like I was fifteen again. It was a matter for debate whether our meeting in the quad was entirely accidental or whether it had been planned by one or either of us. Maybe both.

'So, I was wondering if you wanted a coffee,' this was pretty brave for me given the circumstances, particularly when you consider how out of the blue it was and with no lead up.

'Sure, why not?'

So, we went to have a coffee and started chatting and that is where it all started from. We found that we were able to talk easily in each other's company and we talked about everything that you could imagine in such a short space of time. It's fair to say that we developed the beginnings of a pretty good friendship, but then there is the invisible line which you can cross that takes you beyond friendship. I can't explain how it happens. It just does from time to time.

I have talked a lot about the girls that I have been with and those that I have fallen in lust or in love with. None of them can compare to Ellie – as I quickly learnt that she preferred to be called. There was a spark of electricity that seemed to exist between us. I know that sounds like a cliché, but it is the only phrase that I can think of to use. It was true; there was real energy and life sparking between us. I had never experienced anything like it before in my life. It goes to show you exactly how strange life can be. I was experiencing something that I only would have imagined I could have felt as a teenager or as a young person in love. I was now approaching forty years old and I had expected that all of that kind of thing had been left long behind me now and yet suddenly I was experiencing something I would never have expected. It also took me by surprise because I was not expecting it. I think I may be forgiven for thinking that it was all over in my love life and then it was suddenly as if I had been slapped across the face.

I am eternally grateful to this day that I had the courage to ask her for that coffee which may seem such a trivial thing to you. The spark of sexual chemistry that clearly existed between us was both surprising and delightful as well as being unexpected, but very welcome. The inevitable followed from this as it must do. You can't really have the level of energy that was flowing between us without having it transpose itself into the physical form. The coffee was something that

287

dragged itself out into dinner and after dinner it became clear that neither of us wanted to go home unless we were going home together. It is almost impossible for me to explain how it is that I felt about this change in my circumstances.

***

The next day I woke up the happiest man that I felt existed. It had been a long time since I felt as happy and contented as I did when I woke up next to Ellie. Come to think of it, I probably never felt the way that she had made me feel. I still could not get over that it was happening and that it was happening to me so relatively late in life.

'It would be remiss of me to not say this, Max,' my father said, 'but although I have always said that you have your own life to lead and I leave it up to you to follow your own path, I have to point out to you that you have jumped in pretty quick in the past. Do you think that you might be doing things a little quick once again?'

'How do you mean?' I knew what he meant of course, but it was something that I was rather hoping to avoid. It was possible to learn from your previous experiences, but where would the fun be in that?

'Well, you have only been seeing each other for a couple of weeks and you have already moved in together.'

'This is true.' It was. I couldn't deny it. 'But, it's just something that seems right, Dad.'

'Yes, my concern is that you said Susie and Bea felt right as well.' You might argue that this was something that was a little below the belt, but it was true he did have a point here and it could have been something that I used as a cautionary tale, but I guess I am just not that kind of a guy when it comes down to it.

'Don't worry, Dad. Everything will be okay. I think I have learnt to go with the flow and if I get hurt again then I suspect that's just the way it is.'

'Well, if you are absolutely sure. You know that I will not stand in your way.'

'It may be quick, but I don't think that it stops it from feeling so right. I can't stop smiling all of the time.'

'Yes, I had noticed.'

'Sorry.'

'Nothing to apologise for.' I suppose my father was getting used to the way that things were with me by now. He probably had me down as a lost cause.

***

'You're a lost cause, you are,' said Jerry as he helped himself to some sugar from the bowl that was on the table.

'Well that's very kind of you to say so, oh brother mine.'

'Well, you do seem to flit about a bit. Are you going for as many marriages as you possibly can? Is it your intention to have a marriage for each decade of your life?'

'Nobody has spoken about marriage, Jerry.'

'No, but you're a serial husband. You can't seem to resist the temptation to marry women all of the time.'

'I think that's a bit harsh. I've only been married twice; technically I'm still married, of course.'

'You haven't divorced Beatrice yet then?'

'There's been no need.'

'I suspect that there might be a need now.'

'You might be right, but I still think it a little harsh. I never married Gina.'

'Well, no one in their right mind would've married Gina. She was unhinged; the poor woman was psychotic. I'm just not sure if she was like that before she met you or whether it was something that you did to her.'

'Oh, brotherly love. It's so kind of you; although your assessment of her is sadly rather accurate.'

He giggled at this and stirred his coffee that he had poured a fair amount of sugar into.

'At any rate,' I said, trying to change the direction of conversation. 'What about you?'

'What about me?' He looked at me with an element of suspicion.

'Well, isn't it time that you got married, settled down and had some kids or something. You seem to be leaving it rather late. You can't put all of the pressure on me.'

'I don't think that it's very likely, do you?'

'Why not?'

He sighed and looked at me with a sad expression on his face which I could only liken to the same expression that a teacher might have for a pupil that after ages of explaining things, was disappointed that they had simply been unable to grasp the fundamentals.

'I'm gay, Max.'

'You're what?'

'Gay.'

'You don't mean happy, do you?'

'No, I mean gay as in homosexual. I'm sure you can think of some other terms that are more colourful in their expression. Eventually you will get the idea.'

'But you like football.' I was clutching at straws here I suppose.

Jerry stopped stirring his coffee and looked at me with an expression that could only be described as pity.

'Sorry, I don't know why I said that,' I said realising that I had suddenly become homophobic without apparently meaning to.

'We don't always conform to stereotypes, Max,; but as it happens I have always found watching footballers running around in shorts deeply satisfying and I suppose I have had a crush on Cristiano Ronaldo for years.'

'Really?'

'Fuck, yeah.'

'But he's an arrogant –'

'It's not really his personality that has been that much of interest to me, Max.'

'Oh, I see.'

'Matt Damon is another one as well, but as neither of those seem all that much interested in me at the moment we just have to get on with things as best as we can.'

'Does Dad know?'

'That I fancy Matt Damon; I doubt it.'

'That you're gay.'

'Of course he does, he's not an idiot.'

'He never mentioned it.'

'Why would he?'

'Fair point.'

I should probably take time here to point out that despite the reaction that I have given to Jerry's news, I am not actually homophobic. Much of the persecution of homosexuality, I feel, has its roots in religion. As a matter of fact, the hatred of many things in this world largely stem from religion in some way.

What I have also found bizarre is the fact that so many people have this stigma about homosexuality and let's be honest, it is male homosexuality. Men don't seem to mind all that much about the idea of lesbians. Women being close to each other, even in a non-sexual way is more acceptable than the idea of two guys being close. It is perfectly acceptable for girls to walk arm in arm down the street or to refer to each other as 'girlfriend' when they mean a friend who is a girl. Two boys walking down the street arm in arm and referring to each other as 'boyfriend' are likely to be lucky if they don't get stoned to death by the time they reach the corner.

I began to imagine what it must have been like for my brother. How must he have felt to have gone through life until his mid-30s and still not have told his own brother what his sexuality was? Did he think I would reject him if I had known? I saw that he had lived a life that I would probably never understand or appreciate what he had gone through.

Twenty-Seven

Things between Ellie and myself went from strength to strength. Just when you think it is impossible for things to get any better, it does and the feeling becomes intensified. Ellie was the most wonderful person in the world and I began to think that it was either fate, or some higher power that had brought us together. No, I wasn't having a sudden conversion to belief in God, but I do think it handed some credence to the belief held by my mother that everything happened for a reason.

My path had led me to Ellie and if there had been any alteration in that path along the way then it might not have concluded with me being with Ellie at the end of it. I trusted Ellie more than I had trusted anyone in my life. It was because of Ellie that I started to think that it was high time that Bea granted me a divorce. It was 2009 and we had been separated for two years, during which time we had really not had all that much to do with each other. In theory, it should have been reasonably easy for me to get a divorce on the grounds of the two years of separation alone; however, I was aware of the fact that should she want to she could have made things very difficult for me and made me wait for a few more years. It didn't really matter I suppose as I was not in a major hurry to marry again. I wouldn't rule it out as a possibility, but there were other considerations on my mind.

She was something of a pain in the arse when I got back in contact with her again. I had no interest in hiding from her the fact that I had met someone else. It is possible that this was an error as she then started to slow things up and make the progression of a divorce more difficult. She felt that it would probably be a good idea to wait an extra couple of years rather than go for the two-year separation. I just thought this was her being a manipulative, selfish bitch who didn't want to see me happy. She was not prepared to allow me a chance to have the happiness that she was never able to give me; or to be more precise, that she was unwilling to give me.

The shortest period of time away from Ellie became almost too much to bare. I make no apologies for this at all. It may cause all sorts of eyes being raised to the heavens by the reader, but it remains a simple fact that we were very much in love.

I never thought that I could experience love so wonderful and intense as I felt with Ellie. I began to realise that everything that I had experienced in previous encounters and relationships had been nothing more than a rehearsal and a lead up to the main event that I was now experiencing. It was the ultimate emotion.

Whilst feeling elated and enjoying myself, I received a text message from Bea saying that she wanted to meet. As I wanted a divorce, I felt that there was little option but to go along with it. We met in a small café not that far from the university. I wanted our meeting on my own territory rather than her choosing one of her expensive restaurants so that she could laud it over me.

'Well, this is a charming place,' she said as she sat down almost dusting the seat as she did so, with her nose turned up looking at the table in front of her. 'Do you imagine it will be safe to consume anything here?'

'I'm sure they could get you a cup of blood or something if you asked them kindly enough. They might even bring it to your coffin.'

'Very droll, Max, very droll.'

'Perhaps you will forgive me if I ask for you to cut to the chase of why it is that you're here.'

'I am here, Max, because I thought we could sit and talk things through like adults. I am not sure that I was right in that belief, but it was my hope.'

'My apologies. What is it you want?'

'Well, as you insist on being so clinical and business-like I am here to tell you that I don't want a divorce.'

'I see.'

'I have never wanted a divorce, Max and I admit to there being a stubbornness on both sides, so I have been waiting to pluck up the courage needed to tell you that we should make a go of it again.'

'To *tell* me that we should make a go of it again?' I couldn't get over the fact that her family seemed to still think that they could command what others should do.

'It's the only sensible option, Max.'

'I think I would disagree with that.'

'You must see the sense in getting back together.'

'I'm afraid I see no sense in that whatsoever. You were never interested in this relationship and you never put any effort into it. You simply were not interested for reasons that I'm assuming only you know. Even if there wasn't someone else on the scene, I would not be interested in getting back with you. It's over. You have to see that.'

She looked at me for a long time, studying my face and looking deep into my eyes as if she was trying to read the truth of it.

'I suppose you are right,' she eventually said, slumping into her chair a little more. 'I find it all rather upsetting.'

'When we separated, I realised how intensely unhappy I was with you. It may not be your fault, we were just not meant for each other. I'm sure I made you as miserable in my own way.'

'I think you are making a mistake, Max. You are turning your back on a wonderful life that you could have had.'

'Bea, with the greatest of respect, we were together for three years and I didn't see much of a wonderful life, and if you are making the reference to meaning money then I have to tell you that there is more to life than money.'

'Well, you would say that, wouldn't you,' she snorted.

***

'All that I want now,' I told Nat over the obligatory coffee. 'Is to be able to get divorced from Bea as quickly as I can so that I can then draw a line under that particular part of my life and then move on without ever having to think about it again.'

'That seems reasonable,' he said whilst flicking through his latest text book.

'The thing is, that I'm not entirely sure that Bea is the kind of person who can be reasonable.'

'It's a shame that it took you such a long time to find out.'

'Thank you for rubbing it in. I think she doesn't like the fact that she has no control over me any longer.'

'Did she ever?'

'In a sense, I think she probably did. Just by being married to me she could have some degree of control. Granted we haven't seen each other for the last two years so that control has been relaxed, but she still maintains the control by the fact that she is preventing me from the divorce that I want so much.'

'Are you marrying Ellen?'

'No, not yet; at least I don't think so, but that's not the point. The point is, by being divorced from her she is separated from my life and no longer a thorn in my side.'

'Sounds like she is trying to play mind games with you.'

'I think she has been playing those games all along. She has always been trying to screw with my brain one way or another. Would you believe that when I contacted her and asked for a divorce she actually told me that she was thinking it was about time that we got back together again and gave it another chance.'

'Really?'

'Absolutely. Somewhere in her own little screwed up world she actually thinks that I'm likely to want to get back together with her.'

She clearly couldn't reason that anyone would not want her and the life that she had to offer. This is the problem that you have when you are brought up to have everything that you want. There was never any suggestion that this was going to be a likely outcome to all of this.

'Too much shit has happened between us for it to ever be a likely possibility that I would want to get back with her. Even if Ellie had not entered my life, there was more chance of me cutting off my own cock than going back to life with her.'

'Well, you might as well have done; it isn't as if it would get all that much use when you were with her.'

'Very true.'

'Of course, it's more likely that she doesn't want you back at all.'

'Meaning?'

'Meaning that she is only trying to get you back so that you split up with Ellie and when you have damaged that relationship beyond repair, she will dump you, leaving you with nothing.' I had to admit that this was a possibility that I had not thought about, but it had an alarming ring of potential truth about it. It was the kind of vindictive thing that I could imagine her wanting to do.

'Well, whatever the reason, it's a pretty good job that I don't want to get back with her under any circumstances whatsoever.'

'So, what's happening now?'

'Well, I'm not entirely sure, but I think we are set to go ahead with the divorce and in the meantime, I shall have to be as nice to her as possible to prevent there being any issues that are thrown into the works to delay things for me.'

'Well, let's live in hope.'

'What I do know is that there's absolutely no chance of her coming between Ellie and myself. She's seriously misguided if she thinks that she has even the smallest of holds on me now.'

As far as I was concerned, the future was looking a hell of a lot brighter than it was a short while before.

I engaged a solicitor and started divorce proceedings off once again. At least it was something that I was used to so I had some idea what it was about. My main concern was that if Bea decided to contest it, I would end up with an enormous bill while 'Daddy' paid for the greatest divorce solicitor in the world to handle things on her behalf.

***

Everything seemed to be going well with the divorce, which was something. The papers were going backwards and forwards. As things were going so smoothly with regards to the divorce, Ellie and I started to talk about marriage. Ellie was keen on the idea, but understood that there might be issues with regards to me. Two failed marriages behind you could easily make you lose the desire to want to do it again.

'Well how do you feel about the idea?' my father asked me.

'I'm not sure. Ellie is someone that's very special to me and unlike anyone that I've ever met before. I know that I have said that before about others, but I truly feel that there are differences here.'

'So, if it came to it, you might go in for a third marriage?'

'I don't really see it as an issue. I don't think that marriage is something that is cursed. I don't think it's something that I should avoid for the rest of my life just because of bad experiences in the past.'

'Well the important thing, as I have said to you before, is that you are happy. If you are happy being with Ellie, then it probably doesn't matter if you are married or not; but I'm sure you will find your own way and do your own thing.'

'I suppose I always have. It hasn't always been successful though.'

'How are things progressing with the divorce?'

'Rather mysteriously really.'

'Oh, how so?'

'Had a letter from the solicitor the other day stating that whereas Bea agreed to the grounds of the divorce, she didn't, as such agree with them.'

'Well, that makes sense.'

'Perfect sense, I agree. She states that she feels that she has equal grounds to divorce me.'

'Does she?'

'I've no idea; it's not all that likely. However, my view is that if she wants to have her own grounds, then I would suggest that she gets on with it and divorces me and saves me the cost of having to divorce her.'

'I can see that.'

'She is a hard-hearted bitch. She states that she will agree to the divorce providing it's built in that we are not going to go after each other's money, now or at any point in the future.'

'I didn't think you had any.'

'Well, I don't. Clearly, it's something that she wants done so that it will prevent me trying to take any of her Father's precious money. It's all that she and her family have ever been interested in. As far as I'm concerned, they can shove it. Still, with any luck it will progress quickly now. I find it hard to believe that I ever wanted to marry the bitch in the first place.'

'We are all allowed to make mistakes. Now tell me about this apnoea thing. What's that all about?'

'Well, I only have Google to rely on.'

'Doesn't fill me with the utmost confidence then.'

'It's rather amazing what you can find on the internet when you're prepared to look into it slightly.'

'Okay, so what did you find out about it? What is this sleep apnoea? What does it mean?'

'Literally a temporary loss of breath or inability to breath. I don't know too much about it at the moment, if I'm honest. I try not to believe everything that I read on the internet and will wait to see what the hospital has actually got to say about it.'

'Is it serious?'

'It can be. From what I can gather there is the potential for it to be very serious, even fatal. Nobody seems to know all that much about it though. It's common apparently, but not common enough to be known.'

'I've not heard of it myself.'

'Well nobody famous suffers from it so naturally people are not that interested. If some idiotic, brain-dead celebrity suffered from it then they would probably be getting millions in research money.'

'Are there no celebrities with it?'

'Well, if there are, they won't own up to it. Probably not sexy enough for them.'

'It's a cynical view, but I suppose there could be an element of truth in it.'

'Do you think it's ridiculous for someone to be married three times before they are forty?'

'I don't think anything's ridiculous if it's where your heart is. Sometimes you just have to follow the direction that your heart takes you in, no matter which way it may lead or what other people may think about it.'

'That's true.'

'You have never struck me as someone who is all that bothered about what other people think about them at any rate, Max.'

'No; you're right. Sometimes I do spend too much time thinking about what others will think. Probably a hangover from when I used to act in my younger days.'

'Well at least you stopped doing that and decided to do something more grown up for a living.'

'Well, there are some who would argue that being a lecturer, I never left university, so have never actually grown up.'

'Yes, well I suppose you could argue that.'

***

'I had a terrible night last night,' I said as I sat in the coffee house with Nat. I was starting to feel more tired as each night went by. It was probably psychological as I had been made aware of it by Ellie so I was more conscious of the events that were happening.

'More terrible than usual?' Nat sipped his latte and flicked through the text book that he had chosen for the day.

'Seems it, now I'm aware of this disorder I have that makes me stop breathing and then wake up – even though I still have no recollection of actually doing it.'

'It must be strange. I wonder how long it has been going on for.'

'Your guess is as good as mine. It has probably been something that has been going on for years which I have been blissfully unaware of; only realising anything was wrong when I would wake up feeling like shit and aching all over.'

'Well, I told you to go and see a doctor.'

'Yes, I know you did. Maybe I should have listened.'

'So, what was different about last night?'

'It was about two o'clock. I was violently brought awake and sitting bolt upright in bed. I struggled and realised that I was not breathing.'

'That must have been terrifying.'

'I would be lying if I said otherwise. After a few seconds, I was able to start breathing again, but those few seconds seemed an eternity. It left me with my heart racing and a mild form of panic.'

'Well, I suppose you would panic. Only mild though?'

'It may have been a little more than that. I cannot begin to describe the level of pain that I felt in my chest from a simple act of getting breathing going again. I felt like someone had used a defibrillator on me.'

'In a sense they did, it was your own natural defibrillator.'

'How the hell can I ever sleep again knowing that this kind of thing is probably going on all night long? Most of the time I obviously manage to wake up and start breathing again without any knowledge that it has happened, but what will happen if it takes me like that again? Part of me also wonders though, if I brought it on myself because I now know about this illness.'

'And how do you feel now?'

'I have a pain in my left arm which I imagine must have been caused by the tensing up. I did strain my muscles rather a lot.'

'Is there some cure for this?'

'I'm not sure,' I reached for my coffee. 'I only have the information that I have found out on the internet, which is not necessarily the most reliable source.'

'Well, that's true.'

'From what I can gather, though, there is no "cure" as such. There is treatment, but there doesn't seem to be a way that it can be cured forever, at least not yet.'

'What's the treatment?'

'It would appear to be having to sleep with some kind of mask on your face that blows air down your throat all night long and keeps the airway open and prevents you from stopping breathing.'

'That doesn't sound a lot of fun.'

'No, I don't think it will be fun at all. I can't imagine how I am likely to get on with such a thing. Suddenly the concept of going to sleep is not as attractive a proposal as it perhaps once was.'

'How's the divorce going?'

'It's coming along. The first hearing has gone and she didn't turn up to say anything to stop things so I have that six weeks and a day period now before the Decree Absolute comes through.'

'And then you will be a single man once again?'

'Well, then I will be divorced once again. I won't be single as such as I'm with Ellie.'

'And going to marry her?'

'Well, time will tell on that one. I think I have rushed in rather too much in the past. I don't think it will hurt any to take it easy for a short period of time.'

***

I've said it before and I will say it again. You lucky people who don't suffer from insomnia or sleep disorders really don't know how fortunate you are. How can I explain to you the dread that comes from knowing that it is time to go to bed and the fear sets in about what will happen over the course of the night? If it is an alien concept to you, you that fall asleep and think nothing of it as your slumber starts as soon as you hit the pillow and then awaken in the morning refreshed and bright, ready for the next day, then how can you understand the difficulty and the trouble that has wracked me for all of my adult life?

I envy you if this is the position that you are in. I wish that I could be like you; I hope that you never have to suffer the terrors of the night that I have had to cope with for all the years of my life since I was about sixteen. It is often the case, though, that we take for granted what we don't know about. If you are lucky enough to be one of these people that falls asleep and has good quality sleep most nights then you probably don't realise that there is an alternative. It is the nature of things. You may very well be afflicted with something that I have no knowledge of and in turn you may say, 'Ha, only sleep problems, you should try and go through all of the problems that I have. Then you will know what it is like to have real problems.'

Everything is relative.

Twenty-Eight

My troubles were far from over, but what I didn't know was that they were about to start immediately after leaving my consultation with Dr Black.

We were shuffled off into a side room where the nurse that had caused me so much concern for her own health was waiting for me with a look of pure maliciousness all over her face. This was clearly the part that she really enjoyed about her job. It turned out that the purpose of this was so that I could be fitted for the mask that I would need and various other things so that they could work out the best CPAP machine to send me. It was at this point that I experienced the most terrifying thing that I have ever experienced in my life.

The nurse showed all the care and attention that you would expect from her appearance and having decided that I would be best suited to wear the mask that covered my mouth and nose, she clamped one to my face and turned on the CPAP machine that it was attached to. Immediately, I was unable to breathe. I struggled, but it was like having the air sucked out of me even though it was pushing air into me. I suppose it was similar to standing in a wind tunnel and not being able to catch your breath due to the force of the wind blowing at you. I assume it was like this, I don't really know, I have never stood in a wind tunnel.

Ellie later told me that there was a look of absolute panic and fear in my eyes the like of which she had never seen before.

'I can only assume that I suffered a panic attack from this, I'm not entirely sure; I've never been prone to panic attacks in my life up until this point.' It was coffee time once again and I was keeping Nat in the loop.

'Seems that you have the short, fat nurse to thank for that,' he replied whilst demolishing a doughnut.

'I pretty much knew then that getting used to this therapy was going to be a struggle.'

'Well, you can't be entirely certain of that. You've got to give it a go.'

'Of course, but I have learnt that I have a phobia for things being clamped rigidly over my face.'

'No gimp masks for you then.'

'There are up sides to everything then.'

'So it would seem.'

'The ultimate problem for me was that I felt that the air was being pushed into the mask quicker than I could actually breathe it in. I couldn't cope with it. This made me start to gag as I was unable to regulate the breathing.'

'Well, it does sound like a panic attack.'

'I always assumed that panic attacks were based on irrational fears. What is there that is irrational about not being able to breathe? Seems pretty rational to me.'

'So, what happens now?'

'A long struggle with getting used to something that is unnatural, I suppose.'

***

The 'machine' as I had started to come to call it, arrived a few days later. This was something that would ultimately become my nemesis.

My first night of trying to sleep with it gave me a good indication of what was to come over the months that were to follow. Each time in the night when I felt tired, I would fit the mask in the hope of a good sound sleep only to have the bloody machine wake me up. It would wake me up because I would become aware of the rush of air all of a sudden. It would wake me up because the mask would shift and I would have air shooting out into my eye, or in some other position that would cause discomfort. It was extremely off-putting and once I was awake then I was awake, with no chance of getting back to sleep. It was frankly hell. I struggled with it, but the more I struggled the more difficult it became to relax and sleep with it. Due to all of the warnings that the consultant had given me about sleeping without the machine, I tried my best to sleep only with it and if I couldn't sleep with it then I wouldn't sleep at all. This may have been a misinterpretation, but I had no desire to increase my chances of a heart attack if it were not necessary. The upshot was that I was sleeping in 20-minute segments and was more sleep deprived than I had ever been before. I was virtually a zombie during the day.

With the lack of sleep you would have thought that I would be so tired that it would become comparatively easy to sleep with the mask due to exhaustion; but this was not the case. I would make several attempts each night and all I would achieve was frustration. I was feeling tired and drained before I started having therapy, but now I was a thousand times worse and could barely function throughout the day.

I could only imagine how frustrating and difficult it must have been for Ellie as well. She had to try and sleep whilst I was next to her, frequently banging my head against the pillows in frustration. My inability to deal with the problem also made me feel that I was letting her down in some way. I felt that I should be able to cope with this, but I was not able to. I explained all of this to my father on one of my visits to him. Visits which I was now having to undertake on the bus or by getting lifts from other people as I was unable to drive there myself.

'It seems a difficult one,' he stated after I had moaned at him for what was probably a good twenty minutes.

'I'm left feeling tired, drained and frustrated. I actually feel worse than I did before I started the therapy.'

'But it's not something that you can stop doing.'

'No, it isn't. I now start to dread the idea of going to bed at night because I know that the little evil bastard mask and machine are there waiting for me.'

'It will probably work itself out in time.'

'Probably, but until it does it is going to be a very hard struggle.' The irony of the fact that I was sleeping less and feeling worse than I had done before I started the therapy that was supposed to make me feel better, had not escaped me in the least. 'It's a disaster, Dad.'

'I wouldn't go that far.'

'You don't have to try and sleep with this monstrosity strapped to your head every night.'

'True.'

'I can't stand the smell of the thing, the texture of it and the suffocating nature of it. It's like being tortured every time that I want to go to sleep.'

'I can't imagine.'

'I have to admire the medical profession that is able to come up with a treatment that is actually worse than the illness. I feel like I am banging my head against a wall. I'm trying to cope with it, but there is less that I'm actually able to do.'

'He did warn you to persevere with it though, didn't he?'

'Yes, he did. It doesn't stop me from wanting to smash the machine into a thousand pieces though.'

'Well if you did that, I would imagine that they would only present you with a rather large bill for the machine.'

'I've hardly slept at all. It's now virtually impossible for me to sleep with this damn mask and after everything the consultant told me about what could happen if I don't sleep with it, I'm terrified of just getting some normal sleep.'

'Surely you're not alone in this? There must be other people who have gone through all of this as well. What your consultant has to say about it is one thing, but he's not actually suffering from the condition himself is he?'

'No.'

'So perhaps it would be better if you were to speak to those who suffer from this illness, who have been suffering from it for years, so you can see what they have to say about it all. Their experiences have to be far more useful to you than struggling in the dark on your own.'

***

Actually, this wasn't such a bad idea and it was typical of my father to be able to come up with the solution to the problem of isolation for me.

The internet was a fantastic tool for teenagers (and adults) all over the world to be able to find the porn that they wanted so badly; but I also found that it was extremely useful for other things as well. You can pretty much find out anything you want to and after a few minutes of research, I was able to find a forum where people with sleep apnoea got together to talk about the situation that they were in and to exchange experiences. When it came to the internet, it seemed that you were never alone and there was always someone to talk to; I couldn't vouch for the level of intelligent conversation that you might get from them, but there was always someone to talk to, no matter what the time of day or night.

The general outlook wasn't brilliant and reassuring though. All I was told by the people that had gone through all of this before me was to keep at it and eventually it would become second nature to sleep with it on. I really couldn't see how this was going to happen. I was still at the stage of ripping the mask off after a few minutes of wearing and throwing it across the room. Sometimes it would only take seconds. They presumably made these things out of durable plastic so they survived being thrown across the room as frequently as I was throwing it. I tried to sleep, but the moment the mask went on, that was it; game over.

'I know it has only been a couple of weeks,' I told Nat.

'But you're still having trouble coping with it?'

'If it's meant to be getting better, it's actually getting worse. It's getting worse and I feel trapped without a way out of it. I feel that I've gone from a sleep disorder that made me feel tired to a treatment that makes me feel a thousand times worse. I feel that I'm starting to suffer from the symptoms of sleep deprivation now.'

'Weren't you before?'

'Not as far as I was aware.'

'How is Ellie coping with it all?

'She is stressed out, but tries not to show it. She's probably only sleeping a little more than I am.'

'It must be difficult for you both.'

'It is. In our own ways.'

'So, are you going to stick with it?'

'What choice do I have? Aside from the obvious health issues were I to quit, if I were to give it up, the DVLA would have my licence off of me in a heartbeat and I would never be able to drive again; or if I were it would not be until I had mastered the use of the machine and then it would probably be very difficult to get my licence back.'

'So, there's no turning back now?'

'No, there's no turning back now. I am bound upon a wheel of fire.'

Nat looked at me in a strange way. '*King Lear,*' I said.

'Oh.'

'It was particularly difficult to sleep last night.'

'Any reason why?'

'Today my solicitor is applying for the Decree Absolute.'

'Why should that worry you?'

'Last minute fears that she will change her mind and decide to cause issues for me at the final hurdle. Anything to delay the inevitable and to make my life a little bit more miserable than it already is.'

'Do you think that likely?'

'I sincerely hope not.'

'So, they were applying today?'

'Yes.'

'So, in theory you might be divorced already and just not know it yet?'

'Possibly, although I think it will still take a few days before it's finalised. It just means that if today goes off without any objections from her then she has had her time and there is nothing that she can do to prevent the divorce from going through,'

Nat raised his coffee cup.

'Well, here's to divorce then.'

***

Things went on like this for a few more weeks. I was prepared to suffer in silence, well that is not entirely true as Nat and my father would undoubtedly tell you that I was anything but silent about all of this. I am sure that Ellie would tell you the same.

What I mean is, I was not making a fuss to the right people. It was Ellie that eventually gave me a kick up the arse and told me to contact the people who made the CPAP machine and talk to them. She probably did this out of desperation at not being able to get to sleep herself. I eventually took on what she said and contacted them. The upshot of this was that they said they would send me a humidifier to fit to the actual CPAP machine which might make it slightly easier to cope with and to prevent me from waking with a dry throat from using it; not that I was probably using it enough to be a judge of that. They also said that they would speak to my consultant about the possibility of temporarily lowering the air pressure so that it was a little more comfortable and easier for me to try and get off to sleep with.

One simple, brief telephone call and a couple of potential issues were resolved. Ellie rolled her eyes at me. I would imagine that by now she was getting used to me and my ways. I was a right pain in the arse at this period in my life (if I were not actually a pain in the arse at all other points as well); it amazes me that she put up with me. Don't forget that although our relationship was one that had progressed quickly, we were still in relatively early days. I can't imagine that there was much romance for her in having to go to bed with a dysfunctional Darth Vader each night.

The thought occurred to me that I was lucky that this happened when it did. I suddenly imagined what it would be like trying to date someone whilst having to strap a lump of plastic to your face each time you want to go to sleep. You have to admit that it is not the sexiest of images that a potential partner would want to see. It was rather a bizarre case as in most cases you would need to have a partner to be able to be diagnosed with sleep apnoea, as they would be the ones most likely to notice that you were not breathing. If you then went and had another partner you would have the difficulty of introducing the CPAP machine into your romantic adventures.

'You had your worst night of sleep I've seen so far last night,' she told me at breakfast one morning.

'Oh?' I had no recollection of the night being any different to any of the other nights that I had suffered through. 'How so?'

'You were restless; even more so than you normally are. You were muttering and moaning for most of the night. You couldn't seem to settle.'

I had no memory of this at all. I was sleeping primarily without the mask at this stage as it was impossible for me to make it for more than about half an hour without ripping it off out of sheer desperation. I know that it was potentially extremely dangerous for me to sleep without the mask, but it was either a choice of sleeping without it and risk a heart attack, or stay awake and die from the insanity that would eventually set in from not sleeping for more than half an hour at a time. Difficult choice really. Screwed either way was how I looked at it.

The simplest of tasks would wipe me out. Going to the local supermarket to get the weekly shopping was about the equivalent for me of running a marathon and I would just want to drop dead when I got home. My eyes were so tired that my face hurt. Even my eyeballs would hurt, I was that tired. You ever been that tired? My legs still hurt like crazy and from time to time the same thing would apply to my wrists. It will come as no surprise to anyone, therefore, that I was on the verge of a physical collapse.

It was becoming painfully obvious that if I was unable to function in a normal capacity then something needed to be done. As you will be aware I had never been a fan of going to see doctors, but I returned once again to my GP with the intention of seeing if there were some way that I could collect points on each visit that would save me air miles. I went to speak to my doctor about my general condition and the level of feeling hopeless that I was in.

'Would you say that you are depressed?'

'No, I would say that I am frustrated, irritated, frequently annoyed and above all incredibly tired, but I would not say that I was depressed no.'

He seemed to be disappointed by this, one might almost say depressed by it. It seems to me that depression is a label which is thrown around rather easily these days. It is a medical condition that I do not in any way intend to put down or belittle. Depression is a serious thing, but what strikes me as strange is that everyone seems to suffer from it now. For God sake teenagers suffer from depression now and half the university students that I teach. Most of them are not depressed, they are just typical teenagers doing the usual thing that they get up to. There are genuine cases, but most of them just need a good kick up the arse. What is the saying: 'depression is anger without the enthusiasm'?

Previous generations never had the problem with depression, so why do we? The answer is simple. The invention of the motorcar. We drive everywhere now, even on the smallest of journeys whereas our ancestors would think nothing of walking 10, 15, 20 miles to go to work and then back again. You don't believe me? Read Thomas Hardy. We walked everywhere, that is the key. We got exercise and we got fresh air, we were therefore physically fit and felt well within ourselves.

I explained to my doctor exactly what the problem was; namely, my feeling of general panic when I wore the mask, the inability to settle with it and in general this leading to all the consequences. After much agonising and debate, he decided that I wasn't fit to go to work as even though my job was not physically demanding, I was likely to either fall asleep at my desk or due to lack of sleep go mad and kill an undergraduate (I tried to point out that there was not necessarily anything wrong in killing undergraduates, but he seemed to disagree). He therefore signed me off work for a few weeks to enable me some time to try and adjust to my life-changing condition.

In order to try and make this vaguely a possibility, he prescribed me some medication. Two doses, in fact. The first, a painkiller which might actually help take the pain away from my legs which was due to the lack of oxygen circulation and which in turn made it difficult to settle in bed because they were aching too much. He also prescribed some pills to help me relax and calm me down with the intention of

311

being able to ward off the panic attacks. I have always been sceptical when it comes to pills, but by now if he told me I had to dance naked in the moonlight and sacrifice a wild animal to the bloodlust of some pagan deity, then I can't say that I wouldn't have gone rushing off to the woods with a knife in my hand that very moment. Sleep deprivation does strange things to your judgement which is why so many countries have used it as a form of torture.

I stood up and held the prescription in my hand as tightly as if he had given me a sheet of paper on which he had scribbled directions to the last resting place of the Holy Grail – I don't believe in it, but finding it would certainly have made my name.

'Are you sure you're not depressed?' he said to me with a longing look as I went to open the door.

'I'm afraid not, doctor.'

'Oh, well, never mind.'

***

'I feel terrible,' Ellie said to me one evening whilst we were sitting on the couch at home watching some film or other and I struggled to stay awake without making it too obvious that I could barely keep my eyes open.

'Why?'

'Because it's all my fault.'

'What's your fault?'

'All of this.'

'What?'

'I was the one who first told you that there was something wrong, that you were not breathing.'

'So?'

'So, I was then the one that insisted that you go and see a doctor.'

'Yes?'

'So, because of me, you now can't drive and you are worse off medically than you were before.'

'Babe,' I came across to her and took her hands in my mine. 'All of that is true.'

'You see!' She virtually wailed this and it probably wasn't the line that I should have opened with.

'But you're missing the point. You brought to my attention a life-threatening illness. If you hadn't have done that, then the chances are that at some point in the future, I would have had a heart attack in my sleep. If anything is true here then the truth is that you have saved my life.'

She looked up at me.

'As a matter of fact, the more I think about it, then it's possible to say that you have saved my life on a number of different levels.'

This was true. After the delights of being married to Susie and Bea, Ellie was like a breath of fresh air. Aside from the issues that I was having from a medical point of view, my life couldn't have been any better. For the first time in my life I felt that I actually had a woman who loved me and actually, genuinely cared about me. Everyone else was obviously working on their own agenda. The only problem that concerned me now was: was I worthy of her?

'Ellie, you have been wonderful to me and I can't imagine life without you.'

'You really think so?'

'Yes, I do, and I rather think you might feel the same about me.' Hopefully this didn't come across as too arrogant.

'That's true.'

'So, will you marry me?'

Now I should point out at this stage that I hadn't planned this. There was no romantic music playing or candlelight flicking across the room whilst we drank wine and enjoyed each other's company. Instead, it was bland and ordinary. A standard, cold day with grey skies and drizzling rain on the windows. If I had planned to ask her to marry me, I would like to think that I would have planned it better. It was something that just came out all of a sudden with no preparation. It was as if I had no control over my brain and my mouth. They seemed to be doing their own thing and had decided that they wanted to marry Ellie and that was an end of it.

Sometimes it is really funny how your life can move off in a direction that you hadn't really thought about.

Twenty-Nine

'Is it your intention to marry everyone?'

'No, Jerry, it isn't.' He could barely contain his laughter when I had told him what had happened.

'I suppose it would do no good to say that you never learn?'

'That seems a bit harsh. At any rate, we may be engaged, but our plan is to have a longer engagement than I have had previously.'

'In case you change your mind?'

'No. It's because we don't want to rush things.'

'Well, that would be a novelty.'

'Wouldn't it just?'

'In all seriousness, Max, are you absolutely sure you know what you're doing?'

'Yes.'

'Only you're not yet forty and this will have been the third time you have been married.'

'I was aware of that. Ellie is different though.'

'You thought they were all different.'

'Yes, but Ellie is the only one that seems to actually care about me and it feels so much different to previous relationships.'

'Well, far be it from me to stand in the way of things if you truly are happy.'

'The happiest I have been in a long time, Jerry.'

'Then I suppose you will have to go for it then.'

In the back of my head, I wondered if Jerry was any closer to finding the one that he would end up being happy with. He never seemed to talk about anyone that he might be dating and for all I knew he didn't date at all. Everyone deserves some happiness.

***

'You don't look that bad,' remarked Nat when we met up for coffee.

'That is one of the problems with having a medical condition that is not visible to the naked eye. If I had a broken leg or something, then everyone would have something to relate to; instead, they can't see anything wrong so assume you're making it up or are a freeloader in some way.'

'I never said that.'

'No, but it's what some people are thinking.'

'Well, if they are thinking that then they probably are not worth bothering about. How are you feeling?'

'Rough. I'm only managing about half an hour of sleep at any given moment. Normally I get half an hour with the mask, and for whatever reason it then wakes me up and for the next two hours or so I can't get back to sleep. When I do, the whole cycle repeats itself. It's extremely irritating.'

'I imagine that it must be.'

'The pills the doctor gave me seem to be slowly helping. The other night I managed an hour and a half before I eventually gave in.'

'That's good.'

'And then I'm back to half hours again. It seems I take a step forward and then two back. At that rate, the target level of five to six hours of sleep a night seems a long way off.'

'It might be a long way off, but you will get there.'

'I hope so. It seems impossible at the moment. Most days I get a headache all day long because of it. It makes me feel sick and tired.'

'So how long do you think you will be off work?'

'I don't know. I have no idea how long this is going to take for me to reach a level that they think successful. I can't drive until I hit the right level and I suppose that is the benchmark to set the standard of knowing how well I can function in normal life once again.'

Nat nodded his head slowly as he listened to what I had to say. 'I have tried a different strategy to see if it helps.'

'What's that?'

'I have moved the machine out of the bedroom and placed it next to an armchair in the living room. I then put a film on, recline in the chair and try and snooze with the mask on.'

'How do you think that will help?'

'It takes the pressure away from the bedroom and feeling obligated to lie in bed suffering. I am not entirely sure that my medical team would approve as it does mean I'm not sleeping in the bedroom with the mask at all.'

'Isn't that meant to be risky?'

'Yes, but I figure that if it helps me build up tolerance to the mask, it's worth it.'

'And is it?'

'Well, it was whilst in the chair that I got the hour and a half of sleep the other day, so it's proving to be more responsive than it was just trying to put up with it in bed.'

'Little steps.'

'It seems to be the only way. The progression has been slow though, so my doc has agreed to extend my sick leave.'

'I bet that will go down well with the management.'

'To be honest, they are the least of my concerns at the moment.'

***

The idea of moving it from the bedroom to the living room was to try and get used to the idea of wearing the mask. All the online forums that I had engaged with seemed to suggest that there would come a time when wearing the mask would become like second nature. Indeed, there were a number of people who said that after all the years of wearing it, they were now unable to sleep without it. I found this claim to be almost beyond belief, I could hardly imagine a time when I would feel that I couldn't sleep unless this hunk of plastic was attached to my face. At a push, I could imagine that there would come a time when I would learn how to sleep with it, but to become so used to it that I could never sleep again without it seemed to be something that was pure imagination. However, if history has taught us anything, it has surely shown us that when they put their mind to it, humanity is capable of almost anything. Granted, for most of the time they are too lazy to try, but the potential is there. Let's be honest about this and put all those conspiracy theories to one side, shall we? Aliens did not build the pyramids or Stonehenge. They were built by humans because when we want to be, we can be quite clever. If we could do all of that then I am pretty sure that I should be able to sleep with a lump of plastic on my face, otherwise I shall feel like I am letting the side down.

I know that I should really have moved the machine back to the bedroom, but I was afraid that if I put it in the bedroom before I had mastered the panic attacks and learnt how to cope with it, then it would be a never-ending battle to try and sleep with it. Most of the time I really didn't know what to do for the best. I suppose the medical help could have been there if I had asked for it, but I felt like the evil fat nurse had packed me off into the wilderness with an evil machine that seemed to have it in for me and as far as they were concerned, I should just get on with it. They probably couldn't understand why I was being such a baby over it all.

After another week, I moved the machine back to the bedroom with very limited success.

'It's just impossible to get comfortable in it,' I moaned to Ellie, who by this time was probably becoming used to me moaning about this machine.

I am not a naturally calm sleeper at the best of times and I can often have a restless night of sleep as I try and find the most comfortable spot to settle into. When you add the wearing of a huge mask and hose to that then it is not something that is likely to end well.

The hose; it occurs to me I have not mentioned this. It is something that went from the mask to the machine that carried the air down it. There was sufficient length of hose so that you could move about and turn over in the night without bringing the machine flying

317

with you. It was also soft so that despite waking up from time to time with the entire thing wrapped around my neck from where I had tossed and turned, it was not possible to strangle yourself with it. At least I hoped that it wasn't; that was the theory at least.

Oh, and while we are on the subject, that is another thing that I would like to clear up. When I explain all of this to people they assumed that I am wearing some kind of mask linked up to an oxygen tank. It isn't oxygen from a tank that is being blown down my throat - the machine sucks air from the room and blows that down my throat, with a little more intensity to ensure that the throat doesn't close up.

It probably became very frustrating for Ellie and I was sure that she probably reached a stage where she wondered why I just didn't get on with it. Of course, I wanted to be able to drive again and sleep without feeling terrified, but the machine just turned bedtime into a horror story. No matter what happened, I just could not get comfortable with it. It simply wasn't a natural way of sleeping and I simply couldn't imagine sleeping with it. I had such difficulty with my sleeping before that, all of this was making it impossible for me.

'Perhaps it would be a good idea to go back to the hospital,' replied Ellie.

'I was thinking something similar myself.' I didn't particularly want to see the evil nurse once again, but needs must. 'Perhaps they can try me with other masks or something.'

'I understand that in America they are pioneering techniques to put a pacemaker into the brain that somehow controls the apnoeas.'

'I can't imagine that brain surgery is a good idea. Besides, a pacemaker in the brain, how the hell does that work?'

'I don't know.'

'All I do know is that doing nothing is not an option. Aside from the heart attack, stroke and potential brain damage that can result in not being treated I also see now that they are linking cancer to it.'

'Yes, but to be fair, they link cancer to everything. There is hardly a week that goes by when they don't announce that certain products will protect you from cancer or cause cancer. I think the bottom line is that they simply don't know, but don't want to admit it.'

That sounded about right. People like to think of the medical profession as infallible, but the truth is that there are times when they don't have any more of a clue as to what is going on than the rest of us do. They just don't like us to know that. After all, they did invent the word *idiopathic*. The word comes from the Greek word *idios* meaning 'one's own' and *pathos* meaning suffering or, well pathos. This put together then means a disease of its own kind, which is pretty much as meaningless as it sounds. In other words, they don't know what it is. Rather than say, 'we don't know what is wrong with you' they will say 'your condition is idiopathic'. A better definition for the word would be idiopathic as in 'idiot' because they don't know.

At least it would be more honest.

***

'I'm trying my best with the mask, but I am coming to the conclusion that perhaps my best is just not good enough,' I said to my father about a month after having gone sick.

'I'm sure that isn't true, Max,' he said as he put *David Copperfield* to one side and gave me his full attention.

'At the moment, I seem to find it easier to try it during the day. I still can't manage it at night.'

'Why do you think there is a difference?'

'Between day and night?'

'Yes.'

'I don't know. I would imagine it's psychological in some way. Something to do with the dark demons of the night coming out and causing problems that don't seem to exist during the day.'

'Yes, that would be psychological.'

'Perhaps if I were to be more successful and confident with it during the day, it might take to being used at night. I can only try.'

'And now you are engaged to be married once again.'

'Once again.'

'Do you get a discount on the third wedding?'

'Don't you start; I have had enough with Jerry taking the piss. He finds it highly amusing.'

'I'm sure he cares about you in his own way and is just worried that you seem to be going through wives in the way that some people go through cars.'

'Well, one of them is more expensive than the other.'

'I won't ask which.'

'Probably not a good idea.'

'I'm not going to ask if you think you are doing the right thing. I think I know by now that you will always do what you think is right.'

'I have made a few mistakes along the way, but I am sure about this.'

'Making mistakes are all part of what life is about. Anyone who thinks that they have gone through life without making mistakes either hasn't lived properly or is supremely arrogant in their attitude and worth ignoring. Do you really view your previous marriages as a mistake though?'

'Perhaps mistake is not the best word. Misguided may be more apt.'

'But you learn something from everything that you do. If you had not married Susie and Bea, then you would not have arrived at the place where you are now.'

'And I wouldn't have met Ellie.'

'At least not the way that you have. So, whatever you do, every infinitesimal decision that you make has a knock-on effect to the way that you are now and changes the path that you are walking down. Change one of those decisions in the past and it is like pulling out a thread that may unravel the entire thing.'

'That would seem very philosophical.'

'Well, there are elements of your Mother that have rubbed off on me over the years.'

'So, you think I should be grateful for what I've got.'

'I think you have to accept the fact that decisions you have made in the past have made you the person that you are today. Nothing can change that now. Don't wish away the bad things that have happened, they are part of the good things that happen as well.'

'That would make sense.'

'You never mentioned if the divorce came through.'

'Yes, sorry, with everything else that's going on I must have forgotten to tell you.'

'Well, you have had a lot on your mind. How do you feel about the divorce?'

'Relief. That would be the word that I most associate with it. Relief that it's over and that she is now unable to interfere with my life or do anything to prevent me from being happy. Nor can she prevent Ellie and myself from getting married. It makes me feel like a great weight has been lifted from my mind.'

'I can imagine that must feel good.'

'It feels fantastic, if I'm honest. It took me far too long to realise how miserable I was.'

'But the important thing is that you did realise that you were miserable *and,* you then did something about it.'

I nodded and thought about this for a moment. How many couples are there out there that know in the bottom of their hearts that their relationship is wrong and that they are, in essence, going nowhere? How do these people cope going through their lives being unhappy, but for whatever reason not doing anything about it? Not doing anything about it for the sake of the children that they may have. Not doing anything about it because they are so lonely that they would rather be with someone who makes them miserable than to be alone.

'Have you been back to the hospital?'

'Yes, we had a discussion about the problems that I have been having and they gave me a new mask.'

'What's different about it?'

'More lightweight, less cumbersome and to be honest, something that's a great deal easier to get on with.'

'Why couldn't they have given you that one to start with?'

'Apparently, it's a new mask that has only been available for a short period of time. It wasn't about when I was initially sent the kit.

As soon as I put the thing on for the first time it made such a difference and was a relief. I'm confident that it will make a difference for me.'

'Well, let's hope so.'

'Ellie has been wonderful throughout all of this.'

'Good.'

'She has been unlike anybody that I have ever been with before. If I'm honest and without wishing to cause embarrassment, I feel as if she is the first woman that I have been with that truly loves me and cares about me.'

'I felt the same about your Mother. There was a connection between us that was unlike anything I could have imagined. And there is not a day that goes by that I don't miss her.'

Sometimes we don't think of our parents as having the same emotions as we have had. We seem to think with each new generation that we invented it all. Maybe they felt the same about their parents.

***

As it happened, I did not get on as famously well with the mask as I had hoped that I was going to. It was not all that long before the frustration set in once again. I would go to bed tired and drained, ready for a good night of steady sleep only to be woken up by the air pressure. That was assuming, of course, that I had been able to get to sleep in the first place. There were other times that I would go to bed, put the mask on and then within seconds, the air pressure would have me wide awake again before I had even had the chance to nod off.

The new mask was much of an improvement on the first, but the bottom line for me was that it was just not working out and the bloody thing was not happening. I cannot begin to express how frustrating this was.

'I can't get to sleep with it on,' I moaned at Ellie one night, although I'm not entirely sure why it was that I was telling her this as she must have known by now. I was actually impressed with her level of tolerance for me now that I look back on it. 'When I do manage to get to sleep, I'm at the point of exhaustion. I'm drained throughout the day and can barely make my way through.'

'I know,' she said somehow managing to find sympathy for me in her voice rather than just expecting me to get on with it.

'The entire thing is a bloody nightmare, Ellie. I feel trapped. I wish I could just call the whole thing off and tell them I'm feeling much better now, thank you very much, and I don't need this bloody thing.'

'But you can't.'

'No, I can't. They've got me by the bloody balls now. If treatment is rejected or fails they can just go and tell the DVLA and I could lose my driving licence forever. The whole thing is a damn, bloody mess.'

I feel guilty when I look back at it that I was voicing all this to her who already felt guilty herself for putting me in this situation, or so she viewed it. Mouthing off and complaining couldn't have made it any easier for her. I am surprised she stayed with me, to be honest.

It was difficult for me, though, all of the time. I was told to just get on with it, usually by people who simply do not have a clue what they are talking about. 'This mask will *never* work. It's simply too intrusive.'

'It will work, baby,' Ellie tried her best to comfort me. 'It's just that it's going to take a bit of time, that's all.'

I wasn't entirely sure how much time I had. Things certainly couldn't continue for too much longer the way that they had been going. Four months into the treatment now and two months into my sick leave and things were really not working out for me at all. It seemed to me that the treatment had missed out on the point of what it was that it was supposed to be doing.

My doctor was still reluctant for me to return to work because of the fact that he could see easily enough that it was impossible to function in anything like a normal capacity throughout the day whilst struggling with this condition. Work, however, did not seem to be so sympathetic.

'Just be aware that there are rumblings,' Nat said to me on one of our regular meet ups which I still tried to do even though I was not back at work myself. Naturally, this was difficult because when you were off sick people didn't expect you to be able to go and have coffee, eat or in any way appear to be normal. They expected you to be in bed all of the time, on the brink of death. Obviously, if you were seen drinking coffee in a café then you must be fine.

'What kind of rumblings?'

'I don't think they appreciate you being off sick so long and because they have never heard of sleep apnoea they just can't get their heads around why it is that you are not at work.'

'They've got it in for me, haven't they? Just because of Bea and the divorce. They feel that they have lost some potential money even though she wasn't giving them any since that first night when we met.' She hadn't given me any since then either, but that was a different story.

Thirty

Things progressed like this for some time if I am honest. I would make some small steps of progress building it up until I was at a stage where I was sleeping for two and a half hours. I would have other issues as well, such as the fact that I was also suffering from a toothache around this time. Tooth pain is one of the worst pains that I can imagine, but then I have never given birth. It is a unique kind of pain, though, and anyone who has suffered from it will know exactly where I am coming from. Imagine what it is like having tooth pain with a mask blowing cold air into your mouth, aggravating the pain by working its way into the crack of the tooth. Imagine then trying to sleep with all of that going on.

I could never wake up late in the morning and dash out quickly without washing and seeing to my appearance. Sleeping with the mask would leave red marks on my forehead where the rest would sit and marks around the mouth and nose where the mask would sit and rub. Furthermore, there would be two lines in the hair on either side of my head where the straps went through which would give me a haircut vaguely reminiscent of Henry V's haircut (google it) or a feeble attempt to look trendy with lines cut into your hair, something that my generation really shouldn't go in for.

From this point, though, the progress was very steady and I was pleased to see that there actually was some progress after four months of being in limbo. From two and a half hours of sleep a night, I progressed to four hours sleep a night. I found this staggeringly successful and the kind of achievement I cannot begin to communicate.

'If I'm able to keep things up at this level then I really think that I'm on the road to recovery,' I told Ellie with enthusiasm.

'Well, just take it steady and don't push yourself too hard. It's good progress so far and there should be no reason why it shouldn't continue.'

'Time will tell. I'm actually starting to feel less tired so it obviously has the ability to work.'

'Fingers crossed then.'

And from here there was a sudden leap. One night without any warning at all, I slept for seven hours straight without interruption. I had no idea why it was that things seemed to be working all of a sudden after so many weeks of failure. Nothing had changed over the last few days; it had just suddenly clicked into place with no real obvious reason. To me, it was a miracle having gone from the half hour sleep that I had previously undergone; making the gigantic leap to seven hours was the difference between walking up a slope and climbing Everest. Many people could never understand the excitement that seven hours of sleep caused me.

I was feeling pretty pleased with myself about this which probably cost me, as a couple of nights later I plummeted down to four hours once again; however, I had to admit that even four hours was a damn sight better than half an hour. I think the problem on this particular night was simply not being able to get comfortable with the mask, no matter what it was that I did. It is inevitable that on the path to the recovery there will be, from time to time, the odd setback thrown into the works. I just had to remind myself to try and remain positive about it all.

'You also have to take into consideration,' said Nat when I had told him all of this, 'that you now have to undo years of damage that has been caused by having this condition and never knowing about it.'

'That's a lot of time for a lot of damage to be caused.'

'I don't suppose there's any way that they can tell you how long you have had this?'

'My own personal guess would be that I would put it in my mid-twenties. It was round about then that I started to feel shit and achy a lot.'

'I suppose you have to be thankful that they figured it out when they did.'

'Well, it's Ellie who must take the credit for that, and Ellie alone.'

The issue that few people, particular my bosses, could understand was that sleep deprivation takes a long time to recover from. One doctor I spoke to stated that if you cannot sleep and are awake for one night, it will take at least twice that long to recover from not sleeping. Sleep debt adds up very quickly. I had one hell of a sleep debt that I was having to wade through which could possibly never be recovered from. It could easily take the rest of my life to recover.

'When will you return to work?'

'I don't know yet. My doc wants me to stay off longer as he wants to ensure that we get some kind of reasonable stability with the usage. Plus, of course, he then wants to make sure that my recuperation is complete before rushing back to work too early.'

'Seems like they are being sensible for once.'

'Despite some good runs of the mask, there are still moments when I feel pretty terrible.'

'I spoke to Reynolds.' Reynolds was my supervisor and a bigger arsehole I have yet to meet.

'Oh?'

'He doesn't really get it, does he?'

'You may have to narrow the field for a bit there. He doesn't understand a lot of things. What is it in particular that he doesn't understand?'

'He doesn't understand why it is that you are off sick for such a long time for, as he puts it "being tired". He basically doesn't get it at all. His advice is that you should just get a good night's sleep and everything will be fine.' This is the kind of dumb-ass opinion that I was having to fight against.

'I have had a little communication with him myself. Not a great deal. I tried to explain why it was that I was off and what sleep apnoea is, but he seems to confuse it with narcolepsy.'

'Why doesn't that surprise me?'

'He also suggested that the Board would take a very dim view of the idea of a lecturer who is off for so long and, therefore incapable of performing his job.'

'What does that mean?'

'I think it was a veiled threat of dismissal.'

'He can't be serious.'

'He was very serious. He said the entire thing was considered to be very unsatisfactory.'

'But he does know that you are signed off by a doctor who has taken the advice of a professor of respiratory medicine who has diagnosed you with a lifelong medical condition that's life-threatening?'

'Well, he does now; but I'm not entirely convinced that it makes the slightest bit of difference to him. You see, the thing is that he simply doesn't understand what sleep apnoea is. He's never heard of it. Because it's not something like cancer, he diminishes the seriousness of it.'

'Let's be honest, if you had cancer he wouldn't have had the balls to suggest dismissing you because you're ill.'

'Of course not. If he had, then I wouldn't have known whether to go to a solicitor first or *The Daily Mail*. Either way it would have destroyed his career, and wouldn't have done a huge amount for the university either.'

'So, what happened when you had this discussion?'

'I explained to him the way that things were and that any constructive dismissal would result in me seeking legal advice for breach of the Disability Discrimination Act.'

'Really?'

'Apparently, it's an illness that is covered by it.'

'Doesn't seem to be anything that he can do then.'

'Whatever annoyance that he may feel is nothing compared to the annoyance that I have felt over the last few months.'

'Well the man's a prick; we can't expect anything else from him really.'

My supervisor was a prick. His singular lack of understanding for my condition had made my blood boil. Once again it was a case that because I didn't look physically ill, he felt that I was faking it. No doubt if I had been covered in bruises and with the odd leg in plaster then he might had believed that I was not fit for work.

I imagined that it must be akin to the way that someone with a mental illness feels. When you have a mental illness, whether it be depression or a more acute illness that means you cannot function in society at all without being a risk to yourself or others, you suffer, but there is nothing that is visible to the outsider. Inside, you are as fit to go about life as someone who has been beaten severely and is bedridden, but because nobody can see it they are convinced that there is nothing wrong with you. This is a prejudice that has existed for a very long time and if there were one thing that I would like to change from my time on this planet, it would be the ability for people to understand that you can be seriously ill without looking like you are.

Unfortunately, my supervisor didn't have the intelligence to realise that by making threats about my career, he had put my recovery process in jeopardy. All of this had started to worry me and get me down; it would place me in a black mood and then I would have more difficulty in sleeping than I would have had with or without the mask.

'Are you looking forward to eventually coming back to work?' Nat asked, breaking my thoughts.

'I'm not entirely sure. Before he threatened me with that I would have said, yes; but now I feel as if my soul has somehow gone out of it. I have lost my faith in the system. I remember one of my early role models telling me to work hard and have faith in the system and it would all work out well. He was wrong. You can work hard and the system will just run right over the top of you and not give a toss about you.'

'Are you not bored after being off for so long, though?'

'Funny you should say that. No.'

'No?'

'Not in the least. Some people go on about how boring it would be to be at home all day and how they would have nothing to do and become bored. I feel sorry for them if that is the case as it means that all they have in life is their work. They have no social, private or home life, call it what you will. One day they will retire as we all must, and the very next day nobody will give a damn about them or what they did; it will mean nothing. All the years that they poured into whatever it was that they did will be meaningless. I want to find my meaning.'

'You don't get bored?'

'There is always something to do if you only want to find it. Boredom is a disease. Perhaps most of the time when we say we are bored we are actually just saying that we are too lazy to find something to do.'

***

'This Ellie is someone that I think is good for you,' said Jerry.

'What makes you say that?'

'You seem far happier than I have seen you in a long time.'

'I am happier than I have been for a long time.'

'She's good for you then. You should marry her.'

'I'm going to.'

'Good.'

'What about you, Jerry?'

'What about me?'

'Is there someone who makes you happy?'

'Oh well, there are some on and off, but I have never been one for long term relationships.'

'Any particular reason?'

'I just don't see myself as the settling down kind of person, or maybe I just haven't met the right man yet.'

'I hope you do.'

'Do you?'

'Of course, I do, Jerry.'

'Why?'

'Because you're my brother. I love you and I think you deserve to be as happy as anyone else, but as particularly as happy as I am.'

'Bless. So how is the treatment going?'

'It seems to be going well; my weekly average usage is about six and a half hours at the moment.'

'Is that good?'

'Pretty good considering that last month it was an average of about thirty minutes per week. I won't deny that at times it has been a bloody effort. Does mean that I can start driving again soon. Few people would probably realise what I had to go through to get that result; well, not just me, Ellie as well.'

'I can imagine.'

'In the hope of not being too premature, I think things have settled down a bit now and we seem to be well on the road to recovery.'

'No issues?'

'Well, there are a few, but that is only to be expected.'

'Like?'

'Well, there are still environmental factors that make sleeping with the mask unsuccessful.'

'For instance?'

'For instance, the concept of trying to sleep during a heat wave with a lump of plastic strapped to your face.'

'I can see how that might present a problem in trying to get to sleep.'

'Then there are things like trying to sleep with it whilst you are suffering from a cold.'

'That sounds like it has the potential to be disgusting,' said Jerry, grimacing.

***

And I suppose that is that really. Is this the end of my story? No, my story is still going on, but I have to draw a line under this at some point, and this is probably going to be as good as any other place. So, what is it all about? What have I learnt?

Well, that's a good question. I have learnt a number of things. What is it that motivated me to write this story and share it with you? I suppose it is because a lot of people don't understand what sleep apnoea is. People are quick to criticise what they don't understand and are quick to dismiss you because you don't have physical symptoms. This is wrong. I have never understood why some people are always so quick to judge other people, but so many people seem to make a hobby of it. I suppose, if you have read this, I am hoping that you now understand sleep apnoea a little better than you perhaps might have done before you started reading my story. If you suffer from it yourself, then I hope you take away the fact that you are not alone out there.

Sleep apnoea is a killer. It can kill the person who suffers from it, we have already discussed heart attacks, strokes and brain damage; how many people who are reported as having 'died peacefully in their sleep' have died as a result of a heart attack or a stroke due to not breathing because of sleep apnoea? We have discussed all this but what we have not discussed is when sleep apnoea turns you into a murderer. You've seen it on the news. Train crashes, car crashes and so on, all caused because the driver has fallen asleep. Not all of these drivers will be suffering from sleep apnoea, of course. Some will just be tired for whatever reason, because of lifestyle choices perhaps? But there will be incidents caused by a driver who doesn't know that they are suffering from sleep apnoea and are therefore juggling with their lives and the lives of other people due to sleep deprivation.

Think about it. Have you ever been driving a car and felt tired and not known why you feel tired? Have you ever dozed off for a few seconds whilst at the wheel and it isn't because of the fact that you have been up all night? It might happen when you are driving to work in the morning when there is no reason why you should be feeling tired after a night of sleep. You might not have sleep apnoea, but you might. Think about it. Get it checked out.

The only other thing I would ask from you is to pass it on. Let others know the story and the danger that can happen when you are asleep. Pass it on so that awareness levels raise and more people join the campaign. One day, perhaps a major celebrity will have the courage to stand up and say, 'I suffer from sleep apnoea.' Once they get past the idea that it is not a 'sexy' illness to have, then maybe they will. Although there is the possibility that it will then become counterproductive; it will become 'trendy' to have a CPAP machine and it will make a mockery of the entire thing.

I have had issues and they still impact on my everyday life. I have to get permission to take the CPAP machine on an aeroplane. I have to sleep with this everywhere I go, which is something that some people just don't seem to be able to get their head around. It has to be used everywhere that you want to sleep. Hopefully, this means that I will never be able to sleep in a tent again. It does mean I will never be able to climb Everest or trek across the South Pole. Oh, well.

It isn't all linked to weight, which is what a lot of people will try and fob it off with. Weight has an impact but it is just as often as not genetic and weight is a by-product of sleep apnoea. You are so tired because you have no energy from lack of sleep so you require more sugar to give you energy and because you are not so active because of the pain in your legs and the general tiredness, you are not exercising it off.

Why do I tell you all this, over and over again? Imagine it is you or if it helps (as we all have a habit of ignoring our own problems), imagine that it is someone that you love that you suspect has sleep apnoea. Imagine that they run the risk of a premature death. Chances are that they have no knowledge that they have it, but you might be the one to tell them. So, tell them. Save their life in the same way that Ellie saved my life. They might not thank you in the short term when they are struggling with the mask and unable to drive, but they will realise soon enough that you have saved them.

***

And where am I now?

I am now in my 40s, I have come to terms with my mask and my condition. I have good days and I have bad days, but there are more good days than there are bad ones. Sleep apnoea has caused me to have high blood pressure and I have to take tablets for that daily and am resigned to the fact that I will probably be on these for the rest of my life as well as the CPAP machine. Tests are still ongoing to see if there are issues that have been caused to my heart over all the years that I was untreated. I have palpitations and chest pain frequently so it is possible that there has been some strain put on me there. The medical visits and reviews are ongoing and that will be something that I am stuck with for the rest of my life as well.

Ellie and I have been married for a couple of years and we are very happy together. In fact, all seems to be going very well with my life. We are very happy together and very much in love. We have not become used to each other and therefore complacent. We thank each other that we found each other and fell in love every day that we are together and when we are apart from each other, we can't wait to be together once again. After all the years of mistakes and false starts, I have finally found the one that I was destined for all of the time. The one that truly makes me happy and that I hope to spend the rest of my life with.

Dad is still reading his books, and although he misses Mum beyond words, he carries on each day. Jerry surprised all of us by announcing when gay marriage became legal in Britain, that he was going to marry a man called Roger. Ignoring all obvious jokes about rogering, they seem to be very happy and hopefully he won't have as many marriages as I have gone through. Even Nat has found someone recently and it looks like it might be getting serious. He always denied that he would ever meet anyone and that he was perfectly happy as he was, but I think he has realised now that there is more to life than staying in with your nose buried deeply in a complicated physics text.

So, have I any final words to pass over? Well I am not the philosopher that my mother was and it is possible that if she were here today she would have something wise and meaningful to say. I wish she was here, because I would like to tell her how much I appreciate her and I would like to hear what she has to say myself. You will have to make do with my own cod philosophy, though. I stand by a concept that I formulated a little while ago. The meaning of life is something that people waste years looking for and in trying to understand when it really is very easy, at least in my opinion. Yes, I have discovered the meaning of life.

The clue is in the question really. What is the meaning of life? The answer is a life with meaning. That may sound trite, but I think that if you have some meaning in your life, no matter what it is, then you are reasonably complete. The meaning doesn't have to be earth shattering in a Nobel Prize winning way. It can be anything. Anything at all. Your children, your family, your job, the enjoyment or meaning that you might get from a warm bath, a beautiful sunset, an exquisite piece of music or poetry; literally, anything you like. It really doesn't matter so long as you have some kind of meaning in your life. That is what you must look for; meaning.

There is also a difference between living and existing. Many of us merely exist. We go about our lives working and earning money and in general getting caught up in a lot of petty issues. Things that really don't matter all that much when it boils down to it. Eat, sleep, work. This is existing. Living is something that I think of as a much higher, nobler level. That is where you are more likely to find your meaning. In many regards, this fits in with the concept that our souls are unable to develop because we are distracted by mundane, everyday events. It sounds highly likely to me.

So, where am I? Where has this journey led me?

I am settled now. My breath has been taken away by many girls and women over the course of my life and then my breath was taken away by my wonderful wife before it was taken away by my medical condition, and then returned to me because of the love of my woman. Sometimes it takes a number of roads to travel down before you find the one that you are looking for.

So, to quote Shakespeare, *I say we shall have no more marriages.*